MY
SISTER

MY SISTER

MICHELLE ADAMS

HEADLINE

First published in 2017 by
HEADLINE PUBLISHING GROUP

1

Cataloguing in Publication Data is available from the British Library

ISBN 978 1 4722 3658 6

Typeset in Sabon by Palimpsest Book Production Limited, Falkirk, Stirlingshire

Printed and bound by CPI Group (UK) Ltd, Croydon CR0 4YY

Headline's policy is to use papers that are natural, renewable and recyclable
products and made from wood grown in sustainable forests. The logging and
manufacturing processes are expected to conform to the environmental
regulations of the country of origin.

HEADLINE PUBLISHING GROUP
An Hachette UK Company
Carmelite House
50 Victoria Embankment
London EC4Y 0DZ

www.headline.co.uk
www.hachette.co.uk

I dedicate the first copy of this novel to you, Stasinos, because without you it would never have come to be.

Every other copy belongs to those individuals who have at some point felt worthless. I hope by now you know you were wrong.

1

The buzzing of my telephone is like the scuttling of a cockroach underneath the bed. No real danger, yet still I am terrified. The same fear that a knock on the door just before bedtime brings, always bad news, or a murderer there to live out a fantasy. I look back and see Antonio sleeping by my side, naked save for a white sheet draped over his hip like an unfastened toga. His breath glides in and out, comfortable, at peace. I know the dreams that come to him are good, because he smacks his lips and his muscles twitch like a contented baby. I glance at the red numbers glowing on the alarm clock: 2.02 a.m., a warning sign.

I reach for the phone, my movements slow, and glance at the screen. *Unknown number*. I press the green button to answer the call and hear the bright, cheerful voice. But it's a lie, designed to fool or blind. 'Hi, it's me. Hello?' It waits for an answer. 'Can you hear me?'

I pull the sheet higher, protecting myself as a chill spreads across my skin. I cover my breasts, the left of which hangs just a bit lower than the right. The beauty of fifteen degrees of scoliosis. It is Elle's voice I hear, the one I knew it would be. The last remaining connection to a past I have tried to forget. Yet still, even after six years of absence she has managed to scramble up the walls of the chasm I have gouged between us, wriggle her way back in like a worm through mud and find me.

I reach up, turn on the lamp, illuminating the darkest monster-filled corners of the room. When I raise the phone to my ear I can still hear her breathing, creeping out of the shadows, waiting for me to speak.

I roll away from Antonio, wince as my hip throbs with the movement. 'What do you want?' I ask, trying to sound confident. I have learnt not to be polite, not to engage. It helps not to encourage her.

'To talk to you, so don't you dare hang up. Why are you whispering?' I hear her giggle, like we are friends, like this is just a normal conversation between silly teenage girls. But it isn't. We both know it. I should hang up despite her threat, but I can't. It's already too late for that.

'It's the middle of the night.' I can hear the quiver in my voice. I'm shivering. I swallow hard.

There's a rustle as she checks the clock. Where is she now? What does she want this time? 'Actually, it's the early hours of the morning, but whatever.'

'What do you want?' I ask again, aware that she is picking at my skin, creeping under the layers.

Elle is my sister. My only sister from a previous life from which I have kept few memories. The memories I do have are blurry, as if I am looking back through a window drenched in heavy rain. I'm not even sure if they represent reality any more. Twenty-nine years is a long time for them to morph, transform into something else.

My second life, the one I am stuck in now, began when I was three years old. It was a bright spring day; the frosts of winter had melted and the animals in the nearby woods were venturing from their dens for the first time. I was wrapped in a thick woollen coat, so many layers of clothes that my joints were immobile. The woman who had given birth to me pulled red woollen mittens on to my hands without saying a word. What a three-year-old remembers.

She carried me along a dry, muddy path intersected by grass until we arrived at a waiting car up ahead. I was a late developer, and parts of me, like my hip (a poorly formed socket held together by loose, stringy tendons), hadn't really developed at all. I hadn't managed the whole walking thing. I didn't put up a fight when she pushed me into the back seat and strapped me in. At least I don't think I did. Maybe I don't really remember anything, and this is all just a trick of the mind, to make me feel that I have a past. A life where I had parents. A past with somebody other than Elle.

Sometimes I think I can remember my mother's face: like mine, only older, redder, wrinkles like a spider's web weaving around her lips. Other times I'm not so sure. But I'm sure that she didn't offer any last-minute advice to be a good girl, no quick kiss on the cheek to tide me over. I would have remembered that, wouldn't I? She slammed the car door, stepped back, and my aunt and uncle drove me away from her like it was the most normal thing in the world. And even then I knew something was over. I had been given away, cast out, dumped.

'Are you listening to me, Irini? I told you I want to talk

to you.' Her sharp voice comes through quick as a blade, wrenching me back to the present.

'What about?' I whisper, knowing that it has already begun again. I can feel her on me, slithering back into place.

I listen as she draws in a breath, trying to calm herself. 'How long is it since we spoke?'

I edge further away from Antonio. I don't want to wake him up. 'Elle, it's two in the morning. I have work tomorrow. I don't have time for this now.' It's a pathetic attempt, but I have to try. One last effort to keep her away.

'Liar,' she spits. And I know that's it, I've done it. I have made her angry. I throw the covers off, swing my feet out of the bed and brush my fringe from my eyes. My pulse is racing as I grip the phone to my ear. 'It's Sunday tomorrow. You don't have work.'

'Please, just tell me what you want.'

'It's Mum.' The word jars me when she uses it so casually. Drops it like a friend might use a nickname. It feels alien, makes me feel exposed. *Mum*, she says. As if I know her. As if somehow she belongs to me.

'What about her?' I whisper.

'She died.'

Moments pass before I breathe. She's gone, I think. I've lost her again. I cover my mouth with a sweaty palm. Elle waits for a response, but when I offer nothing she eventually asks, 'Well, are you going to come to the funeral?'

It's a reasonable question, but one for which I have no answer. Because to me, *mother* is nothing more than an idea, a childish hope. A dream. But my nagging curiosity spurs me on. There are things I need to know.

'I guess,' I stutter.

'Don't force yourself. It's not like they'd miss you if you didn't.'

I wish that didn't hurt, but the knowledge that my presence would not be missed is a painful reminder of reality even after all these years. 'So why ask me to come?' I say, aware that my mask of confidence is slipping.

'Because I need you there.' She speaks as if she is surprised I don't already understand, as if she doesn't know that I dodge her phone calls, or that I've changed my number twenty-three times, and moved house, just to stop her from finding me. Six years I have kept the distance, my best run yet. But she weakens me, and to be needed by her makes me limp. Pliable. 'And you still owe me, Irini. Or have you forgotten the things I've done for you?'

She's right. I do owe her. How could I have forgotten? Our parents might have given me away, but Elle never accepted it. She has spent her life clawing her way back to me, her presence littering my past like debris after a storm. 'No, I haven't forgotten,' I admit, as I turn and take a look at Antonio still fast asleep. I squeeze my eyes shut, as if I can make it all go away. I'm not here. You can't see me. Childish. A tear sneaks out as I clench the sheet tight in my fist. I want to ask her how she got my number this time. Somebody must have it. Maybe Aunt Jemima, the only mother figure I have ever known. If she was still taking my calls I could contact her to ask. Let her know what I think of this latest familial betrayal.

'Call me tomorrow if you are coming,' Elle says. 'I hope you can. Don't make me come to London to find you myself.' She hangs up the phone before I have a chance to answer.

5

2

I sit stunned on the edge of the bed, watching as the clock changes from 2.06 a.m. to 2.07 a.m. Just five minutes was all it took to undo six years of effort, and now Elle is back in my life as if she's never been gone. I get up, unsteady on my feet, as if even gravity has shifted. I wrap my dressing gown around me and knot it tightly, dodging the packed overnight bag sitting by the end of the bed. Antonio must be planning to go somewhere, most likely without me.

I nudge his bag aside and slip my feet into grey cashmere slippers. They were a gift, one of many that Antonio has given me during the three years we have been together. At first it all seemed so easy. But then reality started to creep in, and the idea that Elle could turn up at any moment to ruin things started to take its toll. Of course he didn't know anything about her at the time, so when things started to go wrong, he thought gifts might help. Now, as I look at him sleeping in the umbra of our old life, his overnight bag packed like so many times before, I realise that no amount of gifts could ever have prevented this distance between us. Elle is my destiny. Utterly inescapable. She is back, here to ruin things, just like I always knew she would be.

I glide silently over the laminate floorboards of my depressing end-terrace house in a dark corner of Brixton, and step from the bedroom. I look along the street from the landing window, find it shrouded in shadow with not a soul about. Identikit houses merge into the distance, the warm glow of the city just visible as a marker to remind me where I am. A city so large you can disappear in plain sight. Almost.

If Antonio was awake he would hold me, listen as I spoke, and then tell me that I should feel better now that I had got it off my chest. It's an expression he picked up, like people do when they learn a new language, dropping phrases at inappropriate moments. Phrases that are too generic for the situation. Like the time I told him that Elle once killed a dog. Her dog. He said it was all right because I had got it off my chest. As if talking about it made it all go away, and the dead dog with its caved-in head would come sprinting back, tongue hanging out, excited as Toto. There's no place like home. What a crock of shit that is.

I pace down the wooden stairs, taking cautious steps as I move about in the dark, one hand on the wall to steady me as I find my way to the kitchen.

So, I think. My mother is dead.

I stand at the worktop and fiddle with a stained wine glass, swirling around the last dribbles of Chianti at the bottom. I set it aside and take two mugs from the cupboard, taking care to make some noise. Maybe Antonio will wake up if he hears me. Perhaps he will come and sit with me, tell me everything is going to be all right, like he always used to. I could do with that. It might help settle the panic that Elle's return has brought with it. I even take a step towards the bedroom, certain that his presence would soften the loneliness. But then I remember the bag on the floor waiting for his exit, so instead I reopen the cupboard quietly and put the second cup away. Is he going to leave me? Maybe. Destiny, I suppose. I'll have to get used to being alone once he's gone. I slide a pod into the coffee maker, and when the light on the machine turns red I pick up my cup. The steam hits my face as I take a lip-burning sip.

I edge along the wall, turning on all the lights before I sit at my unimaginative glass desk and switch on the computer. I prefer new furniture like this. Bland objects with no history or story to tell. Stuff you don't mind leaving behind. I set my cup at my side and open the browser, bathing my face in cool blue light. I am still for a moment, staring at the screen. Barely even breathing. What am I doing here? Am I really going to go? When I think I hear something behind me that sounds like footsteps, I turn, hopeful that it might be Antonio, but instead I find nobody there. I lean back, look up the stairs, one last check, but see only the dark from where I came. I turn back to the computer and type *Edinburgh* in the search box to look for flight options, still unsure if I am awake enough for such a decision. Am I really going to go back? Next box. *Return* or *one-way*?

'What are you doing?' Antonio asks.

'Shit!' I shout, almost jumping out of my seat. 'Don't creep up on me like that.' My heart hammers in my chest.

'Christ, Rini.' He staggers back, surprised. 'You're the one creeping around in the dark. You scared me.' He is standing in a pair of white trunks that look too small for him, one of my low stilettos in his hand like a weapon. His voice is rich as chocolate, strong as my espresso. 'What are you doing down here?'

'Looking at something online,' I say, still out of breath. He moves in close, sets the shoe on the desk, and I smell my perfume on his skin as he leans over me. He brushes his hands over my shoulders, and when I don't push him away, he rubs at my neck before letting his fingers slide across the top of my breasts. He has never stopped being tactile. Even when he is angry with me, he still wants me close.

'Just relax, OK? Take a deep breath,' he says, kneading his fingertips into my skin. I remember what we were doing only an hour ago and wish I could go back to that, as awkward as the post-argument sex was. Nothing between us is easy any more. He continues rubbing at my shoulders as he leans forward to read the screen. Then he stops, looks at me, a flash of disbelief. 'You going somewhere?'

I think again of his packed bag and how I could ask him the same thing. Instead I take another sip of coffee, just glad that I am no longer alone. 'Cassandra died,' I say.

It takes him a moment to register the name because he isn't used to hearing it. 'When?' he asks, once the pieces fall into place. He crouches down and my gown slips open, exposing my legs and the bottom of my scar. He rubs a strong hand against my weaker left thigh, running it all the way up to the thick red wound. He completes an assessment of my face to see how I am taking the news. I am empty, reticent as a blank sheet of paper. 'How?' he asks as I shuffle away from him, his fingertips irritating the raised flesh of my scarred hip.

Only now do I realise that I didn't ask Elle what happened to our mother. I don't know if she died in her sleep or in a bloody car wreck. I don't know if she died in pain or peacefully. I'd love to say that I didn't ask because I don't care, but I know that I do. I still care, even though I have tried for twenty-nine years not to.

'I don't know.'

Antonio doesn't push it, even though I know he doesn't really understand my detachment. He has too many of his own beliefs about family. They all start with marriage. But he is here, and he has forgiven me for the argument I caused the previous night, something lame that began with his apathetic approach to domestic detail and ended with my unwillingness to become a mother.

'Are you going to go?' he asks.

I shrug my shoulders. There are so many reasons not to. I could still get out of this, change my phone number, move before Elle has a chance to discover where I live. Pretend that I don't owe her a thing. But if I go, there are truths my father could tell me. How can I pass up the chance to know why they gave me away and kept Elle?

'Well, I suppose you have to,' Antonio says. He reaches for the mouse and begins to scroll through the available flights. He makes a selection for 3.30 in the afternoon and drags the cursor in a circular fashion to catch my attention. 'This one looks good. You could be there by late afternoon.'

I nod and smile, understanding his belief that the only right thing is for me to be there. 'Pass me my wallet,' I say as I click on the link with a shaky hand. I select the one-way option, not knowing when I might be able to come back, and immediately feel less confident. Antonio doesn't suggest coming with me. Perhaps he'll just be glad of the space. Perhaps we both will be.

'Now, come back to bed,' he says.

We walk back together, Antonio leading the way, holding my hand as though I'm a teenage girl about to get laid for the first time. We slip back into the sheets and he wraps his arms around me, something I have come to miss in the weeks that he has been distant and unreachable. I rest into him, wishing that I still felt like I used to. But I don't. His touch is angular, like we are two pieces of a jigsaw that don't fit together, and his presence beside me no longer blurs the past as it once did.

I look at the clock, which now reads 2.46 a.m. Time is already slowing, already pulling me down beneath the surface, no matter how hard I fight and kick. Soon enough it will start counting backwards, tick-tock, tick-tock, until I am right back there with the silent woman who was supposed to be my mother. And now, in the dark of our bedroom in Antonio's arms, I wonder what the hell I've done.

I should have told Elle I wasn't going. I should have ignored the voice telling me that I owed her. I should have run from her like I did fifteen years ago, dressed in my pyjamas with tears streaming down my face and blood running down my arm, knowing the only chance of a future was if I let her go. What happened that day forced us apart, but it's also the day that will bind us for ever. The day she saved me and terrified me in equal measure.

But it's not just my thirst for the truth that lures me back.

11

I want Elle, too. I am drawn to her, despite the danger. I can't help it. All these years I thought I could push her out, but I can't. I thought I didn't need her, but I do. And what a terrifying thought that is, because when Elle explained that our mother had died, there was a reason that I didn't ask how. I assumed I already knew; that it was Elle who killed her.

3

The last time Elle found me was in the emergency department of the hospital where I used to work. I watched from the safety of a first-floor window as she fought her way across the car park. When she landed a punch on the cheek of the nurse who was trying to restrain her, a colleague of mine joked about how one of the psych patients must have escaped. I laughed along, added in a few snide comments of my own about the way she was dressed. Just for the record, Elle was wearing a season-inappropriate woollen jumper. It was oozing out from underneath the cuffs and collar of what looked like a school shirt, which she had buttoned incorrectly over the top. Hot pants. Doc Marten boots. Dressed as if she was on her way to a rave in the thick of winter. It was June, and the sun was bright. She called out to me, her flailing arms trying to reach me as the nurse buckled at her side. Security ended up tackling her to the ground, pulling her across the car park, ripping her shirt. They couldn't take any risks because of the kitchen knife she was gripping in her hand.

She never did get to speak to me that day. But she knew I was there. I could feel it as my skin contracted across my body, as her eyes met the glass behind which I was standing. I had handed in my request for a transfer by the time I left for home, and for the next six years I ran as far away as I could. Little good it did me.

Because now here I am, in spite of everything I know about Elle, going back to find her. I called into Queen's College Hospital on the way to the airport, organised three days of emergency leave. I didn't tell them that the emergency is mine.

I sit down in seat 28A, pulling my seat belt tight across my lap. The tiny cabin begins to shake as we rattle our way up the runway, and I feel my stomach turn as we leave the ground. I make a last-minute wish that the wing will buckle, or that we will fall from the sky in a devastating, newsworthy incident. But my wish isn't granted. Instead we climb up and up, London a city in miniature below, until we stutter into a thick layer of grey cloud.

In my bag I have two changes of clothes, a pack of cigarettes, an unmarked bottle of Valium, which I snatched from the hospital this morning, and a book I know I won't read. I snap the top off the bottle and flick one of the tablets to the back of my mouth, washing it down with a brandy. The medley of narcotics would be enough to knock some people out, but I am accustomed to it. Perhaps being an anaesthetist I have more courage when it comes to self-medication. It's only with my family that I am weak. The Valium gets to work, taking the edge off the fear to the point that I stop grinding my teeth.

I pull out my phone and scroll through the messages, realising that I have missed one from Antonio. I press the envelope icon and the message pops open.

My Sister

Have a safe flight. Let me know when you land. Ti amo,
A x

I was attending a conference about pain management when I met him. He was serving dinner, handing out bread rolls, leaving a trail of crumbs. In those first blissful weeks I had no idea about the sedate girlfriend he was hiding. Then she found out about me and threw him out while I waited in the car outside. That very same day he moved in with me, talked about what a relief it was to be free. He made it sound like his dreams were coming true, but in hindsight he had nowhere else to go. I couldn't believe how easily I took it, or how understanding I was. But lying in bed with his naked legs draped over mine allowed me to forget about my past, pretend that life started only then. I felt consumed by him. With Antonio I felt like I stopped existing. But that was a good thing; I didn't have to be me any more, poor old lonely Irini. Irini turned into us. I belonged to us. So, he had played me along a bit. Big deal. It wasn't like he had done anything comparable to what my family had done to me. And besides, he wanted me.

It was lucky we met in an Elle-free period, because it gave us the freedom to live our lives, as simple as they were with our shared love of nature documentaries and his home-cooked food. For the best part of two years I didn't even tell him that I had a sister, and living in that lie was bliss. Once I had him, I stopped needing her.

It was after a trip to Italy to meet his family that he started talking about marriage and kids. I refused. What kind of mother would I make when I had never had one of my own from whom to learn? We've been falling apart ever

15

since. In fact, those final days of our lazy Italian summer, curled up on the same lounger, watching the sun dip beneath the horizon, were the last I can remember where we resembled something based on happiness.

At first I thought he was going to leave. But he stayed, cried, said he couldn't be without me. It was a relief, because I wasn't sure that I could be without him either; what would I do on my own? Disappearing into my books and work was an option, but I had done that before and knew the emptiness it held. I had tasted connection with Antonio, and I knew that even a flimsy attachment to him was sweeter than isolation. I didn't want to be Irini again, the girl with no family and no friends.

But now everything is changing, like we're rotting, getting moth-eaten. I am slowly becoming Irini again, and the union that I have been hiding behind is disappearing. He doesn't understand my decision to exclude marriage and kids from our future, and I can't admit to him that actually I want a family too. Because even to want it feels dangerous. I can't tell him the truth, so I throw the phone back into my bag and order another brandy.

The plane touches down to unnecessary applause and I stand, hobble forward, my hip sore from the awkward position. I can feel the nerves growing as I get ever closer to reunion, the nausea in my stomach, the slight difficulty in breathing. I remind myself that the trip will be short, that I will stay in a hotel, and that I only have to turn up at the funeral. I tell myself that I chose to come here. That I won't even have to see Elle alone if I don't want to. Last-minute bargaining with my nerves and memories. Sense bubbling to the surface. But as I walk through customs, I see her waiting at the gate, even though I haven't told her what flight I am on.

I realise that her appearance has changed during these latest years of absence, and despite my dry throat and sweaty palms I allow myself to hope that it's an indication things can be different. Before, there was always an outrageousness about her presence, an inability to conform to the ideals of society, physically or mentally. Everybody could see it. The rave gear outside the hospital was just one example. But now she appears refined, her hair neat and blonde, cut in a sharp bob. Tight sporty clothes hug her lithe frame, and she is clutching a bottle of Evian water. There are pearls the size of marbles in her ears, so big and dull they could be carved-up chunks of bone. An active Stepford wife, perhaps with two perfectly turned-out kids, a casserole in the oven, and the courtesy to wipe her mouth like a lady when she has finished sucking you off. Could she be different? Is that a smile I can see? She has the appearance of somebody who is connected, who actually sees what the rest of the world sees when she looks in the mirror. The only thing that hasn't changed is the triangular pink scar on her forehead. Neither of us scars very well. Bad healers.

I find myself wondering who Elle really is beneath the surface. Superficially she is everything I am not. She walks with her head held high, whereas I have the remnants of a limp that gets worse when it's cold, thanks to a dysplastic hip. She is slim; in comparison I am verging on chubby. The only exception is my left thigh, which refuses to develop even with all the attention it gets. Antonio always makes an effort with it when we have sex, kissing and stroking it, gliding his hands over the wrinkly skin like it's one of my erogenous zones. It is not. Perhaps it's to remind me that I am a cripple, that I should be grateful for his love and therefore make more of an effort when he asks me to marry him. No man would dare do such a thing with Elle.

But as I get close, I see her jaw tightly clenched, her teeth set. It wasn't a smile I saw, and I watch as her unblinking eyes search the crowd. I pick up my pace and slip around the barriers, swallowing down the lump in my throat. Elle spots me, her eyes locked on her target as she pushes past a woman with a crying toddler, knocking into the pushchair. She tuts, the way adults without children do in order to shame parents when their child has unintentionally annoyed. It is a reminder of her unapologetic certainty that, unlike me, she has never once doubted who she is. That confidence is captivating, and I realise that nothing has changed. She might look different, but she is still Elle. And this reminds me that there is only one thing of which I can be sure when it comes to my sister: she is the one person who never tired of trying to find me.

At first I made it easy for her. A simple change to my phone number, a new address in the same town. Being alone was hard, and despite what happened to make me run from her at the age of eighteen, to know she was searching for me felt good. So I started to test her by raising the stakes with false trails and dead ends, forcing her to prove her resolve more and more each time. The knowledge that she was searching for me was narcotic, and I was addicted. Oh, to be wanted. What a joy it is. Yet the only thing worse than her absence was her presence.

'I wondered how long you were going to make me wait,' she announces. 'I've been here since I got your message.' She looks me up and down, sizing me up, her jaw still tight, her lips drawn into a sickly grin. I smile, try to look friendly, and like I haven't been avoiding her for most of my life.

'I haven't been here long. I just spotted you,' I say, fiddling with the handle of my brown tote, not yet able to make full eye contact. Then she reaches forward, unexpectedly taking me in her arms. I wobble towards her on my dodgy left hip and catch a middle-aged man with a swollen gut smiling at us, enjoying our reunion. Elle spots him too and makes a bigger effort, pulling me tighter, throwing off little breathy sounds of contentment like a purring cat. My cheek brushes against her cold neck, and a shiver runs down my spine. Her fake smile is instant when she realises there is an audience to please. Then she pulls back, slips an arm around me and begins drawing me in her direction. I try to tell myself that her grip isn't any tighter than it needs to be, but I can already feel my self-confidence flapping, like the storm-torn sail of a boat, ragged and good for nothing.

You chose to come, I remind myself. You want the truth. But what next? Five minutes here and I am already falling under her spell, following her blindly as she leads me away. By tomorrow, who am I going to be?

'Look at you,' she says, her words thick with false sentiment as we move towards the exit. 'You got so fat!' She says it with such enthusiasm, and even nibbles at my cheeks with her perfectly manicured fingertips. She pulls my bag from my hand and I offer no resistance. She pushes through the crowd, coercing me along behind her.

We step outside into a strong wind and my eyes begin to water. I dab at the corners with the back of my hand. I stop, forcing her to stop too. 'Elle, before we go any further, I have to ask you something.'

But it's like she doesn't hear me. 'It's been too long,' she says, turning to look at me. She swallows hard and for a moment I think she is about to cry. I feel a pang of sympathy, guilt even. But I know this is one of her tricks, the ability she has to make me think that she needs me.

I try again. 'Elle,' I say quietly, knowing that if I don't ask now, the strength to do so will disappear. 'How did she die?'

Elle stares back at me with a glint in her cold, ice-blue eyes. She takes hold of my hand and slides her fingers through mine, like she might have done when I was a child if we had ever been given the chance to be sisters. I feel the pressure as she secures her grip. She says nothing at all as she leads me across the car park, a left-sided sneer inching on and off her face. I am sure her silence is proof of her guilt, and I can feel what's left of my confidence slipping away.

And I realise what is happening here. All those years without Elle have allowed me to forget who I really am. I pretend to be somebody other than that little girl who was abandoned. But now that we are reunited, I exist. I came here for the truth, and now, within minutes of being with Elle, I have the first part of it: I will always be that little girl, the one they decided they didn't want. It doesn't matter how hard I fight it, or how I lie and tell myself my relationship with Antonio is everything I need.

I think of all those times I have run from Elle, trying to get away to finally be myself. All that time with Antonio thinking that we had found something good, that I had been completed by him and had finally said goodbye to poor Peg Leg Irini. Years of study to become a doctor, a mask so people wouldn't see the real me. All that wasted time. I can already feel Elle slipping back into the cracks of my life like a poison, filling me up, making me whole. I want to cry as I watch the sharp cut of her bobbed hair slash like a knife with each step she takes. Because now I realise that there was only ever one person I have the right to be. Me, the unwanted little girl, just as I existed from birth.

4

Elle hands me my bag as we climb into the bullet-grey E-class Mercedes, taking cover from the harsh Scottish wind. She turns the key and a chorus of operatic music screams through the speakers as the engine roars into life. She reaches for the CD player, sinking us into silence. Inside it is cold, even with the heaters on full, and the air is blasting at my face, squeezing out tears. I sit like an idiot in the passenger seat, with no clue what to say because she still hasn't answered my question.

'Elle,' I say quietly, my voice apologetic as I brush my fringe from my eyes. 'I asked you to tell me how she died.'

She fastens her seat belt, adjusts the tension across her chest as if I haven't spoken. 'Shall I take you to have a look at her?' she asks, scrutinising the dials and levers with the same care with which a pilot might check a cockpit before takeoff. 'I think it would be nice for you to meet her,' she suggests, her smile sickly and her stare vacant. 'The little butterfly returning to the nest after all these years.'

'I don't think so,' I say with a quick shake of the head, my eyes wide and nervous. I've felt like this before, moments as a teenager when I wasn't sure where Elle was leading me.

She continues to test the wipers, even though it's not raining. They flop across the windscreen, *thwack, schweep, thwack, schweep,* before she adds in a squirt of foamy green water. I look back at Departures as she pulls away, gazing at the passengers who are travelling somewhere new, smiles and laughter all over their faces. 'Why would I want to see her body? Especially when you won't even tell me how she died.'

'She just died, all right? Dead. She is D E A fucking D. What else could you possibly need to know?' She sighs. 'So where do you want to go if you don't want to see our dead mother?' It is as if we are bargaining between a visit to Costa or Starbucks. She glides on to the nearest motorway, heading towards the English border, test-perfect control of the car despite her frustration.

The open green space of the countryside seems endless, with only sporadic views of the elevated castle and the grand clock tower of the Balmoral Hotel flashing through weaker sections of hedgerow. I could cope there, I think, swallowed up by concrete and crowds, despite the memories I have with Elle in this city. But the countryside is like the open ocean, deep and vast, unbreachable. As though there is no escape. 'If you don't want to see her, let's do something together.' She pats my leg like a mother might to offer a child gentle encouragement. Like I saw Aunt Jemima do once to one of her own children, the children who, she liked to remind me, had always been part of their plans. But all it does is make me shiver, tense up. I feel as tight as a coiled spring.

'I want to go to a hotel,' I say, trying to sound confident, trying to remember the person I have endeavoured to be in the years leading up to this moment. I want to take a bath and sleep. Smoke a bit, drink some wine. Chew a few Valium. That would really help. Anything that doesn't involve Elle will help. But her silence in the wake of my request is unnerving, and it makes my attempt at certainty feel like bad judgement. I can see now that I shouldn't have come here. 'Something close by. Whatever hotel you think,' I add nervously, an unconvincing attempt to cushion the impact of my certitude.

Without glancing at her watch she says, 'It's only five past five. What are you going to do in a hotel at this time of day when we have only just reconciled after,' and she turns to look me straight in the eye as we drive at eighty miles per hour along the motorway, 'six years? The only place you are going is with me.' It's enough to let me know that I am not the only one who harbours mixed emotions, pent-up feelings that for the sake of politeness remain hidden.

'I'm tired from the flight,' I maintain, but even as I say it I know I have lost this argument. She has waited six long years to see me again. It was easier for both of us when I was younger. I was always more willing back then. But who isn't when they are only thirteen?

That's how old I was when Elle first turned up unannounced, despite our parents' best efforts to keep us apart. She walked into my life a hero, saved me from Robert Kneel and his band of bullies. How he regretted making me his target that day after she had finished with him. Then there were the late-night trips to the park when Aunt Jemima thought I was asleep in bed, the shoplifting Elle did on my behalf. The alcohol she bought for me, and her tentative care when I puked it all back up.

'Well, you will not be staying at a hotel,' she says, spittle flying, her patience exhausted. I know what she is going to say. She means for me to stay with her, at the house. My almost family home. But to stay in the place that could never have been my home is unthinkable. A joke. 'Besides, we live in the middle of nowhere. There are no hotels. You will be staying at the house with me.' I open my mouth to protest, but I am pathetically powerless. It's like I'm driftwood caught on a wave, at the mercy of the sea. She just pats my leg again, her composure regained, and we continue our drive in silence. I can't believe how easy I have made it for her this time.

After a quiet hour on the road I sense we are slowing down, weaving into smaller lanes, taking us to the village that I have been told lies just north of the border. I steal a glance outside for the first time since she told me she was bringing me here. I see little more than overgrown hedgerows and distant mountains, all blanketed by a low layer of oppressive grey cloud that appears set to swallow me up. There is no hiding place here. No orange city glow to remind me I'm in London. I can't even see the sun. But I see the sign, smudged with dirt and surrounded by pink foxgloves: *Welcome to Horton.* And I know this is the place. We are nearly there.

By the time we reach the entrance to the family estate, I have nibbled a tear around the edge of my thumb, a childhood habit that never quite disappeared. The skin lifts and blood rushes to the surface as we pass a slate sign engraved with the words *Mam Tor.* I wrap my fingers over the wound, scared to look up and see what is outside, because somehow

I know that we have arrived. We follow a long driveway, the ground lumpy and poorly formed. We slow down as we approach the gates and I force myself to take a look. Beyond the lofty corridor of trees I see a house. I feel a wave of nausea as we drive towards it.

The property is a double-fronted monstrosity, big enough to house five families. As we pass through the gates I spot a conservatory on the left, and beyond a field full of trees that I assume is an orchard and to which a layer of fog clings. I look right to find another building, a block of garages, six in total. Six fucking garages.

'It was built by my father's construction company in the seventies,' Elle says in the style of a tour guide, before laughing to herself. 'Sorry. I mean *our* father.' My lips flicker into a sort of smile/seizure combo. The windows bulge out in mock-Victorian bays, and behind I can make out swathes of drapery, big and heavy, smothering the frames. Beyond that I see nothing, like the whole place is just one giant black hole, waiting to suck me in.

Elle pulls up outside the garage block, the gravel crunching under the tyres. She gets out, slams the door, making the car shake, then breaks into a half-hearted jog, springing light as a feather towards the double-fronted doors in her ultra-high-fashion sportswear and trainers. And in the shadow of this house, her expensive clothes and shoes matter like never before.

Because before, it was easy to tell myself that my birth family were poor. Poor, and all as mental as Elle. That there was some benefit to not being with them. But it isn't true. At least not the part about being poor. The realisation of their wealth makes me want to vomit, and I wonder, if I did, whether Elle would hold back my hair and wipe my cheeks like she always used to.

It matters because I was always the kid in the hand-me-downs, the unbranded clothes that scratched at your skin and never quite fitted properly. Discarded things for the discarded child. Aunt Jemima wasn't inclined to spend her family's money on me, choosing instead to stick to the allowance my father sent her, which never seemed to stretch very far. One time I was handed down a pair of Reeboks, brown and scuffed from previous wear, but nevertheless Reeboks. And for the first time in my life I felt proud. I walked into the school gym that day on top of the world, like I was dancing on the clouds. But this house shits all over those shoes. This house is so big that whoever lives inside it could have afforded hundreds of new Reeboks.

I get out and slam the door, trapping the edge of my woolly jacket. I yank it out and watch as a thread pulls out in a silvery slither. I breathe in, tell myself to calm down. 'You're here for the truth,' I whisper to myself. I look through the window of the car, past the reflection of my face and the house, and see that I have left my bag inside. I pull on the door handle but the car is already locked. 'My bag,' I call to Elle, and wait as she reaches backwards and clicks the button on the key. The lights flicker on and off and I test the door handle again. Still locked. I hear her laugh, taunting me as she disappears into the house.

I crunch my way across the driveway, the sound of broken bones underfoot. I look back as I hear the screech of metal to see the iron gates closing me in, the trees of the driveway twisting and curling into a gnarly canopy. Beyond the conservatory the land rises abruptly in the shape of a hill, peppered with rocky outcrops, the ground black and saturated after recent rain.

Elle has left the door ajar, a heavy oak thing that I push open. Behind it I see nothing in the hallway except for space filled with elongated shadows and clouds of dust. I hear the ticking of a clock somewhere in the background and I push the door open a little further. Not to go in, just to allow some of the late-afternoon light to slip in through the gap. I don't want to go into the dark.

Oil paintings adorn the walls, a mixture of noble faces that all somehow look the same. The eyes, perhaps, which I note are not unlike mine. Ancestors? Family? There is a Chinese urn mounted on an obelisk next to the door, and the whole place bears the mark of a museum, right down to the musty scent. In some ways, that's exactly what it is, a museum of my history, the one I was never allowed to know. I am like an archaeologist, Indiana Jones without the cool hat and trusty sidekick, digging at the earliest years of my life. I gaze along and find a sweeping staircase that snakes its way into the upper levels of the house. I don't want to know what is up there.

Elle breezes back through in that light, springy way, clutching a fresh bottle of Evian. She hits the light switch and a harsh glow spreads out from the chandelier, patterns dancing about like cut-out paper snowflakes.

'What about your bag?' she asks. She is deadly serious too, as if she really expected me to be carrying it.

'The car is locked. You locked it.'

'Well, you'll need it, won't you?'

She offers me the water bottle, but as thirsty as I am, I refuse. 'No thanks,' I say, one foot inside the house. She glides towards me, pulls me inside, and then pushes the front door shut. For a second there is silence, just the two of us alone. And then I see him, stationary, watching me from halfway up the staircase.

'Irini.' It has to be him, my father, although I can't see properly, his face cast in shadow. I open my mouth to speak as I feel Elle's grip tighten around my arm. I move my lips, but no words come out. What would I say? Where would I begin? I make a sound but it is just a squeak. 'You're here.' He sounds . . . warm. 'Why don't I arrange some tea and we can—' he begins, but Elle doesn't give him a chance to finish, and he takes a step back as she swings around to face him.

'She's tired from the trip,' she tells him. I feel a shiver run through me, rough like a fissure through ice, as she pats the top of my hand, leading me away. Never once does she take her eyes off him. I look down as she guides me, her grip tight, snatching stolen glances here and there. Despite my desperation to ask him *Why? Why me?* I say nothing. 'Let me show you to your room.'

'Yes, maybe that's for the best,' he calls after us as we walk away, edging his way down two more steps. 'We can talk when you're feeling up to it.' I feel like my heart has stopped, and I can't open my mouth. I gasp, but no air gets into my lungs. He really wants to talk to me.

Elle drags me into the kitchen and closes the door behind us. It is brighter in here than in the hallway, and the air feels cleaner, less stale. I'm still thinking about my father, but as I take in the bare windows and the detailed tiling of the floor, a memory hits me. Comes out of nowhere, smack in the face. I stagger back, perhaps only saved from falling by Elle's grip. I see myself as a baby, dragging my limp little body along the black and white floor, laughing as somebody calls out *Well done!* from behind me. A woman's voice. Strong arms, I think. I always had strong arms. They had to be strong because I couldn't walk. I remember how cold the floor used to feel, with the exception of one tile near the sink where the heat from a hot-water pipe escaped. Is this real? Is it possible I have memories of this place?

Elle pulls me onwards, breaking the vision. I look back before we slip through another door, the memory, if that's what it was, already gone. With a jerk of my arm she leads me along a maze of corridors that meander through the house like a jagged network of tunnels, gradually getting darker and tighter until we arrive at a stairway. I can feel the dust in my throat. It's like we have stepped into an unused wing of an old castle, a place of work and servants. I can even hear the boiler ticking over. In comparison to the stairs leading away from the hallway, this is a small staircase, straight, running up the side of a wall. There is little in the way of decoration; no portraits, paintings or fancy heirlooms adorn these walls.

We climb the stairs, covered in a deep red carpet that looks like it has been here since the house was built. The cornicing is decorated with edges and curves, ornate filigree to excite the senses. Everything feels old, antiquated somehow, as if it has been unused for years. It is so different from my house in London, where I have done all I can to bleach it of personality. We arrive on a landing, dimly lit like the hallway. There are a couple of panelled doors with elegant wrought-iron handles leading from it, plus one dead-end corridor no more than a metre deep. There is a tall dresser with high shelves against this wall, covered in photos. I lean in to take a look, but Elle steps in front of me.

'Bathroom,' she snaps as she points in one direction. 'Bedroom.' She points in the other. Her casual and lofty demeanour has vanished. There is a weight on her shoulders, bearing down on her from above. She is hunched and quiet, and she slips back down the stairs without so much as a goodbye. I watch as she leaves, unsurprised by how quickly her mood has changed. It's another reminder that she is still the same old Elle. I turn and look at the pictures, wondering if I am in any of them. But when I hear Elle and my father's raised voices in the kitchen, I am overcome by an urge to get away. I might want the truth, but this feels like too much too soon.

I push open the bedroom door, jiggling the handle, which is stuck. When the door gives way, I see that the inside of the bedroom is not much better. It smells damp and mouldy. The bed looks small, and as I sit on the edge of it, a cloud of dust encircles me. There is a smattering of old furniture, a lame butterfly painting on the wall, colours muted, or faded. Some sort of hook above the bed that was probably part of an old lighting fixture. The window is a narrow slit, poor-quality double glazing with a diamond pattern on the glass. The whistle of a light breeze glides past outside, and as I try to open the window, I see just how flimsy the frame really is. The kind a child might fall through if they leaned against it. I open the window and let in some air. It is a welcome relief. Finally I breathe.

Just off to the left, behind the six-car garage, I see workmen busy on scaffolding. I watch as they hack at the conifer trees that line the entrance to the nearby woods, and I search my mind for another memory. Do I remember those trees? I try to imagine them without three decades of maturity, squat like bushes. Maybe the garage wasn't even built back then. But nothing else comes to me, not like in the kitchen. I spot another maintenance man working in front of the garages, wiping over the car that I arrived in. He has the doors open, and I see my bag inside. My two jumpers and changes of underwear. My cigarettes and Valium. And my phone. My loose connection to the outside world, the one without a history, where memories don't jump out at me because they simply don't exist. I am struck by the realisation that I should have made things better with Antonio before I came here. Because right now he is the only remaining connection to the person I want so much to be, which makes him the only life raft I have. I look to the door, willing myself downstairs. I really want that phone, really should talk to Antonio. But now that I'm here in this room, I feel trapped.

I look around and spot an old phone on the bedside table. It is black, the flex fragile and in places exposed. An old rotary thing. I edge back on the bed, dust billowing upwards as the mattress creaks and groans, my knees bent up because the bed is so short. I pick up the handset to call Antonio.

But instead of hearing the tone of a working line, I hear voices.

'Yes, she is here,' says the first. A man. Him? My father?

'So, she insisted?' asks another man.

'Yes.' There is a long pause, the sound of breathing. 'But it won't be for long. Hopefully she will remain manageable.'

'You'll soon be rid of her, Maurice. Not long to go now.'

Maurice. Yes, Maurice. That was his name. Maurice and Cassandra. The almost parents.

'Quite. How quickly can you get here to finish the paperwork?'

I slowly push my finger against the switch, replacing the receiver on the hook. I slip down on the bed, put my hands over my ears.

'I don't want to be here,' I whisper, but even as I say it I know that it isn't really true. Deep down, I know why I came. To discover the truth that nobody would ever tell me. Not Elle, not Aunt Jemima. I came because I need to know why. I have always needed to know why. Why did I have to leave this place and my family to go and live with a woman who didn't want me? Why did they keep Elle and send me away? And now, after all these years, what is so wrong that they can't wait for me to leave? I came for the part of me that's missing, for the part of me that got left behind, and for the part that I always knew I would never be able to find anywhere but here.

5

The first time Elle found me was at my school when I was thirteen years old. I had delayed my exit because there was a boy, Robert Kneel, who had taken a dislike to the way I walked, which at the time was with a considerable wobble to the left and a rectifying stride to the right. That, coupled with my mildly hunched back, had earned me the nickname Bison, an unpleasant alternative to Peg Leg Irini.

Kneel was a skinny little runt, arms too long for his shirts, his ankles visible below his trousers. He was poor, and it showed. His skin was always a sickly grey pallor, like he wasn't getting enough iron in the free school dinners that he had to eat because his parents couldn't afford to feed him. Every day without fail he would hang around outside the school gates waiting for me.

I thought I had waited long enough, but forty minutes after the bell he was still there. By the time I saw him, there was no going back. So I put my head down, began walking faster. *Hhhhhhhuuuummmmmm* came the noise, the sound of a bison, guttural and as deep as his half-broken voice would permit. *Hhhhhhhuuuummmmmmm* began his band of three followers, soon erupting into a chorus of chanting.

They let me pass, a twist in the game that unsettled me even more, but they were soon on my tail.

That was when Elle appeared in front of me, a vision like I had never seen before. She was seventeen at the time. Her pink hair was in bunches, and the ring in her nose shone as the sunlight caught it. At first I thought she was a stranger, but then I noticed a small triangular scar on her forehead that jogged a subtle memory from my childhood. The memory was of our only other reunion, when I was nine years old. It was my parents who'd arranged that meeting, but they lived to regret it. Afterwards, Aunt Jemima said we had to move house so Elle wouldn't be able to find us again. She would have moved to a different country had Uncle Marcus agreed. Then Elle found one of our cousins in Edinburgh and followed her back to our new house. Finding my school after that was easy.

'Hi,' she said to me, as cheerful as you could imagine. The crowd of boys pulled up behind me, their hands on their knees as they caught their breath. She said it like we were old friends, as if I knew her.

'Hi,' I said back, my voice wobbly because I was close to tears, my cheeks flushed pink from effort, pain and embarrassment. But she walked past me, heading straight for Robert Kneel, and all that cheer drained from her face. The boys tried to run, realising the game was up, but she caught Robert by the hood of his jumper. That was what the tough kids did in 1996, wore illegal jumpers under their uniform blazers. Even the dirt-poor ones.

'You are a little cunt,' she said to him as she slapped him across the face. He fought and wriggled, his legs flailing and kicking, and all I could think was that tomorrow, when she wasn't there, I was really going to get it. I thought maybe he might even kill me.

'Get off, you crazy bitch,' he shouted. He had barely finished speaking when she threw him to the ground. And I mean *threw* him, like she was bowling or plate-smashing or something where there was an intent to break. I felt myself squeal, jump back as he hit the ground. One of his front teeth shot from his mouth like a bullet, followed by a trickle of blood down his chin. She turned to me and smiled, raised her eyebrows a bit, then kicked him right between his legs. He cried out in pain, but she just laughed. I couldn't believe it. I looked around for witnesses, as if I was the guilty party. But nobody was about. No houses overlooked this stretch of road. She had picked her spot well.

'Little cunts don't need balls between their legs,' she said as she kicked him again. 'I've been watching you for weeks.' She kicked him twice more before grabbing my hand and starting to run. I trailed behind her, my backpack bobbing up and down, covered with my cousin's scribbles from the year before.

We arrived at a green Volvo estate that was parked just around the corner. I remember thinking how lucky it was, because my hip wouldn't have taken much more effort. I sat in the passenger seat, watching her as she drove us to McDonald's, unable to believe what she had just done. We ate Big Macs and shared six portions of fries, Elle laughing about how much she had hurt Robert Kneel. I laughed along, but not very convincingly. I couldn't focus, the untameable fear of what would happen the next day at the forefront of my mind. Afterwards she bought me hot apple pie, and in my eagerness to appear grateful I burnt my lip. All the while we ate, she burnt matches down to her fingertips. At one point I could even smell her nails as the flame licked against them.

'You know I'm your sister, right?' she asked later as we sat on a bench feeding gravel to hungry ducks. I could feel her eyes upon me as I watched the ripples on the water, but what should I say? I wasn't sure, so after a long silence I nodded without really knowing it. 'That means we have to spend time together.' She reached over to my face and turned it in her direction, picked strands of my hair out of my eyes. I stared at her nose ring, unsure where to look. 'They don't want that, you know. Not since the last time. You remember what happened the last time, right?'

This time I nodded without delay. I didn't want to think about what had happened that day when I was nine years old, or the ambulance, or the cold, or the fact that Aunt Jemima's whole family had to move in order to keep me away from her. 'Yes, I remember.'

'Good. Because they can't stop us, Irini. Nobody can.' She leaned in, kissed me on the lips. I felt her tongue poke into my mouth, wet, sweet as the apple pie she had just eaten, yet cold from her chocolate milkshake. I didn't move. It wasn't sexual, more like the way a frog might catch a fly. I just think she wanted to know if I would let her. After watching her kick Robert Kneel in the balls, I would have let her do pretty much anything. Even though I couldn't deny that background level of fear, she was like a hero to me, and for the next five years the pattern was stuck.

'Nothing can keep us apart, you have to know that. But this is our little secret,' she said, before leaving me there with my milkshake and no way to get home.

Robert Kneel never bothered me again. He was taken to hospital by his parents, where one of his testicles was surgically removed because it was twisted and starting to go black. Everybody called him One-ball after that. The school asked me about the incident, and I admitted to being there. I said I had no idea who the attacker was, and that I got away from her by hitting her with my backpack. It helped that one of the other boys thought her hair was pink, and another blue. The next time I saw Elle, it was black.

That was the end of it. Elle had got away with it. Of course, Aunt Jemima knew the truth, and there were several fights between her and Uncle Marcus about her brother's *fucked-up family*. Aunt Jemima wanted to move again. Uncle Marcus refused. They wanted me to change school. I refused. I should have felt sorry for them perhaps, for all the difficulty my presence was causing. But I didn't. After all, they were trying to keep me from my hero. From Elle.

I should have felt sorry for Robert Kneel as well, but I never did. Even now, as an adult, I cannot muster any sympathy for his loss, even though I dream about him at least once a month. In fact I think he should be grateful for what Elle did to him, because when it would later come to setting up Margot Wolfe, someone else who hated me, he was still away from school recovering from the surgery. Otherwise he might have ended up a one-balled rapist.

6

I stand at the window and gasp at the chilly evening air. It is so much colder up here in the north, without the simmering heat of the city concrete to warm me. I scrabble in my pockets, pull out a pack of cigarettes and light one. I breathe in the smoke, suck it down. I look outside again as I exhale and notice that the short man who was straining over the Mercedes has left it unattended, doors wide open. I drag in one last lungful of smoke before stubbing out my cigarette on the wall, then waft the smoke through the window and march towards the door. I brace myself for confrontation, listening out for ghosts as I snatch it open, but I hear nothing and see nobody. I sacrifice silence for speed and rush through the house along the red carpet like some kind of VIP. I thought irony was supposed to be funny.

I move through the corridors, wishing I had been paying attention to the route when Elle brought me here. There are only two possible turns, but they look essentially the same, and taking the wrong one, stumbling into another household member, doesn't exactly fill me with fuzzy family feelings.

I plump for the left turn and strike lucky, arriving in the kitchen. I revisit the memory I had on the way in. Again I see myself as a baby, crawling along the floor. *Well done! Brave girl! Now spread your wings*, I hear, as if she, whoever she is, is here with me now.

Into the hallway. I hear voices in the background, coming from one of the adjoining rooms. I'm sure that one of them is the voice I heard on the telephone. Elle isn't here to divert me away. I could go and speak with him now. But I have to get my phone. So I skip awkwardly to the door, and breathe only once I get outside.

I can hear somebody moving about in one of the garages as I approach the car. I don't want to be seen, so I reach in, snatch up my bag and start back towards the house. I rummage inside to check the contents and realise that my phone isn't there.

'Is this what you are searching for?' I turn to see the portly man who was wiping over the car. He is holding up my phone.

'Yes, it is.' I snatch it from his hand. There is a perfect hole in the centre of the screen from which a series of jagged rings fans out.

'You must have dropped it on your way out of the car.' He pulls a dirty rag from his overstretched belt and begins wiping his hands. We exchange a light handshake, which he steers to a natural end by pointing at the ground. 'I found it just down here.' He tucks the rag back into his belt, and folds in a stray piece of his shirt. It is filthy, with a line of dirt engrained into the belly from where he has repeatedly brushed against the sides of the car.

I crouch down and run my fingers across the ground like a detective looking for clues. I find shards of glass and nod my head affirmatively before standing back up. I push the *Off/On* switch a few times, and a flicker of life flashes across the screen like the final beats of a heart just before death. The phone is fucked, and my annoyance whinnies out of me like a stroppy teenager. 'I can't believe it's broken.'

'Maybe you stepped on it,' he says, peering in to take a closer look.

'I don't think so.' I hold up my small left foot for his inspection, as if its minuscule size proves innocence. 'Who knows? Whatever. Anyway, thanks,' I mutter without sounding remotely thankful. As I begin to slink away, hoisting my tote over my shoulder, I hear him call out to me.

'Miss Irini,' he says. It is strange to hear my name used in this place. As if I belong, as if I have a place in the life that happens here. I turn, find him investigating the gravel of the driveway with the toe of his shoe. 'If there is anything you need while you are here with us, I'd be happy to oblige. Any time you want to leave, you just say. I will drive you anywhere you want to go.' I nod my head, smile in a way that doesn't look unappreciative. 'But in the meantime, go easy with Miss Eleanor. She, um . . .' He pauses, and I wonder what it is that is so hard to say. 'She doesn't take kindly to having to answer to anybody. I know it can be claustrophobic in there. The atmosphere . . .' He trails off, patting the disturbed gravel back into place. 'Oh,' he smiles, lets out a little chuckle, 'listen to me going on when you have only just arrived.'

'It's OK,' I tell him. 'But what do you mean?' I already

knew that there were secrets hidden in the creases of this house, and something about the way he looks at me, so pityingly, makes me certain that at least some of them are about me.

'Oh, you know, just a big old house,' he chuckles, but he doesn't seem amused. 'Creaks and bumps in the night.' I look back at the 1970s-design flat wooden panelling smothering the upper floor, the ugly double bay windows and the Corinthian columns holding up the porch. Even uglier in today's grey light than I imagine it might be in the summer. It's a hotchpotch design of whatever my parents might once have thought elegant. 'Anyway, anything you need, you just let me know. My name's Frank.'

'OK, thanks, Frank,' I say as I start to walk away. When I get to the front door, I glance back to find that he is still looking at me, watching me with a level of compassion I find hard to understand when I am nothing but a stranger.

I arrive back in my room and drop my bag at the side of the bed. I lie down, my legs curled up, my feet brushing against the foot end. I turn on to my back and stare at the ceiling. It is white with occasional patches of brown, water stains that must have been making steady progress for years. My eyes move across the objects in the room, searching for details upon which I can focus. I stare at the image of the faded butterflies and remember the words I heard in the kitchen. *Well done! Brave girl! Now spread your wings.* After a while I get up from the bed and take the picture down, creating a clean window of lemon paint. I shove it behind the chest of drawers. I take an ornament from the top; a little boy sitting on a mushroom, fussing with the fur of a rabbit at his feet. I open a drawer, place the ornament inside.

I lift the receiver of the old rotary phone. I dial my home number and hope that Antonio answers. I need to talk to somebody outside this house, and who else do I have? He picks up after three rings.

'Hey you,' he says.

'Hi,' I answer, surprised. 'How did you know it was me?'

'Rini, hi.' He pauses. 'Caller ID, distance call. Good guess, I suppose.'

Silence follows and I know he is still pissed off with me. Not for the argument we had the previous night, but instead for the things that remain unsaid. 'I made it safely,' I say, starting with something easy, stating the obvious. 'But my phone is broken.'

'I'm just glad you're OK.' He is quiet again for a long moment, but then I hear him physically soften, his voice sweeter and kinder. 'How are things?'

My turn for silence. Realising how fragile things are between us, I settle on a lie. 'I'm good. No problems.'

'That's good,' he says. Yes, everything is good. Perfect. Fine and dandy. Two idiots lying to each other because neither wants to face the truth. The word 'sorry' is right there on the tip of my tongue. It feels right to say it, but I'm not sure what it is I'm sorry for. I'm not sure I'd know where to begin. 'The flight was OK. She picked me up from the airport.'

'Your sister? Oh, really?' he says, not waiting for confirmation. 'How is everything?' he says again. I breathe in deeply before I reply.

'OK, I suppose.' I pause. 'She brought me here to the

house. I'm in one of the bedrooms now. I'm using their phone.' For a second he doesn't say anything, but he quickly tries to cover up his shock.

'What is the room like? Is it comfortable?'

'It's OK.' I edge up in the bed and roll over on to the pillow. I have stopped listening out for signs of family life on the other side of my four walls. Instead I watch the tops of the trees sway behind the garages, where the workmen are trimming them back. I can feel tears welling in my eyes and I hope my voice does not betray how I really feel.

'When is the funeral?' he asks. I hear him light a cigarette and it makes me want one, so I rummage in my pocket, pull out the pack of Marlboro red and take one with my teeth.

'I don't know,' I say, getting up from the bed to light my cigarette. I pick up the telephone base and take it with me as I move towards the window. I pull out more dust and fur balls as I lasso the non-elastic flex out from behind the cupboard. 'I guess soon.'

I lean against the window and gaze outside, and that's when I see my father. Goose pimples shiver across my body. He's holding something, a beaker with something brown that makes me salivate. He is watching the workmen attend to the trees, casually puffing on a cigar. A car pulls up and another man, short, thick around the middle with bright red cheeks and a flash of orange hair, steps out. My father walks forward to greet him, and they shake hands. The second man retrieves a briefcase from the car. As they turn to the house my father glances up at me. This time there are no shadows to distort what I see.

I dodge back into the room. I am not ready to put a real face to my idea of what he looks like. I have imagined him so many times, a character playing a role in my fantasies of family. He was always strong, broad-shouldered, and I was always small and in need of his help. Perfect father–daughter. If I grazed my knee I would imagine it was him tending to me while Aunt Jemima dressed the wound, his large hands on my cheeks, telling me that everything would be OK. The same if I woke from a nightmare. But now he is there in front of me, more diminutive than I had hoped. I pull the window shut so that I become nothing more than a shadow behind the glass. We are two strangers, but he must know it's me. Just in the same way I know it's him. The call of DNA from our bones.

Despite my hesitation I edge forwards, glancing down, revealing myself as the last light of day streaks through the window. I realise that although his face isn't familiar, he looks like the portraits on the wall in the hallway. I can see from here that he has the same slate-grey eyes as those painted faces, and his chestnut hair resembles mine. Nothing like the straw-yellow colour of Elle's. His long, angular nose, sharp and square as a meat cleaver, casts a shadow across his cheek.

'Rini, are you there?' comes the voice on the end of the telephone line. I watch a while longer until the two men disappear into the house. 'Rini, can you hear me?'

I step back into the room, curl up like a foetus on the bed as I hear Antonio speak. There was no joy in my reunion with my father. I thought at first he was pleased to see me, but after hearing his telephone conversation I realise that I am not the thing he aches for. Not the thing for which he cries at night. For the first time ever I wonder if what I hoped to find here even exists. But at least now he cannot pretend that *I* don't exist. Now perhaps I have been elevated from *distant memory* to *painful reminder of a badly made decision.* Perhaps he can feel me in his stomach, like the throb of an ulcer. I would take that over nothing.

'Rini, are you there?' There is desperation in Antonio's voice.

'Yes,' I whisper, my voice shaky. 'I am still here. I was . . .' I am not sure what to say. I'm not sure what exactly I was. I take a big breath before I whisper in hushed tones, 'It's *him.*'

'Who? Your father?'

'Yes,' I say, as I fiddle with the flex of the telephone. I look around the room, searching for something to tell me I belong here. I find nothing. Antonio is here on the phone with me, and yet still I feel alone. I feel the tears streaking across my cheeks. 'I have to go in case they pick up the phone. I'll call you back later.'

I hang up while Antonio is still talking. I stand and grab my bag and rush to the door. I even open it, as if I'm really going to leave. I could march downstairs and get Frank to whisk me away, if only I could just push myself through the doorway. But I can't, because where would I go? Back to Antonio? Home? If I did that, what about the reason I came here in the first place? I have to know why this place stopped being my home, and why my parents spent so many years keeping their distance. I drop my bag on the bed and take another Valium.

Chemically pacified, I dare myself down the stairs and into the kitchen. I can't stand this feeling of hiding, as if I should be ashamed that I am here. I came here for a purpose, and I have to fulfil it. So I edge towards the hallway, following the voices with every scrap of confidence I have left, sure that if I can just talk to him this could be easier. I'm close enough to hear the mumble of voices, but not close enough to make out their words. And as I follow the dark corridor, I see them, the two men, one of whom is my father. I hide in the recess of a doorway and watch him for a while.

'Just once, there.' My father is leaning over a desk with only a dim beam of light from an old brass lamp to help guide him. He is writing something, under instruction.

'And this one too?' he asks.

'Yes, I'll keep a copy,' says the other man. 'Better that way in case she creates a stink about it.'

My father nods in agreement but whispers, 'Keep your voice down. She is upstairs. I don't want her to overhear.' He straightens the papers and turns. I hear him say, 'No thank you. That will be all.'

I attempt to edge closer, but just as I begin to creep forward, an elderly woman dressed in a white pinafore slips out of the office carrying a tray. At first she doesn't see me. But when she looks up and catches sight of me trying to hide behind the grandfather clock, she dashes back, closes the office door. Shut out. My confidence slumps, limp as a wilted flower. I retreat into the kitchen and close the door behind me. Is there anything left for me here?

I root through the cupboards until I find an old bottle of sherry behind a bag of solidified flour. When I hear footsteps approaching from the hallway I hurry to the bedroom, curl up under the dusty sheets, my left leg hanging off the bed, sore from the stairs and all the running. I feel cold, so pull another jumper out of my bag, slip it over my shoulders. I become still and inanimate, something forgettable like the paintings and ornaments that have been left in this room to fade. This room and I are stuck in the past. A closed book, a sealed chest. It is only me who is still searching for people who don't seem to exist.

Just before I fall asleep, I hear the sound of a vehicle. I sit up and glance out of the window. I see four men, strong, dressed in black suits. I immediately know who they are, and what they are here for. I watch as they open the back end of the car, slide out a black coffin. They carry it low at their sides, and disappear through the front door of the house.

7

I awake the next morning with a head heavier than lead, and full of regret. All those years I erroneously thought returning home might provide a sense of belonging. It was the nonsense of a child. There is no calm from being here, and no hush has descended to quieten my pain. I'm still Irini.

My stomach is gurgling, rabid for food. I haven't eaten anything in hours. I reach for my phone on the bedside table before remembering the thing is broken. I look at the house phone and consider using it to call Antonio. But I decide against it, even though I think I remember telling him that I'd call him back.

Light is streaming through the window, and I catch sight of the little patch of lemon on the wall from where I removed the butterfly painting. I sit up, swing my feet out of bed. It is a beautiful day, the clouds have dispersed and the sun is shining. In the distance I can see mountains; somewhere closer still a village with a church. There are several impressive houses scattered in the nearest hills, and the view is quite beautiful. I reach for my bag and pick up the bottle of Valium, but put it back down again without taking anything.

Today is a new day, I tell myself.

I find a small photo frame in my bag, stowed in an inside pocket. Antonio bought it a couple of years ago. He put a picture of us in it, and it usually sits on his bedside table. He must have slipped it in when I wasn't looking. I consider leaving it there, but in this place of unknowns, the presence of Antonio's face can't hurt. At least seeing us together in this memory of Italy is a reminder that I was capable of building a life for myself, no matter how flimsy it might have been. We were even happy when this picture was taken. I take the frame out and set it on the side.

I cross the landing quickly and splash my face with scalding water. At some point the bathroom was painted a soft shade of baby blue. It's tired now, the paint peeling in giant eczema-like patches. I rinse my mouth, run water through my hair, then grip the sides of the sink because my legs feel weak. I run my palm across the mirror, and as my reflection appears it reminds me of just how little I resemble my father.

I reach over and turn off the tap. As soon as the water stops running, the floorboards creak on the other side of the door. I look down and see a shadow moving, visible through the space where the door doesn't quite meet the floor. Perhaps it's the old woman from last night. Perhaps it's Elle. I reach out and drag the locking mechanism into place just as I hear the handle being tested from the outside. I jump back as the door rattles.

'Are you in there, Irini?' It's Elle. She tests the handle again and pushes her weight against the door. I see the frame budge slightly, hear the subtle splintering of wood. I push back, willing her to stop. What does she want?

'I'm in here,' I say, stepping away as she releases the handle. Why does she want to get in? 'I just finished showering.'

I jump back as she tests the door once more. When it doesn't budge, she says, 'Come for breakfast. Hurry up,' with more than a little irritation.

I watch the shadow of her feet from my position on the edge of the toilet. When I am sure she has left, I wait in silence for another five minutes before leaving the bathroom. It feels just like being thirteen again, hiding in the school toilets in the hope that Robert Kneel would tire of waiting for me. Only this time it's Elle I'm hiding from, who back then was my hero. But a lot has changed since then. A lot has happened since that day she saved me.

I step into the hallway and cross to my bedroom, one eye on the stairs in case she is waiting for me. I take one last look at the picture of me and Antonio, sitting in front of the Fontana di Trevi on my surprise trip to Rome that he paid for with my money. At first it seemed logical to give him access to my bank account, when I knew he didn't earn much and I was desperate for him to stay. But during our time together I have purchased myself many beautiful Italian pashminas on his behalf that I never wear. And then there were trips abroad. Meals out. I didn't mind at first. But he started to buy himself gifts too. I was forced to open up a secret account into which I could siphon off enough money to pay the bills. I realised that my money was one of the things he loved about me, and when the funds grew smaller, so did his affections.

But I push that irritation aside, because I'm sure the frame is in a different spot from where I put it. I look at the bag on the floor, certain that I left it on the end of the bed. Is the Valium I took yesterday making me delirious? Or has Elle been in here, going through my stuff?

No memory hits me this time as I walk into the kitchen. Instead I am met by a small woman working at the sink, wrinkled and well into retirement. She is wearing a grey slip dress, a white apron over the top. Staff, the same woman who was here last night. She either ignores me or doesn't hear me as I approach. But as I cross the room, she catches the movement in the corner of her eye. She turns and smiles, one half of her face rising, the other frozen in time.

'Good morning,' I say. Her face is kind, simple, without frills or decoration. The kind of face you would like for a grandmother. There is no make-up on her skin, no effort to her bobbed hair, with the exception of two grips that hold it in place behind her ears. At some point she has suffered a stroke. Her left arm doesn't look as strong as the right, swinging without purpose at the side of her leg. I have a natural affinity for the afflicted, so I walk forward without any effort to cover up my limp, which after last night's comatose sleep in a bed too small is worse than usual.

'Good morning,' she replies, with only the slightest hint of a slur, something a good speech therapist has probably tried to help her overcome. 'Are you hungry, Irini?' She comes towards me, takes my hand in hers. She looks me up and down, paying special attention, I note, to my offset hip. 'What an unexpected treat to see you, in the most unfortunate of circumstances. You must be finding it all terribly confusing.' She doesn't wait for me to answer, and in fact looks somewhat embarrassed. Probably about shutting me out last night. 'If you are looking for Miss Eleanor, head straight and take the third door to the right.' She motions in the direction of the hallway, before glancing away as if she has suddenly gone shy. 'They take breakfast in there.'

I nod, and the old woman offers another lopsided smile. With my eyes to the floor I pass the galleried hallway and the stairs, heading straight along the corridor. I pass a selection of rooms, none of which I glance into for fear of what I might find, unsure if it is the living or the dead which scare me the most. As I arrive outside the third door on the right, it opens.

My father stops the second he sees me, halfway in, halfway out. I back away to the wall behind me. He glances left and right for an exit, his cheeks bright pink from where he has forgotten to breathe. Knowing that feeling of suffocation a little too well, I oblige his need and step aside so that he doesn't have to look at me. I wait for him to storm away, perhaps make a minor adjustment to his tie to avoid looking uncomfortable. But he doesn't take the opportunity I have presented. Instead, his eyes scan me up and down, snatching embarrassed glances on each pass. He sees a knee, then his eyes dart away to the floor. Fingers, then back to the floor. A scarred hip if he uses his imagination, or perhaps memories that we don't share. My heart is racing, my stomach bottoming out. I slide along the flocked wallpaper, my palms brushing against it like a cat's fur coat. He looks up again, sees my chest, then my chin, followed by the quickest flash to my face. He opens his mouth to speak, but before any words come out, the old woman from the kitchen shambles forward with a trolley straight out of 1970, gold legs topped with a white plastic tray, and pushes it between us.

Her presence breaks the tension, or connection, or whatever it was that was holding us both here. He scurries away, one hand held to his bowed head. The old woman is ushering me into the dining room, using the trolley to round me up like a farmer would a lost lamb. I glance over my shoulder and look at my father as he staggers along the corridor, willing him to turn around. But he disappears around an unknown corner, and with no other distractions I let myself be pushed into the room.

I find Elle sitting at a large oval table, watching the scene unfold. I clutch at the edge of my jumper, my palms damp at the sight of her, and take a seat. The room overlooks a vast grass lawn, so perfectly shaped and even in colour that it looks man-made. For a moment I think I can smell the grass, feel the wet mud on my knees as I drag myself along with my strong arms. Another memory? The sound of the door closing behind me breaks my concentration. When I look up, Elle is staring at me, her brow furrowed and eyes fixed. I can feel her gnarly fingers in my brain, trying to root around in my thoughts.

'Your presence upsets him,' she says, without a hint of acknowledgement that his could also upset me. I have no idea if she is trying to excuse him, make me feel better, or just simply tell the truth. It could be any one of those possibilities. There is a fourth: that she actually wants to hurt me. But I cannot bring myself to entertain it because I can't bear the thought that we have arrived at a place where she enjoys my pain.

'My presence here upsets me somewhat too,' I reply bravely. 'That's why I suggested staying in a hotel.'

The old woman sets a plate of toast and scrambled eggs in front of me, followed by a glass of watery juice. I shuffle in the wooden seat, trying to mould it comfortable. The eggs look cold, but the old woman's smile as she looks down at me makes me want to please her. I take a big mouthful, make an effort to show my appreciation. 'Very nice,' I mumble, and she smiles again, resting her hand on my shoulder.

'Not likely,' Elle comments as she bothers the tabletop with the tip of her knife. 'Since she nearly died, she hasn't had the same steady hand. Always overdoes the salt.' The glint of the blade transports me back to that day when I was eighteen, when I knew I had no choice but to cut Elle from my life. I can hear her words as if it was yesterday. *I'll fucking stick you with this, I promise you. I'll fucking slaughter you if you go near him again.* Without warning I reach up and touch my throat, and the sliver of a malignant smile creeps on to her face. I know she is thinking about it too, and what she did. I just know it. I can feel it, as if we are one and share the same thoughts.

She grinds the knife into the wood, her eyes never once leaving the cook's face. Shocked and desperate to move the situation on, I smile as I swallow the mouthful of salty eggs and touch the woman's arm to distract her from Elle. But I see that Elle's comments have hurt her. 'What?' Elle continues, unabashed. 'You think you're the same as before? He should have got rid of you, the same as the doctors should have let you go. Don't know what any of them thought they were trying to save.' She looks to me as I chase down the eggs with a gulp of juice. 'Of course I guess you'd disagree,' she says. 'You're one of those doctors after all. Think you can save the world and are too good for the rest of us.'

'They're very nice,' I repeat quietly as the old woman slinks away, pushing her trolley back to the kitchen. When she closes the door, I say, 'That was rude,' hoping it's loud enough to be heard on the other side.

'You used to like that about me,' Elle says, taking a triangle of toast and layering it with butter and then jam. 'You told me so. You used to like the ability I had to upset people. The undeniable way I could hurt our parents.'

'They are not my parents,' I say unconvincingly. I shovel in another defiant forkful of salty eggs.

'Yes they are. I remember the day you came sliding out of the dead woman in the very next room.' I cough and drop my fork, spilling lumps of egg on the crisp white table linen. A snide little giggle slithers out of her, as inappropriate as it would be if we were at a funeral. I hear my childhood wish reverberate in my head: *Make her want me, make her want me.* 'So,' she continues, neatly placing her knife and fork on her plate. 'We have a few things to discuss. She has arrived. Late yesterday, while you were upstairs with the sherry and the Valium. She is in the main sitting room, and you will have a look at her later. The funeral will be held in two days' time.' I put my napkin back down on the table, setting it alongside an unused cereal spoon. 'You are going to need some clothes, because you haven't brought anything acceptable with you. And there's no need to look so surprised and offended. So what? I've been in your bag. Big deal. We are sisters, you know.'

'Why?' I ask, without expecting an answer.

'I came up to talk to you. I don't get to do that much, do I now, especially not since you *stopped answering my calls*.' She enunciates the words so that there is no doubt about whose fault it is that we have lost touch. She wants to claim the upper hand, play the wounded victim. 'It's been six years since I knew how to reach you. Only now would Aunt Jemima give me the number, and that was only to avoid having to talk to you herself.' She snatches up another slice of toast from a rack on the table, dabs a knife at the butter and pushes it around the triangle. The mention of Aunt Jemima is enough to shut me up. I knew it was her who must have given out my number. I should be angry about it. I was a couple of nights ago. But here in this place, summoning that anger is not so easy.

My aunt and uncle tried to be there for me after I left to go to university, despite their obvious reservations. But the cat-and-mouse game I was playing with Elle, moving house and changing phone numbers, made it hard for them. They would turn up only to find that I had moved, leaving no forwarding address. Eventually we just lost touch. I tried to rekindle it once, not long before Antonio arrived in my life. But it wasn't the same. I belonged even less as an adult than I had as a child.

'I have to catch you unawares now,' Elle picks up. 'In the early hours of the morning, from an unknown number. I'm not sure what I did to make you hate me so much, other than being wanted by our parents.'

My cheeks flush from embarrassment. 'They are not *our* parents,' I say. 'They are *yours*, and yours alone. How many times do I have to say it?'

'I can see through your lies, Irini, but fine. Whatever you say.' She tosses her uneaten toast triangle on to her plate. She is straight back to chipper, actually rubbing her hands together like a good plan is coming to fruition.

'So, as I was saying. *My* mother came back late yesterday. We'll have a look at her soon. Then we will buy you some clothes.' She runs her eyes over my baggy black jumper, then shakes her head as if whatever thought came to mind was intolerable. 'Don't worry, *my* father has plenty of money. I will buy them for you.' She pauses as if going through a mental checklist of Irini-related tasks, counting them on her fingers. Operation Get Irini Ready for the Funeral. 'Then we will go to the gym. You've got so fat since the last time I saw you. You need to work out. The last thing we need is for you to embarrass us.'

She stands up, walks towards me and with a look of utter disappointment on her face slides the plate away from me as I swallow the last mouthful of eggs. 'I'll be back to collect you soon.'

She slips from the room, leaving me alone. I have no way out. I am unravelling. Being unravelled. Rather than give me answers, this place could destroy me. I finger the small roll of skin that curls over my waistband and wonder if you could call that fat. Maybe, but only if you were trying to be cruel.

I stand up and walk towards the bay window to look out across the lawn. The box hedging that lines the grass and the row of trees at the far end of the grounds have been neatly trimmed in preparation for the funeral guests. My eyes drift to a little white cross and I just know that that is where they buried the dog. The one that Elle killed.

It happened after the failed reunion when I was nine years old. I overheard Aunt Jemima on the phone not long after, describing how Elle had stomped their dog to death, blood all up her leg, all the way to the knee. Our parents had found her in the garden trying to dissect it with a butter knife. They held a ceremony the next day where they buried it, laid some flowers, erected the cross. I heard Aunt Jemima suggest that saying goodbye this way might help teach Elle about compassion.

I see my father again, making his way across the lawn. He is holding a tumbler of brown liquor, perhaps a brandy, sipping frantically. He sees me watching and looks at me for a second, then glances away again, shaking his head before it drops to his chest. Despite the fact that now he can barely bring himself to look at me, yesterday he wanted to see me. It wasn't coincidence that he was there when I walked through the door, and it was his idea to sit and talk. It was Elle who stopped him. She moved me along, put a stop to any hopes he might have had. And she was here again today when he couldn't bring himself to speak. Is it possible that he is afraid of her in the same way that I am? Do we share the same secrets, or does he hide more of his own?

Now I understand the look on my father's face as he left the dining room. It wasn't fear. It wasn't disgust at what he had created. For the first time I see something in my father that I recognise. Something we share other than a love of strong liquor at inappropriate hours of the day. It's something Elle knows nothing about, and this makes her vulnerable in a way I could never have imagined. It is shame that I see in my father. Not of me, but for himself.

8

I am grateful that we manage to leave the house without paying a visit to the dead body lying in repose in the sitting room. We don't have time, Elle informs me as she ushers me forward, skirting up behind me, rambling about our plans for the day. Sisters' Day, as she has labelled it, like we are a couple of twelve-year-olds who are about to learn how to put on lipstick and practise kissing on our teddy bears. We are to travel to Edinburgh, shop, go to the gym to combat my fatness so that I am not an embarrassment, talk and divulge secrets about our lives. Her excitement is on overload, and any earlier irritation that she may have felt seems to have been surpassed. I smile and laugh, mostly on purpose, an effort to make this as bearable as possible. But sometimes I even find myself laughing without trying. It is one of Elle's good points, her wit.

It was the thing that snared me the first time she found me. I was so used to being the target that to suddenly be on somebody's team, watching as her insults flew faster than her fists, was like the first breath after nearly drowning. In that moment when she burst into my life when I was a thirteen-year-old victim of just about everybody and everything, she made me feel like I was part of something.

United. Safe behind her walls. It was easy to put to one side what had happened four years previously, when our parents had attempted to reunite us.

Elle tours me through five different shops looking for suitable clothes to see me through the next two days. She parades me into each, announcing our presence with elaborate hand gestures and sweeping motions around hanging rails. By shop five we agree on an outfit: brown jeans with too much shine, and a beige jumper with the word *FEEL* written on it. She argues that if I won't accept the sportswear-as-everyday-wear idea, then she will flat-out refuse to buy me anything that adheres to my 'doctorial' tastes. She relents when it comes to the gymwear, allowing the purchase of a black workout set: leggings and a crop top, neither of which she will allow me to try on. The only thing I insist on is a pair of Reeboks. When we arrive at the gym and change – me in a private cubicle – it is obvious that the new workout gear is too tight. The small roll of soft skin that escapes over my jeans is being strangled like a hernia, bulging over the cinched-in waist.

'I can't wear this,' I say as I walk out, palms spread wide. When I eventually look up, I find her naked. She is balancing on one leg, her hip bones jutting out as sharp as our father's meat-cleaver nose. She catches me looking at her smooth skin, finely covering her salient bones. She looks like an anatomical drawing, sketched to perfection. She glances at her hip, and then back to mine. I look away, my eyes scanning newsletters about lost dogs and hippy yoga classes pinned to the wall for a distraction.

'Ha, there you go,' she says, pointing at me. 'I told you you'd got fat.'

'I'll put my T-shirt over it,' I huff as I reach for the shirt. But her arm flies up, intercepting me. She snatches the T-shirt from my hand, perfect tits and arms flying everywhere, the left one nearly catching me on the cheek. Her body is as bald as a baby. She tears the shirt, shreds it in two. *Rrrrriiipp.*

'Now you *have* to wear that,' she says, looking satisfied but flushed as she throws the shredded garment down and stomps on it as if it has caught fire. 'They are not too tight. You are too big.' She snatches at her bag, takes out her own workout gear. She pulls on a pair of hot pants but she is all of a dither, pissed off at me. She shoves her bag into a locker, slamming the door shut with such force that it seems to work loose from its hinges. My anger bubbles as I think of the people who will laugh at me trying to exercise my imperfect hip in this ridiculous outfit. But I don't want a scene, so I remain silent. There are people nearby already aware of our presence, and it would be much easier if this was understood to be an insignificant blip in an otherwise happy sisterly day. 'Hiding under the baggy layers just enables you to forget that you got fat,' she says as she takes a pinch of my abdominal skin in her hand, 'and I am not about to become your enabler.'

A few eyes remain on us as she hurries on a skimpy bra top. Socks, shoes. Headband. Mirror check. She snatches my hand before strutting towards the exit door, pulling me behind her. One woman especially appears to feel sorry for me, so I offer a smile and laugh it off. She seems unconvinced, scoops up her bag and moves away from us. 'I don't know how you ever managed to become a doctor looking like that,' Elle calls out loud enough for all to hear, as if my imperfect stomach has any bearing on my intellectual capabilities.

She insists we drink water before we begin, because *dehydration is a killer*, and then we complete an orientation circuit of the gym. She points out a couple of men she likes, a couple of women she doesn't, and one whom she knows to have chlamydia because she slept with her boyfriend and he confessed. After a series of stretches in front of the mirror that I cannot complete on account of my less than perfect anatomy, we start on the cross trainers. And I am enjoying myself, kind of. Sisters' Day, I think. Not so bad. I even consider probing the past, asking her what she knows about why I was given away. I have tried a few times before, the last when I was about sixteen years old. We had been out for the night, both got a bit tipsy. When I dared ask why they'd never wanted me, she grabbed me by the throat and pushed me up against a wheelie bin, much to the amusement of other revellers nearby. 'Our mother is a whore,' she told me. 'You don't need them. Don't listen to what they tell you.' Then she cried and held me in her arms like an overgrown baby, rocking me back and forth as we sat on the kerb. I was so mortified I never dared ask her again. But years have passed now, and she seems in a good mood at the moment. I decide to wait until we have finished the workout.

So we pedal alongside each other, one of her judgemental eyes always trained on me because I am going too slow. She might be thirty-seven, but she has the body of a teenager, and I am impressed. Enough to straighten my back and focus on not limping. I pull up my left shoulder to even up the line of my breasts.

Several men amble up during the workout. They hang out next to Elle's cross trainer, offering varying degrees of attention, and she smiles and giggles like a schoolgirl as they look her up and down, using their imagination to remove the tiny garments she is wearing. They speak to her chest, and she helps them out by stretching up like a cat for petting. One of them rests his hand on her ass and she pushes back into it. She looks at me in a way that can only be described as pitying, as if I should somehow be jealous of the mauling she is getting. I try hard to focus on the exercise, but the Valium and alcohol from the night before linger in my system, and the coffee I would normally have drunk by now is conspicuously absent. My face is flushed, beads of sweat trailing across it, salt licking at my lip.

After the ass-grabber moves on, the next victim saunters over wearing a T-shirt that says *Live to the Max!* Elle pays her newest admirer no attention. 'Looking good, working hard,' he says. At least this one speaks. He completes a quick circuit of the machine, casting his eyes up and down. There's another guy with him who looks over at me. He's a little shorter than the first, his eyes softly formed, with long lashes, his lips pouty and moist. He looks kind rather than beautiful like his friend. I knuckle down and push on, keeping my left shoulder held up. My speed increases like a rocket, and my hip complains, sending shooting pains ripping through my thigh.

'Always,' Elle replies, not once breaking her stride. 'You haven't been here for a while, Greg. Where have you been?'

'So you've noticed?' says Mr Live-to-the-Max, working his tongue into his cheek before nibbling on his own lip.

Gross. Elle smiles and pushes her tits out even further. He offers her his towel. She refuses, but stops driving the machine and picks up her own, dabbing it across her face and then her bulging chest. He watches her, shifts his weight in a way that makes me think he got hard. It is enough to break my concentration, so I stop and grab my own towel.

'Not really,' she says. 'It's been too long to remember you. How many others have been on my mind between then and now?' She rolls her eyes upwards in a daydream, holding up her fingers to count what I'm sure are not imaginary men. Somewhere in the background I can hear the drumming of feet on the floor as an aerobics class starts, an over-enthusiastic voice booming across the speakers. 'More than enough to forget you,' she concludes as her counting fades out somewhere before the tenth finger. She flicks the tip of his nose, butt stretched right back and angled upwards as if she is just waiting for him to mount her.

'Only on your mind?' he says as he slides one hand over her slick, wet thigh. I step from the machine, desperate to put some distance between us. Greg nudges his buddy in the side without taking his eyes off Elle. He says, 'Matt, where do *you* think they've been? In her mind, or elsewhere?' His hand disappears from view and Elle squeals as if she is on her way to climax right here in the middle of the gym. There is a pensionable woman behind her with a good vantage point, who without any doubt can see exactly what is happening. She makes a disgusted noise, half snort, half yelp, and brings her hand up to her mouth as if she is about to be sick. She steps from her own machine and heads to the treadmills on the other side of the room.

'No idea,' says the one called Matt, uninterested. I'm impressed by this lack of attention for Elle, reassured by his easy Scottish accent. He's doing that thing that Antonio did when I first met him, paying attention only to me and ignoring everybody else. But he's different, too. From the first moment, I knew Antonio wanted me physically. He made it clear, like Greg is doing with Elle. But Matt isn't doing that. He doesn't feel dangerous like Antonio did. 'Maybe they were visiting her at the loony bin,' he mutters under his breath, just loud enough for me to hear. I can't help but giggle, and I realise what a traitor I am. Only minutes ago I was lounging around in the idea of sisterhood, thinking that we were connecting. Now I'm laughing at her expense.

'Who's your friend?' Greg asks Elle. 'Not seen her before.'

'She isn't my friend,' says Elle, laughing as if he has just told the best joke in the world. He laughs too, pleased and smug with himself without really knowing why. The kind of guy who would get some of his ribs removed so that he could give himself a blow job. That's how impressed he is with himself. 'She's my sister.'

I can tell that Greg is thinking *no fucking way.* Elle smirks as she rubs up against him. I bring an arm around my chest, let my shoulder slacken.

'Nice to meet you,' says Matt, holding his hand out to me. He looks embarrassed about the loony-bin joke, so I take his hand in my sweaty palm and manage a proper smile.

'You too,' I say, noticing that Elle is already halfway to the door with Greg. Fortunately I am flushed from the exercise and it masks my embarrassment. Why it matters to me that Elle is slutting it up all over the gym, I'm not sure.

'I think we've been stood up,' Matt says.

'Well you're in a better position than me, because I'm going to have to wait for her to get back.' He is laughing too now, but I don't think he seems like the type who would try to belittle me. He is too movie-good-guy for that, handsome in a simple way, hair foppish, slicked to his wet forehead. 'What's so funny?' I ask.

'You'll be waiting a long time. Last time they left together, I didn't see him until later on that week.'

'Great.' I shrug, tossing my towel back down. I take a glug from my bottle of Evian water. 'What am I going to do now?'

'I can take you home if you like,' he offers. 'Wherever you want to go. My car is just outside. Give me a minute to get my stuff.' He rushes off without waiting for an answer, but I don't think I would have refused even if he had given me all the time in the world. I go and get changed, grab my bag.

He comes sprinting from the changing rooms with wet curls and pink cheeks. We head out and walk in silence to his car, and I lag behind a step or two, watching him as he moves. He looks so relaxed. He opens the boot so I can toss my new gym bag in.

'You see,' he says, casting his hand left and right. 'No ropes, handcuffs or bottles of chloroform.' I laugh. 'You'll be quite safe.' I climb into the passenger seat and reach across for the belt.

9

'Now, where am I taking you?' he asks as he gets in the car. Where the hell am I supposed to tell him to take me? It's not like I have many choices.

'Do you have Elle's phone number? Maybe I should try and call her.' Surely that's the best plan. I'm not certain I could find my way back through the maze of country roads that lead to the village where my family's home is. Which is a shame, because I could have used this time to try to talk to my father.

'Aye, I have it,' he says, stifling a smile. 'But do you really want to call her now?' He gives me a knowing look, like I have been naive not to consider what Elle is doing.

'Good point. I'll call her later,' I say. I make a mental note to call Antonio later too. 'Maybe we could go for coffee, wait for them together?' Other than linger at the gym, what else am I going to do? What would Elle do? Certainly not mope around waiting for me, that's for sure.

'Sounds good.' He starts the engine and we pull away.

We drive through twisty lanes away from Edinburgh, the endless countryside without border or restriction, segmented by hotchpotch walls and sudden outcrops of rock like the one behind my family's house. The sunlight slices in through the window in golden blades of light, intermittently blinding me like some kind of torture device. Eventually he pulls up outside a country pub, an ancient building that has been repainted in a shade of bone grey, decorated with finely cut topiary bushes in spheres. A sign hangs outside: *The Dirty Dog, Gastro Pub*, like they needed to advertise what they were just in case somebody got confused.

'This OK?' he asks as he pulls the keys from the ignition.

'Yes,' I say, and he nods his head, pleased with himself.

We go inside, my hip not doing at all well with the steps after all the exercising. The smell of beer and wine floats past me, mixed with a lavender-scented wood polish. There is an acoustic mix on the stereo playing well-known rock songs: a woman singing 'Losing My Religion', followed by a poor rendition of U2's 'One'. Matt orders the drinks while I stake out a table and stretch out my left leg. He returns with two large glasses of straw-coloured wine and pulls out his chair. Before we have even exchanged a word, half of my wine has gone.

'Needed that.' I try to speak lightly, as if this whole situation is normal. To be here with a stranger at the best of times would be tough – I'm not really one for small talk – but today, on Sisters' Day, it somehow seems even worse. I'm disappointed at how I allowed myself to believe that it might have been different, that maybe I would have spent the day with Elle talking about something worthwhile. That maybe by the end of it I would have been left with the truth.

Matt eyes up my glass and the remaining wine. After a moment he picks up his own and gulps it back in an effort to catch up. 'So, tell me. How come I never knew that Elle had a sister?' He has a cheeky smile; he is confident that this is a safe subject between two strangers. I consider truth or lie, but realise that if I admit anything less than the truth, Elle will call me out on it later and I'll look stupid.

'Because she doesn't, not really.' He scrunches up his eyes, confused, and a deep line forms between his eyebrows. He says nothing, waiting for me to clarify, knowing that the safety net he thought he was in just fell apart. 'We didn't grow up together.'

He appears relieved, nods along, all-knowing. 'Divorce is hard. My parents too. Weekends with Dad, one holiday a year.' He shakes his head like the part-time-parent memories are as bad as he could possibly imagine. He's trying so hard to empathise with me, sharing the tough moments of his past. I could almost feel sorry for him, if it wasn't all so ordinary. But I know that isn't the whole story. People always keep something back. He leans in a little and the scent of his shampoo drifts across the table, a familiar smell. White Musk, the smell of my teenage years; it was what Elle used to steal for me to cover up the smell of cigarettes. 'I wouldn't choose it for my kids,' he continues, 'and I'll never get divorced. No matter how hard it gets.' He sips at the little bit of wine he has left. 'That's if I ever get married and have kids,' he adds as an afterthought, and for a moment, just in the way his eye twitches, he seems terribly sad.

'Actually, that's not it. She lived with our parents. I didn't. Our parents never got divorced. I lived with other family members from the time I was three years old.' It feels good to hear it aloud. I think of all the times Antonio has told me that I will feel better once I get it off my chest, and see now that perhaps he was on to something.

'Oh. That must have been hard.' Matt is kind of lost, stumbling about in the dark, fiddling with the menu card on the table. But I can see there is fight there, a determination that all is not lost. He is wondering how he can still pull this back and make the next few hours bearable. 'Siblings are really everything, though. I have a sister. Love her to bits.' He rocks his head to the side, left and right as if his neck is a weighing scale. 'My parents, not so much. They didn't make the best choices. But me and my sister stuck together. Don't know what I would have done without her.' He smiles, I smile. We're both smiling, and bizarrely, in spite of everything, I don't feel so bad. But there are other memories buried in there that he hasn't shared yet. I know that look, trying hard not to reveal so much of yourself that you scare people away. I like him even more because of the things he might be keeping hidden.

'Maybe we should call Elle,' I say, wanting to let him off the hook, change the subject. 'Do you have her number?'

He looks confused. 'Don't you have it?'

'No, my phone is broken.' I pull it out of my jacket pocket and show him, as if I need to prove myself.

'Looks nasty,' he says, tracing a finger over the cracked screen.

'Can I use yours?'

He passes it over. I sit with it in my hand. He directs his attention to my phone, wondering if it is salvageable. He is a fixer, just like Antonio. But after a moment he looks up, realises that I don't know the number. I think maybe that's not so weird. After all, who remembers telephone numbers nowadays?

'Check the phonebook,' he says. 'I have her number stored in there.'

I scroll the names, make the call without saying a word. When nobody answers, I slide his phone back over the table, avoiding the beer rings that have been left by a previous occupant. 'Obviously still busy.' I raise my eyebrows, realising again that he finds me funny. I smile, without trying, the realisation of which makes me smile more.

'Let's get another drink,' I say as I swill the last of my wine down. Matt nods, jumps to his feet as if what I said was an instruction. He returns with two fresh glasses, and I see how the first has already touched him, wobbling down the steps from the bar, the whites of his eyes pink and glassy.

'I think we should get something to eat, too,' he announces, and I nod in agreement. He quickly settles on a steak with chips. I order a heavy pasta dish in the hope that it will be enough for the rest of the day so that I won't have to suffer another meal in the dining room at the house. Until the food arrives we chat about the weather and how it has been a mild summer. He tells me about his work, even though I don't ask, and it turns out he is a successful investment banker. He works with Greg, who I learn has a bit of a thing going with Elle. The food arrives, and he digs into his before I have even picked up my knife and fork.

'So tell me more about you,' I say, wondering if it sounds like I am flirting. He slices through the steak, takes a chunk of it in his mouth.

'What do you want to know?'

'Tell me more about your family.'

He finishes swallowing, takes a sip of his wine. 'Well, I don't remember my parents together all that much. Dad was a good guy, but they couldn't make it work. He claims that she was difficult and controlling; she claims the same. Said he was a womaniser.' He shrugs his shoulders and gulps down more wine. Now I realise why he seems like such a good person. He doesn't want to be like his father. Perhaps. 'They are both great people, but not when they're together. Like I said, they made some bad choices.'

'What kind of bad choices?'

He sets down his knife and fork, aligns them on his plate. He's thinking about telling me, but something holds him back. I want to tell him that I won't judge him. That I know what a shitty childhood feels like, and that I'll understand. That was something Antonio could never fathom. But I keep quiet, and end up feeling guilty for having asked.

'I'm sorry,' I say after the long silence, my cheeks flushing. 'That was nosy. You don't have to tell me anything.'

'No, no,' he says, flying into action. 'It's OK. It's just, well, I'm always worried how it sounds.' He allows himself a brief glance out of the window for courage before turning back to me. 'I didn't take their divorce all that well. Went a little out of control. I had to spend some time with a therapist. In a clinic.'

I answer quickly so that he doesn't have a chance to wonder if I'm uncomfortable. 'Maybe that was one of their good choices. For you to get well.'

His head drops before he turns away, gazing out of the

window. He doesn't offer anything more and instead fills his mouth with food.

I change the subject. 'So what about Elle? Have you known her for a long time?' It is a risk, because in some ways I don't want to know things about her. I know so much about her already, terrible things I wish I didn't. Yet I can't help myself, because there are whole years that passed by when we were apart.

'A while. A year maybe. I met her at a charity fundraiser.' He stops when I nearly spray him with wine, bringing my hand up to catch the drips that escape through my surprise. *Charity? Elle?* 'You OK?' he asks. When he is sure I am not about to choke, he continues. 'It was about a year ago. A kid at the gym got cancer and needed to go to the States for treatment. Had some rare type of bone cancer.'

'How old was he?'

'I'm not sure.' He shrugs. 'Not more than eighteen, nineteen.'

'Probably Ewing's sarcoma.' I might only put people to sleep for a living now, but there was a time when my knowledge was good.

'That was it. I remember now. How do you know about that?'

That's when I realise I have given away another snippet from my life. No turning back now, I think, on this road of truth. 'I'm a doctor.'

'Oh,' he says, glancing at the dodgy *FEEL* jumper and two near-empty wine glasses. For the first time, I feel judged. But there is no point in being angry about it. After all, he knows Elle, and that we share the same blood. 'I didn't realise. I thought—'

'That I was like Elle?' I finish on his behalf. 'A bit empty?' We both smile and I shake my head. 'No. I am nothing like her,' I say, aware that I don't really believe that is true. We *are* alike, both craving the attention of those who make us feel good.

'Anyway, that's where I met her. She was heading up a cake stall of things she had made.' That I doubt, remembering the cook and her salty eggs. I can imagine Elle standing over the woman in the kitchen, demanding and shouting out her orders. 'Greg started fussing over her, had fancied her for ages. You know, it's easy to be drawn in by Elle at first. She's a bonnie wee lass.'

'Yes, she is very pretty,' I admit.

'But it doesn't take long to realise that there is more to her than that. And I don't mean that in a good way. Oh!' He palms at his face in despair. 'I shouldn't have said that. Being rude about your sister, yeah, way to go, Matt.' He gives himself a sarcastic little cheer, raising his fists like he is a self-appointed champion jackass. I realise he is trying to impress me, and that I like it. 'Anyway, she was cold for a long time with him. But that just drove him on. Then they started hanging out.' He hangs his head, nibbles on an otherwise well-manicured thumb as if he is embarrassed to continue.

'What?'

'Your sister. She is kind of . . .'

'Weird?'

He shifts a bit, trying to get comfortable in his seat, before relenting. 'Yeah, but also kind of scary. She sleeps around with people at the gym, runs hot one minute, cold the next. Drives like a total maniac. But Greg is an idiot, and he thinks there's something between them. He is a total slut too, though. Oh, hang on, I didn't mean that she is.'

'Yes you did. It's OK.'

'It's not just Greg that she has a thing with, you see. There are others, too.'

'Yeah, I figured that out for myself.'

He moves in close, leaning over the table to share a secret. He beckons me forward. 'She had a thing with this other guy. He doesn't go to the gym any more. They had a one-night stand, but it turned out that the guy had a girlfriend who also used to go to the gym. When it came out about his fling with Elle, it all kicked off.'

'You mean his girlfriend found out and went crazy?'

He leans in closer, his voice dropping to a whisper. 'No. Elle went crazy. She kicked off with the girlfriend. Said he was hers and that she wouldn't share. She ripped out a chunk of the girl's hair.' He pulls at his own hair and I imagine the poor girl defeated, lying on a yoga mat with the clump of hair on the floor at her side. But I can't say I'm surprised. If I was prepared to consider whether Elle might have been responsible for our mother's death, picking a fight with an unsuspecting girlfriend seems pretty mild. Her words from the day I ran from her ring in my head. *I'll fucking stick you with this, I promise you. I'll fucking slaughter you if you go near him again.* It was a moment when I had never needed her more, and when I had never needed more to get away. Attacking a girl at the gym

76

doesn't even register on Elle's scale. 'I warned Greg, but he said he knew she was crazy. That the crazy ones are the best.'

'Well, I don't know Elle all that well,' I lie, 'but I have always known she had problems.'

He seems troubled by my lack of surprise. 'So why do you still see her?'

'I don't. In fact I avoid her for this very reason. But our mother died a couple of days ago.' He is visibly shocked, all slack-jawed and slit-eyed. He sits upright in his seat as if I have just told him the moon is orange and the sun is white. That, or somebody shoved a stick up his backside. 'I came for the funeral.'

'She *just* died?'

'Yes.' I can see his mind working overtime, trying to figure something out, like I have just put forth a convincing argument about the world being flat. 'What? You look surprised.'

'I am. Elle told me that her parents died years ago. In fact, now I come to think of it,' he says, his cheeks flushing as he scratches at the back of his head, 'she told me that her sister had died too.'

There is silence for a while. I shake my head and know that he wishes he could take back what he has just said. 'She's a liar. Our mother died a few days ago. My father is still alive, and so am I.'

He is grateful for my stoicism, grips on to it in order to help us move forward. 'I'm sorry for your loss.' He reaches over, touches my hand.

'Thanks, but since I came here I'm struggling to see what it is that I have lost. I always hoped that one day I would return to my family home and find a family. At least find out why I was given away. But I'm not sure there was anything left for me to find. According to you, my sister labelled me as dead a few years back. And as far as my parents are concerned, I've been dead to them for even longer. Since I was three years old. Even now my father has hardly spoken to me.' I nibble at my lip, and then at my already sore thumb. My hip starts to throb and I reach down, try to rub some heat into it. 'They gave me nothing to lose,' I say, pulling my hand away from his.

'Don't say that,' he says, reaching further across, his fingers brushing against my forearm. 'They gave you lots. That face, for one.' He is smiling, really trying to make it all right. Like he just ripped my past away from me and is now responsible for giving it back.

'Matt, they gave me away and kept Elle. I was never wanted by them, and I never will be.' I pull my arm away again, link my fingers together and rest my chin on my hands. 'Other than the truth about why they rejected me, I want nothing from them, or anybody else.'

He tries not to look hurt as he returns his hand to his lap. 'That can't be true.'

'Why not?' I ask, my chin cocked forward like I'm ready for a fist fight.

'Because we *are* our parents, Irini. We are what they make us, either by their presence or through their absence. Has a day gone by that you haven't thought about them? I bet not. And when they die, there is a part of us that dies with them whether we spent our lives together or not. They take part of us back, the bit that always belonged to them and that we never realised was theirs to keep. When it's gone, it leaves a space in us. It's all right to be hurt by that, but you can't deny it.'

'That's rubbish. They already created enough space in my life. Their death won't change anything.' As soon as I have said it, I want to take it back. It leaves me sounding needy, spiteful, hurt. I don't want to be any of those things, and I suddenly wish Elle was here, just like all those times before when I have wished she was still around to make me feel wanted. 'I just mean that nothing can change the past. They didn't want me. It's simple.'

And then he says something that changes everything, like a light switch illuminating the darkest corners of my life. An eye suddenly open. Awake. 'But for three years they did want you. They kept you, loved you, no doubt.'

I think of my father's face this morning, unable to look at me, ashamed. It might be the first time that I see there is another version of events apart from the one I have created. In my version of my life it was always about me and what I have lost. I never considered anybody else in this sad little story. I never assumed they didn't have a choice. I never considered that maybe they had lost me just like I had lost them.

'If I was you,' Matt continues, 'I wouldn't be asking why they didn't want me. I would be asking what happened to make them believe that after three years of being your parents, they couldn't do it any more.'

10

When I was eight years old, Aunt Jemima decided to take me to Kiddiwinks, a parent/child club. She had been going there with her children for the last three years, but they had never taken me before. So it was a big day for us. For me. Out with the family instead of home with a sitter. They told me I was to behave. I was to be a good little girl and act like they had taught me. I wasn't to cause trouble. That's what adults tell kids who have a tendency to misbehave. And I had a tendency.

That was what Miss McKenna had said at the parents' evening the week before. The new school year had just started and I had been acting up, being disruptive, destroying other children's work. It had come to a head when I planted a sharpened pencil into another girl's hand. Straight through it went, like a knife through soft cheese. Margot Wolfe. I thought she was a precious little cow. She always looked too perfect. She had better clothes than me, a better bag than me, and her pencils were all new whereas mine had been sharpened down, things filtered out from my cousins' belongings. I was the kid in hand-me-downs with snot slipping across my face. And I hated her for it.

So when parents' evening came, it was a big deal. I had to go too, and I was kind of excited because it was the first time I remember having to do something as a parent/child combo. I knew they weren't my parents, but that didn't matter. All the way there I was looking forward to it, and the bloody hole in Margot Wolfe's hand was barely even a memory. I didn't realise my behavioural issues were going to be discussed.

After Miss McKenna laid out the case that I was uncontrollable, an effort that brought her close to tears, the headmistress, a stocky woman with big calves, suggested a psychotherapist. I remember Uncle Marcus stating that it was a familial problem, which made Aunt Jemima drop her head in shame. Shame that she was part of the family with the problem. She was my paternal aunt after all. It was her genes, and her brother's decision to get rid of one of his kids that had thrust me into their midst. Uncle Marcus even suggested it was a genetic abnormality, that I was the same as my sister. I didn't understand what he meant at the time.

But, they stressed, making absolutely certain that it was understood, *they* weren't my parents. What were they supposed to do? This night wasn't even for them. It was for parents and teachers. They had been lumped with me, like a kitten found in the back garden that you don't really want but you haven't got the heart to watch starve to death. So you take it in and pretend to like cats, hope it will become tame. That's what Aunt Jemima and Uncle Marcus were to me. The reluctant guardians who watched helplessly as I left a trail of kitten shit all over their nice organised lives, full of ordered and pretty children with good hips who didn't wear hand-me-downs and who had been wanted from the start.

So Kiddiwinks was an effort to make me a better child. The psychotherapist said it would help. I was supposed to learn how to integrate, as if all that was needed was a few simple play dates. We were supposed to ignore the fact that I knew my parents didn't want me, that kids at school called me Peg Leg Irini and that I shared the Harringford genes. Soft play with kids I didn't know. The apparent answer to all my childhood problems.

But even at eight years old I was sceptical. Climbing over rubber cubes and swinging from nets, sliding down spiral slides and bouncing on trampolines is all fun and ball games when you're able-bodied. But I wasn't able-bodied. I could walk by that point, didn't even need my frame. I was still lame, but most people ignored the limp and the slight tendency to veer to the right. Climbing wasn't fun, though. Clambering wasn't fun. Running wasn't fun. Still, when they encouraged me into the soft play area like an animal into a circus ring, I was expected to perform. I saw them watching with horror at my lack of integration, that elusive something that apparently could be found at the bottom of a ball pit. So I smiled and waved and made an effort. I pushed myself deeper into the land of foam and watched Aunt Jemima pray for a miracle. I managed to climb over one obstacle, then slipped head first into a pit of balls. The only other option had been a climbing net made of rope, and there was no way I was following my cousins over that. So in I went, letting myself sink. I thought at least I could hide there until it was time to leave.

But when they couldn't find me, all hell broke loose. I

called out but they couldn't hear me over the commotion. My dodgy leg wouldn't balance with all those plastic balls underfoot, and I couldn't swing it back round to gain any purchase on the good leg. The police were called, along with the fire brigade. They had to dismantle part of the play area and empty the balls out one at a time from the top. They reached me after another hour. Of course they assumed I had done it on purpose. Attention-seeking was what they said. Family trait, Uncle Marcus claimed, one judgemental eye cast towards Aunt Jemima.

That was the last time we went to Kiddiwinks. We scrapped the search for integration, and the psychotherapist who suggested it in the first place. *We have three children of our own, you know. We can't afford for you to see a therapist, just because you can't learn how to behave.* There was no money for hare-brained schemes like that, not even with what my father was sending.

So, out of fresh ideas, they began to wonder if a reunion with my sister might help. Aunt Jemima told me at the time that Elle had begged them for it. I was so excited. This was, after all, what I wanted. For my family to want me. Elle had apparently made all sorts of promises about how good she would be if only they would let her see me. I guess they still had hopes for who she might become.

My father brought her to Aunt Jemima's house. My mother came too, but all I remember of her was listening as she cried in the hallway while Aunt Jemima did her best to comfort her. I had worn my best dress in the hope that my mother might like it. Aunt Jemima had braided my hair with a red ribbon tied on the end. I thought that if she could only appreciate the effort I had made, she might realise her mistake and take me home. But they ushered us outside to play in the garden before she even got a chance to see me.

For a moment at least they must have got distracted, because within fifteen minutes I was standing half-naked on the railings of Slateford Aqueduct, watching Elle floating face down in the water below. It was my turn to jump, just like I had promised her. I wanted to impress her, but I remained unconvinced how that could happen if we were both dead. Maybe that's why I didn't jump, and instead let myself be coaxed down by a friendly passer-by. Any ideas regarding family reunification were scrapped after that. Instead, Aunt Jemima moved house, taking me with her, and hoped that might be the answer.

The story of my childhood assault on Margot Wolfe gained notoriety in the following years. Margot, of course, hated me for what I'd done, and would show everybody the scar that Peg Leg Irini had given her. And yes, it still hurt, even after all those years, thank you for asking. Even though she deserved it, I hated the sympathy that Margot Wolfe got. I hated the fact that she hated me. So after Elle found me four years later and we put Robert Kneel in hospital, I decided to finish what I'd started when I was a kid. Reunited with Elle, I felt unstoppable. Nobody even knew that we were seeing each other. I saw being with Elle as a way forward, and a chance at something better. A chance to put the past behind me and become somebody who was wanted. It was time, I thought, to teach Margot Wolfe a lesson. I had no idea the lesson would end up being mine, and one I would live to regret for the rest of my life.

11

Matt and I spend another hour mulling over the trivialities of my adult life: where I work, how it feels to anaesthetise a patient, how it feels to watch one die. Then Greg calls. Elle is with him, and they have finished. She insists on picking me up from The Dirty Dog. After an awkward goodbye kiss on the cheek from Matt, I get in her car. Elle is full of it, excited and anxious to resume Sisters' Day. But the idea that what happened all those years ago was beyond my parents' control remains at the forefront of my mind, like a fly bothering at a light bulb. Could they have been as influenced by Elle as I was? I have never let my parents off the hook before, and the idea that it wasn't their fault is tempting. But Elle's chatter soon takes over, and she starts filling me in on the whole story of her and Greg with more detail than I care to mention.

'Anyway, enough about him,' she says eventually. 'He is boring. BOR-RING. You know all he talks about is the slide in crude oil prices.' She puts on a mock accent, impersonates some hoity-toity slimeball. 'Let me tell you about the latest active deals and the summer internship I'm about to take in New York. And then I'll fuck you while I talk about mergers and acquisitions and my fiancée and yada yada yada.' She snaps her fingers to emphasise the fact that he never shuts up. I settle into my seat, thankful, sort of, that Sisters' Day has resumed. But the mention of Greg's possible fiancée reminds me of the poor girl Elle attacked at the gym. If there *is* a fiancée, I wonder if she knows about Elle. 'All the damn time. I should tie him up and ice-pick him to death like in that movie. What was it called?' She bursts into hysterics, motions furious ice-picking action, snorting as she laughs.

'*Fatal Attraction*,' I say, as we continue along the straight road. Large grey houses rise up all around us. People. Other lives. A place where I could blend in. I let out the breath I've been holding.

'Yes, that was it. *Basic Instinct*. That lizard man Greg is always talking about was in it. You know the one.'

She approaches a roundabout and doesn't slow down. I push my foot on to an imaginary brake and cling to the door handle in order to stay upright as she takes the exit. A familiar feeling surges over me, the same as I had when I was balancing on that bridge, right before somebody dragged me from it. *Don't show her you're scared.* Horns wail behind us, and I wonder where the test-perfect driving of yesterday disappeared to.

'It was Michael Douglas in both of those movies,' I say, barely able to keep up.

She snaps her fingers again. 'Yes. Gordon Gekko. That's who he wants to be.' She swerves out wide to miss a pedestrian and then slams on her brakes. She is fuming, her cheeks flushed pink, her breath whinnying as she turns back to take a look. I turn too, find an old lady who probably didn't see or hear the car at the speed Elle is going. 'Fucking blind bitch,' Elle says, before opening the window and chanting, 'Oi, are you fucking blind or something?' There is such hate for the old woman, her teeth set and lips stretched tight as she turns back to hold the wheel. As she pulls away, she shouts, 'Fucking bitch,' before turning to me and saying, 'Anyway, I'd rather fuck Charlie Sheen. He could strap me down with those red braces.' She titters to herself as she glances in the internal mirror, smoothing her eyebrows into shape. 'Let's go home so that I can introduce you to her.'

I watch in the side mirror as the old woman crosses the road, a passer-by there to steady her after her run-in with Elle. They are both staring at the car, disbelieving. 'Elle, before that, I have to ask you something. I've tried time and time before, and now there's no point in hiding it any more. Not now that she's dead.' I swallow hard, try to feel brave. 'So just tell me. Why did our parents give me away?'

Her speed slows a little and she checks the tension of her seat belt. Licks her lips. 'What?'

'Why just me? What happened?'

'It was a long time ago. How do you expect me to remember?' She shakes her head, laughs in a way that makes her appear uneasy rather than amused.

'Well, you were there. You would have been old enough to understand what was being said. And now there's no reason to protect anybody any more. If something major happened that—'

She doesn't let me finish. 'Like what?'

'Well, I don't know, just something.'

'What major thing?' She reaches out, grabs my wrist.

'What did Aunt Jemima say? I'll tell you now she was lying.'
I snatch a glimpse at the speedometer and watch as our
speed plummets. 'She's a fucking bitch, I'm telling you.'

'She just said our mother was depressed, that was all. But
now she's dead, there's no reason for secrecy.' Elle's grip
tightens. 'I just need to . . . Wait, stop. Elle, let go of me.
You're hurting me.' I try to snatch back my wrist, anxious
that she has got hold of me. I hear the sound of horns and
see the flash of lights behind us. The first car overtakes as
we stop in the middle of the road. 'Elle, let go.' Without a
word she releases her grip, completes a mirror check, flicks
her finger at one of the overtaking cars whose driver felt it
appropriate to make his displeasure known. Thank God he
doesn't stop. She glides back into the stream of traffic, and
I breathe a sigh of relief.

'I said I wasn't there. I was away,' she snaps. I can hear
her breathing, rapid and shaky. She looks at me. 'I wasn't
there,' she says again, defiant as a child.

'OK, Elle. Forget it.' I shouldn't have pushed it. I'm out
of practice. I've forgotten her limits, and I'm not getting
anywhere. 'We'll talk another time.' I just want this conversation finished.

She is scratching at her forehead. The skin looks red, so
I reach up and gently brush her hand away, only to see that
she has almost picked a hole in it.

'Leave that alone,' I suggest, and she lets me withdraw
her arm. 'You're making it sore.'

She turns and looks at me, and the smile that appears on
her face is so genuine, so thankful, that I let my hand drop
to her leg and stroke her like I might a pet. She does the same.

'Beautiful Irini. You always cared. I knew that, you know. I never forgot.' She lifts her fingers to her lips, chews at the skin.

Moments like this were what kept me coming back. The slightest glimpse of what I always convinced myself was the real Elle. Kindness, and connection. I wanted us to be the same. Even now I still love to see it, even though I'm no longer sure that this softer version is anything more than a guise. But I don't fear her today like I once did. The knowledge that I share something with my father, even if that something is shame, has given me a certain power. It detaches Elle from us both, gives us the strength of insight.

'I need to call Antonio,' I say as a distraction to put the last minute behind us. She hands me her phone. She doesn't question why I don't have my own, or who Antonio is. I dial the number and the call goes through. At the last minute I realise the Bluetooth is still connected but I manage to sever the link by the time he picks up. She looks visibly disappointed, her hands grinding at the wheel in disapproval at being cut out. Her anger is palpable. The real Elle is back.

'It's me,' I say as we glide along winding roads, passing sprawling countryside estates, leaving the noise of the village behind.

'*Buongiorno*,' he replies, in flat, nonchalant tones. This is not a good sign. Language is the barrier he uses when he doesn't really want to talk to me, or when he wants to talk *about* me. Plus I can hear it in his voice, that spiky tone of frustration as he breathes.

'I'm sorry I haven't called.' I look at my watch and see

that it is approaching 6 p.m. Way too late to be acceptable.

'I tried the house. The number you called me from last night. I think it was your father who answered.'

'You called the house? What did he say?'

'That you were out. Didn't know when you would be back.'

'That was right, we were out,' I confirm, freaked out that Antonio has spoken to my father. That's more than I have done. I see Elle glance in my direction. I make the mistake of eye contact and she throws me a little wink. At least she has calmed down.

'Doing what?' Antonio asks.

Shopping? Going to the gym? Having lunch with a stranger? While I am no expert on the etiquette of mourning one's dead mother, I am pretty certain that none of these are acceptable. Especially not to Antonio. But realising how weird it would sound to describe our day makes me wonder what the hell Elle is doing. Elle was raised by our parents, yet she is out shopping for sportswear, burning it up at the gym, picking up fuck-buddies. She actually seems to be having fun, and that nagging doubt about whether she might be responsible for our mother's death creeps back in.

'Just making preparations for the funeral.'

'When is it?' he asks.

'In two days' time, and then as soon as it is over, I am out of here.' I add that in for Elle's benefit, but also for his. I want him to think I am desperate to get back to him, and that he should stick around. For now at least. 'I'll call you from the house later.'

'OK.' He ends the call before I can say anything else.

'OK then. Love you. Bye,' I add while I listen to the disconnect tone. He couldn't wait to hang up, but I covered it up the best I could.

'Why didn't you just tell him the truth?' Elle asks when I hand back the phone.

'The truth about what?' I ask, as if I don't know.

'About what we've been doing. Shopping, gym. Boys. OK,' she reasons with herself, weighing up the options with her head wobbling left and right, 'you could have left the part about Matt out. But the shopping and exercise. What was wrong with that?'

'Matt and I were not on a date, you do know that, right? I wasn't doing anything wrong. I was waiting for you.' She smiles as if we both secretly know what I just said to be a lie. At the same time I remember how he flirted with me, and how I liked it. At least I think he was flirting. I definitely know I liked it. 'But Antonio wouldn't understand,' I say, folding my arms and staring out of the window as we whip around corners.

'Why?'

'He would think it bizarre.' For a moment she looks like she is about to delve further into my private life, but at the last minute she backs away, attracted to activity outside the car. There has been an accident, a cyclist knocked off, an ambulance straddling both lanes of the road with all the urgency the paramedics could muster. A small crowd of people has gathered, some hanging back to watch, others fussing about trying to help. I turn away, not wanting to see.

'Do you think we should stop?' asks Elle, the car already

stationary. She is staring at the blood pooling on the road. 'You're a doctor. Maybe you could do something.' There is a hint of pride in her voice, and I'm almost tempted to try.

'No. Keep going,' I say. I see a paramedic running from the ambulance with a defibrillator. The other cuts the clothes away and sticks the paddles to the casualty's chest. *Clear!* The body jumps and they start chest compressions. 'Looks like he has a traumatic head injury.' She looks to me for confirmation. 'He won't make it.'

'Really?' She smiles at me, rubs her hands together. She is again perhaps mildly impressed, and I enjoy the briefest moment of her admiration. I use her good mood as a chance to remind both Elle and myself of my purpose for being here.

'You know, there is going to come a point when we have to have that conversation, Elle. I have to know exactly what happened.'

She looks down at her hands before snatching a shy glance back at me. Then she turns back to the scene of the accident and kills the engine of the car.

'Maybe,' she whispers, her breath fogging against the glass. 'Maybe not.'

12

I see the roof of the house over the treeline as we approach. Now that I know where to expect it, I am able to pick it out from the surrounding greenery, as if it were in hiding. Elle pulls up at the side of the road not far from the driveway. Birdsong plays out overhead. She glances across the hills that rise up in the distance.

'Elle, what is it?' I ask as we sit in silence broken only by the distant rumble of an aeroplane.

'So you're sure he died?' she asks. She must mean the cyclist; the paramedics gave up on him after five minutes of effort. We waited, watched as it all unfolded, until they zipped him into a body bag just before we left.

'Yes, I'm sure.'

'Shame.' She turns, points at the view. 'When bad things happen, you need a place to retreat in order to forget them. Like this view. You can get lost in it, pretend you're some-where else. Isn't it beautiful?' she says, resting her head on the glass. 'I come here sometimes and just stare at it. Like it's an escape.' I look across the land, my eyes scanning the outcrops of rock as they push through the green mounds of earth. She's right. It is beautiful. 'It's like it's endless.'

'Yes, Elle. It is.'

'If only it wasn't for that place.' She motions to a stately looking building that at first I think is a church, big and white, a steeple poking from the roof. It seems to spread out in all directions, high on the brow of a hill, looming above everything else. It is protected by a dense perimeter of trees. 'But it's derelict now. That's something, I guess.'

'It doesn't look derelict to me. What is that place?' On second thoughts, it isn't a church. It's too big. What building of such a size would be hidden away in the hills of Scotland? As a cloud passes overhead, I catch the sunlight reflecting off the windows, picking out the irregular shapes of the broken glass. The building is so large it seems to cast a shadow over the rest of the landscape.

But Elle has stopped listening to me, and instead starts the engine. We meander down towards the house, and I see the sign, *Mam Tor*, rocking in a light breeze. We bump along the driveway, the black iron gates opening as Elle edges the car ever closer. The only sound I can hear is the tyres as they roll over the ground. No sound arises from inside, and there are no signs of life. The house is holding its breath, waiting for me to approach.

We slip from the cool evening air into the even cooler air of the hallway. The faces of my ancestors stare back at me, their stern beaky noses casting doubt on my right to be here. There is music playing in the background. Something I think I have heard before. A woman singing an aria, so mournful, bereft. Elle is pulling at me, dragging me towards the post-mortem introductions that are coming about twenty-nine years too late.

'Elle,' I say, a last-chance effort to protest. I pull back slightly, but she is bigger and stronger than me, and her grip only intensifies. Her nails dig into my wrist.

She pulls me along the corridor and we burst through the door of the sitting room, breaking every unspoken rule concerning behaviour around the dead. The room itself appears to be in mourning; the light beige tones and pastel floral drapery look dark and sombre, as if the petals are ashamed of their cheery mood. The sun refuses to cast its light here today. The sofas have been pushed aside to make space for the shiny black coffin with the fancy handles, balanced in the centre of the room on tripods decorated with ornate roses and faces of angels. But as Elle steps forward, I see something else that I was unprepared for. My father is here with the body, conducting a vigil at his dead wife's side.

'Eleanor, Irini.' He stands with a degree of effort, whispers something in the direction of the coffin. 'I didn't hear you come in,' he says, moving towards the stereo, where he silences the music. He is looking at me, I think, but I can't bring myself to meet his eyes. 'It was your mother's favourite,' he explains. And I realise it was the music that I heard in the car when Elle picked me up from the airport. Then he reaches towards the body, perhaps to close an open eye, the unnerving wink of the dead. Maybe he brushes a stray hair away from an overly made-up face. I don't know what it is he does, but the way he looks down at the body before him hurts me. It is with such affection, wet eyes brimming with held-back tears.

'Here she is.' Elle beams, pulling me forward, ignoring

our father. I glance at him, and for a second we make eye contact. It's me that looks away first. 'Have a look at her face,' Elle says, urging me on. 'See how weird they made her look. I'm telling you, I swear they gave her Botox.' She steps behind me, blocking my exit. I feel her hands slide around my body, her grip tight as a nut, her nails digging into my arms even through the fabric of my clothes. 'Won't you just take a look?' she says, moving me forward with the weight of her body, her breath tickling at my hair. She is as impatient as a child trying to show off a new toy. She glances back towards our father and tuts, as if I am just so damn difficult. *Still the same, that one. Nothing but trouble. Thank God we got rid of her when we had the chance.* But he doesn't say anything. He continues to look at me, but doesn't try to speak. Instead, he watches me, then Elle, then his eyes move back to me. Together again, two sisters, like he has travelled back in time.

I step forward and he steps back, looking away to the floor. Elle grabs my hands, her wristwatch catching my bone, cutting through skin. I flinch, but she pushes me up close, forcing my hands down on the edge of the coffin. I feel it shake beneath me. We all hold our breath for a moment in case it topples over, but I hold it steady, my fingers brushing against the soft satin lining, Elle's hands suffocating mine.

'Doesn't she look weird?' Elle whispers in my ear as she relinquishes her grip. From the corner of my eye I spot her poking at the skin on our mother's face. I look down, telling myself, *just a dead body, just a dead body, just a corpse, nothing there but death.* But I can't help wondering if there's a wound hidden somewhere underneath her summer-blue dress. If the evidence to implicate Elle is right there in front of me.

'Don't do that,' our father snaps, grabbing at Elle's exploratory finger. She allows herself to be pulled away. He lets go with the same urgency as when he reached out and grabbed her, like he is dropping something hot. He holds his hands up apologetically, as if he momentarily forgot himself and now understands his mistake. For the second time today I see that we are not so very different, my father and I. He understands who is in control just as well as I do. Elle pulls her hand back, shakes her head in disgust.

'She is dead now,' she reminds him. 'She doesn't care if I touch her now that she is dead. Irini, take a look. Come on, don't be shy, she won't bite.' She urges me on with a nudge from a bony elbow in my side, but her eyes don't leave our father. 'Don't you think she looks like you?'

'Eleanor, I really think perhaps we should give Irini a little time alone with your mother.' My father steps forward. 'What do you think?'

'I think Irini has a tongue,' Elle says. 'She can tell us if that's what she wants.'

But I'm not listening to them. I am focusing on my mother. I see the look of the embalmed before me: typical plumped-up features, overly pink skin covered in clown make-up. A beautiful pearl necklace looped around her neck. At first I don't spot anything that resembles the face I see when I look in the mirror. But as I carry on studying it, taking in each feature, I start to wonder whether something might be familiar. The curve of the eyebrows perhaps, and the way they arch up towards the outer eye. The square tip of her nose, and the little bone that appears crooked just at the bridge. My features. I glance back at the man who is my father just as he looks up at me. I know he sees it too. I am her and she is me. Just like Matt said. We are our parents. We are what they make us, through either their presence or their absence.

'Yes,' I say, my grip on the edge of the coffin strengthening. 'I do look like her.' And then the image of me dragging myself across the kitchen comes back to me. *Well done! Brave girl! Now spread your wings. Push up, I know you can. Do it for Mummy.* The missing pieces of the memory come flooding back and I see her face. She is there, picking me up, smiling at me, encouraging me as if she loved me.

I glance back down at the glued-together eyes and stitched-up mouth, sad that a person who looks so much like me physically has absolutely nothing to do with my life. I look up at Elle, and then at my father, and I see that she doesn't resemble anybody.

'I'll give you some time,' my father says.

'Where are you going?' Elle snaps as he tries to push past her. She grips his arm, the same way she did mine when she wanted to drag me in here. I see the whites of her knuckles, the intensity with which she is holding him. I have placed one hand across the open coffin, protectively covering my dead mother. I look up as my father takes a step forward, but Elle switches her footing and manages to block him.

'Now, Eleanor, stop this. Remove your hand from my arm. I only want to give you some time together. Irini and I can talk later.' Then he looks to me. 'I would like that, Irini, if you and I could sit down and talk.' I don't say anything. All this time I have wanted to speak to him, but yet here in this moment I am lost for words. 'Just the two of us.'

'Without me?' Elle asks, but nobody answers her question. My father is still staring at me, and for the first time I see something other than fear, shame or guilt on his face. It looks like an apology. An *I'm sorry that you have to see this*. For the first time ever in my life I can really believe that it was better that I didn't grow up here, that perhaps, maybe a one-in-a-million chance, he gave me up because he wanted something better for me.

'I should go,' I say. 'I shouldn't be here.' It is perhaps the most truthful thing I've said since I arrived, and the first time I might actually believe it. I forget my fear and craving for the truth and take a step forward, but Elle holds out a hand and shoves me backwards. I hit the corner of the coffin and feel it wobble again. I reach behind me instinctively to steady it. My father takes hold of my arm to catch me. I don't need his help, but I let my weight fall into his grasp.

'You're not going anywhere,' Elle says. 'You are our guest.' Only then does she seem to notice our father holding me, and with that, he lets me go.

'It's for the best,' I plead with her. 'For me, and for him.' Because I want to protect him too. From her. I want this horrible scene to be over. 'I don't know why I came here.' I push forwards, but again she shoves me back.

'Yes you do. You came here because you want to know why they gave you away. You said it in the car. You just asked me, remember?' She turns to our father. 'So? Are you going to tell her?' she spits, a finger wafting in his face. 'Is that what you want in your little tête-à-tête? To tell her the truth? Do you want her to stay? *She* would want it after all, wouldn't she? That's what she always said. Always said she wanted *her* here and not me. I used to hear you, you know that?' I realise that Elle is crying and I reach out to try to help. She knocks my arm away. I turn to look at my father and see that his gaze is unfocused, guilty, unsure. 'Whispering at night when you thought I was asleep. But voices travel through the vents as clear as day. Couldn't bear me to touch her, could she? She never stopped resenting you for the choices you forced her to make.' She slips into a nearby chair, her body shaking, curled up like a baby. Tears run down her cheeks, and suddenly she seems so small. Weak in a way like never before. I look at our father and see him holding back. He knows as well as I do that this quiet won't last.

'Eleanor, don't get yourself worked up.' He holds out a hand, yet still he is cautious. He takes a step forward and I follow his lead. But then he swings his hand towards me, uses it as a barrier, ushers me back. He crouches down at her side and I stay where I am, my back against the coffin.

'Always her, right?' Elle says, her voice weak, shaky. 'I need to know, *Daddy*. That's why I got her here. So I could know. So I could know if you still think you made the right decision.' She reaches out and clutches at his arm, desperate. 'So? What is it? Do you still feel the same?'

He doesn't say anything to Elle; he doesn't even look her in the eye. Instead, he maintains his broken gaze in my direction, the weight of a defeated army on his shoulders, and tells me something I knew all along. 'You should never have come here.' Then he leans in, cradles Elle in his arms as her crying intensifies.

Never have I felt less a part of anything than right now. There was a point just a short while ago when I thought my father and I shared something of worth, something that set us apart from Elle. But now I see they share so much history, and I am once again little more than a spectator.

I step forward. 'But you still want to talk, right? Just the two of us?'

He shakes his head. 'Can't you see that now is not the time?'

I look away from them both, and with my eyes cast to the floor, I rush from the room.

13

Sometime during the night, my father came to my room. He whispered my name, his deep voice hoarse but instantly recognisable. I gave no answer. I didn't want to see him, not after what had happened. He tried the handle, opened the door a crack. I closed my eyes, pretended to be asleep. After a few seconds he retreated, left me alone.

When the earliest birds begin singing, I am already awake, watching the darkness retreat to the shadows of the bleak northern countryside as an invisible sun rises in the sky. Even at this hour I feel sticky and warm, hot like an overdressed baby in the summer. I hear the cook, Joyce, who brought me drinks and sandwiches as room service last night, rattling about in the nearby kitchen. More than once I hear footsteps on the gravel of the driveway, and even at times in the hallway outside my room. Now I just want out. Yet still I am here.

When I venture downstairs, I find Joyce in the kitchen. She spots me at the bottom of the stairs looking hesitant, so pulls out a chair and sets a glass of juice on the kitchen table. A get-out-of-jail-free card so I don't have to go to the dining room. If she was in the house, there is no doubt she heard what happened yesterday afternoon. So I proceed to eat a plateful of salty eggs in the kitchen with Joyce scurrying around me.

'I'd love a coffee,' I say quietly, not wanting to be heard beyond this room. She sets down a giant mug, and I sip at it, burning my lips. When I hear footsteps in the hallway I make an urgent but silent move to stand. But Joyce is straight to my side. She places her good hand on my shoulder and I sit back down.

'He went out early, and she won't come into the kitchen,' she whispers.

I watch as she wheels the serving trolley away, loaded with coffee and juice. I wonder if he instructed her to keep me away from them, now that he has admitted I shouldn't be here. Either way, I am grateful for Joyce's help, and I slip back up the stairs to grab my bag. I remember how brave I was on the first day here, creeping downstairs to find him. It feels like a long time ago. The memories of my mother are strangely silent today.

'Thanks for breakfast,' I say as I walk back into the kitchen. She smiles at me from across the room as she dries a beaker with a soggy tea towel. 'I'm going to go out for the day.'

She steps towards me and gestures to the back door. 'On your own?' I nod. 'Well, she won't hear you leave if you go out this way,' she mumbles. I try to smile but I just feel ashamed. I can feel my cheeks flushed pink, my eyes red and swollen.

'Why are you helping me?' I ask.

She looks down at the glass, balanced over a useless, gnarled hand. 'The funeral is tomorrow. Just stick it out until then. You never know, you might want to hear what he has to say about her.' I fight not to cry. 'Then you can go back to your life and forget about it all.' She backs away but I reach out and grip her arm just like Elle did to me.

'What life? I'll never be able to do that. Not now I've been here.' I wipe a tear from my cheek and tell myself I have got to get it together. 'I need to know what happened. Did he tell you to help me today? Did he tell you to keep me away?'

She gently pulls her arm free and I loosen my grip. She casts a quick glance down at her reddened wrist but doesn't make anything of it. I spread my fingers to show her I mean her no harm. 'Some doors are better left closed,' she whispers. She drops the glass to her waist and lets out a sigh. 'And some are better left closed, locked and stuck behind a cupboard full of photographs. Never to be opened again. It's for the best,' she says patting me on the arm. She hasn't answered me, but she is quick to get her good hand on the door handle.

'But I need to know why they gave me away.'

'No you don't. You just need to be strong for another day or so.' She ushers me out with her weight behind me before I can ask anything else.

I slip through the gates, dodging Frank and his cheery demeanour. I keep my head down and push on along the dusty driveway. I look up only to see where I am going as the path twists and turns. Which is when I see my father up ahead, a newspaper tucked underneath his arm. Up until yesterday I was desperate to talk to him; now I look behind me in search of a way out. But the path only leads to the house, cast in a grey shadow, visually impregnable. By the time I turn back around he has seen me too. He has stopped, his body tight with fear. He takes a step forward, me a step back.

'Irini,' he says as he holds out his hands. The newspaper drops to the ground, forgotten. He is only a few metres away from me. I could almost reach out and touch him.

'Don't you . . .' I say through uncomfortable breaths. But I'm not sure what it is I don't want him to do. So I cross to the other side of the driveway, head down, unable to look at him.

'Irini, please. Wait,' he says as he glances to the house. 'About last night. I'm so very sorry.' He nibbles on the inside of his lip and I back away. 'Bloody hell, that sounds so trite. Please forgive me, Irini. You must've been able to see how she was behaving. We have to talk, now, while she's not around. Come quickly.'

I am shaking my head. I try to walk away but he steps forwards to block my path. 'Let me get past,' I say. He reaches to grab my arms but I back away towards the trees, my pulse racing.

'Come on, Irini. There's not much time. I need to explain so many things. Like why I thought it best to let you settle with Aunt Jemima, not to disrupt you by turning up out of the blue. You must try to understand, we had to keep you apart,' he says, edging towards me. This time I don't move. 'Surely you must understand that.' He tries again to reach out. Again I back away, but this time with less conviction. 'Irini, I have something I want to give you. It's important. But I can't do it while she's around. It's not good for her,' he stammers. He takes a look back at the house. 'She mustn't know that we are talking, I realised that last night more than ever. You must understand what she is like. There's not much time,' he repeats.

'I never wanted anything from you but the truth, and now I've got it. I shouldn't be here, remember? Your words.' I am almost shouting. 'What happened all those years ago?'

He winces, looks back to the house. 'Please, keep your voice down. If you are quiet, we can talk. Come on, let's go for a walk together, away from the house.'

'Irini, are you still there?' We both hear Elle calling. We look to the house and see her standing on the porch. My father pushes me behind a conifer tree.

'Just me, Eleanor. Irini's already halfway to the village,' he shouts, and then turns back to me, whispering so quietly that I can barely hear him. 'It's too late now, there's no time. But I have to give you something. Later on. We must find a moment.' He swallows hard, wipes a bead of sweat from his brow. He reaches out a hand and touches my hair. 'Your mother, she loved you, but the depression, it was—'

'No.' I pull away. I don't believe him. Nobody would give away a child because they were depressed. 'It's just another one of your lies.' I break into a poor effort at running, putting as much distance between us as I can.

As soon as I step on to the main pathway that heads towards Horton, I take out a cigarette and smoke it fast. I manage two more during the twenty-minute walk to the centre of the village.

The green blanket around me is broken up by a multitude of grey houses, all made fancier than they once were with the addition of garages, hanging baskets and neatly trimmed lawns. The sickly scent of honeysuckle drips through the air. The church stands proudly in the middle of the village, flanked by green fields and punctuated by decrepit gravestones covered in ivy and moss, as if nature is trying to reclaim them.

I rest against the church wall and watch the activity at what I think is the post office. Beyond that I can hear the cries of children. Perhaps a school or nursery nearby. Perhaps the school I might have attended, should I ever have been allowed to live here. After a few minutes and one more cigarette I push on, past the village pub, the Enchanted Swan. I'd be in there if it wasn't closed. There is a man outside it, ruddy-faced and rough around the edges. He looks like what I would expect from this part of the world: weathered by the winters, battered by the wind. If he was a boat, his sails would be torn and his paint peeling. Yet still he would sail true, returning his passengers to shore. He tips his flat cap to me and hollers, 'G'morning.' He sets out a stand that advertises *Haggis pie with neeps and tatties*, stretches an overworked back with his hands on his hips.

'What time do you open?' I ask, waving back across the road from the edge of the graveyard. A good measure of whisky would really help, maybe followed by a wine or vodka. Whatever they've got. I had a glug of sherry before I left the house, but I kept off the Valium and there is still an edge that could tip the wrong way if I was pushed.

'Twelve today, usually eleven.' He taps the board. 'Do a nice dinner too.' He offers a half-wave and I check my watch. That gives me two hours to kill.

I follow the noise of the children, letting my hand drag along the cold, sharp surface of the stone wall. I'm drawn by their cheer, and the carefree sound of childhood happiness. I pass the post office and corner shop, arriving at a small grey-brick building with a sign outside that reads *Foxling's Nursery and Infant School of Horton.* I glance past the fencing and see little red jumpers charging around in the school yard. The teachers who stand along the perimeter look casual and relaxed, not a care in the world as they sip at their cups of tea. I rest against the fence a while, watching and listening to the sound of a childhood I never knew. After a few minutes I take a step away, wondering where I can kill a couple of hours. But curiosity gets the better of me. Maybe this place would have been my school. I could have grown up here, had I stayed. Behind these walls I might have become somebody different.

I push open the front door to the school and a little bell rings out. Inside the overheated lobby there are children's self-portraits taped to the walls. The eyes are misplaced, the mouths drawn gaping wide. The hair is shaped with wool, glued in place. *Gavin, 6. Isabella, 5. Theo, 7.*

'Can I help you?' a voice asks from behind me as I gaze at the children's work, suspicious of the stranger who has entered the school. I think about running but decide that will most likely result in a worried phone call to the police. So instead I stay, turn around, smile at the wiry receptionist, and begin with a lie.

'Good morning. My name is Gabriella Jackson.' I reach out my hand as the lie glides easily from my tongue. She takes it, but I see that she also takes a good look at my chewed thumb and the four nail marks on my wrist from where Elle dragged me in to see our mother last night. 'I was hoping to discuss schooling for my children. We are moving to the area.'

Her suspicious attitude softens, and the worry is replaced by a smile. She is thinking, *How dangerous could she be? She is a mother, after all.* The international stamp of goodness.

'Oh, in which case, please forgive me. You know, you can never be too careful.' She shakes my hand with extra vigour to negate any offence she might have caused. 'I didn't realise you were a mother. Let me fetch our headmistress.'

The woman scurries away, and after a moment of mumbled conversation behind a partially closed door, she returns with a fierce-looking schoolmistress. Not head. Not teacher. Mistress, her torso overtaken by breasts, tamed behind a tight, high-necked blouse. Her thick calves balance on wide ankles, bound in sensible shoes. Proper, unrelenting.

'Good morning,' she says curtly, her Scottish accent soft and breathy. 'I understand you would like to discuss the potential schooling of your children.' I nod agreeably, but lose my smile and replace it with seriousness. 'Usually such meetings are organised in advance and occur by appointment. Especially since we have just got started with the new school year.' She wants to remind me who's in charge, but the very fact that she has bothered herself, wriggled those hips out of a chair no doubt too small for her, means she isn't going to turn me away. I try to be charming.

'I know, I am terribly sorry.' I augment my accent, try to sound a little more upmarket than normal. Like the kind of woman who doesn't have to work. I hold out my hand and she takes it, somewhat reluctantly, but her grip is firm. 'I happened to be in the area and just stopped by in the hope that you might be able to see me. Not to worry if it is too difficult.' Her exterior cracks a little, a simper of a smile breaking through like sunlight after a storm.

'No. It's all right.' She reaches behind, pulls her office door closed. 'If you are going to join us, let's not get off on the wrong foot. My name is Miss Endicott. Schoolmistress for thirty-five years. It's a long time, but I have plenty of years left in me yet.'

Miss Endicott marches down a corridor and into a large hall with parquet flooring set in a dogtooth pattern. I follow. It reminds me of my first school. The one where I hardly spoke, despite the speech therapy the school provided, and where I walked with a frame I christened Henry.

'As you can see, we are a small school. It was not the case when I began my working life here. But slowly, as the years pass, families are enticed by the towns and cities, and therefore there are fewer children left in the village who require schooling.' We arrive at a galleried corridor that looks out over the school yard. Although it is difficult to count the moving targets, I estimate there are probably no more than twenty pupils. 'We used to take in many more children from a much wider catchment area, but there are newer schools now.' She says it like there is a bad taste in her mouth. *Newer schools*, like *what do they know?* 'I won't lie to you, Mrs . . .'

'Jackson,' I say.

'Mrs Jackson. There are other options. Larger schools closer to the city. But what we offer here is focused learning, developed with your child in mind. Individualised educational programmes. We have five members of staff. That is only five children per teacher.' She opens another door to reveal a bright room that smells faintly of mud. She takes a quick sniff. 'The children have been creating clay pots in the style of the Aztecs and Egyptians. Very good for dexterity with their hands and development of creativity. Plus, we are keen to enrich their learning with a taste of other cultures. It's important they learn empathy for all, especially those who are different.'

'I agree, very important,' I say, wishing that somebody had taught such a concept at my school. I was different, and I don't remember a single child who demonstrated any empathy for that. Not until Elle showed up and taught one of them a lesson he would never forget. 'I really would like my children to attend the local school. I want to get to know the village, Miss Endicott, and build our lives here.'

She smiles and looks flattered as we head up the corridor. She opens another door, presenting the science room. 'Three science sessions per week, per child. There is no larger school that can replicate that at this key stage in development.' I have a nose inside, spot a few Bunsen burners and battery packs left lying out on the laboratory benches. They even have gas taps, which I'm sure can't be safe for such little kids. 'You have come to the right place, I can assure you. I have been teaching here for nearly all of my thirty-five years of working life, and I am Horton born and bred. I have lived in the little end cottage just along from the post office all my life. That's why the garden is so well developed.' She stops herself, giggles at her own apparent naivety. 'What

I'm trying to say is that you will not find anyone who knows the village and its history quite like I do.' She closes the door and takes a good look at me. 'I'm sorry to intrude, but are you all right? Your eyes are very red.'

'High pollen count,' I say, reaching into my pocket for a tissue. I dab at the corners of my eyes and she carries on up the corridor with a sympathetic hand placed on my shoulder. 'As you were saying, Miss Endicott, about knowing the village so well . . . that's most fortunate for me.' I wonder if perhaps my father is not the only person who can answer my questions. If the people at *Mam Tor* believe that things are best left behind closed doors, I'll find someone who knows how to open them. 'I'm sure there are many questions you could help me answer.'

We continue the tour and she shows me the classrooms, the computer area where they have just installed a PC with Windows; Miss Endicott announces this with an inappropriate sense of pride, as if they have made a revolutionary development. I wonder why anybody would choose this school and rely on this dinosaur for their child's education. 'The village must have changed a lot over the years,' I say, driving the conversation in my chosen direction.

She nods in agreement as she plods forward in her heavy lace-up shoes. 'We have seen many children come and go. All on to bigger and better things. That's what I like to think, at least.' She turns back and flashes me a big smile, full of brown teeth from the cigarettes she smokes in her office. I can smell them on her clothes. 'I like to create memorable childhoods, and an environment that enriches the children's emotional development.'

'And I assume you share a special relationship with the local families. For generations, perhaps,' I suggest. We pass a set of entrance doors from the yard and she stands aside to let the rowdy band of sweaty children hurry inside. She pats each one on the head as they race past.

'Of course,' she announces as she closes the doors behind the last one. She almost looks offended that I should even have questioned it, her gaze lingering a little too long. 'There isn't a child that has gone through this school whom I don't remember. But I must say, I am surprised you are here today. As far as I was aware, there are no houses for sale in the village. Where did you say you were moving to?'

I stumble briefly as I cobble together an answer, borrowing from my surname and mother's first name to create a couple of imaginary children. 'We are still looking for a property. We found the village first and just fell in love with it. We were here only a few weeks ago, and little Harry and Cassie were running around . . .' I look off to the ceiling as if I am lost in the memory of them gambolling in the fields like a couple of von Trapps.

Miss Endicott steps back, her face pale. She ushers me forward, and for a second I wonder if I have offended her, although for the life of me I can't think how. I try to move the situation on.

'We just have to settle on a house. It is very hard to find one in such a small and beautiful place. But there are some wonderful properties nearby. There is one in particular I saw on the way in. A fairly new place, double-fronted, with a large circular driveway, set back from the road. That would be perfect for us.'

She stops just before the reception area, smoothes her hands over the dog-eared corner of a child's wall-mounted painting. 'I'm not sure of the property you mean.' Her inability to make eye contact intrigues me. It's impossible to believe somebody who can't look you in the eye. That's how I knew my father really meant it when he told me that I shouldn't have come here, because he looked straight at me.

'Oh? You can't miss it,' I push. 'The last house on the right before you hit the main village, if you're coming from Edinburgh. About twenty minutes on foot from here. It has a name plaque outside. *Mam Tor*.' I have to make her admit she knows my family home. There is no way she can't know the house, which means there is no way she doesn't know my sister. She remembers every child, after all, and where else would Elle have gone to school?

'Oh, that one,' she says unconvincingly. 'Yes, I know the house you mean.' She takes a long look at my face, twitches her nose, shakes her head before adding, 'But I don't think it's for sale.' I consider pushing it further, suggesting that I have seen people coming and going. I want so much to ask her about my sister, my family, whether she remembers me and if she knows why I was given away. Somebody must know. Before I can think up the next question, she is speaking again. 'Anyway, Mrs John—'

'Jackson,' I interrupt, as if the facts of my fictional life are important.

'Sorry, of course, Mrs Jackson. I really must be getting back to work. Should you wish to make a further appointment, I would be more than happy to see you again. If you would like to leave a number, I will contact you if I hear anything regarding properties for sale.'

She escorts me through the lobby and we chat about the weather, the forthcoming church fete, and the local topiary club, of which she is president. I add that I can't wait to show Harry and Cassie where they will go to school, and she smiles, although I note less enthusiastically than before. I leave my actual telephone number and take the steps from the building, past some very nice topiary planters for which, no doubt, Miss Endicott is responsible. Just before I reach the pavement, she calls out to stop me.

'Mrs Jackson, may I ask you something?'

'Yes,' I say as I turn around. 'Of course.'

'Do you by any chance have family in Horton? Any distant cousins or aunts, for example.' She tries to make her question sound casual, like the answer is irrelevant and she doesn't really want to know. Yet I doubt there is anything casual about Miss Endicott.

'No. Not that I know of. Why do you ask?'

'No reason in particular. Just a final thought.' She holds up the paper on which I have written my telephone number. 'If I hear of any properties for sale, I will be in touch. I hope your eyes get better soon.' Without waiting for an answer, she closes the door.

14

The morning of the funeral has a buzz about it much like I would imagine a family wedding would, should I ever have been to one. Frank and Joyce jostle about the house; him out of place, unsure of where anything is, her hindered by her gammy leg and weak hand. I can hear Elle bellowing instructions, the first resounding up the stairs as though she is using a megaphone at about 6.25 a.m., by which point I am wide awake with all the lights on. *Put a table here. Locate some flowers in this alcove. Move the Chinese urns from the hallway. No, you are doing it wrong, you stupid, stupid cripple.*

She flaps into my room before I am out of bed and catches me in the jumper she bought me. I haven't taken it off since the trip to the gym; I still can't bring myself to undress, because to do so would mean slipping into an ordinary routine. Something natural, an acceptance of being here. After my father told me I shouldn't have come, I just couldn't bring myself to pretend that anything about this place was normal for me. I haven't even showered, and as I hide myself under my dusty covers, I catch a whiff of my armpits. It isn't good.

She sweeps in, black dress in one hand, carrying a small leather box in the other, here to ready me. The last time I saw her was as I ran from the living room two days before. But there is a seriousness about her this time, refined and businesslike. This isn't supposed to be fun like Sisters' Day.

'Don't think you're going like that. They will all know who you are and we cannot have the whole village talking about you.'

Following my trip to the school, I spent most of the day in the Enchanted Swan. The pub was full, with interested eyes cast towards my seat at the bar for most of the night. They were all wondering who I was, an outsider in their midst. I think I stumbled back to the house around 9.30 p.m., no doubt already the subject of village gossip. And that's before they realise I'm a Harringford.

Elle drags me out of bed and bundles me into the bathroom. At first I protest, much like a child might. I keep my arms by my sides, hesitant, not looking at her. But she tugs and yanks at my jumper, dragging it over my head, pulling at my ear lobes.

'All right, all right,' I say as I accede to the removal of the jumper. 'Just get out. I can shower on my own.' Reluctantly she leaves, turning to look at me as I turn the shower tap on. She is standing in the doorway as she whispers something to me, but I don't hear what she says.

I reach back and turn off the tap. 'What did you say?' I ask.

'I said, we are sisters, you know. You don't have to be shy. I know what you look like underneath those clothes. I know about the scars that cover your hip. I know the way your belly button is an outie and not an innie. You should let me in, don't push me away. There are lots of things I know about you.' She shuffles awkwardly and smiles, runs her fingers up the brittle frame of the door. 'Like the fact that you liked mashed-up banana for breakfast as a baby, and always used to pee as soon as they took off your dirty nappy. Plus, I know how you feel. I know how it hurts to be unwanted.' She waits there, staring at me, reminding me that I was, and remain, unwanted. I have to grip the sink for support. Then she closes the door behind her without waiting for a response.

I leave the bathroom fifteen minutes later, skin clean and dripping wet. I pass the cupboard of photographs, keeping my head down so I don't have to look, because to get through the next couple of hours will take all my strength. When I open the door to my bedroom, Elle is sitting on the edge of the bed, the sheets draped across her. My bag is beside her, spilling open.

'Do you remember that time when I jumped from the aqueduct?' she asks me, without any introduction or appreciation of the fact that I am virtually naked, wrapped only in a towel too small for my body. She sets the picture of me and Antonio down on the bedside table. Last night, in a moment when I was sure I was about to leave, I packed it away. I take the bag from her and rustle inside for some fresh underwear.

'Yes, of course I remember,' I say, almost able to feel the cold wind that whipped against my skin as I stood on the railings. It was a winter's day, no more than three degrees. A crisp layer of frost was clinging to the ground. There were patches of ice on the water below where it had started to freeze, and a big hole where Elle had fallen through. She only kicked for a moment, until the cold got her.

The moment when we left the garden was probably the only time they took their eyes off us. Just a second for her to lure me away. That was all it took. Perhaps they were distracted by my mother's tears. Elle said she wanted me to go with her, something she had to show me. I hesitated, maybe because Aunt Jemima had told me never to follow a stranger. I suppose there was a chance I was scared of what she might show me. But the truth, if I'm honest, was that I was scared of her. I could see there was something about her, as clearly as if she had a birthmark across her face.

'You would have died if that passer-by hadn't dragged you out.' Jumping, Elle said, would unite us. They would never be able to separate us again. But there was something in me that couldn't go through with it. All the while I was standing up there in only a T-shirt, shivering, watching her floating, I wondered why I hadn't kept my promise. Any distant hopes that our parents had of reuniting our family died that day. 'Why are you bringing it up now?'

'After that, they wouldn't let me see you any more. You know, that's the last time we saw each other for years.' She rests back on the bed and pulls the covers up tightly under her chin, never appearing more fragile. 'Until I found you again.'

'I know. Aunt Jemima moved house so that you wouldn't know where I was.' I sit down next to her limp body, holding on to my towel. I remind myself that it is the day of the funeral, that I should be softer with her, sweeter. 'I know all this, Elle. Why won't you tell me the things I don't know?'

She ignores my effort at truth-digging. 'But I found you, didn't I? They couldn't stop me; I found you.'

'Yes, you always found me, Elle.' I think of the first time, when she attacked Robert Kneel. The last was at the hospital when security dragged her away. Every time she found a way back. And every time I felt a wave of relief that she never stopped searching. Even this time, if I'm honest. I shuffle up towards her head, rest my hand on her arm and rub it.

'I had to. You understand that, right? You understand now why I had to find you?'

'Because we are sisters,' I say as I stroke her hair from her eyes.

'No,' she laughs, sitting up. 'It's got nothing to do with being sisters.'

I stand, snatch up the dress she brought with her. I turn away so that she cannot see my scars, even though she knows they are there. I pull the dress over my head slowly, waiting for the flush of embarrassment to pass. When I turn around, she is staring at my hip.

'So what is it then?' I snap. I fasten the zipper and think how this time she got the size just right. It's a nice black shift dress, three-quarter-length sleeves. Something I would buy. 'Somebody to do crazy shit with you, like jumping off bridges or taking drugs?'

'No,' she says, raising her gaze in the direction of my face. 'To learn the truth, Irini. You have no idea how hard it's been for me. But I knew that one day you would be here

120

in this house, back in your old room, and that finally I would know.' She breathes deeply, lets out a long, steady breath. 'I'm a patient woman, Rini. And now I do.'

The words hit me like a train wreck, and I stagger back, gripping the frame of the tiny bed to stop myself falling.

'This is my old room?' The words stutter out, shameful and afraid. My eyes skirt around the details, the lame picture that I have hidden away behind the furniture, the drawer where I have stowed an ornament. Mine? 'My room when I was a baby?'

She screws up her face, as if what I am asking is one of the dumbest questions she's ever heard. 'Where did you think I had put you? This is your room, exactly as you left it.'

I glance around, looking for proof, trying to jog a memory. I find nothing. 'So where is the cot?' I challenge her. 'This can't be my room. I was a baby. I would have had a cot.'

'You couldn't sleep in a cot because you had your legs all plastered up, dangling from that thing on the ceiling.' I look up, following the line of her finger, her once-perfect manicure bitten down and chipped. Sure enough, there is the hook I assumed was for a lamp. Now I realise it is an outdated traction system used for fixing my hip. 'I used to run up the corridor from my bedroom and sit with you when you couldn't move, draw butterflies on your plasters because you liked them. I told you that one day they would make you fly.' She wriggles her fingers against my arm, all the way up to my shoulder. When she starts fluttering her tongue against the roof of her mouth, the sound of wings, I remember her childhood face above mine, peering over the bed, making the same fluttering sound. The same delicate touch of a child's hand against my bare torso. The tears hit me as fast as the vision. I go to the chest of drawers and pull out the faded picture of the butterflies from behind it. Something I liked. Something that is mine from childhood. Butterflies. 'But all of this is irrelevant now. Just like your tears. Because now I know.'

I am holding the butterflies in my hand, the faded wings never more beautiful. I am barely listening to what she is saying. 'This was my room,' I stutter. 'You were here with me.' I swallow hard, try to breathe. 'You were sweet with me, and I remember . . . you drew butterflies all over me.'

'I was a child,' she says dismissively, with a shake of her wrist. 'Of course I was sweet.'

'I liked butterflies,' I say, smiling down at the framed watercolour. 'You even used to paint the wings different colours, right?' She nods. I want to ask her to make the sound again, flutter her fingers over me like she did before. But something holds me back. I should reach out and hold her, thank her for making me remember. But she is staring at me, her eyes so dead that I don't dare.

'We all liked butterflies,' she says. 'Don't you remember how she used to play the *Madam Butterfly* soundtrack? She always loved it. Even before,' she says, giving me the strangest look. Before what? 'Mother used to tell us the story and play the songs over and over on an old vinyl. You were scared of the crackles of the needle at the beginning, before the music started.' I sit back down next to her, the faded butterflies in my hand. 'She used to hum the tune, say that one day you would grow into a butterfly. That you were a brave girl and would spread your wings.'

'That's what Dad was listening to the other day,' I say as the memory of seeing my mother's body comes back to me. 'And you in the car. It was *Madam Butterfly*. I remember.'

'Yes, but regardless, like I was saying, you are free of me now. I will never look for you again. I always knew that one day I would get you here, put you with him, and then I would know. And now I do.'

'Know what?' I ask, wiping my wet eyes, the memory of the mournful music still loud in my head.

'He told you that you should never have come here. It proves that he doesn't regret what he did for me.' She looks around the room, scans past me as if I am nothing more than an inanimate object. 'It means that I was wanted. That he still chooses me over you.' She gets up, picks up the little leather box from the side table. 'Finish getting ready.' She tosses the box at my chest, as if she has lost all interest in me. It falls on to the glass of the picture. 'And wear that. The cars will be here soon, and like I say, we don't want the whole village talking about how awful you look. It will reflect badly on us.'

She leaves me clutching the faded image of butterflies, the sound of *Madam Butterfly* playing out in my head. She slips from the room, turns the corner, and I buckle, collapse on to the sheets, the shaking of my hands rippling into the rest of my body.

After a few minutes I get my act together. I go back to the bathroom, wash my red, puffy face. But this time on the way back to my room, I don't walk with my head down. I stop, turn to face what sits in the alcove: the dresser covered in photographs. There is a layer of dust, but the pictures are clean. I pick one up and notice that there is even dust beneath it. The photo has been placed here recently, perhaps for my benefit. I look at the image of what is clearly Elle. I am also in the picture, no more than eighteen months old. I am giggling, and she is staring at me with icy eyes. There is some kind of smile on her face, but it isn't a happy smile. There are other photos too, but I can't face them all today. I toss the frame back down, scattering the other pictures like ten-pin bowls.

I see now why my feet touch the end of the bed. It was not made for an adult. I pull up the sheets and find extendable side rails that might once have stopped me from falling. I open the drawer where I stowed the ornament and find terry-towelling nappies and a pot of pins. Untouched for years. I open another and find a collection of pink babygros that range from birth to eighteen months. My things. Things I would once have worn. I pick one up, smell it, but the covering of a fine dust layer makes my nose itch. I pick up the ornament and cradle it to my chest, edging back on to the bed. I reach for my phone, remember it is broken. *Breathe*, I tell myself. *Stop crying*. I pop a Valium and wait for it to work. When it doesn't, I wipe my eyes and call Antonio on the house phone, and then hang up when he doesn't answer.

I stir once I hear the cars pulling into the driveway in that slow processional fashion reserved for funerals. I stand up, spot five black Jaguars, one a particularly large affair at the back with the rear doors wide open. A gaping mouth ready to swallow up the coffin. I catch a glimpse of my reflection, my shoulder-length hair and fringe kinked and wavy, still wet, hanging in clumps. The pallbearers exit the house, slide the coffin into the car just as a knock arrives at my open door.

It is Joyce. She spots my tears and makes what should be a reasonable assumption: that I am sad for my loss. It is true, but it is not my mother for whom I mourn. It is the life I lost. The baby I once was. The child I never got a chance to be.

'There, there,' she offers, taking me by the hand. She does a quick scan and notices that I am barefoot. She looks around the room and sees that all I have are the flat black boots I was wearing when I arrived and a fancy pair of new Reeboks. She picks one up and checks the sole. 'Stay here,' she mutters as she pushes me into a sitting position before scurrying from the room.

She returns after a few minutes with a pair of sensible black lace-up pumps, the kind she herself wears. When I remain unresponsive to her suggestion to put them on, she crouches down and, even with the left-sided weakness, fastens the laces for me, propping my feet on her knee. She looks up when she has finished, spots the leather box on the bed alongside the ornament. She picks up the box and opens it. Inside is a pearl necklace. She turns so that I can see it, looking to me for answers, perhaps wondering if I took it.

'Elle gave it to me.'

She purses her lips, and at first I think she doesn't believe me. But then she nods, like a self-affirmation. 'Which is why you won't be wearing it.' She closes the lid and reaches back, shoving it in my bag. She helps me up, slicks down my troubled hair. She pulls a tissue from her pocket and dabs at my red eyes, but her kindness only brings about more tears.

'Oh, Irini, you have to settle. I don't want her to see you like this. Nor that father of yours. Come on now, girl. Get it together.' She puffs out her chest and braces herself, as if showing me how I am supposed to pull myself together by mirroring her actions. I nod and wipe away my tears on the back of my sleeve. Arm in arm we shuffle down the stairs. She grips on to me for steadiness.

Well done! Brave girl! Now spread your wings.

When we arrive on the driveway, I spot my father, who looks so small, as if he has been crushed. He is being held up by a man I have never seen before. The squat little man who was here at the house on the first night I was here is also nearby. I don't see Aunt Jemima. Elle is directing, ordering people into cars, arranging flowers. Roses, the flower of both love and death. Before the last people climb inside, she steps back and assesses her arrangements with a satisfied smile. She beckons me forward and I try to follow. But Joyce tightens her grip on my arm, preventing me. Instead, she edges me into another car, with her.

'Best you come with me,' she whispers as the driver closes the door behind us. Elle doesn't appear too bothered. The cars begin their slow, painful journey of deliverance.

'Where's my Aunt Jemima?' I ask Joyce, but I'm not sure she hears me over the sound of the car's tyres on the gravel.

We pull up outside the churchyard after just a few minutes of procession, and one by one the people vacate the cars. Ours is the last. The congregation links arms for support amongst a crowd of waiting villagers. A random stranger, a woman in a floral shirt and royal-blue hat, takes my free arm in hers. We all shuffle into the church, following behind the minister and the coffin. Incense burns and clings to the back of my throat, forcing out a little cough. I take a seat in one of the pews and look around for Aunt Jemima and Elle. I spot Elle up at the front. She looks distraught, although I know only minutes ago she was composed and calm. Is it an act? When I realise that I still don't know how my mother died, I wonder if Elle is trying to cover up something she has done. I'm not sure she is as heartbroken as she would like us to believe. I look around at the congregation of friends and family and wonder who really is mourning if neither of the deceased's daughters are. I can't see Aunt Jemima anywhere. Why wouldn't she be here?

I hear the minister say, 'Blessed are those who mourn, for they will be comforted,' and I realise that even in her death there will be no peace. Not for me. Not for any of us.

15

'Forgiving God, in the face of death we discover how many things are still undone, how much might have been done otherwise. Redeem our failure.'

Joyce clings to my arm as the mourners shuffle left and right, assuming position. I am frozen, rooted to the ground. A tree without fruit or leaves.

'Bind up the wounds of past mistakes,' the minister continues. I wonder whose failure and mistakes he is referring to: mine, my mother's, or everybody's in my family? 'Transform our guilt to active love and by your forgiveness make us whole. We pray in Jesus's name.'

'Amen,' I say, the response taught to me as a child at school. Speak when they speak. Wait your turn. Follow the lead.

I hear the shuffling of bodies, the crumple of jackets. The minister's words are lost on me. Somebody unwraps a sweet behind me and I hear another person hush them. I try to focus on Elle, as I am sure many of the congregation are doing. She is a snivelling wreck at the front of the church. Her face is perfectly made up, yet her eyes stream, her shoulders shake. Hollywood tears.

'Though I walk through the valley of the shadow of death, I will fear no evil; for you are with me; your rod and staff, they comfort me.'

I try not to listen, glance around at the mourners. Who is here to say goodbye? There are maybe thirty people besides those that came with the cars. The villagers, most of whom are in excess of the age of sixty, are dressed in black, a flock of crows around a carcass. I spot the schoolmistress, Miss Endicott, shuffling in late, alone at the back. A man in a long overcoat greets her, offers her a place near the front, which she declines. I turn away in the hope she hasn't seen me. Joyce takes my movement as a worsening of my mental state and pulls me in close. I bury my face in her shoulder, and although I'm concerned that this diverts attention my way, I cannot risk being seen by Miss Endicott. So far, in spite of Elle's warnings, nobody else seems to know who I am.

I'm surprised to see that Miss Endicott's arrival has piqued Elle's interest too. She has twisted in her seat, transfixed as several other attendees jostle about the teacher, offering respectful smiles and warm welcomes. I look back to Elle's grave face, her wet cheeks glistening, her eyes narrowed to acrimonious slits. She goes to stand, but our father senses her movement, and after a quick look over his shoulder he settles her back into the pew with an encouraging stroke of his hand and a few words in her ear. I look back at Miss Endicott and see that she is huddled up to the wall, almost like she is trying to disappear. Elle takes one final look in her direction before turning back to face the casket. What is it about the school-mistress's arrival that has bothered her so?

Moments later my father stands, more composed than before, though his head still hangs low. He steps up to the lectern and a chill passes over me, radiating from the bare stone walls. I realise that he is about to read a eulogy, and the very idea of it draws me like a moth to a flame.

'I would like to thank you all for coming here today to celebrate my beloved Cassandra's life.' Only now does he look up and glance at those of us packed inside the small church. He avoids me, which convinces me that he knows where I am. 'Cassandra's life was cut shorter than we would have hoped, taken from her by a terrible disease. Many of you here have watched as she battled cancer, and many of you supported us and helped. I thank you all for being there when we needed you, now, during her disease, and in times past.'

The crying intensifies around the church. Gentle sobs turn into proper tears. Handbags rustle and noses are blown. I am composed and calm, the antithesis to my sister, who is wailing, and who for the first time I can absolve of any guilt. It was cancer that killed her. Just another average death, in another average family. Because I think I am starting to ascertain that that is exactly what we are.

'But I do not wish to dwell on such times,' my father continues. 'It is not how I want to remember my wife, my friend. My partner. I choose to remember her as the fair-haired girl of seventeen who complimented me on my bicycle and asked me to take her for a ride. I will remember her as a keen painter and collector of antiques.' I think of the faded butterflies and know, just know, that they are hers. Painted for me. 'How she used to drag me out into the surrounding hills whatever the weather. Our happiest times were in youth, when our family was young, when our memories were fresh.'

And then he glances at me. I see the tiniest flicker of his eyes, like the glint of a distant planet in a dark night sky. But it disappears as soon as I look at him. I think Joyce notices it too, because I am sure that she clutches my arm a bit tighter at that moment.

'I am sure many of you can attest to Cassandra's generous soul. She was always there to help when a friend or stranger was in need. She was a woman who would sacrifice her time for the sake of another. A wonderful wife who loved to cook, and who never tired of making me laugh.' By this point I can hardly stand to listen to the fairy tale. The eulogy; a version of the truth with all the ugly details scratched out. It's me Photoshopped, so that I have no scars and my bones are perfectly aligned. He pauses to wipe his eyes, and somebody dashes to offer him a tissue. They hang around supportively at his side, but he reassures them he is all right to continue, and they return to the second row. He clears his throat.

'Cassandra was a selfless mother, always doing what she thought was best for her child.' A rumble of interest whips through the crowd, and I'm sure a few heads turn my way. Do they recognise me after all? Again my father looks to me. For certain this time. Joyce seems bothered by this last comment, and her grip on my arm keeps strengthening. Maybe she thinks I am a flight risk. But I'm not going anywhere, because the thought that he can describe her as a selfless mother while looking at me has to mean something. Why did he want to see me alone? What couldn't he tell me while Elle was there? What truth is he still hiding? More than ever I think my mother loved me, wanted me, and did what she did believing it was for the best. He is telling me that they had no choice, that it hurt her too. Otherwise he wouldn't be able to say it, not with me here. Perhaps I can learn to mourn. Perhaps I will be comforted and find peace.

A little while later, we disperse from the church. I hang back from the crowd, not wanting to get too close as they lower the coffin. While the diggers shovel soil into the grave, the crowd buzzes around my father offering good wishes and kind words. I stay hidden behind a large gravestone, from where I keep an eye on Elle. Miss Endicott is close by; she must have been quick out of the church, one of the first. She appears awkward, lingering behind the wall of the porch in the same way I hide behind the gravestone. Soon she begins hurrying away, making her way across the road to either the school or her house.

Joyce mutters something under her breath as she watches the schoolmistress leave. I don't quite catch what it is. 'What did you say?' I ask. 'I didn't hear.'

'Never mind, Irini. Nothing important.'

My detachment from the crowd is noticed by more than a few inquisitive eyes, and I see people whispering to each other while casting sneaky glances over their shoulders. It is quite obvious to me now that they know who I am: the lost child, returned. It makes me feel like an intruder. But Elle soon starts rounding them up, ushering them in the direction of the Enchanted Swan, her behaviour bordering on inappropriately cheerful. Nevertheless, I am grateful, because as she directs the crowd, she doesn't spot me in my hiding place. And soon enough, with the exception of a few unknown faces hovering in the graveyard, perhaps visiting their own relatives, I notice that my father is alone. After reassuring Joyce that I am going for a walk to catch my breath, I make my approach.

'We have nothing to say to each other,' he says, before I have even got within an arm's length. He is steadying himself with the help of the wall that bounds the church, standing next to a small gravestone. The wall is supposed to keep the nearby sheep out, yet now it keeps him from running away. He will listen to me. He has to. 'You heard everything I had to say in there.'

I take another step forward, not wanting to let him off the hook. Doesn't the fact that I have just attended my mother's funeral mean anything to him? I have recovered from our previous meeting, and know that now is my chance, whether he wants it or not. Elle isn't here, and he is broken. This is as strong as I'm ever going to feel.

He turns slightly, taking all of me in. He brings his hand up to shield his eyes from the sun, casting his face in shadow. The weather is glorious, an unexpected late summer's day. I cannot see his eyes, but I can feel them upon me. After only a few seconds he shifts, angles his head to the distant hills where Cassandra used to drag him out whatever the weather. 'Elle is right,' he says softly. 'You look so much like her.'

I take a breath. 'There is only one thing I want to ask,' I say. 'Then I will leave, and I promise I will never bother you again. I know that's what you want.' He looks hesitant, so I add, 'I think you owe me that.'

'I don't owe you anything,' he says. 'I gave you every last shred of my soul many years ago. I have nothing left to offer. I can't talk about this today. Not now. Not to you.'

'Please.'

He takes a breath, clutches the wall. 'Just ask me what it is you want to know.'

'When Elle said that she always wanted me here – my mother, I mean – was it the truth?'

He looks back out to the hills, catches sight of a blackbird circling ahead, follows it as it settles on the pile of earth covering the freshly dug grave. It pulls out a worm and makes off with it. We both watch as it flies away. I look back to my father, who is nodding his head.

'Then why did you tell me that I shouldn't have come? Even now, to her funeral. If she regretted what she did,' I say as I edge closer, 'if she regretted giving me away, it would have been good for me to know that. It would have made me feel less worthless throughout my life.' I am crying again, but I do not try to stop it this time.

'You are not,' he says in the softest voice anybody has ever used with me, 'and never were worthless, Rini.' My crying intensifies when he shortens my name, teardrops falling like rain to the ground. He looks at my flushed face. I see a flicker in the muscles of his hand, and for a moment I think he is about to reach up and wipe away my tears. I am close enough, and I wouldn't stop him, even though I now know that he must have been the one who forced my departure. The flicker amounts to nothing as he sets his hands on his hips. 'You were and still are worth everything. That's why, for you, I was prepared to pay with everything I had.'

'So why would you tell me that I shouldn't be here? Surely I deserve a chance to say goodbye, properly this time.'

He draws a long breath in before saying, 'Because you open up old wounds, Rini. For me and your sister. Wounds that will never heal.' He takes a step closer and again I think he is about to touch me, his lips parting; perhaps a kiss, a final goodbye as we both stick to the deal that was made all those years ago on my behalf. But again he stops himself. 'I don't wish you harm. Quite the opposite, in fact.' He looks to the pub, nervous, and then back to me. 'But you should leave. Leave now while you are still able to get away from us. You'll see it's for the best. Now that she thinks she knows the truth, she will leave you alone.' He just about manages a smile. 'There is nothing left for you here.'

16

So it's true. My father has confirmed my darkest fears. I should accept that I don't belong here, go. But it's a hard concept to face, the idea of having nothing. Of truly being alone.

When Elle burst back into my life with her attack on Robert Kneel, I wanted so much to be around her. She saved me that day, made me feel that we were a team. Her sporadic input into my life made me feel better about myself. Her presence gave me a position in the world, in the beginning at least. It didn't matter that I had no friends at school, or that they called me names. Even that became little more than whispers behind my back after the attack on Robert Kneel. Now it was a risk to ridicule me. You might lose one of your balls if you pissed me off. I marvelled at the way Elle's presence gave me power, but I didn't realise that Elle felt the same about me. I didn't understand that I was her pawn, a game piece that she could toy with, manipulate. But I would learn soon enough.

We used to meet regularly, Elle and I. When I suggested I spend my Saturday mornings at the library, Aunt Jemima thought that I wanted to improve at school. She was cautiously impressed. But she also knew Elle was back in the picture. I'd heard her talking about it on the phone with my father after the school questioned me about the attack on Robert Kneel. *Keep that bitch away from us*, she had told him. So she only agreed to the idea of the library if she could take me and pick me up. But it was easy enough to slip through the fire exit at the back, where Elle would be waiting.

Every Saturday we got two hours together. At first it seemed that Elle wanted to test the water with me, so the first few meetings were pretty safe. Nothing too rash: spitting on the pavement, smoking cigarettes, scrawling the names of my teachers on toilet walls, with telephone numbers for fake chat lines. She would plant some hair in her burger and complain to the staff. It was nothing to be pleased about really, because we had to give up the best part of one meal to get a replacement. But it was the principle of it, and we got to keep the chips. What she wanted was for me to see that she was in control. That she got what she wanted. That she could make people do things.

The graffiti grew more enthusiastic. I made sure to find excuses when it came to bridges and bodies of water, but otherwise you could see our handiwork across the city. The cigarettes turned to weed, and she taught me how to skin a joint while we sheltered from the rain in a bus shelter. The disgusted looks from passers-by made it even more appealing. But we were always limited by our two-hour time frame and we were both sensible enough to realise that intoxication levels had to be minimised if we wanted to keep our meetings a secret. She told me that I had to earn my aunt's trust. She told me that I had to earn hers, too.

The first time she made me wait outside a shop alone, I knew it was a test. She was gone for what felt like hours, and all I could think was that Aunt Jemima was probably in town killing her two hours of waiting time and might see me at any moment. I was trying to hide as best I could, blending into the crowd, dipping back and forth to check the Balmoral Hotel clock tower on Princes Street, when suddenly Elle appeared, strutting down the hill with a grin splashed across her face. She didn't stop walking as she gripped my arm and led me forward.

'Keep walking, don't look back,' she said. I did as I was told.

She ploughed on, dragging me along as I hurried to keep up with her confident strides. We walked in the shadow of the Scott Monument to our left and Edinburgh Castle to the right. We dropped down to the lowest level of Princes Street Gardens until the sound of the departing trains could be heard in Waverley railway station. She pulled me to the grass and we sat under the shady canopy of a large oak tree, where, like a magician, she began pulling a bright orange cloth out from up her sleeve.

'You did good. It was easy this time. Here,' she said, shoving the material at me. 'This is for you.'

'What is it?' I asked. I held it up and it dropped into shape: a vest.

'I got it for you,' she said, and winked at me. The idea of her buying it flashed through my mind, but I knew that was wrong. I knew from the smile, the cheeky little wink. She *got* it for me. Stole it for me.

I ran my fingers across the ribbed-knit vest, which was

exactly the one I wanted, cut high to show my midriff. That was cool in 1996, and I wanted to be cool. But the spark of gratitude was short-lived, replaced instead by the realisation as I fiddled with the security tag that for the first time in our joint history I was actively involved in something bad. The Robert Kneel incident wasn't my idea. I didn't ask for it, and I didn't feel responsible. But I had complained only half an hour ago that Aunt Jemima only ever gave me hand-me-down clothes. I had complained that I wanted something new. This was my fault. Elle was a thief because of me.

I didn't say anything, though, and instead I snuck back into the library with the vest in my bag. Elle had managed to get the tag off with a minimal amount of effort. I was sure everybody knew it was there. Aunt Jemima picked me up, and when she asked, I told her that I had been reading about Shakespeare. She asked me which play, perhaps as a test, so I said *Othello*, because I had seen the 1995 version with Laurence Fishburne a few months before and remembered roughly what it was about. She seemed impressed, and when we got home she offered to make me a hot chocolate because there was a chill out. Instead I went upstairs, hid the vest in my cousin's drawer. I saw her wearing it under a tartan check shirt only a month later. Nobody questioned where it was from.

After that temporary moment of shame, I got quite used to Elle's thievery. It came in handy when I wanted something new, or if I just liked the look of something. It was easy to turn a blind eye, and most weekends she would turn up with something for me, or steal it while we were together. She took great pride in getting me what I wanted. Sometimes she even stole stuff that neither of us wanted. We just dumped those things in a bin later on, laughing about how unstoppable we were. One time she stole a man's scarf, and when I suggested she give it to a homeless person in one of the bus shelters, she hugged me and said I had a sweet heart. I felt proud about that, especially the way she looked at me, like I had done something good.

So when Elle told me that it would be her birthday the following week, I knew there was only one option. I didn't get a pocket-money allowance, so it was time to be brave. I fished around for ideas about what she would like, but she gave very little away. I sneaked out from school one day, went into town. It wasn't even that hard. I waltzed into Elle's favourite shop and lifted a massive pair of gold hoop earrings and an A-line denim skirt with buttons running up the front. She would love me for these things. She would see how much I wanted her to stick around. The morality of the theft didn't even register.

I met her out the back of the library the following Saturday and told her that I had a surprise for her. She seemed so excited, so I built it up a little on our way to the nearest McDonald's, saying it was for her birthday and that I hoped she'd like her gift. Her surprise. She laughed along at my side, hugging me, holding my hand, saying how great it was that I had bought her a gift. She wanted to know where I got the money. What did Aunt Jemima say? Did I think they might let her come and visit? I was too naive to see that her eagerness was bordering on mania. By the time we reached our seats with the burgers on our trays, she was uncontrollable, pawing at me, desperate to find out what it was.

I was all of a fluster when I finally gave it to her, my cheeks flushed from the embarrassment of putting myself in the line of her judgement. But she loved it. She put the earrings straight in, waggled them about with her finger and shook her head so that they slapped against her cheeks. She stood up and wrapped the skirt over her baggy jeans and said it was perfect. It was too big for sure, but it didn't matter to her and so it didn't matter to me. She reached over, hugged me, drew me in to her. My heart nearly stopped it felt so good.

'What did you tell them the money was for?' she asked.

And there was my moment. It was what I'd been waiting for, the chance to admit what I had done. For her. That I was like her. That we were the same. I smiled, winked just like she had when she first gave me that orange vest.

'I got it for you,' I said.

'You stole it?' she asked. I smiled collusively and bit into my burger. With that she grabbed my arm and shoved me backwards, the burger falling apart in my lap. 'You stole it?' she asked again as my head cracked against the mirror behind me. I heard it shatter. 'You don't. Fucking. Steal,' she spat. She sat back, letting my arm go.

I was so stunned, I didn't move for a second or two. A few other people noticed the scene, and watched as she ripped off the earrings. One came out all right, but the clasp on the second got stuck and she tore her ear lobe in the process. Blood dribbled down her finger when she touched it. She took a bite of her burger before licking the blood from her hand.

'I wanted to get you a gift,' I tried weakly, but my defence

141

only angered her more. She jumped out of her seat, grabbed me by the wrist and pulled me up. I lost my footing and fell to the floor, sauce all over my face, pieces of burger trailing behind me. She stumbled as I fell, almost landing on top of me. A boy laughed, and for a second I thought she was going to attack him. He shut up as she got close, at which point she turned back to me, looking down at me as I covered my face with my hands. She pulled me by my left foot out into the street, and my hip swelled instantly in pain. Shards of mirror scraped against my head.

She unbuttoned the skirt and threw it at me. It slapped me in the face, catching my cheek, leaving a red welt that buzzed hot as fire. A crowd gathered, like I had seen happen at school when a fight was about to go down. But nobody chanted, and they all just seemed to be looking on, feeling sorry for me. I could hear the words *Bison* and *Peg Leg* going around in my head like the Robert Kneel incident had never even happened.

'You're so fucking stupid,' she shouted. 'You don't do that. What if they find out? Huh? Did you think of that?' She was leaning over me. Somebody suggested she calm down, but Elle turned, shoved them out of the way. 'They'll think I put you up to it, and that'll only make things worse. Something else that she'll say is my fault. Another fucking reason to hate me, and again it'll all be because of you!' She kicked me once, right on my hip where the scar was, before saying, 'You better hope Aunt Jemima and Uncle Marcus don't find out, because if they do, *they'll* get rid of you too, and then there will be nobody left that wants you. Then there'll be nothing left for you anywhere.'

Somebody helped me up after she left, and a kind lady wiped the remnants of the burger from my face and clothes. I'd got my act together by the time I returned to the library. Aunt Jemima asked what had happened to my cheek, and I said a book fell off a shelf and hit me. She said I always had been clumsy. Later she asked if I had finished *Romeo and Juliet*. I had told her that I was working my way through Shakespeare's tragedies.

I wouldn't have gone back to the library the next Saturday if Aunt Jemima hadn't insisted upon it. But she did, saying it was really helping with my schoolwork and attitude. That my behaviour was getting so much better. So she watched me walk in, and as soon as I got through the doors, I saw Elle sitting there waiting for me. She motioned for me to sit down.

'I could tell them what you did, you know that, right? They'd believe me, because I know you better than anybody now. They'd say you were just like me and get rid of you. You'd lose me, too.' She sat back in the chair, folded her arms. 'Is that what you want?'

'No,' I mumbled. My hip was in agony, as if it could sense the very threat of her. 'Please don't tell. I won't do it again.' I felt my shoulders curling in, my throat aching as I desperately tried not to cry.

She stood up, walked around to my side of the table and put her arm around me. 'OK, I'll keep quiet. But don't you dare fuck up any more.' And then she took a pinch of my arm between her fingers and twisted. I winced, and felt her cheek curl up into a smile next to mine. 'Otherwise it's all over. Without me, you'd have nobody left for you anywhere.'

143

17

My father doesn't wait to see me collapse. By that time he is already crossing the road, running towards the Enchanted Swan. I feel like I have lost things that were barely mine all over again. The closer I get to the truth, the more it seems to hurt. I bring my knees out from underneath me, brush away the mud and wipe the tears from my cheeks. That's when I realise I am sitting on top of a grave.

The headstone is small, white marble, half covered in moss. It reads, *You live on in her.* Nothing else. I stagger to my feet, take a quick pace back, stepping on somebody else's final resting place. Before I know it, one stray foot has landed in the mud on top of my mother's. I am in a carpet of graves, so I hotfoot through as fast as I can and run for the house. When I reach it, my hip complaining, my cheeks and armpits sweaty, it is by sheer luck that I find the back door left unlocked. I dart through the house, no more fear of stumbling upon my mother's dead body, weaving through the corridors until I arrive at a study, the same one in which I saw my father on the first night. A desk made of solid oak sits before me. No computer. But there is a telephone, so I call Antonio, desperate to go home.

'Antonio,' I say, my voice still fragile from the tears.

'Oh, it's you. I thought you wouldn't call. I thought it was over.' He sighs, his voice shaking in the same way as mine. Is he crying too? *'Grazie a Dio!'*

'I need you to book me on the next flight home.' I take a seat in the green leather chair, twiddle the telephone cord between my fingers. I look down at the desk, not wanting any more details of this place, or this life. 'I have to leave. Now!'

'You are crying. It was the funeral today, right?'

I nod as if he can see me. 'It's finished. Everything is over; there's nothing left for me in this place,' I say, my voice slowly coming under control as I wipe my tears. 'But I learnt something here. Something important.'

'What?'

'That my mother did want me. It was my father that didn't, and he still doesn't. But there was a reason, I just don't know what. He isn't angry with me for being here. He is sad. He said I open up old wounds and that I should leave while I still can. I know it has something to do with Elle because she as good as told me so, but I don't know what.' There is silence for a moment. I will him to say something, but then realise there is nothing he could say that would suffice. Then, just as he takes a breath, he finds it.

'Mio amore.' My love.

I can hear his relief on the end of the line. His breathing has deepened, the worry in his voice replaced by love. I think back to that sad little bag he packed with his clothes, and how far away it all seems.

I always thought that because I supported him and enabled him to stay in his crappy waiter's job in an effort to gain restaurant experience, life with me was too much to give up. Failing to leave even after I refused him a child felt like proof of that. That life was easier with me. But what I realise now is that life would be easier *without* me. It is not easy to love a person who is cold, or who always shuts you out. It is not easy to stick around when you want so much more than they are prepared to give. Yet he did. 'I need to get home as soon as possible,' I tell him. Perhaps there is something there that can be saved.

I hear him shuffling along in his sloppy slippers, the sound of the computer waking up. 'Just a minute,' he says, the ruffle of his chin against the receiver. The keys click as his fingers strike them, entering the search. 'There is only one more flight today. Hang on, let me open it up. It's at 9.45 p.m. You will arrive at 11.15. Is that OK?'

'It's fine. Book it.' The relief is instant, knowing I will be away from here soon. I glance out of the window while he makes the booking, towards the well-maintained lawn. Today there is a table out there, a few sad-looking refreshments on top for those who choose to return to the house.

'That's it. Booked. Shall I email you the reference?'

'No, read it out to me. I don't have my phone, so I'll check in at the desk.' He reads out the number and I write it down on a notepad embossed with my father's initials.

'What will you do between now and then?' he asks.

'I will get my things together and call a taxi. The sooner I leave, the—' I don't finish my sentence, because I spot something half-slipping out from a cupboard next to the desk. A face. A face I recognise.

'Rini?'

'The better,' I finish. 'The sooner the better.' I reach down and pick up the photograph. The face of my mother stares back. It could be me, looking back in time. We are so alike, no wonder Miss Endicott felt compelled to ask if I had family in Horton. Must have been like seeing a ghost when I turned up.

'Rini, are you all right?'

'Yes,' I say, not even sure if I know the real answer to that question.

I open the door to the cupboard and find a row of old blue photograph albums, lined up in date order. One of them has fallen over; I stand it up to see the spine, which reads *1978*. I finger my way along the rest and find that three from the sequence are missing: 1984, 1985 and 1986. I flop to the floor with the phone balanced on my shoulder and leaf through the fragile pages of 1978, old glue falling away like dust. The faces of history gaze back at me.

'What is it?' I hear Antonio say.

'Nothing,' I reply as I close the album. 'I think they are coming back. Let me go and get ready. We'll talk later, before the flight.'

I hang up and reopen the album at the desk. It shows my parents in their younger days. Outside the Louvre before the pyramid was built. Boating on a gondola in what I assume is Venice. Happy, unlined faces, free from anguish and pain. *Our happiest times were in youth, when our family was young, when our memories were fresh*. There are empty white spaces in the album where images once sat but have since been lost. Then a picture of them with a baby. Their firstborn. Must be Elle.

I grab another album, 1983, the year after I was born. I run my fingers along the faded gold lettering, then open the cover. The first image is of Elle standing at a table with a birthday cake on top of it. The fondant glistens and the candles flare bright, blurring the image. I count five flickering flames. There are other children at her side, but there is distance between her and them. Not one of them is smiling, and in fact, one is crying, his arms raised in the air, asking to be taken away. I push aside the thought that it means something.

I turn the pages, image after image of a growing family. Then it is me and Elle together. Elle running along chasing a dog, the one that she would later kill, me in the background on a push-along tricycle. Bright yellow seat, curls cascading over my chubby face. I flick to the next photo. It is the same wintry scene, a white sky, frost on the ground. Only this time I am on the floor, pushed from my tricycle by the looks of things. Elle is snatching it away from me, and the dog is jumping in the background. I smile at the idea of us together, just being a family. Domesticity, something I never experienced. Not first hand, anyway. I only saw it as an observer, a watcher from the sidelines. But here in this image, with my face red from the cold, my eyes wet with tears because my sister has stolen my tricycle, I see the normality of family. We were that, once. I turn the page, hoping the story continues overleaf, but the sleeve is blank. The next picture has been lost.

I hear the front door open. I push the album back in the cupboard and make it into the corridor before anybody sees me slip the fallen picture of my mother up my sleeve. It is Frank who arrives first, and I breathe a sigh of relief.

'Irini. We were wondering where you went.'

'I left early. Can you please take me to the airport?'

'You are leaving already?' He looks back towards the front door, expecting company.

'It's for the best. Really it is.' He nods as if he understands. 'In the next ten minutes?'

His shoulders drop with disappointment, and I know he is about to let me down. 'I'm sorry, Irini, but that won't be possible. In a couple of hours, once the wake is finished, is fine, but if I leave now, Mr Harringford will string me up. Today of all days.' He takes a step closer. 'Anyway, you should stay. It wouldn't be right to leave now.'

Embarrassed, I reluctantly agree, and soon enough the house fills with guests. What's a couple more hours? Elle has stopped crying, and is now playing hostess. She has Joyce running back and forth in uncomfortable court shoes. I look down at my pumps and wish guiltily that she was wearing them instead of me. There is tea and coffee, champagne, sherry, whisky. Anything you want, as if we have arrived at Willy Wonka's. I knock back a couple of whiskies, linger on an old Queen Anne chair in the corner of the drawing room. The hit from the alcohol is fast because I haven't eaten anything for almost twenty-four hours. Feels good, too. But still, in the hope of staying clear-headed, I stand up, pick up a cocktail stick of cheese and pineapple, quickly followed by a square of quiche Lorraine.

It seems nobody is interested in talking to me. And I am grateful, because their sly over-the-shoulder glances are enough to unsettle me. I remember that Elle told me everybody would know who I am, and I realise she was right. How could they not when I look so much like the woman they are here to mourn? So I slip into the study and grab the flight-booking details, which I left there in my haste, before retreating to my bedroom, whisky in hand, to wait out the last couple of hours.

I set the tumbler on the bedside table and shove anything of mine into my bag, including the image of my mother that I took from the study, and the sherry, which I have decided doesn't need to be returned. They owe me something, and since it is difficult to give back a whole life, I settle on the remainder of a bottle and mark off part of the debt as paid. I slide the framed butterflies into the top of my bag. But now that everything is packed, the room seems a little more dead than it was before. Like I am being removed twice over.

I hear the creak of the stairs, followed by the rattling of the door handle. I do up the zip and turn around just as the door opens.

'Frank tells me that you want to leave,' Elle stutters as she inches through.

'Yes.' I'm less unnerved by her now, and I can't feel her like before. 'I'm ready to go home. Back to my life.'

'When?'

'Tonight. Plus you should know I'll be changing my number tomorrow. This time, don't search for me.' I need a clean start, another chance at life away from her. 'I can't play these games with you any more, Elle.' I sit down on the edge of the bed, close to tears, spurred on by Dutch courage. I look at her for the first time since she arrived. 'We have nothing left to say to each other.'

I have spent my life believing that it was here that I belonged. Now that I know that isn't true, I have to get away. I have to stop dreaming of what this house and these people could once have been. I have what I needed from the past. My mother wanted me all along, just like I used to wish for. Anything else is superfluous, Elle included. I'll trade knowing the rest for a future, one where I can look back and say that perhaps I don't understand everything that happened, but I can accept it was done for love. Learning any more than that is a risk. I can settle for what I know now.

'You really mean that, don't you?' She looks visibly deflated. 'You said that once before, remember?' She sits down next to me, my bag between us.

'I'm sure I said it many times, Elle.' I am calm, the tears stemmed. I feel like something is over.

'But you used to say it without meaning it.' She huddles inside a big black cardigan that she has thrown over the slick dress she wore to the funeral. I can hear Joyce downstairs in the kitchen, my father's voice bidding farewell to the final mourners. 'There was only one other time when you actually meant it.'

'When?'

'When I killed my dog. After that, you said you didn't want to see me again.'

I think back to the satisfaction I felt when I overheard

Aunt Jemima on the telephone only months after our failed reunion, telling my father how he had to expect this kind of thing from Elle. That he should never have allowed her to be around animals. How pleased I was that my parents' lives were falling apart, all because of Elle and one dead dog.

'Did you really kick it to death?'

'No. I stamped on it and cut it open.'

To hear it from her own lips, so matter-of-fact, is as scary as it is exhilarating. It really happened, I think. 'I was pleased you killed that dog because I thought you had managed to upset our parents.'

'Good, because I did it for you. Aunt Jemima had moved house and they wouldn't let me see you again. I did it to upset them. Afterwards she wanted to send me away again so the doctors could try to fix me, but he wouldn't allow it. Not after what happened the time before.' She stops for a moment and glances at the window, stares off into the distance. 'Shame for you, really. You might have got your wish if they had. Her too.'

'What time before? What wish? What are you talking about?'

'In the mental home. The nut house,' she says, rapping her knuckles against her temple. 'They have drugs that make you say stuff that you would normally keep secret.' She fiddles a piece of dirt out from underneath her bitten fingernail. 'They got it all down on record the first time I was in there, before our parents could get me back. Lucky what happened to me really. For me, at least. Not so good for you, I suppose, but otherwise I'm not sure they would have ever let me out.'

'You're not making any sense to me, Elle.' I think I am past caring. 'Except for the fact that you really did kill the dog. I always wondered.'

'Yes, of course I did. But you knew that already. That's why you told Aunt Jemima that you didn't want to see me again. That's what they told *me*, anyway.'

'I don't remember.'

'Could be another one of their lies. That's what I always hoped. When I found you a few years later, you did seem pleased to see me. Maybe they were lying after all.' What I realise is that she always needed me to want her just as much as I needed her to want me. She turns to me and grips my arms. Tightly to the extent that it hurts. But it is not anger on her face, it's desperation. 'Stay.'

I shake my head. 'I have to leave.'

'But not yet you don't. If you really mean it, about never wanting to see me again, just do one more thing for me. I need you, Rini. We just buried my mother. I feel so alone. Let's go out together now. A quick drink somewhere nearby. It's still early.'

'I have a flight to catch.'

'The place I'm thinking of is ever so close. We can get back here, grab your things, and still be at the airport on time. I promise. We'll say goodbye there.' She tries a smile, unable to hide how she really feels, which makes me pity her for the first time in my life. She leans into me, strokes my face. 'It will be exciting; like Hollywood or something.' She is nearly crying when she says it.

'This morning you told me that I was free of you. That you would never look for me again. That you knew how our father felt, and that he would still choose you, like everything was better without me.' I can feel the tears coming on too. 'What's changed?'

'Just one drink. A last goodbye. One good final memory.' She looks pathetically broken as she clings to me. 'Together.' The limited past we share tells me that nothing good can come from this. But how can I say no? Today of all days, how can I run from her again?

'Just one drink. And from an unopened bottle,' I warn her. 'Don't think I can't remember what you did to that poor girl at my school.' She looks hurt when I bring up Margot Wolfe, and shakes her head.

'I wasn't even there. I was somewhere else.'

'It was your plan. You knew what would happen. I was too young to understand.'

'You were old enough to know the consequences of what you were doing, and more than pleased with the result.' She enjoys watching as I squirm, remembering what we did. 'It was one of the best things that happened to you at school. But as *if* I would do the same to you. You're my sister.'

18

We leave the house at 5 p.m. and head into town, me back in my *FEEL* jumper, Elle in a snazzy pair of leggings and a T-shirt that might or might not be designed for exercise. I am ready and braced for any possible erratic responses as we set off, gripping the door handle before we even leave the driveway. Yet she is calm and mild-mannered. In fact, she is nothing like Elle.

By the time we park up at the pub in the nearby border town of Hawick, it is approaching 5.20, the wind blowing, a summer storm brewing. She has parked and changed her mind three times, but eventually she settles on the Bourtree. She is quiet and reserved, almost to the point of unresponsive, like she knows something is over too. I encourage her along, pointing out a table just inside, and she follows. I suggest bottled beer and she agrees. I tell her that I thought it was a nice service at the church, and she smiles and says the reverend is a kind person. Throughout she burns matches from a box bearing the name of the pub. She strikes one, watches the flame, waits until it is burnt all the way to the end before dropping it in an empty glass. She tests her tolerance of the fire, drawing patterns with the flame across her hand, occasionally catching the down on her arm, filling the air with the scent of burnt hair. I have no idea who the impostor in the chair opposite me is, but it makes me nervous.

The silence between us is difficult, and I can't think of anything mundane to fill it. So I plump for something real. 'Will you be all right with our father once I leave?' It's a dangerous question, because if she tells me no, I'm not sure what I will say. It's not like I would ask her to come to London with me. It's not like I'm planning to come back and check in on her.

'I think so,' she says, and I breathe a sigh of relief. She spots it, pretends not to. 'It will be better now, anyway. I think once he gets over it, he too will find it easier.'

'What will he find easier?'

'Her not being around. It was always strained between them. Mainly because it was strained between me and her.' She looks up at me and sees that I am waiting for clarification. She drops a lit match on to a beer mat and watches as it starts to smoke. I bash it out with the edge of my fist, but it's like she doesn't even notice. 'She blamed me, you see. She always knew there was something wrong with me. It's not like it's a secret.' She lights another match and we both watch it burn down as she holds it steady between us.

I maintain a silence. I pity her beaten resolve, quashed by her own insight into the nature of who she is. 'You said something earlier that I didn't know about,' I say. She shrugs, inviting me to elaborate. 'That you went into a clinic. Why did they send you away?'

She looks surprised, like I am the one with the problem. 'Why did they send me to the nut house? Because they didn't know what to do. They thought the doctors would help. So they put me in there as a show of action, to make them feel better about things. Anyway, whatever. It's a long time ago, not that long after you were born. But let's not sit here all night talking about that like somebody died.'

She jumps from her seat and heads to the bar. I see her making a phone call before she comes back with two more drinks. Just like she always did, trying to lure me in. Hardly a surprise.

'I said only one, and from a bottle. I'm not drinking that. Plus, you're driving.'

She rolls her eyes at me in the classic Elle way, as if I am just a miserly fun-spoiler. A party-pooper. I've seen this look many times before. She takes a sip from both drinks as if to prove they haven't been spiked. I take the one closest to her, give it a sniff. I don't know what I am looking for, but it just smells like whisky.

'Come on. We're drinking to your Elle-free future,' she says without a hint of irony, her unblinking eyes fixed upon mine. If her comment was designed to make me feel bad, or her stare to make me uncomfortable, it's worked. She is holding up her glass so that we might raise a toast. I strike her glass with mine. I sip cautiously and see that it tastes fine. *As if I would do the same to you. You're my sister.* 'It's a good one,' I say, hoping the compliment on her whisky choice can sweeten her mood.

'I know it is. This *is* Scotland, and I know a good whisky when I see one, just like I know a person who likes a good drink. You and he are not so different. Go on, knock it back.' I humour her and swallow the drink. 'That's better,' she says.

We pass the next half an hour talking about our shared experiences, of which there are few. Of course we discuss the dead dog, the fact that it happened, and that indeed the white cross at the end of the lawn represents not only where it was buried, but also where it died. She raises some of the more questionable things she got me to do. She tries to bring up the last time we saw each other before I left for university, but I dodge the subject by mentioning the time she jumped from the aqueduct. For some reason I find it amusing, and instead of reprimanding her for it, I finally see the funny side. I laugh as I remember the horror on the face of the man who pulled her out, jabbing at her naked body with a fallen tree branch. The leaf that clung to her eyelid like a pirate's patch. Haha! I'm actually giggling out loud, and amidst my humour I realise the trick. I look down; her whisky remains untouched.

'You spiked my drink,' I say as I try to stand. 'You said you wouldn't, but you did.' I don't manage it, slip back into my chair. She steadies me and I lean on the table for support.

'Don't be pissy with me. They'll be here soon.'

'Who'll be here?' I ask, trying to fight the drug in order to remain angry.

'Greg and Matt.'

This revelation forces me back up and out of my seat, but my legs are less than stable. I wobble a bit before gripping the edge of the table, and reach to cup my hip protectively. Then I slump back down, defeated. 'You bitch,' I say, laughing. 'You fucking drugged me.' The thought is, in the moment of realisation, hilarious.

I see Greg walking towards me. As he approaches the

table, Matt slips out from his shadow. He smiles at me, and I smile back, and my first thought is that he looks good. Before Matt sits down, he picks up the glass of burnt-down matches. He motions for Elle to give him the half-empty box; once she relinquishes it, he drops it into the glass, which he sets on another table.

'Well, well, well. What are two beautiful ladies doing drinking on their own?' says Greg. Elle cracks the biggest smile as he pulls up a chair. It makes me laugh too, and I don't find him quite so repulsive tonight. Not quite. 'We will have to rectify that,' he says as he slides up next to her. I wonder where his fiancée is, and I almost ask him, but I am distracted by my foot in a wet patch of carpet. I try to remain sensible.

Matt sits down and leans in towards me. 'Everything OK?'

'Yes,' I say as his hand brushes against mine. It feels amazing. I have never been touched that way before. I slide up close, press my body against his.

'Hey, easy there,' he says as I rub my face against his neck. His stubble is as sharp as needles, and I am purring like a cat. I reach up and stroke his face, and my skin shivers, tingles from head to toe. Somewhere inside of me the real Irini is screaming, *What are you doing?* but the fact that it is so much like a distant echo makes it easy to ignore.

'Rini, are you OK?' I hear Elle ask. She stretches across the table and I take her hand in mine.

'You are my sister,' I say. 'We are family. How can I leave you?' I lean in to her as I finally manage to stand up. I brush my fingers through her hair, find it smooth as silk.

She reaches up and touches my face, and it sparks a memory, drunk or high I'm not sure, of us sitting together on a kerb. That night was the beginning of the end. Back then, to leave her was the only thing I could do. I try harder to listen, to concentrate. She is talking but I can't differentiate the words.

'You can't leave me. Now close your eyes,' she says. I feel the wind on my skin, brushing over me like the feathers of a bird. I open my eyes to find Elle blowing gently on my face, running her fingers up my arms like butterflies. I know in that moment that it will be the happiest memory I ever have of her.

'Come on,' I say, reaching for Matt's hand. 'Let's go outside.' I can't stay here with her. I don't want to give her the chance to spoil what she has just done.

I pull Matt along behind me until we leave the pub. I swirl around in circles, dancing in the wind with my arms outstretched. Passers-by stare at me as they wander the Victorian streets of this little town, their eyes bulging out on stalks at my stupidity, my freedom, but I don't care. We skirt past the sand-coloured buildings and gaudily fronted bars offering cheap beer and Sky Sports. In the distance I can see the tower of the town hall, which looks more like a French chateau. We run like maniacs up the high street, Matt trying to catch me as I hide behind a statue of a horse. Before he reaches me, I jump out from behind it, scare a person who happens to be passing by. But then I feel Matt's arms around me, hear his laughter. I lean in to brush against his stubble, but instead my lips catch his. I kiss him, his lips so wet, so hot, and it drives me crazy. He spins me around, pushes me against the monument, the weight of his body bearing down on me. Grounded.

'You know what this horse represents?' he asks me as he runs his hands through my hair. When I don't answer, he tells me. 'Victory over the English invaders. That's what you are, you know that? You've invaded me, taken over.'

'I leave tonight,' I say, only half listening. I hear a rumble of thunder shudder through the sky. 'I told her I'm never coming back. But I love her. I love Elle. How could I leave her for ever?' Or do I just need her, crave her, desire her in some sick way that means I can't let her go, like an addiction? He brushes his hands across my cold cheeks and I let out a moan.

'You can't; she's your sister,' he whispers. He tightens his grip, pulls me in close. 'It wouldn't be fair on her.'

'My family,' I say, as I kiss him again. 'I'm not myself. This isn't—' He interrupts me with another kiss, and any resistance that I still had begins to melt away.

We walk, stopping every few steps to kiss and caress each other, because I am addicted to his touch. I break free at times when something catches my eye. Once a coin on the floor, the next a bush flickering in the breeze. Somehow I always end up back in his arms, being whisked along, carried forward. At some point we end up in an alley, me against the wall with his hands fumbling under my clothes like an eager teenage boy. I don't want it to stop, but somebody chases us away. Somewhere inside of me I feel that something is different, warmer, like a buzzing in my belly. In this moment I totally belong. With him. With me. There is no other place I should be. No Elle. No Antonio.

I can feel my teeth chattering, but I might just be talking. I can't be sure.

'Putting people to sleep is weird, like you see them one minute and they are wide awake, and then the next.' I smack my hands together in a giant clap and the shock wave shudders through my body. 'Bang, they are under. So quick. So easy. Easiest thing in the world.' I feel spots of water hitting my face, and I look up at the sky, watch as the buildings darken in giant streaks as the rain begins to pour.

'Then they wake up and they've been somewhere else entirely.' I roll around his body, complete a full loop like I too have been away and now I am back, facing him.

'I wish somebody would put *me* to sleep for a change. Find that same kind of peace.' I jump up on a wall, walk along the edge like a gymnast, spring off the end with my arms up in a theatrical *ta-da!* He takes me in his arms and I look up into his wide eyes. 'But I would never want to wake up again.'

Before long, and with little memory of how I got there I find myself on a bed. The sheets are white. They look smooth, but the weave ripples against me as I spread and glide my hands over them. They brush against my legs too, and I look down and see that I am not wearing my jeans. My bare feet dangle over the edge. Then I see Matt. I should tell him this is a bad idea, that's what I think. But he straddles me, kisses my neck, and it feels so damn good that I can't tell him no. He slides my jumper up and over my head, and as I turn to pull my head out of it I see an alarm clock on the nightstand. Where are we? *8.41 p.m.* flashes back at me and I remember that I am supposed to be getting on a plane. I should get up, but the voice telling me to stay is too loud to ignore. The sheets feel so good. His lips, his stubble, his hand and the way he pushes it against me and pulls at my breasts. In this moment I don't even care if they are lopsided. I lie helplessly as he unfastens the last of my clothes, peeling away my layers until I am just me, exposed, unhidden and free. He rubs his hand across my stomach, trailing down to my scars. But he doesn't linger over them like Antonio does.

'I want you,' he says as his wet lips slide over my thighs. The shadows rise and fall as his body moves in the soft light of the moonlit bedroom. Rain strikes the window.

'I want me too,' I say, and when he doesn't question it, I know I am in the exact place that I should be, for the first time ever in my life. Here with a stranger, I have found peace. And in that moment I tell myself something greater than anything that has gone before: that I deserve to feel this good. That just like my father told me, I too am worthwhile.

19

The sound of running water wakes me. At first I think it is rain beating down outside, but the first thing I see as I open my eyes is Matt's face. He is standing in a towel, his skin glistening and wet, with steam billowing out of the bathroom in soft, fluffy clusters behind him. That's when I realise I'm in a hotel. I realise too that I am naked, the only thing covering me a creased white sheet.

I lie still, trying to remember how I got here. I remember flashes of the previous night, his smiles, Elle's laughter, us kissing, but cannot place any of these events in a timeline that leads to this room and this moment. Matt smiles as he sits down on the edge of the bed and brushes his hand against my foot. I pull it away, snap it back to me like tight elastic.

'Sorry,' he says, appearing hurt. He holds up his hands in surrender, and I feel an instant hit of regret. Partly for him, but mainly for Antonio.

'No, I'm sorry,' I say as I let my foot slip back towards him across the sheets, which disappointingly just feel like sheets in the light of a new day. Regular old sheets that don't ripple underneath my skin like I thought they did. 'You didn't do anything wrong.'

He lets out an audible sigh of relief. 'I thought for a second there . . .' He doesn't finish his sentence. 'You were pretty drunk, I think, but I asked you plenty of times if you were sure. You just kept telling me that it felt so good. Not to stop.' He smiles at the memory, but then finds it inappropriate and straightens himself up. He looks down at his body, his chest covered in hairs, surprised, like he only just realised he was naked.

'I wasn't drunk,' I say. 'I've been drunk plenty of times to know how that feels. I was high. Somebody slipped me a roofie.'

'I didn't—'

I don't let him finish. 'Don't worry. I know it wasn't you.' My head is throbbing, my mouth dry and sandy. I reach for a glass of water at the side of the bed, all the while keeping a firm hand over the sheet that covers me. It matters now, the scars and the lopsidedness of my body. I guzzle down the water and then slam the glass back down on the bedside table. 'It was Elle.'

'Your sister? Why would she do that?' He looks genuinely scared. I can see him thinking about all the times he thought she was a bit nuts, when he warned his buddy to stay away from the crazy girl without any real or substantiated concerns. Even when she attacked the girlfriend of one of her victims.

'You think this is the first time she's done something like this?' I say, covering my mouth with a fist, remembering Margot Wolfe. 'Elle's a fucking nut job. Always has been, and I just keep getting sucked in by her. God, I'm so stupid.'

'Even if that's true,' he says, doubtful of my accusation,

'you're her sister. I would have expected some kind of familial immunity.'

I shake my head, realising that I did too. I believed her. Trusted her. 'We are nothing to each other,' I spit, finally understanding the sad truth of it. 'We have never been sisters, not as such. Yesterday I told her that I wanted nothing more to do with her, and she did the same. And we both meant it. I was planning to leave and—' I suddenly remember. 'Oh my God, my flight. I missed my flight home.' All I can do is shake my head, cover my eyes with shame. 'She's a bitch. She did this on purpose so I would have to stay. Where are we?'

'Hawick,' he says, more than a little scared. 'I'll take you to the airport if you like. You can be there in less than an hour.' He rushes for his clothes, but I motion for him not to bother. 'Home then?' I glance up, my face reminding him of the stupidity of the word, then slouch backwards under the weight of my mistake. 'I'm really sorry about this. I never thought . . . I just . . . I never anticipated—'

'It's not your fault,' I say as I adjust the sheet to keep myself covered. He looks about the room and picks up my bra and jumper, offers them to me. I take them, feeling guilty for his embarrassment. 'But when I find her, I'm going to kill her.'

'Well,' he chuckles, then stops himself as I slip my arms into my bra. 'Perhaps I shouldn't tell you this, but she's just next door.'

I bolt up like a jack-in-the-box, hanging on to the sheet. I point at the rest of my clothes and motion for him to pass them to me. He crouches and picks up the scattered remains of my dignity. 'What is she doing here?' I ask, spinning my fingers to indicate that he should turn around. He does so without question, and I dress.

'Greg brought her here. I don't think he wanted to go home.'

'Probably because of his fiancée, wouldn't you think?' It's a chance to throw that one at him, test it for truth. From his silence I assume I am right. Turns out that not everything Elle tells me is a lie.

I pull on my fancy Reeboks and barge past, pulling open the door. I point left and right, looking for an answer from Matt. He indicates a door and I hammer my fist against it but get no reply.

'Where are they?' I demand.

'Probably at breakfast,' he says.

I huff and puff, my displeasure almost at the level of last night's pleasure. If I had to hazard a guess, I would say it was Ecstasy that she gave me. Heightened sensations. Open and chatty. Everything I am not. I snatch a glance in a hallway mirror and see that my pupils are still the size of saucers.

'Wait a minute.' Matt reaches out and takes my hands in his, still wearing nothing but a towel. I feel none of that electricity running across my skin from the night before. But there is something. Perhaps a memory of something good suppressed by the guilt of the morning after. For this reason alone I don't push him away. 'I know you weren't quite yourself last night, but I had a great time with you. You're single, and unlike Greg, I'm single too. And a decent guy, if you don't hold it against me that I took advantage of you.'

'You didn't take advantage of me. I was more than willing.' I think I should tell him about Antonio, but the prospect of the truth doesn't fill me with excitement. I realise that to him I must look like quite a catch. Single, averagely pretty, good job, great fun. Uninhibited in bed with a little bit of chemical assistance. I think back to the night before, flashes of memories of all the different ways we had sex. We were like a couple of teenagers at it for the first time with our hands on a Kama Sutra. I couldn't get enough of him if I remember correctly. I can still feel the after-effects of it now, the throbbing between my legs, the ache of my hip. I feel my cheeks flush at the embarrassment and pull myself away.

'So let's do this again. Next time without the drugs and the crazy sister.'

I smile as my eyes scan his body, the towel that is only a few more steps from falling. I don't want him to feel bad, but the pitying look on my face has told him all he needs to know.

'Or not,' he concedes, defeated.

'It wouldn't be a good idea.'

I wait in the corridor while he dresses. We find Elle in the dining room, Greg sitting opposite her. I walk towards their table, Matt just behind me. He is whispering frantic warnings as we pass the travelling reps and foreign holidaymakers pouring tea and slicing bacon. The warm aroma of bread lingers in the air. Smells good. Homely. By the time I arrive at her side and sit in the chair, she still hasn't noticed me.

'Elle,' I snap, but she doesn't respond. Instead she continues buttering a dry triangle of toast. I watch her as she spreads it thinly, the layer perfect and even like that from an advert on the television. 'Elle,' I say, louder this time. 'What the fuck did you do to me last night?' Still she says nothing. I lash out, smack her hand. Force is all she understands. I feel an immediate sense of regret and fore-boding as her triangle of toast flies from her hand, lands in Greg's coffee cup. He lunges backwards, but still the coffee splashes over his plate and shirt.

'What the—' he begins, but I cut his words short.

'I said, what did you do to me last night?' I hear the sounds of the restaurant quieten as a couple of the nearest tables stop what they are doing and turn their attention to us. I brace myself because I must be firm. Hard to do when she is still acting as if I am not here. Matt takes up position next to Greg, warning him not to interfere. Elle picks up her napkin and wipes her fingers. She offers it to Greg, who snatches it, eyes daggering into me as he mops up the spillage. 'You drugged me, Elle. You made me miss my flight.'

She looks up at me with her nose and chin in the air and asks, 'I'm sorry, who are you?'

Her arrogance sends me into a spin, and I reach out, quick as a fox, latching on to her wrist. I tighten my grip around her skinny little arm and get a good hold of her. She doesn't resist, even though I am certain she could out-strength me. But that's the thing with psychopaths. Sociopaths. Whatever you want to call her. They don't fear or react to outside stimuli because they see no threat. Instead she uses her other hand to knock over a glass of juice that is waiting in the empty table setting. It pours into my lap, and I see a smirk creep on to Greg's face. Matt is calm; grabs a napkin and tries to mop it up. I grip her tighter as juice pours down my legs, seeping into the jeans she bought for me.

'If you remember correctly, as of today I no longer have a sister,' she says. 'We have nothing left to say to each other. That's what you told me yesterday, when you broke my heart. So what, I slipped you an E. Big deal.' She pulls her arm away and I don't resist. She reaches for another triangle of toast and begins buttering it in the same prescriptive style.

'Big deal?' I demand. 'Of course it's a big deal. And it was you that told me you didn't want to see me any more.'

She slams the knife down on her plate and tosses the toast down next to it. Her fingers remain on top of the blade and I edge backwards at the recollection of what she is capable of. *I'll fucking stick you with this, I promise you.* She remembers her words too, I'm sure of it. My mouth goes dry.

'I only wanted for you to enjoy yourself, for once in your pitiful and empty life. To feel something other than hate for all of us.' She slurps at a glass of juice, but most of it runs across her chin. She sets the glass back down, spilling more juice on the white cloth. Even Greg looks anxious now. 'You loved me last night. You questioned your desire to cut me out. And as far as I can tell, what with you being here in a hotel and him following you to breakfast,' she jabs the knife towards Matt, 'you had a pretty good time on it.'

'That's not the point,' I say, trying not to look at Matt. But it's a hard truth to face. I had a great time. It was true that nothing had ever felt so good.

'I will take you back to *my* house so you can get your bag. Then I will take you to the airport and ensure you get on a flight that takes you away from me for the rest of your miserable life.' She says it all very matter-of-factly, as if her speech came with bullet points. 'I'd say that makes me pretty fucking selfless if you ask me, considering I had no intention of ever trying to cut you out. Just because our parents didn't want you, it doesn't mean that I didn't. I wanted you. I cried when they took you away from me. I needed you, Irini. You were so small. You couldn't hurt anyone. I wanted to keep you, paint you with butterflies, but they wouldn't let me, just because I made one or two mistakes.'

She stands up and I follow, my jeans wet and sticky. I offer up a half-goodbye, half-apology to Matt, and take with me some of the best memories of my life from the night before. I wait in the lobby while she goes to her bedroom to collect her things. She returns dressed in fresh sportswear, carrying a small overnight bag. For a split second I wonder if she had all this planned. But then I clench my teeth, shake it off. What does it even matter?

'Can you give me your phone?' I ask as we begin to walk out of the lobby. She hands it over without question and I dial Antonio's number, trying to think of an excuse as to why I am not with him. Just as he picks up, I hear Matt calling my name. I hit the *End Call* button and spin around.

'Irini, just a moment,' he puffs, his hair messed up in gentle blonde curls, cheeks flushed, dressed in last night's clothes. His sprint drops into a jog as he arrives in front of us.

'Matt, I really have to go. I have to get a flight home.' Just as I say that, the phone starts to buzz in my hand. It is of course Antonio, returning the call that I dropped.

'Just hold on a moment.' Matt reaches out and touches

my free hand. 'Aren't you going to answer that? I'll wait,' he suggests as he looks down at the phone.

I open my mouth to speak, but before I do, Elle interrupts. 'Actually, that's my phone. Hers is broken.' She snatches it before I can react and answers the call. 'Hello, who is this?' I hear her ask as she whisks the phone away. Within only a few short steps I cannot hear what she is saying over the hum of the busy lobby.

'Good, she's gone,' Matt says, taking my empty hand in his. 'I wanted to talk to you. Just for a moment before you go. I wanted to tell you something.'

'Matt, there's no point to this.'

'Maybe not, but regardless, I want to say it.' He takes a long, bolstering breath in, lets it out quickly. 'I want to say that I know what this trip has been like for you. I know it has been a nightmare. And I'm so sorry about your mother, and all the shit with your family.' He snatches a glance at Elle and my gaze follows. She is still talking on the phone, moving towards one of the empty seats, and I wonder what further damage she is doing to my life. 'But for me it has been the opposite. As soon as I saw you in the gym with Elle, I thought, just, wow.'

'Stop it.' Whatever anybody thinks when they look at me, *wow* is not on the list of possibilities. For Elle, maybe. But for me? No way.

'Really, that's the truth. I'm not like Greg. I don't go to the gym to pick up girls. I find it hard to open up to people, or to let them get close.' He steps closer, drops his voice to a whisper. 'The things I told you, about my parents, and about having a therapist . . . I don't tell people that stuff.

172

Greg doesn't even know. With you, I can be honest. There is something about you . . . about us, together, that feels right. I feel I can be myself with you.'

'You don't know me at all. We've only met twice.'

'Aye, but the first time we met I told you things about my past that I haven't told anybody before. I've been looking for that all my life. That has to mean something. I don't know what you think of yourself, but you are amazing. Last night was—'

'Because of Ecstasy.' I glance over at Elle, who is smiling, laughing. She is sitting on one of the plump lobby chairs next to a businessman dressed in a sharp suit with a laptop propped on his knees. He looks only mildly interested in what is on his screen, considerably more interested in who has sat down next to him. Elle is the sister who turns heads, makes minds and bodies stray. Not me. People do not say *wow* when they meet me.

'No. Last night was amazing. I know how you felt. I could see it. I could feel it. And I know how I felt, too.' He reaches into his pocket, pulls out a business card. 'I want to see you again. This is my number. When you get back home, think about it. Think about me. And if you want, call me.'

I take the card and nod. 'OK. I'll think about it.' He reaches forward and kisses me. He goes for the lips, but I turn slightly and he catches my cheek instead. His stubble grates at my skin, feels like it has left a red mark like a graze on a child's knee. Matt's lips purse, a smile of understanding that nothing today is the same. It is as if he realises that his effort is futile. That familiar feeling I know so well;

that there is nothing you can do to change things already done.

'Take care, Irini,' he says as he lets go of my hand before walking away.

I look over at Elle, who has already ended the call. I beckon her over and she meets me at the glass doors. They slide open and shut as people pass in and out, warm air from outside mixing with the chill of the air-conditioning vents. 'What did you tell him?' I ask as I watch Matt slip back into the dining room.

'I told him that last night, when it came to leaving, our father broke down in tears and begged you to stay just one more night. That he was so very sorry. That he wanted a chance to put everything right, even though he realised such chances didn't exist.' I can imagine Antonio hearing this, happy that perhaps finally my demons might be put to rest. That now I will agree to marry him and have a baby. 'He asked why you didn't call, but I said that it was an upsetting time, that you had taken it hard. That we had sat up talking all night. I told him that we would soon be on our way to the airport. That you were better, and that we would try to organise a chance to meet at some point in the future of our reunited family.' She lets a fake smile bounce on and off her lips.

'What did he say to that?'

'He seemed very happy,' she says as we walk through the doors.

'Thanks for covering for me,' I mutter, embarrassed that my psychotic sister has the chance to play a part in this deceit. That I have proven myself untrustworthy in her presence. She says nothing as we step out into the car park. We sit in her Mercedes in silence until she starts the engine. Was it her that brought us here?

Her driving is slow and cautious, like that first day. Outside is grey and overcast, the air cooler after last night's storm, the colours muted by the rain. We skim through the town and follow the country lanes, passing pimple-like hills in the distance. A low-hanging layer of mist still clings to the ground, and after a while I can stand the silence no longer.

'I'm sorry it has to be like this, Elle.'

'No you are not,' she says, her words formal and enunciated. The voice she adopts when she wants to be strong, to show she has set her mind to something. 'It is what you want. I knew the day would come. People do not tolerate me for long. Remember, that's why you lied to me about which university you were going to.'

'It wasn't a case of not tolerating you. I was scared. Don't you remember what you did before I left?'

'Of course I remember,' she says. 'Perhaps you are the one who has forgotten that I did it for you.'

'You threatened me with a knife.'

'But it wasn't you I used it on, was it?' We sit in silence at the memory neither of us wants to recall. 'And anyway, you lied to me about where you were going before I did what I did.'

We arrive in Horton and she stops at the side of the road, looks out across the view she claims to love, the derelict building she claims to hate. She traces the hills against the glass with her finger. 'I am never enough for people, Irini.

No matter what I do for them. That was always the problem.' She pulls away again and heads towards the house. We pass the sign for *Mam Tor*, and as she turns into the driveway, I see the house looming in the distance, the reflection of clouds cast in the windows. She parks up in front of the six-garage block. Frank is there, working on the windscreen of another car.

'Elle, you're wrong. It was me that wasn't enough. Remember, it's you they kept. You were enough right from the start.' I say this not really believing it any more. But I have come to understand Elle now. As tough as she seems, she is weak. As strong as her words are, she is frail in spirit. She feels betrayal perhaps even deeper than I do.

'If only you knew how wrong you were.' She kills the engine and turns to face me. 'I have watched you in this house over the last few days. I know you understand now that she wanted you, even if you don't understand why he forced you away. It was a close call, you know. Me or you. But she is dead and the past is better left untold. The important thing is that he doesn't regret his choice, and I only know that because you came here. Thank you,' she says, a little softer than before, to the point where I think she might mean it. 'I'll be all right. Without us, perhaps you will too.'

She steps from the car and I follow, thinking about the first day we arrived here. This place doesn't feel as strange any more, and I do not feel like such an alien. I even think as I look up at the house, knowing that this will be the last time I step inside, that it is quite a beautiful place, in a moody sort of way. As I step through the open doors, Joyce is sweeping crumbs from the hallway rug. Remnants of yesterday's mourning. Elle is just up ahead.

'Morning, Joyce,' I say. 'Are you OK?'

'Yes, Irini. Thank you.' She spots Elle walking towards the stairs and calls out, 'Miss Eleanor, your father is still sleeping. He retired early last night and asked me not to disturb him this morning.'

Elle raises a hand to dismiss her, and the only sound to break the silence is the grandfather clock ticking in the background. I roll my eyes at Joyce, offer a gentle smile to show my understanding. In my head I say, *Typical Elle*, before dismissing the thought as flippant. Joyce just shakes her head.

'I'm leaving today, Joyce. Thank you for your help while I have been here. Especially yesterday. You've been kind.' She stops sweeping and reaches out to hug me. She rubs at my arms, then moves a hand down to my scarred hip.

'It's so nice to see how you have grown up. I remember you as a baby, do you know that?' I shake my head. 'I nursed you in that room you've been staying in. I used to sit in an old chair in the corner with you in my arms. I missed you when they sent you away.'

Lost for words, I pull her close and squeeze her tightly. To know I was loved, held, that my presence was missed, means more than I could ever explain to her.

'Thank you,' I say. Just that. Nothing else.

'They did want you, you know that, don't you?' I pull back, shocked by what she has said. 'They *both* wanted you. If your dear mother had got her way, it would have been the other one who left this house.' *It was a close call . . .*

Me or you. 'She deserved it after what she did. If only they hadn't discovered what was happening, they would never have brought her home.' Then she shakes her head, purses her lips. 'Oh, I know I shouldn't say that. She was just a little girl and I shouldn't wish that upon a child.' She reaches up, places her good hand over her chest where her heart is. 'Not even her, God forgive me.'

'Joyce, what are you talking about? Why did they send me away? What was happening?' The similarity of this story to what Elle began telling me after the funeral is indisputable, and the proximity of the truth swells up inside me, blocking my windpipe. All this time I was sitting holed up in that room, and if I had just pushed Joyce about what happened, she might have told me everything.

'He didn't feel it was right after learning what they were doing to her. They had to bring her home, but it was too risky to let you both stay. He just felt so guilty. So many lies had already been told, what was one more?' She swallows hard. 'He didn't think anybody would be able to care for Elle if they learnt what she had done. So he kept her here, kept it all quiet, and sent you away. Oh,' she says, touching her head. 'I forget myself. However could I have said that it would be better if nobody knew? For that to happen to a little girl . . .' She steps away and I reach for her arm. 'No, I shouldn't be saying this. Like I said, better left behind closed doors.'

My mouth parts to speak, but I don't get my words out in time. Instead the cry flies down the stairs, shrill and urgent.

'Noooooooooooooo! Whhhaaaaaaaaaaaaanoooooooooooo!'

Desperate cries, mauled baby, strangled kitten cries. I let go of Joyce and charge up the stairs, round a dog-leg bend into unknown territory. I pass a dead end on the right with a small table next to it and swing around the banisters as I follow the wailing. '*Breeeatthe!*'

As I run, I can hear Joyce shuffling along behind me calling out to Frank. I arrive at an open door. The room is dark, curtains closed. Elle is on the bed, rocking back and forth, wailing. I see my father underneath her. I have seen enough of death to know that he is gone. I have spent my adult life watching the sleeping, and I do not confuse the two. I creep forward, invisible, and look into his dead, half-open eyes. I know there is no point trying to save him. He died hours ago, and the empty bottle of Valium on the bedside locker next to an empty bottle of Scotch is all the evidence I need to know that it was suicide. I pick up the pill bottle with no name on it. It is mine.

I step backwards, unable to help. Snapshots of the room blink at me like the flash of an old-style camera: the heavy velvet curtains, the striped dressing gown on the end of the bed, the brown duvet cover, the empty water jug. I slide the bottle into the pocket of my jeans and edge away. Joyce is hobbling along the landing as I reach the door.

'Call an ambulance,' I mutter as she arrives next to me. She yelps when she sees him, wobbles, and I catch her before she falls. 'Call an ambulance,' I say again. I take one last look at Elle, flailing about on the bed, distraught. She is beating her hands like a wild animal against our dead father's chest. We are orphans, I realise, something else that binds us. What can I do? Nothing. I cannot save him. I cannot save her. This time, just like every other time, I can only save myself.

I run down the main stairs and up to my bedroom and see that my bag is still sitting on the end of the bed, ready to go. It looks undisturbed. I grab it, ignoring the commotion from the adjoining room, the screams filtering through the air vents. I charge through the door, letting it swing to the point that it slams into the plasterwork. I hear something crack, break, flutter to the ground, but I am back down the stairs in a flash without a second thought. I slip outside through the back door, and as I approach the front of the house I see Frank running towards the main entrance. I wait for him to pass before I continue. I can still hear Elle. She is hysterical, making no sense. I think that maybe I should stay, try to help her, even though I know I will fail. But it would be futile.

I throw my bag on to the passenger seat of Elle's car and climb in. The keys are still there. The tyres crunch on the gravel as I pull from the driveway, heading for the airport. The village with what should have been my school is just up ahead. The grave of the woman I resemble so much is only minutes away. I look into the rear-view mirror and watch as the house that should have been mine fades into the past, just like Elle, and I know for the first time that there is nothing salvageable left behind.

20

Once I'm through security I stake out a quiet corner, one of the seats that nobody wants because of the limited views towards the departure gates. I buy a new phone, one of the cheap disposable things that I will bin as soon as I get home and change my number. I push in my old SIM card and wait for it to register. Within thirty seconds I receive seventeen missed-call notifications. Each one Antonio. The tears that struck me on the way to the airport resurface, so I put the phone down and brush them away. My eyes are hot, so red-raw that my vision has become blurry. I know I should call Antonio, and I even make a couple of attempts to dial his number. Half an hour later I still haven't made the call.

I head to the toilets and wet my face, letting the water wash into my eyes. A woman at a nearby sink watches me, sees that I am troubled. She considers an approach, a Good Samaritan shoulder to cry on, so I grab a paper towel and get the hell out of there. I buy a coffee and sip it before it gets the chance to cool down, burning my lip and tongue again. My head is throbbing, either from the swelling of my Ecstasy-fuelled brain, or because of what I have done as a result of it. So I find an empty seat near a kiosk selling souvenirs, where the noise is not so overpowering. I take out the new phone, knowing there is no point in waiting. Nothing is about to change. I dial Antonio's number.

'I love you.' The first thing he says, and in English too. There is no anger in his voice, and no confrontation. 'I am so sorry for everything.' It makes everything so much worse, because at least if he was angry at me I could claim injustice. Whatever it was that Elle told him, he sucked it in, drank it up like baby milk.

'I . . .' I can't get my words out. I want to tell him everything and be forgiven, yet at the same time I cannot bring myself to admit what I have done. The only thing flowing is a tear across my cheek. 'I . . .' I say again, but my voice cracks and it's no use trying to hide it. Another kindly looking woman initiates a movement in my direction, so I turn away, stagger towards an exit. There is a large sign hanging across it that reads, *Use only in an emergency*.

'Don't say anything. It's OK. I should have gone with you. I should have been there.' I can hear that he is angry with himself. As if he is the selfish one for not coming.

'I wish you had been here,' I sputter, a line of snot streaming from my nose. I don't know why I feel so sorry for myself, because the things I feel most sorry about are all my doing. Sleeping with Matt, and abandoning Elle at the time when she has perhaps never needed me more.

'I will be at the airport waiting for you,' he says.

And he is. He carries no flowers or extravagant gifts. Just him, dressed in the leather jacket I have always protested I hate. But when I see it, there is something instantly familiar about the way it makes me feel. He reaches out and I grip him, the smell of leather and garlic filling my nose. He wraps his arms around me and holds me, whispering in my ear in a mixture of English and Italian that is impossible to understand. But I do catch one phrase: 'I will never stop being here for you.'

Suddenly nothing of what has gone before in our relationship matters. As if all the arguments and problems never existed. Somebody always there for me, is that what's on offer? I can handle that, can't I? No matter who it is. I wonder if I said something to elicit such a response. I'm not sure. I sink into the crumpled leather, let him muffle out the world. For a moment, it is just me.

At the house, I see that standards have slipped. Beer bottles are stacked up by the sink; there's a smear of pizza sauce on the white tiles of the kitchen. Things that wouldn't normally be there. But it doesn't bother me, not even the haphazard way that the cushions have been tossed about. Not even the fact that it looks like he slept on the couch last night. That's a whole lot better than where I slept.

'Welcome home,' he whispers. 'This is where you belong.' He snuggles in close, but the relief of being with him, away from them, isn't as fresh as it was at the airport. I'm starting to think more like myself now that I am in my home, and I begin to suspect that he can smell Matt on me, like some sort of primitive instinct.

'Thank you,' I say, taking the cup of tea he makes for me. 'I'm going to have a shower. Then we need to talk.' I set the mug on the table. 'There are things I need to tell you.' There is only a hint of concern on his face, which he hides well with a smile.

I run the water hot to the point that my skin turns pink. I scrub my lank, greasy hair free of the dust from my childhood bedroom. I slough off the hairs from my arms and legs, and then proceed to the small strip between. By the time I finish, I am as hairless as an on-set porn star. As hairless as Elle. I scrub my body, avoiding only the scars on my hip, desperately trying to work out what it is that I want to tell Antonio.

I grab a towel and wrap it around my scalded body, my scars raised and inflamed. I leave the bathroom, determined to tell him everything. I go into my bedroom and push my feet into the slippers he bought for me, but then kick them off, feeling that to wear them is a liberty I shouldn't take. I dig further into my bag, see the butterflies flapping to get out. I take the picture, drag my fingers over the delicate strokes. I set it down on my bedside table, propped up against the wall. I see the photo of my mother so retrieve that as well, but slide it quickly into my bedside drawer. I rummage for the small toiletry bag in search of lotion that I haven't used in days. But as I pull it out, something else comes with it: a manila envelope. It falls to the floor and lands next to my bare foot. I look down and see that on the front of the envelope there is a name written in old-style calligraphic handwriting.

Irini Harringford.

'Rini,' I hear Antonio call up the stairs, 'I made you another tea. Hurry, while it is warm.'

'OK, I'm coming,' I shout, sliding my arms into my towelling dressing gown, which smells like home, crossing over the ties at the front. I sit on the edge of the bed and reach down for the envelope. A few drops of water fall from my hair on to the ink, obscuring the letters. I curse under my breath, snatch at the white towel and dab at the drops. I turn the envelope over, feeling the weight, trying to guess what is inside. I slide my finger into the seam and tear it open, pull out the contents. The first word my eye catches is *testament*.

I, Maurice J. Harringford, of Mam Tor *House, Horton, declare that this is my last will and testament. I revoke all prior wills and codicils created prior to my wife's passing, and I . . .*

I stop reading when I see Antonio leaning against the bedroom door frame. The door frame that he painted. Such details make my infidelity seem much more hurtful.

'What are you reading?' he asks as he sits next to me, fiddles a finger into my hair.

'Nothing. It's not mine,' I say, folding the pages over. He picks up the envelope from my lap and holds it out in front of him.

'It has your name on it. That makes it yours.' He turns his body and edges towards me, and I smell his familiar perfume, spicy ginger and cardamom rich on his skin. 'You wanted to talk, yet now you lie? Why?' He doesn't wait for an answer. 'You have something here. Something for you. It looks important. Tell me. Tell me *something*,' he begs. 'Let me in so that I can help you.'

I swallow hard, impressed by his dedication. 'A lot happened these past few days, Antonio. None of it was good.' He looks a little nervous, almost sad. I offer him the pages and he begins to read. It takes time, because it isn't like any English he knows. After a while, he pushes them back into my hand.

'I don't understand. What is this?'

'It's my father's will. His wishes and instructions after his death. It is a legal document. I found it in my bag.'

'In an envelope with your name on it?' I nod. 'Your father's handwriting?'

'I'm not sure. I guess so.'

'So, your father wanted you to have it. But he's not dead. Why would he give it to you now?' My face gives it all away: the little swallow, the jittery eyes, verging on tears. 'Your father died?' I nod, look away. He reaches for me but my body stiffens. 'What happened?' he asks.

'He killed himself. Overdose.'

'But you spent all night together, talking and working things out. That's why you didn't come home last night.'

I start working on an explanation through the fog of lies. Elle's lies, which I don't fully know. I feel like I am the one who murdered him and am now trying to make up an alibi, lie my way out of trouble. 'We did. It must have been after-wards. After he went to bed.' But as soon as I say it, I know that my story contradicts something he thinks he knows.

'But you . . .' He pauses, before changing his mind. 'Never mind.' He flaps his hand dismissively.

'What? Go on,' I urge him. I lean into him because I want to know what mistake I have made, what part of my story already smells like a lie.

'It's nothing,' he says, reaching down to the will. He pushes it towards me. 'What does it say?'

I follow his lead and remind myself not to be too specific about what it is that I am supposed to have done. Turns out I'm not quite ready to divulge the whole truth.

'I don't know. I haven't read it yet.'

'Well, go on. Read it.'

I skim the five-page document as best I can, trying to rake through the legal jargon and pick out the important facts. I recount them for Antonio as I find them. 'He survives his wife, Cassandra Harringford. He declares he is of sound mind.' When Antonio looks confused, I add, 'That he knew what he was doing when he wrote it.' I turn the page, trail the words with the tip of my finger. 'His funeral expenses should be covered by his remaining capital. And . . .' I pause, not certain if I have read it correctly. 'Just a minute. Let me read this part again.' I swallow hard, gulping for breath as I take in the words. I look to Antonio, who is waiting, his teeth gritted together with the excitement of finally being involved.

'What?' he urges.

'He left me the house.' Antonio takes the paperwork from me. 'Article four,' I say, directing him to the relevant section. He reads while I stare at the butterflies sitting next to my bed.

'He left you the house.' Antonio flicks through the last pages, turns over the whole document and looks at the back in search of hidden secrets. 'There is something written here. A number.' He points to a handwritten series of digits, scrawled on the back in the same calligraphic handwriting: *0020-95-03-19-02-84*. 'What does that mean?' he asks.

I shake my head. 'I've no idea.'

'Phone number?'

I look again at the numbers, the delicate blue ink. 'I don't think so. At least not in the UK.'

'And not Italia,' he confirms, as if there was a chance. I

187

smile, because it reminds me of just how much he wants to be useful to me. How much he wants to be an integral part of my life. How much he used to try. And for that reason I think of Matt, and just how guilty I feel for what I have done.

Antonio continues skimming through the document, certain that we must have missed something. Then suddenly he jumps to his feet, tapping at the papers with the back of his hand. He thrusts them at me, pointing at the signature. 'There, look. The date.' I shrug my shoulders to indicate I don't know what he is so excited about. He points again, pushing his finger into the page. 'That's only a couple of days ago.'

And he is right. The will was written on the same day I arrived at the house. I remember my father in the study. Wasn't he signing something that night when I went to find him? Is this what he wanted to give me? I snatch up the picture of the butterflies and drive it with a strong forearm into the wall. Antonio staggers backwards in shock. I watch as the glass shatters into tiny pieces, parts of the painting tearing as it falls. Instantly I regret what I have done.

21

'We should look into the number. The number has to mean something,' Antonio insists, not for the first time since we came downstairs. The radiators are kicking in and I can hear them clanking in the background as I sip on a glass of red. There is a chill in the air, and the house feels smaller than it once did, like Antonio and I are stumbling over each other. He reaches for an oversized sweater draped over the edge of the couch. A light drizzle whips at the windows.

'I don't even want to think about the number. I just want to forget about it.' If I am entirely honest, what I want to do is get drunk, pass out, and wake up tomorrow as a different person. Again. I settle for saying, 'I don't want his money, or his house.'

Antonio nods, but seems less than certain. He tries to hide his displeasure at my unwillingness, but he doesn't do it well. I have known him too long for him to be able to mask it, and I know what he is really thinking. He believes this document creates a connection to my family. That he can exploit it, heal my wounds, and finally I will give him what he wants. He tries to settle next to me on the couch for a while as we watch some inane show about the mating habits of the dung beetle, but it doesn't take long for him to get the fidgets. He sets his wine glass down untouched, heads over to my desk. I can see him working on the Internet, typing the number from the back of my father's will into different search engines.

After a couple of hours and another bottle of Merlot, I am feeling better and he has finished his research. He begins giving me options, possible solutions as to what the number means: telephone listings in Egypt, Fibonacci sequences, and a television show called *Number Alert*. He reassures me that the television show has already been discounted as a dead end. Next up, details about how to calculate an international banking code, instructions on how to create a Swiss bank account, and notes about the instability of the human genome. All from the number scrawled on the back of my father's will. It pisses me off that he seems to have been enjoying himself, creating a treasure hunt out of irrelevant Internet finds, like this is all part of a game.

'This is not a conspiracy theory,' I say, snappier than I intended. 'What is this shit?' I push his pile of handwritten papers away, and when he doesn't take them, I dump them on the coffee table. He looks offended. But I am one too many glasses in, and I cannot string together a convincing charade about how his research is useful. Fucking Fibonacci. Trust an Italian to come up with an Italian solution.

'We have no idea what this number is. We should try to work it out. It's obviously important if your father gave it to you.' He reaches for my hand, but I snatch it away. I don't want him near. His presence is grating, making me itch.

'My father gave me nothing before tonight. If I cared what the number meant, I would find the telephone number of the lawyer who countersigned the document. I'm sure if the number was important *he* would be able to explain what it meant. After all, he would have been there when the document was drawn up, don't you think?' *Keep your voice down. She is upstairs. I don't want her to overhear.* Was it me he was talking about, or Elle? I had thought it was me, but now I'm not so sure. I swill the last of the wine down and set the empty glass on the table, rectifying the topple created by my unsteady hand. It's so silent without the ticking of the grandfather clock in the background. I can't hide here like I once could.

'But he was your father and he left you a lot. For years you have wished that your past wasn't how it was. I thought you had resolved your issues with him. Elle said you had been up all night talking. That you hadn't even gone to bed.'

So there is my mistake. In Elle's version of the truth we never went to bed, and yet that is where my father ended his life. Antonio's hand settles on my leg and begins stroking at it. But in my drunken daze, wrapped up in the wounds of my past, all I can think is how I wish it was Matt who was here with me, a man I barely know.

'If you miss him,' he continues, 'if you are sad, we can work it out together. Plus, he left you his whole estate.'

'But I don't want his whole estate. And why are you so interested?' I say as I flick his hand away, swatting at him like a fly on a summer's day. 'I told you I want nothing to do with them. Not her. Not him. But you won't leave it alone. Is it because you think there might be money involved?

You think we would be set up for life if we claimed this inheritance?'

He jars his teeth, parts his lips. Looks away so he doesn't have to look at me. 'You don't mean that. I know you don't think that way about me.' He is hurt by my accusation, yet my stance doesn't seem to soften. 'You have just drunk too much.' He picks up the empty bottles and takes them into the kitchen. Even though I know that what I am saying is nonsense, it still keeps coming out, my hurtful allegations following him as he leaves.

'Is that why you are still here?' I shout. 'For the money? You were planning to leave me before my mother died. Don't think I didn't see that bag. But instead you stuck around because you think I am about to hit the jackpot. That I can pay your phone bill, order your takeaways,' I say as I remember the pizza smudge on the kitchen floor. 'This place, for example. When did *you* last pay a bill?' And in this instant I'm sure that I'm on to something. When *did* he last pay a bill? I can't fucking remember. He is grinding his teeth, standing in the doorway, trying really hard not to respond. But I wish he would, because in this moment I want him to hate me. It's the only thing that will make me feel better and justify my continued silence. It would show me that he's using me just like I was using him. I can almost convince myself that he doesn't deserve the truth. 'Even when my mother died you couldn't bring yourself to offer to come with me. You don't know how to support me. All you've been doing for the past three years is living off me. Using my money. You think you're *that* good? You think you're worth it?'

He storms towards me, and in a last-minute diversion of

his energy he smacks his hand against my wine glass instead of my face. His hand goes back up in the air, ready for another strike, but as he looks down from his towering position above me, he lets it drop to his side.

'Well, go on then, if that's what you want. Hit me.' I push up towards him, grapple for his hand but find it immovable, stone at his side. 'You think you've fucked up now, don't you? Worried you've lost your meal ticket, the best thing you ever had.'

But he doesn't even hear my last words. Powered by his anger, he drives his fist into the second wine glass, sending it careering off on the same path as the first. I yelp, cower backwards, watching as the veins in his head swell with rage. Beads of red wine splatter up the wall like the bloody remains of us. He shouts something in Italian as he charges through the door towards the stairs. I have heard it before. It means *go fuck yourself.*

For a while I picture us years ago, when everything was fresh. Him shirtless, holding a small sanding pad, moving it back and forth across the skirting board in the same delicate way he touches my scarred leg. Back then he would stop, turn to look at me, caress me with his sawdust-covered hands. Even by nightfall the musky smell of sanded wood would be lingering on my skin. Did he really only stay in order to benefit from my desperate need for somebody who loved me? I'm not so sure now. If only we could go back to those early days. But that was a long time ago.

My heart is still racing when he comes back ten minutes later carrying a pair of thick socks. I watch as he wipes up the wine and scoops the shards of glass into a dustpan without saying a word. He inspects the wall with his fingertips and looks disappointed. In himself, but also with me. Probably. He throws the socks at me and whispers, 'You should put those on so you don't cut yourself. We will talk tomorrow,' then slips upstairs without another sound.

After a while, the isolation of being alone is too much and so I follow the routine I have learnt. It goes something like this. First, fuck him off. Really piss him off to the point that he wants to hate me. To leave me, bags packed, tickets booked. Next, fuck him, a positive feedback loop. The anger brings the sex, which brings the joy, which brings the anger. So I follow him upstairs, strip, slip into bed, where I begin sliding my hand up and down his back. He flinches at first, tenses his muscles, but then I whisper, 'I'm sorry,' and I feel him relax. I reach around to the front of his body and touch him in ways I know he likes as the first rumble of thunder ambles across the moist summer sky. Flashes from last night come to mind as Antonio's skin touches mine: Matt on top of me, squeezing me, licking at me. His breath against my ear. I push the images away.

Antonio turns to me and strokes my face. But before long his gentle touch turns rough, his fingers sliding into my hair, gripping at the strands to pull my head back. But it is Matt's face I see when I open my eyes.

No, no, no. Antonio, Antonio, Antonio, I tell myself. Think about Antonio. He is the one here with you now.

'Antonio,' I say aloud, as a reminder more than anything, but I try to make it sound like desire. His soft lips trace the curves of my crooked body. Yet it does not respond as it normally would. There is no tingle, no fire. No rush of blood. I try to focus on him as he moves across me. He kisses my lips, and for just a second he opens his eyes. He catches my stare before drawing back as if he sees something he has never seen before. He flips me over and pulls me to my knees, dragging me back by my hair. My hip throbs as he pushes into me, my scars hot as his hand pulls against them. I moan in a way that sounds like pleasure, but only because I think I should.

I don't know if it is the comedown from the drugs or the memory of the night before that has numbed me, but I feel no pleasure as he pulls me into the positions he favours. He knows that bent back on my knees like this is painful for me, but he continues regardless, jabbing himself against me. Spears of pain rip through my hip and into my belly. I open my eyes, see the shattered remains of the picture lying hopelessly on the floor. Tears come, a mixture of mental and physical pain. But I do not blame him.

That night Antonio fucks me twice. Both times I am pulled back like an animal, dogged from behind. The second time he wakes me, already on top of me, already halfway there. I make the right noises, do the right things. I smile and stroke his skin afterwards, and whisper his name like an actress in a 1950s movie. 'Antonio, Antonio,' I say. But it isn't the Antonio I know. It is a new one, a vindictive one. One capable of selfish needs. I have created in him the things I despise about myself. For the first time ever it is all about him, and I am just a vessel from which he drinks. I am reminded what being an extraneous character in somebody's life really feels like. I remember just how much it can hurt.

22

It was Elle's plan, and I went along with it at the time because I was desperate. She was still angry about my thievery, and I wanted so much to go back to how it was before, when she was my hero and we belonged together. She felt bad about it too, I think, because she started asking me what she could do to make me happy. Like she wanted a way to put things right. So during our secret Saturday meetings I told her all about Margot Wolfe, and how she had bullied me ever since I'd stuck a pencil through her hand as a child. This was my chance, I thought, to make Margot pay, and to put things right with Elle.

I told her that Margot sang in a choir. That she played the flute. That her neat little sweaters had been replaced by over-sized jumpers with the word *TOMMY* printed on them. Elle told me that made them expensive. I mentioned that she wore black G-strings in gym class that even her friends thought were slutty. That she still hadn't started her periods, because she always took a shower. Getting your period was the only excuse, because no teacher wanted a Carrie-style disaster in the cubicles. Oh yeah, and one last thing that I would live to regret: all the popular boys at school told tales of how she was frigid, and that not one of them had been able to nail her. The only one to have stuck anything in her was me.

I spent a few weeks initiating rumours as per Elle's plan. There were plenty of kids in the lower social ranks of the school who would trade gossip for a temporary elevation in status. Word soon spread that Margot had set her sights on having sex at the next party. By the time I had finished, there were at least four, maybe five boys who thought they were her target. Jessica had told her friend Becky, who had told Hayley, who had told Samantha, who was dating Jack, who subsequently told Nathan that he was going to get laid. Just keep your mouth shut about it. Who told Jessica? Oh, some girl. That was all I was.

There were four or five other versions of this story; some included Margot giving blow jobs. Some suggested she wanted to take it up the ass so that she could technically remain a virgin. I can't remember what I said, or to whom I said it. Most of the stories were Elle's and I was just the messenger. The one about the ass, though, that was mine.

A few weeks later there was a party in the park. It was June, school was ending, and there was an open invite where everybody could turn up to get wasted on cheap cider. I nearly chickened out when it came to it, scared about how I could slip the Rohypnol in her drink without being noticed. Elle was the one who gave me the drug. I had no idea what it was, but she told me that it would make Margot act crazy, wild, and that everybody would laugh. I was only fourteen, and still a virgin. What did I know?

So I kept my eyes on Margot and saw my chance when she placed her bottle on the grass to start a faux-lesbian chase with her best friend. There were plenty of horny onlookers, naturally. So I spiked the drink when nobody was watching. It was dark. Nobody saw me. Nobody ever really saw me.

Within half an hour she had disappeared with Alex Robinson, the highest-ranking alpha male in our school year. He came back with a swagger less than five minutes later, red-cheeked and sweating. When he pointed to the bushes, another boy made his way over. Then another. Then another. I would love to tell you how I intervened, regretted what I had done. Regretted that she got fucked by at least four boys, if what they said was to be believed. But I didn't do anything. Instead I just watched from a safe distance and then laughed about it with Elle for weeks afterwards.

Margot got the nickname Margo-go-go, and the use of Peg Leg Irini slowly faded out. I even made friends with her after that, when the other girls wouldn't hang out with her because they said she was a slut. I was her hero, and I felt pretty good about it. I apologised about her hand and she said it didn't matter, that it didn't even hurt. There was a police investigation into the party, but most of the boys said it was all bravado. That none of them had actually done anything with her. But Margot and I both knew that wasn't the truth. The police examined her for evidence, but too much time had passed. They took blood, but the toxicology reports were clear. Of course they were.

After the police got involved, people gradually started to forgive Margot, started to believe that maybe she *had* been raped. Then it was the boys' turn to suffer. Teachers marked them down, excluded them from class for minor offences.

It didn't matter that they were never charged. Eventually Margot became popular again. Everybody loves a victim. And she took me with her and I became popular too. My grades improved. Aunt Jemima praised me, told her friends when she thought I was out of earshot that she had finally got through to me. That finally I had learnt how to integrate. That I wasn't *all Harringford*. And who made it all happen? Elle, of course.

The gravity of what I had done didn't hit me until I was much older. I lost touch with Margot when we left school, but I often thought about looking for her again, telling her what had happened. One time I even found myself outside the clothes shop where she worked, my intention to admit my part in the ruin of her life. But I chickened out, didn't even make it inside.

Antonio hasn't been home in two days, hasn't even called me. He'd gone by the time I woke up the day after arriving home. I have left eight messages from a new phone number, and another eight from the old one. He isn't replying, and he doesn't want to see me. But he hasn't taken much of anything with him, so I am sure he is coming back. I really hope he is coming back. I wish I could undo all the shit I have done and make him come home. Otherwise, what am I going to do? I wish I could bring myself to go to work, but I can't. I wish I could un-jab that pencil from Margot Wolfe's hand and instead just tell her that the drawing she did was pretty and try to be her friend. But once something is done, there is no undoing it, and you just have to find a way forward through the mess left behind.

23

It is late on the fourth night that I hear the key in the door. I recognise Antonio's heavy boots as they scuff over the doormat, and then as he tiptoes through the hallway, trying not to wake me. I shuffle up on the couch, grab the TV remote and try to make it look like I've hardly noticed he has been gone. I start flicking channels as he arrives in the doorway to the lounge. He doesn't say anything at first, but I feel him staring at me, and I grit my teeth to stop a nervous smile from creeping across my face. My first thought is, *Thank God it's over.* How quickly I have forgotten how to be alone.

It has hardly stopped raining since he left. On and off, constant storms. One minute sunshine, one minute rain. I have only been out once, in order to get a new phone. From the corner of my eye I see him shaking off his raincoat. It is new. I wonder if he spent my money in order to buy it. But I remind myself that I have done worse, and bite my lip.

'Hello,' he says. I flick the channel, ignoring him. I have flicked so much that I have arrived at the God channels, where literally everybody is either getting saved or doing the saving. There are people falling over each other as they crumple to the floor under God's might. I recall the time Aunt Jemima took me to an alternative healer in an effort, she said, to help my hip. But the healer kept talking about the evil inside of me, that he would cast it out and reduce my suffering. Looking back, I think they were trying to exorcise me. Afterwards she told me not to say anything about the visit, so naturally I told Uncle Marcus that night. They argued and she stopped speaking to me for a month. She never took me again.

Antonio takes a step forward and I channel-hop with renewed enthusiasm, pushing the remote towards the television. Freeview Preview appears on the screen, all tits and pouty lips in extreme close-up. Every now and again a girl gets flipped over and fucked from behind, with another guy edging into view to work on her face. My hip is still sore from where Antonio did the same to me the other night. I try to tell myself that he didn't mean to be an asshole, but it's hard to feel convinced. I switch off the TV and set down the remote.

'I'm sorry I didn't call,' he says as he edges into the room. His oil-black hair is dripping wet, his shoulders hunched and apologetic.

'Did you get my messages?' I ask. He nods. 'Where have you been?' The images from the television sex creep into my mind, and I picture him in some seedy strip club, spending my cash and getting his cock sucked in a room out back. Vomit rises in my throat, so I reach for a near-empty glass of wine and drain the remainder. Irrespective of what I have done, it would really hurt if that was true. I see him cast his eyes over the three or four empty bottles at my feet. Might be five or six. He doesn't say anything; just sits down next to me.

'I'm sorry I left. I was very angry. I'm calm now. I don't want to upset you.' I take my first glance at his face. His eyes are sunken in deep sockets, circles of black like smudged eyeliner. Not even his long lashes can pretty them up.

'Where have you been? It's four nights since you were here.'

'Italy.' He edges further back on to the settee and turns to look at me, his body still facing away, as if he has one foot poised ready for a sharp exit.

'Italy? For four days?' I set the wine glass down next to his research papers, which are still lying on the table. 'Why?'

'I couldn't be here. Not with you. When you came home, I was so pleased. I wanted so much to help you and look out for you. I thought maybe it would be a new start.' He reaches across and picks up the research work and tidies it into a pile. 'But you were just like before. And you were right, I was ready to leave you. I didn't want to stay here any more, fighting and fucking. That's all we ever did.' He is crying now and wipes a tear from his cheek. It isn't the first time I have seen him cry. 'We used to be so good, Rini. It was so nice to be with you. But as soon as I mentioned having a family, you changed.' He gets closer to me, risks a touch on my arm. I don't push him away. 'I want a normal life, Rini. Marriage and babies. I want them with you. I came back to tell you that. I will give you time. I will help you if I can. But I want you to be honest with me.' He reaches out, takes my hand. 'If you don't want me, just tell me. I can get my things and go. But I want you to know that I do love you. I don't care about your past, or any problems you or I may have had. I can make today number one. The first day. If you want it.' I wonder how many times I am supposed to restart my life. I'm like a damned cat. He stops, takes a breath, and then, as if he thinks he might not have demonstrated that he is steadfast in his decision, adds quickly, 'But you have to really want it.'

I take the prepaid phone from the table and toss it into the nearest waste-paper basket. It doesn't mean anything really, because all I have done is move it from the table. But it is supposed to be symbolic. It means I am tossing away the old life, the old contacts, and eight of the sixteen unanswered calls to Antonio. Somewhere on that SIM card are Margot Wolfe's details. It is also the number that Elle knows. He understands my actions, moves in closer and holds me in a tight embrace. I should feel relieved, but for some reason I don't.

He whips up some pasta in a carbonara sauce, and while he is cooking, I use the time to check my online bank account. I find that he made a withdrawal of £340 from my account the morning he left. Which means I paid for the coat, and no doubt the ticket to Italy. It matters, but I decide that it doesn't matter enough to raise it and cause an argument, revisit the whole *I support you* thing. We're on thin ice as it is, and I don't want to be the one to stamp my foot and watch as we drown. I'm not ready for him to walk out on me. What the hell would I do? Being alone is fine when you've never known anything different, but now that I have, I can't go back to work-sleep-repeat. Maybe in time it will get better between us. If not, maybe I will get stronger and find a way forward without him.

So I sit and smile and wait to eat. He tells me that the days without me were hell, and I reply the same, which they kind of were. We eat, and then he gives me the look that I know means he wants to kiss me. He does, and we end up in bed. This time it is back to expectations: Antonio being gentle with me because I am fragile, his hand moving up and down over my scars. Afterwards I get up to look at my hip in the mirror, thinking how the marks seem to take on a shape I have never noticed before. I know it is just from where they ground out my bones and fixed my tendons, but they look like the arch of a butterfly's wings, a gentle V shape with a body carved in the middle. I look down at the torn painting and tell myself that tomorrow I will put it away.

Not long afterwards, Antonio gets up and sweeps up the broken glass from the floor. He tucks the painting in a drawer, knowing it must be important if I brought it back with me. It's like he can read my mind. The storm outside still rages, but at least the one in here, inside me, seems to be settling. We fall asleep together that night, wrapped in each other's arms, and I think I am glad he came home. It's the first time we have slept like that in months, and I wonder if finally the demons inside me have found their way out.

24

Over breakfast the following morning, Antonio announces that he is going to open the bistro he has always dreamed of. He has long talked of this. He envisions a small place, beat-up tables and expensive white linen. Like old Rome. Recycled glasses and silver cutlery, only without the view of the Colosseum.

'The bank will lend me half, and I have the other half saved up.' He tucks into a rasher of streaky bacon and shovels in a spoonful of scrambled eggs. I remember Joyce's, and how salty they were. I smile at the idea of Elle driving her crazy now that she is lady of the manor.

'That's a fantastic idea,' I say, doubtful about the bank loan and the savings. But again, as if he is able to read my mind, he gets up, produces the paperwork from the bank. As I scan the page, he steals a rasher of bacon from my plate. On the table there is a carnation in a slim vase, which I assume he put there.

'I organised the loan during the time you were away,' he says, smacking his lips, licking his fingers. 'The first day, when I thought we were finished.'

I smile, reach up and kiss him, not really reading what

he has given me. He backs away, surprised, before slowly relaxing into my lips. 'The eggs are great. If you serve these, I'm sure it will succeed.'

Afterwards we sit together on the couch, snuggle up and watch the Discovery Channel. A lion pride, and how the young survive. Later on, he cooks pesto pasta with chicken and we eat it from our laps underneath the duvet, which we dragged downstairs after we made love earlier. Yes, that's what we did. It was nice, kind, gentle love. The kind I used to back away from but the only kind that has the ability to heal old wounds. Which is, after all, what I am. Or at least, according to my father, what I open up.

But it all feels a little like we are following a script, some made-for-TV movie about how to patch over mistakes and pretend everything is all right. We smile a lot at each other when we don't know what to say, hold hands from a distance. But he is trying, and I suppose for once I am too. It's enough for now. Eventually we fall asleep.

I only wake up when I hear the thud of thunder. A loud clap reverberating through the house. Then again, the exact same sound, and I realise that it isn't thunder at all. It is somebody knocking at the door. I glance at my phone. 11.07 p.m. No good news comes at this time of day. I nudge Antonio awake and then feel sick with the realisation that it could be Elle. It feels just like that night when she called about our mother having died.

'What is it?' he mumbles after first stammering something unintelligible in Italian. More knocking.

'It's the door,' I whisper. He looks down at his watch, stands up, pulls his T-shirt on. Adjusts his boxers, and what's in them.

I slump down underneath the duvet, listening. Although I can't hear what is being said, I can hear the tone of the conversation, and I know straight away that it isn't light or trivial. But I also know that it isn't Elle, so feel relieved.

I pull on my shirt, and less than a minute later Antonio is back in the lounge with two people following. They stand with authority, dripping on my laminate floorboards, the drops running through the cracks. They have left clumps of mud across the runner in the hallway. One of them is a woman. Her face is angular, like a Rubik's Cube out of line, and make-up-free. Her ears are set too low on her head, as if they have slid down, melted. She smiles at me, but I know there is no kindness in that smile. It is formal, a kind of *well, I'm in your house so I might as well look polite* smile. The man next to her is large, over-proportioned in just about every dimension. I know straight away that they are police.

'Good evening, Dr Harringford. I am DC Forrester and this is DC McGuire. We need to ask you a few questions about your sister, Eleanor Harringford.'

I look around the room and make my assessment of what this looks like. There is a bottle of wine on the table to start with, the shape of which could easily be mistaken for champagne. Two empty glasses. The television is playing in the background on mute, and I have that distinct look of somebody who not long ago was having sex. Happy couple, no problems. But these are police and they want to ask about my sister. That means they probably know that my parents have just died. Which means they probably know I am set for a big payout. Elle is probably the one who called them, and I am hit by a somewhat underwhelming fear that this looks like a celebration.

'OK. How can we help?' Antonio steps straight in. Got to love him for trying, but what could he possibly do? He has never even met Elle.

'May we sit down?' DC Forrester asks as she positions herself on the couch opposite. I don't answer, yet Antonio ushers DC McGuire into the seat next to her.

'What about my sister?' I say, kind of tired. I say it casually, as if we might be the parents of an unruly child and are used to visits from the police. *Oh, what has Eleanor been up to now? What trouble has she got herself into? A pencil through the little girl's hand? Oh goodness, what a minx.*

'Your sister has been reported missing, and we are working alongside a team in Edinburgh to help locate her. She was last seen two days ago in Horton, the village where she lives. There are no further reported sightings, not in the village or nearby cities. She hasn't been home, either.' DC McGuire hasn't spoken yet, but he is taking all the details in. No pictures of family, no trinkets placed on the cupboards. The only books are medical or morbid. *Anaesthesia. The Pocket Handbook of Anaesthesia. Pain Management. Tombs for the Living: Andean Mortuary Practices. Pharmacology Success! Killing for Company.* I might as well have a guide on how to murder and conceal a body.

'But you aren't just police officers conducting a search. You're plain-clothes officers,' I say, knowing that already this thing has escalated. Thoughts are racing in my mind, and in just about every scenario I do not look good.

'There are plenty of uniformed officers doing house-to-house, Dr Harringford. Rest assured. But yes, we are from CID. Criminal Investigations Department.' Antonio is doing that thing he does, shuffling from one foot to the other in a way that he thinks looks casual, but that he only ever does when he is nervous. 'Your sister was last seen by the owner of the public house, the –' she stops, flicks through her black notepad – 'Enchanted Swan. She was running around the churchyard late at night in the rain. She hasn't been seen since. Based on what has been happening during the past week, we are trying to build up a picture of her movements. There are anecdotal accounts of mental health issues, so she is what we would call a vulnerable adult.' I almost laugh, and stop myself. I think I have covered it up, but I guess nothing gets past a cop's eyes. 'Is there something you find funny, Dr Harringford?'

'I'm sorry, I don't mean to laugh. It's just, I have never heard anybody describe Elle as a vulnerable adult.' I compose myself, pull the duvet higher. I wish I was wearing knickers. 'In fact, quite the opposite. What can I do to help?'

DC McGuire takes over for a bit. It is effortless the way he just steps in, as if they have rehearsed this. 'We understand that you have experienced a number of losses in your family of late.'

'Shall I put the kettle on?' Antonio interrupts. The break in conversation comes just as a flash of lightning crosses the sky. The thunder follows only a second later.

'White, no sugar,' says DC Forrester.

'The same. Thanks.' McGuire turns to me and links his hands together. 'At times of stress, existing problems are always amplified. We understand that you lost both of your parents recently. Our condolences.'

'Thank you,' I say, kind of coldly. I should have tried to look hurt, like it was difficult for me, but I guess some things are just too well programmed for an automatic override.

'I'm sure this is difficult, but I want to ask about your mother. What was the cause of her death?' he continues.

'I think cancer.'

'You don't know how your mother died?' DC Forrester chips in, squinting in my direction.

I pause, and swallow. 'I believe it was cancer, but I haven't seen the medical records or spoken to a doctor.'

DC Forrester looks around at the books, stands up and wanders over after checking that I don't mind. She picks up *Pharmacology Success!* and flicks through the pages. 'You're a doctor yourself, right?' I nod. 'Were you not interested?' She sets the book back down and looks around at the absence of personal objects. 'Let's look at it like this. One of my family gets involved in a crime, I would want to know what was happening. I'd want to know the details of the case, what facts were known, what hypotheses were being made. Because that's how my mind works. It's my job to be curious. Suspicious.' She picks up *Killing for Company*, a biography of serial killer Dennis Nilsen, a man who kept the bodies of his victims to ease his loneliness. She sets it back down, expressionless. 'I would have thought as a doctor you might like to know how your own mother passed away.'

I tuck my hair behind my ears and brush my fringe from my eyes. Antonio slips back into the room with a tray of tea. I reach over, take mine, all the while clinging on to the duvet.

'Our relationship wasn't very good,' I offer. 'It wasn't what you would call a normal mother–daughter relationship.'

'Yes, we understand you were adopted by your aunt.'

'No I wasn't. I just lived with her.'

'Why?'

'Why didn't she adopt me or why did I live with her?'

'Both,' says DC Forrester.

'I don't know.' Antonio sits down next to me and takes my hand in his. 'I went to live with her when I was three years old. Nobody ever told me why exactly.'

'You never asked?' I shrug my shoulders, letting them know I have no answer. 'Not very inquisitive, are you? We already spoke with your aunt. She told us your mother couldn't cope with two children, that she was overwhelmed. I guess you'd call it post-natal depression nowadays.' Antonio strokes my hand, relieved to be learning the truth. But I know this is crap. Bullshit that even now my Aunt Jemima is happy to accept. I want to know if they realise that Aunt Jemima wasn't at the funeral, but I don't ask, certain that the question would act like a fan to the flame of suspicion.

'I think that's it,' I agree. 'Post-natal depression. Our relationship was almost non-existent. We didn't talk or exchange letters. To her it was like I didn't exist. So when she died, I didn't ask.' I don't add in any of the assumptions I made regarding Elle's involvement.

'So let me build up a picture here,' says Forrester as she picks up a mug of tea and sits back down. 'You had no relationship with your mother. None with your father.' She looks to me for confirmation and I give it with a quick nod of the head. 'How'd you find out about your mother's death?'

'Elle called me.' They look confused. 'Eleanor. My sister.'

'And what did you do?'

'I went there for the funeral.'

McGuire follows Forrester's lead and picks up his mug. 'So you dropped everything and took a flight for the funeral?' he asks.

'Yes.' I slide my hand out from Antonio's.

'Even though you had no relationship with either of your parents.'

'I guess you could put it like that.' It kind of hurts, listening to the past being reduced to the skeleton of details. It feels like we are doing it a disservice somehow, making it smaller than it really is. It makes me sound stupid: *Little girl dashes to mourn Mummy who never wanted her.* I must look really pathetic to them.

'Presumably you went to support your sister?'

'Yes, I suppose you could say that.' While that isn't strictly the truth, saying that I went to find out why they never wanted me seems so heartbreakingly lame that I cannot bring myself to admit it. Especially when I have just agreed to Aunt Jemima's version that post-natal depression forced them to give me away. 'I went there because I wanted to support Elle.'

'Eleanor Harringford.'

'Yes.'

'And how did you find her when you arrived? What was her mental state like?' They sip at their tea in unison.

'I'm not a psychologist, how would I know?'

Forrester looks to McGuire with half-pursed lips, a little wrinkle crease forming on her cheek like the crescent-shaped scars on my hip. She raises her eyebrows in a way that makes me think she has got me down as a wiseass. 'No, Dr Harringford,' she says, irritated, 'you are not a psychologist, but you are her sister. You know her. You share the same blood. You must be able to tell me if she was crying, sad, happy, elated. These are simple emotions, Dr Harringford.'

'She was OK.' Their heads slide in towards me, as if I have just announced that she occasionally turned into an alien. 'Elle isn't like most people. I don't want to paint her in a bad light, but she didn't seem particularly sad at what had happened. Not regarding my mother anyway. If you knew her—'

'So,' she interrupts. 'Eleanor Harringford was in a reasonable mood following your mother's death. Not taking it too badly. What did you do together in the days before your mother's funeral that would lead you to believe that she was in a reasonable mood? Coping with the loss, so to speak.'

I run over the events in my head. Our activities don't look good, and it makes both me and Elle appear heartless and cold. In this moment I hate her more than I ever have. Where the fuck has she gone? 'Not much. Simple stuff. We hung out. We ate dinner. After the funeral, I left.'

'Simple stuff, hm.' She huffs and hums like I might have done when gazing over a weird rash on somebody's skin, trying to decipher what she sees and still appear intelligent. 'But you didn't leave immediately after the funeral, did you?'

'No. Not immediately.' Her eyes are fixed on mine, waiting for me to elaborate. 'I stayed one more night.'

'Where?'

'At the house.' The first outright lie. I am a good liar, this is known. But to the police? In a missing-person inquiry? For a *vulnerable adult*. They exchange a glance that makes me uncomfortable because it looks like they know otherwise. Antonio spots it too and turns his attention to me. 'We did go out for a while that night. For a few drinks. I guess it was all a bit much for both of us.'

'With Mr Guthrie and Mr Waterson.' Antonio stiffens next to me, and the jealousy in his blood rises. Of course it doesn't help that I haven't told him anything about Greg and Matt. That makes it automatically suspicious.

'Yes,' I say. 'They were friends of my sister's,' I add in an attempt to detach myself from their presence.

'And then you left the following morning?'

'Yes.' I know what is coming. I can feel it. It is as if I am watching a freight train, the lights glaring in my eyes because I am standing on the tracks. As if it is coming towards me, the horn sounding, yet I am unable to run.

'Right after your father died.' I nod. 'How did Eleanor take the news of your father's passing?'

'She was upset. I would say she didn't take it very well.'

'When she called you about your mother, would you say that she was upset? Or did she seem calm?'

'She was calm.'

'So it would be reasonable to suggest that she was more upset by your father's death.'

'Perhaps.'

DC Forrester crosses her arms. 'So she calls you, calm and seemingly dealing with your mother's death, and you rush on a flight to get to her because you say you wanted to support her. Yet when your father dies and Eleanor is visibly upset, you take her car and leave. We found it at the airport, a grey Mercedes with the number plate KV58 HGG. Is that correct?'

'I don't know about the number plate. But yes, I took her car. I wanted to get away.'

'From Eleanor? The sister you went there to support?'

'Excuse me, officer,' interrupts Antonio. 'But what has all this got to do with Elle's disappearance?'

'We are simply trying to establish her mindset,' says DC McGuire, stepping in. 'Plus, we found her car with the keys left in the ignition.' He turns to me. 'I'm sure you agree that we would need to rule that out as a relevant fact. So you confirm that you took the car?'

'Yes, I did.'

'Well, that saves us about forty-eight hours of CCTV footage,' he whispers to Forrester.

'And you, Mr Molinaro?' asks DC Forrester. 'Where were you when all this was happening?'

'I stayed here. Irini likes to do these things alone. She didn't want me to meet her family.'

'Why is that, Dr Harringford?' asks Forrester, looking at me.

'It's pretty obvious I didn't have a good relationship with them. You already mentioned that Elle has issues with her mental health.'

'No, in fact we told you there was nothing more than anecdotal reports. I'm sure as a doctor you appreciate that we can't discuss her medical history with you. But, just for clarity, we've checked into her history and there is nothing of any significance reported.'

'But there is, I'm sure of it. Elle told me herself that she spent time in a mental health facility.'

'We are not at liberty to discuss it any further.'

'But it's important. That's why I didn't want her in my life. She was very difficult.' As soon as I have said, it I realise how awful it sounds when I am trying to sell myself as a supportive sister. 'I just preferred it when there was a distance. It was better for both of us,' I lie.

'But still you went there to support her,' Forrester says, too sarcastic for my liking. 'And since?'

'We've been here. I haven't been to work, I called in sick. Instead we stayed home. We needed some time together. To reconnect after the time apart.'

'Well, it looks like you've been doing a good job.' DC McGuire smiles as he stands up.

DC Forrester, the one who seems to be playing the role of bad cop, follows. 'Try to be available over the next few days. I'm sure we will have more questions.'

They walk towards the door and I follow, the duvet wrapped around my waist. 'Oh, just one more thing,' says Forrester as her partner opens the door. The rain pelts down and wets the doormat. 'The name Joseph Witherrington. Does it mean anything to you?'

I think for a second before I say, 'No. I have never heard it before.'

She smiles. 'OK, thanks. Try not to worry. We receive more than seven thousand missing-person reports each year. The majority of people turn up safe and well. In fact, some of them even choose to go missing, especially if they feel threatened or at risk.'

'I don't think anybody threatened Elle,' I say. They don't say anything, only snatch a quick glance at one another.

DC Forrester flashes that same false smile as she did when she arrived. Fixed and set and as unlikeable as mine. 'Most of them turn up eventually.'

25

Antonio is already awake when I surface from a dream about Robert Kneel. He is sitting up in bed with the lamp on. I look at the clock, catch the image of the night sky in the corner of my eye. 3.01 a.m.

'You're awake,' I say, stating the obvious as he sits motionless staring at the wall.

'I can't sleep. I keep thinking about your sister.' He reaches to the side and picks up a bottle of water. He must have been downstairs to get it, because it wasn't here when we fell asleep. 'You were dreaming.'

'How do you know?' I hold my hand out and he gives me the water.

'You were mumbling, saying a few words.'

I swallow, use my hand to wipe the drips from my lips. 'What was I saying?'

'Something about a robber. Robert? I don't know. It was nonsense. Gibberlish.'

'Gibberish,' I correct him. He does this every now and again, when he tries to use unfamiliar words. Repeating them like a parrot, and not always correctly. He doesn't acknowledge the correction or the mistake. I hand the bottle back. 'What do you think has happened to her?'

'I don't know. Remember, you never let me meet her.'

'You spoke to her, though.' He looks surprised, a sharp turn of his head. 'On the phone, before I came back. What did you think of her? What did she sound like?'

He takes a breath, as if he is trying to decide. 'She sounded manic. Excited. I thought maybe it was because you had reconnected, and that your relationship with your father was better. But that doesn't seem so. Not from your behaviour. So I think maybe she is just crazy.'

I don't dispute his conclusions. 'But where would she go? And *why* would she go? She has that whole house to live in now.'

'Actually, *you* have the house.' He guzzles the water and sets it down. I think about the house being mine, wonder what I'm going to do with it. 'You never told me anything about her past. About her being ill. You told me she was crazy, but that could mean anything. I didn't know she was *actually* ill.' He looks away from me, his eyes downcast before flickering up to a star-filled sky. The storm has passed and has left behind an image of beauty. Perfectly twinkling stars. Clarity of a diamond. 'I wish you had told me that before. I wish I had known that she was actually ill.'

I shrug my shoulders. 'What difference does it make?'

He looks down again and picks a little tuft of fluff from his belly button. 'Nothing, now. But tell me something about your past. It was always off limits before, but I think we have passed that. I need you to tell me something about her. To help me understand.'

'What like?'

'Anything. Your choice.'

I consider the stories of Margot Wolfe and Robert Kneel, but decide that neither paints me in a good light. So I come up with another, a later one, when I had realised who Elle was. I don't try to cover myself with the sheets as I sit up, because I am wearing my pyjamas. There was no more sex after the police left.

'One night, before I went to university, she told me that she was taking me out to celebrate. It had been getting harder to be around her; her thoughts and actions were increasingly erratic. She told me she had never had a sister who was going to university before, which I thought was weird because I was her only sister. But she said we had to mark the occasion. So we went to a pub, smoked cigars and drank ourselves stupid. I was eighteen, couldn't handle the booze.' My hip was still dodgy, and I had terrible dress sense, even for 2001. Too much colour, too much denim. Elle was dressed in blue velvet knee-high platform boots, white hot pants and a red latex boob tube, like a human Union Jack. All stolen.

'She took me to a club, a dark place lit by strobe lights and happy house music. Anywhere she went she had her hands in the air, pointing and jabbing them to the beat. By four in the morning I was flat. Done. I wasn't jacked up on pills like everybody else, so I just crashed in the nearest booth. She had been doing drugs all night long, and come eight in the morning, when everybody was leaving, she was still buzzing. Hands in the air like *woo-hoo*.' I make the motion with my hands like I am back there, watching Elle lose herself in the music. He smiles sympathetically. 'The bouncers ended up dragging her out, literally throwing her out of the club, me trailing behind.'

'I was staying with her for the summer, living in a flat she had rented in order to be near me. She slept for a week after that. Woke up sporadically, bursts of mania and depression, one minute crying because they had kicked her out of the club, the next organising nights out that never happened. Even days later she was still angry, screaming that it wasn't right, that it shouldn't be like this, that it wasn't her fault. I put it down to the drugs, found it all kind of wild, you know, like you do when you are just a kid and you think there is only this one crazy person who truly loves you. But I also started to realise that she wasn't good for me. I knew that if I was going to have a normal future, the life I shared with Elle had to end. I didn't hate her. Still don't, even though I sometimes try to convince myself that I do. But neither could I stay. So one day I just sort of slipped away when she was still in bed.'

'Did she follow you?'

I reach over to the bedside table and take a cigarette. 'Yes. But I had told her I was going to Leeds University. She went north in search of me, but really I was going to Exeter. It took her a few months to find me.'

'How? What did she do?'

I light the cigarette and take a long drag. Antonio hates me smoking in bed, yet he takes one too, does the same. 'She trailed medical school campuses until she found me.

Broke down in tears, saying how awful it had been without me. Thanking God that I was all right. She acted like I had gone missing or something. Like it had all been an accident and she was relieved I was OK.'

'And you? What did you do?' I stub out what is left of my cigarette and slip down into the bed, head warm against the pillow. He does the same, brings the duvet up to cover me. I clutch it and hug it close. Our faces only inches apart, the smell of pesto still on his breath.

'I was grateful that she was back. I felt wanted, needed again. I'd been lonely without her, just like I was as a child in the years when they kept us apart.' He rests an arm across me and rubs at my shoulder, pulling me towards him. Our faces touch and it feels, in that instant, so good. So warm. Almost like I could tell him everything. 'I let her stay for a while, until she started sleeping with the boys in my hall. I switched rooms after that, changed my number. But I knew she would find me. I thought about her every day until she did. It became like a game. A game where there were no winners.'

Antonio reaches over, turns off his light, leaving only the moon to cast shadows on my face. The sound of traffic and voices filters through the window. I remember how that reunion really went, Elle turning up at the university, knife in hand, threatening that if they didn't bring me to her she would slit her own throat. I should have expected it after what really happened to make me leave. Yes, there were outbursts, episodes of mania, too many drugs. But that wasn't it. I don't know why I don't want to admit it to Antonio. Perhaps I'm just not ready to hear it again. I wrap the duvet over me, turn away. I close my eyes and pray for sleep. But then he asks something else.

'Rini, what were the names of those men you were drinking with? The night before you came home?'

'Erm, Mr Guthrie and Mr Waterson. I think that's what the police said.' I try to make it sound casual, like I can't remember, as if they were barely part of the event.

'Their first names, I mean. You must have known them.'

'Greg and Matt,' I say quietly. 'They were friends of Elle's.'

He twists away and I feel the pull of the duvet. 'So it wasn't Robert, then.' He sighs, as if relieved, but it could be the sound of his burden I can hear. In the dark, it is impossible to tell.

26

I knew that being with Elle was a risk, and I was nervous when I made the decision to stay with her in the weeks leading up to the start of university. I was young, not stupid. I knew that anything good had the potential to unravel in the blink of an eye. But she was so excited to have rented an apartment for us, and I guess I was still hopeful. And desperate. I still craved a sense of kinship, and she told me so often how we belonged together, it was hard not to believe it.

Life with Aunt Jemima had degenerated into polite confirmation of facts: yes, I have an offer for medical school; no, I don't need a lift; yes, I'll be gone sooner rather than later. Not even my academic success could bridge the Elle-sized gap between us. Aunt Jemima knew I'd been seeing her, and that was enough for her to want me at arm's length. Uncle Marcus had washed his hands of me. I saw Aunt Jemima's indifference as evidence that they couldn't wait for me to be gone. In hindsight, I think she was desperate too, out of ideas. She couldn't fight against the fact that Elle was the only person who demanded my attention, my presence, who went out of her way to get close to me.

Although leaving had left me with a sense of emptiness,

arriving at Elle's flat was like catharsis. It was my home for the foreseeable future, and a place where I was wanted.

Elle was all over me like skin for the first few days. She tended to my needs with such enthusiasm that it was as if I was recuperating from a disease or operation – perhaps my surgical excision from the past, her love dressing the wounds left behind. She would stroke my hair when I was tired, nurse me back to health when the hangovers were bad. I suggested we streak my hair pink to match her own, and she cried with joy at the idea. They were debauched days, hedonistic in a way that only youth allows, and for the short time that it remained just the two of us, the best days of my life.

But there was something that troubled her during this time: I was still a virgin. She couldn't believe it. The stories she told me about her experiences shocked me almost as much as my unbroken virginity shocked her. She asked me over and over why it had never happened. I answered the same each time: I just didn't like any of the boys I knew. My answer didn't satisfy her, though. Probably because it was a lie.

The truth was that since the incident with Margot Wolfe, I couldn't bring myself to even think about sex. Margot had been raped because of me. Four times. I had put that drug in her drink, and despite the help and encouragement that Elle gave me to do it, it was impossible to ignore the satisfaction I felt when I saw the first boy guiding her away from the party. Plus, I supposed my virginity was about the only thing I completely controlled, that was mine to keep for myself. It was the only thing about me that wasn't broken, and I wanted to keep it that way.

But Elle saw it as a problem to solve, a load to lose. Our days and nights began to revolve around the quest for a man for me to sleep with. Any man. Elle listed her friends: blond men, black hair, olive-skinned. She knew a man from Kenya who would be more than happy to help. Another one from Newcastle. She took me clubbing and talked about me to men she knew, and men she didn't. They would leer over me like I was some sort of product, ripe for the picking, available to the highest bidder. I spurned them all, stayed in the toilets wishing we could go back to those first few days when she'd suffocated me with her love. I could have died like that and been happy.

On the sixth night out, something changed. I saw a guy watching me. He was quiet and cautious, seemed less interested in Elle and what she had to say than the others, and that felt good. He wanted me, I knew it. Plus there was something about his look, the way he held himself, his shoulders soft, mouth loose. He wasn't trying, and it was the sexiest thing I'd ever seen.

He wasn't the first boy I had liked. Chris Hughes was a tall blond boy in my year, played rugby for the school and ran cross country at county level. I only had to see him and I felt the flutter in my knees, the rush in my stomach that more often than not found its way to my groin. I would go home, find myself wet and swollen, with no clue what to do about it. I knew what desire felt like, and I felt it now as I stole glances at the auburn-haired man propping himself up against the wall. Looking back, I guess he was a bit like Matt.

But it wasn't until we arrived back at Elle's flat that he

came close to me. He sat at my side on the box-like 1960s sofa and said hello. I could barely hear him over the music and the sound of Elle making cocktails in the kitchen with two other men she had picked up.

'Hi,' I answered, but it came out croaky and hoarse. He reached over, slipped a hand around my head and pulled me in for a kiss.

I pulled back, my body pushed up against the arm of the sofa. But his grip was strong, his eyes wide open, fixed on mine like a missile lock. In my head I was screaming to get up. This could be over in a second; all I had to do was move. I could go to the single bedroom and slip into the musty flannelette sheets to sweat out my sexual frustrations there. But he wasn't trying to restrain me, and because of that I stayed. When I didn't move, he took his chance, placed his Jack Daniel's-coated lips on mine, and I followed his lead.

He left at some point before sunrise, while I was sleeping. I never saw him again. Instead I was left with just the memories of his pimpled skin moving up against mine, the sporadic hairs on his chest, and the salt of his sweat on my lips. Even now I don't know what his name was, because when I asked Elle, it turned out that she didn't actually know him.

Elle woke me that morning by slipping into my lumpy bed, wrapping her arms around me. When I tried to turn to her, she hushed me, turned me away with the shape and weight of her body. I could feel her breathing as she spooned up behind me, hot air whistling across the back of my neck, her knobbly knees pushed into the back of mine. She felt good up against me, protective, one of her arms draped across my chest, pulling me in close. She didn't care that I was naked, and perhaps I didn't either. After a while she whispered to me, 'Did it hurt?' She knew what I had done. Instinctively she knew.

'Yes,' I said, and without wanting to, I began to cry. For some reason I felt utterly sad, like the life I had didn't fit me. I reached down, cupped myself between the legs, thinking about Margot Wolfe. I was bruised, throbbing. But what happened to me and Margot wasn't the same. I had been kissed, stroked. He had whispered breathy sounds of what I took for appreciation when his hands slid across my breasts. At some point he asked me if I was all right, if I wanted him to stop. Afterwards he told me I was beautiful and I forgot all about my scars. Nobody had done that for Margot.

'Don't worry. You'll feel better soon.' I felt her stroking my hair, kissing the skin of my shoulder. 'It gets better. The next time it will be easier.' She held me tight, her body warm. 'I'll never hurt you like he did, I promise.'

And it was such a beautiful moment that I knew it wasn't real. There was disaster around the corner. Her kindness, as sweet as it tasted, was tainted. Like we were in a dream. This moment would end, and at some point, irrespective of her promises, she would hurt me again like she had before. I hadn't forgotten the times she had hit me, or the time she burnt me with a cigarette. She'd said it was an accident, but I had my doubts. I knew I was able to love her more when she wasn't around.

'I'm leaving in a few weeks,' I said. Getting to university had been my ticket out of my life, something I knew I needed after what I had done to Margot. So I'd knuckled down and done my best, which turned out to be more than enough. Medical school. A place where they would give me a new title, and a new start in life. I knew it had to be the end for me and Elle, and this was my moment. 'Will you come and visit?' I turned my face into the dusty pillow. Hoped she wouldn't hear the lie.

'Of course I will,' she replied, squeezing me a little tighter. My tears burned my eyes.

'Good. I'll be in Leeds.' It was the first outright lie I'd ever told her.

I should have left the same day. Got up and gone. But I had nowhere to stay, so instead I waited, hoping to outrun the inevitable. It happened, though. Of course it did. This time it was like nothing that had ever gone before. I doubt even Elle could have predicted the terrible resolution to our time together at the end of that summer, just two short weeks later. There was no way of foreseeing what would happen that day. But it happened nevertheless. And when it did, it drove me away, made me run faster than I ever had before, for my life.

27

Days pass before we hear anything else. I call in sick at work, telling them I have gastroenteritis, even though I know they won't believe it. But this little white lie is designed so that the person on the other end of the phone doesn't feel uncomfortable with the revelation of the truth. It isn't supposed to be believable. Nevertheless, to add a veil of authenticity to the whole thing, I make a phone call to the local GP's surgery to get a note, and because I'm a doctor she agrees to a diagnosis of food poisoning without doing any tests or an examination. That'll shut work up for another week at least.

The mood of the house is sombre. It seems that every time I turn my back, Antonio is picking up his phone, rattling away in Italian, something that seems to have deepened the fissure between us. His telephone conversations have become more frantic, almost as if they are verging on disagreement. On several occasions I ask who he is speaking to. Once he tells me his father, another time his mother. Then a friend I've never heard of before. But the conversation always sounds the same, and it is always peppered with the translation of the word *fuck*. So I know he is lying, because he would never say that to his mother.

I dig out the most recent telephone number I have for Aunt Jemima, in an old address book filled with emergency contacts that she created for me just before I left for university. I call her a couple of times, each effort bringing the contents of my stomach somewhere into my throat. I would love to know if she will tell me the truth now that both of my parents are dead. I would love to know what she thinks about Elle's disappearance. But she doesn't answer. I guess we are still estranged.

DC McGuire calls a couple of times, just to keep us informed. He tells me they are checking the local hospitals, but that so far nothing has turned up. The house-to-house questioning is ongoing. He asks me if Elle has any identifiable features that I can recall, so I tell him about the only thing I can think of, which is the small pink scar on her forehead. He suggests I use social media to begin a search of her friends; that perhaps I could message them and ask what they know. He seems pretty disturbed when I tell him that I don't have any such accounts, and in somewhat of a fluster suggests I could make one. When I say I am not sure how, he stutters out an unorthodox offer to create an account on my behalf, but tells me that he will first need my photograph. I agree, and send it via email, and within an hour he sends me a list of links and passwords. On my behalf he has sent over one hundred messages to the people that Elle is friends with on Facebook.

By the time I log on a few hours later, not one of them has responded. I go through, search for anybody I might recognise, but a quick check of the accounts proves that none of the people she is friends with are from Scotland.

231

No Greg, and no Matt. They are all far away, Americans and Australians. A few Russian names pop up, followed by a sprinkling of other Eastern Europeans. Finally one from Brazil. All men. In fact, there is not a single female friend. McGuire calls back, asks me if I would have any idea what Elle's passwords are, because he is waiting on a warrant to access them. Obviously I don't.

I do eventually get a few responses to DC McGuire's messages, but they amount to a collective disappointment. One is in another language, probably Russian. I have no idea what it says, but the text is followed by a winky emoticon, and so I dismiss it as bullshit without bothering to translate it. Another is from Facebook user 'Randy Ronny', based out of Bullhead City on the Nevada–Arizona border. He suggests Elle should come home soon, offering to spank her cute little ass red raw once she does. Everything is starting to feel a bit hopeless, and thanks to DC Forrester, the idea that I am responsible for her disappearance is growing. So by day three I decide that I need to at least try to do something to help.

I begin with the humanitarian group the Guardians. They have a good website, a photograph of a child that actually makes you want to need them, not just help them. Lots of happy faces: kids, cripples like me, the disabled and drug-addled all living happily ever after in an institutional utopia. Play groups, dance groups, cooking groups. Groups for coming off drugs, groups for finding a home, centres for sleeping, eating. The only thing they need is a brothel and all basic human needs would be met.

I call the number for the office in the Scottish borders. A

woman answers, her voice soft and smooth, trained to make problems go away.

'Good morning, you have reached the Guardians, Alice speaking. How can I help you?'

'Good morning. My name is Dr Harringford.' I start like this in the hope that she will make the basic assumption that I am not complete dirt. Which is a conclusion that, if she knows Elle, she could easily reach. 'I am looking for my sister, who has been missing for several days. Eleanor Harringford.'

'Has she stayed with us before? I can search on our database for her name.' I can hear her tapping on a keyboard, slow, like she doesn't really know what she is doing. At one point I hear her whisper something to a person nearby, as if she is asking for help.

'Not that I know of.' But in all honesty, how would I know?

'Well, I've put the name in here and nothing comes up. It says *no results found*. That's right, isn't it, Bob?' I realise she isn't talking to me, so I wait for Bob to check what she has done. I hear more tapping, and Alice repeats the name to Bob. After a few seconds she says, 'I'm sorry, there were no results found. She hasn't registered with us. How long has she been missing?'

'A few days,' I repeat. 'The police are looking into it.'

'Oh yes, I recognise the name now. I heard it on the news last night. That poor girl from Horton, right? What a terrible shame.' Helpful Alice turns serious. 'They said she was the last surviving member of her family. What did you say your name was?' Nothing like being cut off from a bunch of dead people by local news reports to make you feel good about

233

yourself. I can't even belong to my parents' corpses or my missing sister. I hang up before I give her another chance to rub salt into old, open wounds.

I call several other shelters. The first is for vulnerable women, so before I even dial the number I don't expect to find her there. I can't accept that Elle is vulnerable. Sad, maybe. In mourning, for sure. But vulnerable? There's just no way. Ask Margot Wolfe or Robert Kneel if my sister is vulnerable, and they'll tell you straight. I call anyway, becoming a concerned friend, and when they push me, I tell them my name is Sarah and I live in Hawick. I follow this script for several other shelters, but come up with nothing. One of them must have some kind of number tracker and a suspicious mind, because not long after I finish making the calls, DC Forrester calls me on my home phone, a number I didn't give her.

'Afternoon,' she says as I hear her sipping at some kind of drink. I imagine her with a Styrofoam cup from the canteen, a cheapo alternative to Starbucks. The idea of it seems mildly depressing.

'Good afternoon, DC Forrester. What can I do for you?'

'There are a few things I would like to ask you about. Can you come to the station?' I am standing in my tracksuit with no bra, letting my asymmetrical breasts hang loose. 'There are a few details of your last days with Eleanor that I think are pertinent. You're not at work, right?'

'No, I'm not at work. Sure, why not?' I say, fiddling with a piece of paper on my desk. My response is too casual, my actions those of somebody who has a choice to say no. I hear her sigh, take another sip, shuffle some papers. 'Say in about an hour?' I suggest, trying to sound more serious. I don't ask her where she got my number.

'Great. See you then,' she says, before ending the call.

I hang up the phone, and as I look down I notice that the paper I am fiddling with is my father's will. I stare at it for a while, wondering what to do with it. Wondering why he would put it in my bag and then take my tablets and kill himself. The envelope with my name on it means that he wanted me to see it. And I can't help but think Antonio is right about one thing: that the number on the back isn't there by chance. It would have been helpful if he had written just a brief explanation, but I should be used to this kind of oversight by now.

I sit for a while with the will in my hands, staring at the pages, waiting for the answer to come to me. There has to be something here that I am meant to understand. I remember telling Antonio that if I really wanted to know what the numbers on the back meant, I would call the lawyer who drew up the will. So I flick to the last page, scan with my finger until I find the name. Joseph Witherrington. I know it sounds familiar, but at first it takes me a while to remember where from. When I realise that it is the name that DC Forrester threw out casually when she was here at my house, and once I remind myself that the police don't throw out anything casually, I start to be concerned. It means they have seen this document. They know about my inheritance of my father's estate. And now the only person left alive who could contest the will is missing. The person I say I left at the scene of my father's death. I'm not sure that I could look any guiltier.

I grab the phone and call Joseph Witherrington. He picks up sounding flustered, and I imagine him all red-faced and puffed out. Probably with a cigar.

'Yes.' No secretary, no polite welcome.

'Good morning, this is Dr Harringford. I am—'

'Oh, Dr Harringford. At last. I thought you were never going to get back to me.' I hear him pull out a chair, which squeaks as he sits down in it. 'I suppose you have had rather a lot going on. No time to answer messages. Deepest condolences, by the way. Terrible to lose a father like that.' His sincerity is about as deep as a saucer, but his tone is softer than it sounded when he picked up, and he is not altogether unlikeable.

'What messages?' I ask.

'I left three messages on your answering machine. I was beginning to wonder if you had made off like that sister of yours.' He breaks into a fit of stifled laughter before regaining his composure. 'I say, did you know she's gone off on a wander somewhere? It's all over the news up here.' I consider telling him that I'm about to go to the police station for that very reason, but I'm not sure that getting into the details is relevant or necessary. Regardless, he doesn't really wait for an answer. I get the impression he is accustomed to giving them, not receiving them. 'God only knows where she has got to now. Thank goodness you had the sense to take her car.'

'You speak of Elle like you know her.'

He chortles, a full belly laugh, wheezy from cigars. 'I've known the family for years.' I note how he doesn't say *your family*, but I let it go. 'She's always been a bit of a troublemaker, generally wild, disappearing for weeks at a time. Quite the tearaway, that one. Don't worry about her, though. She'll turn up unharmed. Always does, more's the pity. No offence intended.'

'None taken.' His inability to feel sorry for Elle endears him to me, and goes some way to making me feel better. 'So it wasn't you that reported her missing?'

'Good God, woman, are you as crazy as she is? Not in a million years. It was that Mr Riley who owns the village pub. He called the housekeeper, said that Eleanor was acting weird in the graveyard. She in turn calls the police in a panic and they open an inquiry. Somebody else says they saw her with a man, and a few hours later you have yourself a kidnapping slash murder slash missing person case.'

By *housekeeper* he must mean Joyce, and I can't believe I didn't think of trying to contact her earlier. If ever there was a person who could attest to my immediate disappearance following my father's death, it is her. Plus, she seemed to like me, and so could perhaps even vouch for me that I had nothing to do with the inheritance and last-minute changing of the will. Should it come to that.

'But with all due respect, Dr Harringford,' he clears his throat, as if deciding whether to say it or not, 'she was always with some strange man. She'll turn up. Mark my words.' I open the drawer under my desk, find a pack of cigarettes and light one. I waft the smoke away as if Antonio is here to complain. But he is not. He left the house before I woke up this morning, telling me last night that he had an early shift at work. 'Now, about the transfer of the deeds for the house. How soon can you get up here to sort that out?'

I like his directness. No bullshit. Straight to the point. 'I don't think it's going to be as easy as that, Mr Witherrington.'

'Why ever not, my dear?'

'Well, as you mentioned, my sister is missing. There is an ongoing police investigation. I don't think we can be seen to be transferring the deeds of a property that morally should belong to her.'

'Perhaps. I suppose that is one way of looking at it. But your father was quite specific. What about the money, then? You're due a pretty penny, my girl.'

'Yes, I realise that.' While I was looking at the will, I realised there was a sizeable monetary benefit too. Not that I want it. 'But to be entirely honest with you, I really don't want to do anything that might lead the police to think I am involved.'

'Involved? You? Don't be ridiculous.'

'Well, I am grateful for your confidence, Mr Witherrington. Perhaps the police will want to talk to you at some point. But before we even think about my father's estate, I wanted to ask you something. On the copy of the will my father gave me there were some handwritten numbers. Do you know anything about them?'

He doesn't say anything for a moment. I drag on my cigarette, letting the smoke drift passively from my nostrils. 'What numbers?' he asks.

'It's a series. 0020-95-03-19-02-84. Do you have any idea what it could mean?'

'Um, er, no. No, I don't. It's probably nothing. Call me when you're ready to proceed with the house and I will be happy to help you.'

'Thanks,' I say, but he has already hung up.

I sit on the edge of my desk while I finish the cigarette and look over at the waste-paper bin. My old SIM card is still in the prepaid phone I purchased at the airport. I walk over and fish it out, pushing aside the red-wine-stained tissues and shards of glass from where Antonio cleared up the remains of our argument. Because it is one of those old brick things with a screen the size of a small matchbox, it still has charge. I navigate through the menus, finding ten missed calls and, according to the voicemail service, five new messages. Three are from Wittherington asking me to call him. The next is from DC Forrester asking the same. The last message is from the head teacher at the school in Horton.

'Hello, this is Miss Endicott. We met at Foxling's Nursery and Infant School. I have some information I think might interest you, and I would be most grateful if you could return this call.'

She leaves a number, which I scribble down on the back of my father's will, underneath the hand-scrawled sequence. I resolve that I will call her after I get back from seeing DC Forrester. I wonder if I should call Elle, and even begin to dial her number. But I decide against it this time. Better to let her find me. That's how this game works; I know it of old. I put both the old and my new phone in my bag and head to the police station.

28

It's humid in the reception of the police station, and the smell of sweat and coffee makes my eyes sting. Outside, buses and cars trundle past, the sound of people shopping chirruping in the background. There is a woman inside, overly made-up and wearing very little. She looks like she should be out working the track, looking for the next John to bend her over the back of a car seat. You must have to be surprisingly flexible to be a hooker. There is no way I could pull it off. I'd have to be set up in a brothel, the type where the lights glow red and the carpet smells like old spunk. But even so, they wouldn't put me in a window. Nobody wants to see crooked bones and scarred hips grinding uncomfortably against an imaginary dick. Surest way to make your customers go limp. I wouldn't be good for cash flow.

'He'll be back out soon,' she says to me.

'Thanks,' I say, drumming my fingers against the desk. I linger there for a while, run my hands along the surface, slap it with the palm of my hand like a workman. *Yep, strong and steady.* There is only one other chair, and it is next to her.

'He'll be a while,' she says. I nod again, smile half-heartedly. After another minute I sit down next to her. She smells of cheap perfume and cigarettes, my teenage years. She offers me a cigarette from her pack, and although I don't want one, I take it anyway. She snatches one up with her teeth, fumbles in her pocket for a lighter. She finds one just as an officer arrives at the reception.

'I don't think so, Jules.' He flicks up a section of the desk and marches over with his chest puffed out. He pulls the cigarette from her mouth, crumples it in his hand. I slip mine up my sleeve like, a teenager caught in the act. When the officer turns his back, she rolls her eyes at me. I roll mine too, nod like, *yeah, what a ball-breaker* he *is,* just to show willing. He heads on through the reception, leaving us alone. I feel as if we are outside the head teacher's office.

'Dick,' spits Jules, pulling another cigarette from the pack. 'Thinks I don't got no more.' She quickly sparks up and inhales deeply, sucking through a cat's-ass mouth. She leaves a red lipstick mark on the butt of the cigarette and the backs of her fingers. In her hurried approach she has smudged her lipstick across her cheek, making her look like a little girl who hasn't learnt how to do her make-up. She is jittery, and I spot a purple love bite on her neck. 'Come on, smoke it quick, there'll be another one along soon.'

She reaches over and snaps a well-trained thumb across the wheel of the lighter, and I pull the cigarette from my sleeve, puff on it like a novice. I want it even less when I catch the whiff of old tobacco on her yellow-edged fingers. I look down so that she doesn't see the discomfort on my face, and catch sight of her shoes. They are prettier than I imagined they would be, strappy, with a little butterfly on the side. One of the wings is squashed the wrong way, as if it tried to take flight and she swatted it back into place. But as pretty as her shoes are, nothing can make up for her feet. She has made an effort with a slick of red polish over nails as thick as walnut kernels. I guess for some it doesn't matter how crappy life gets, they never stop trying.

'So who you here for?' she asks, like we have a camaraderie through criminal association. 'Boyfriend?' she pushes as she eyes up my bare ring finger.

'Sister.' She looks surprised. 'She's gone missing.'

'What's her name?' Jules asks, as if she might know her. 'Lots of them go missing, but they turn up eventually.' She sucks in another long drag of smoke. 'Of course, not all of them turn up in the same state as they left.' In her world, a missing girl equals a whore who picked up a bad punter. Might turn up alive, might turn up dead. A disposable life. I can see her going through her mental files. The blonde who disappeared last week and turned up beaten and drugged but otherwise OK. Back out later that same night. The brunette before that with the nose piercing and wings tattooed across her back. The redhead they pulled from the fishing pond on Hampstead Heath, her tits hacked off and the word *slut* carved in her stomach. I heard about that one too.

'Elle,' I say, going along with the story, pretend-hopeful. I wait while the cogs go round until she comes back with a blank.

'Nah. Don't know her,' she says, shaking her head. I take a drag on my cigarette.

Just then a commotion breaks out on the other side of the doors, and Jules is up on her feet, prowling back and forth, head low, shoulders back, ready for a fight. She drops her cigarette and stubs it out with the butterfly shoe. The doors burst open and an angry dude flies out. Skinhead, tattoos of some kind of bird on the sides of his head, just above his ears. He mutters something under his breath, sounds like a threat.

'Baby,' Jules says, fluttering along at his side as he storms out, more pumped than if he was shooting steroids. I see another police officer at the doors, so I quickly drop my cigarette and stub it out, hoping that he hasn't noticed. I watch as Jules fusses at her baby's side, running her fingers over his muscles as they head towards a car. Just before they get there, he gives her a shove, then opens the door and slaps her inside.

'Can I help you?' the police officer says, breaking my concentration.

After a round of questioning, I make it through the double doors, finding myself in a tiny ice-blue room without any windows. They fix me up with a bitter coffee, Styrofoam cup, and assure me that DC Forrester will be along soon.

'Thanks for coming down here to assist us with our inquiries,' says Forrester as she backs through the door. She is carrying a coffee, just as I imagined, a bunch of files tucked underneath the other arm. She sets the coffee down and dumps the files on the table between us, looking at me in a way that I find strange without knowing why. She sits down opposite me, crosses her arms. I wish now that I had called Elle. That way perhaps it would look less like I don't care. 'It's important that you know you're free to leave at any time. You're here voluntarily, OK?'

'That's OK. Anything to help.' DC Forrester nods, once. Sharp and definite, as if she expected nothing less. 'I want to clear this up, find Elle.'

'I take it that Eleanor hasn't been in touch.' I shake my head, sip my coffee. 'Did you try and get in touch with her?' She waits for a response, but when nothing comes, she looks down disappointedly at the file in front of her, lets go of a toxic breath. As she rustles through the contents, I see Elle's face staring back at us.

'I did call the Guardians and a few shelters,' I say quickly. 'Plus I checked the responses to DC McGuire's Facebook messages. Don't think there was anything useful, though.'

She looks up, her head resting on her hand. 'Send any of your own?' I shake my head and she looks back down at the file. 'Well, let's see what we've got so far.'

She spends the next five minutes recapping what we already know. Elle's reported mental illness. The death of my mother. My father. Our trips to the gym, shopping, drinks, disappearances. She scratches her fingers against the table with every new fact, as if carving them in stone like the ancient Athenians.

'I wanted to ask you a little bit more about the night before your father's death. Is that OK with you?' I nod my head agreeably. 'Good. You told me that you and Elle had spent your days doing normal stuff. Everyday, average stuff.'

'Yes, that's right.' I sit on my hands to stop myself fidgeting.

'So what is normal for you? What counts as *everyday*? What kind of things do you do in your life?'

'With Antonio?' She nods, drums her fingers against the table. I can feel her foot shaking. 'We hang out. We go out to eat. Maybe the movies. Normal stuff.'

'Ever lost anybody close to you before, Dr Harringford?'

I find the question insulting, because I have pretty much lost everything since I was born. But I get where she is going with this, and so I go along with it. 'Not through death.' Anybody with any positive connotations to my life is still alive. Uncle Marcus died a few years back, before I lost touch with Aunt Jemima, but that doesn't really count. I didn't even go to his funeral. I was anxious that my actual parents would be there, or even worse, Elle. No wonder Aunt Jemima doesn't call me any more. No wonder she didn't answer my call after Elle vanished.

'I have,' says Forrester. 'Lost my father last year. Took three weeks off work. Took it hard. And I don't have a husband or kids to look after. Just myself.' That doesn't come as much of a surprise.

'What's your point?'

'My point, Dr Harringford, is that losing somebody you care about is tough. It's a challenge to get past it. Your parents' deaths *could* be a good enough reason to go missing.'

'We don't know why Elle has gone missing. This is just speculation.'

She picks up her coffee and looks at me, stares into my eyes, searching. It is me who looks away. 'I am simply trying to understand her actions in the days after the death of your mother, and immediately prior to your father's suicide.' She hates me, I can feel it. Every time she makes eye contact, the corners of her mouth turn down, like I'm a bad taste. 'I am trying to understand her character.'

'How long have you got?' I say, realising immediately that what I've just said makes me look snippy, like I have got something against Elle, a cross to bear. Nobody needs to have something against a missing person. As if to confirm what I was thinking, Forrester pulls a dissatisfied face, lips all puckered, her wrinkle-set eyes stretched as she arches her brows. 'Sorry about that, it's just . . . Elle is kind of complicated. If you knew her—'

'That's what I'm trying to do.' She ignores my apology and says, 'So, you went to the gym.' My hands feel sweaty, hot like fire tucked underneath my legs. The left one has offset my hip and it has started to ache. I pull them out, try to relax.

'Yes,' I say, wiping my palms on my jeans.

'Enjoy it?'

'I guess.'

'I have a statement from the owner of Sportswear For You.' I must look confused, because she goes on to confirm for me, 'You shopped there on your first day with Eleanor. I'll read it to you.' She holds up a piece of paper from the file. *Two women came into the shop sometime after eleven. I remember them because the tall one was very pretty and had nice hair. She was wearing a pink sports fleece, and I remember thinking it was high-quality sweat-wicking fabric. I wondered who else was selling it in the local area.* She says all this without stopping for breath. Irrelevant facts just setting the scene. Then she slows down, which is how I know that what is coming is more important. *'The tall one was in high spirits, kept saying how she wanted to treat her sister. The short one had a hobble, looked upset about something. Everything I suggested was no good, and slowly the tall one, the pretty one, got disappointed. She kept saying, "All I want is for us to be able to do something together." The short one got tired of her begging, even after picking out a high-end pair of trainers, and in the end grabbed a pair of leggings and a racer bra, which the pretty one went on to buy.'*

DC Forrester glances up, looking for clarification about what happened in Sportswear For You. It's because it doesn't suit me, the idea of a racer bra. It's the hobble, which I thought was less noticeable. But it seems that even random people in sport shops notice it. I use my fingers to mark the outline of a crop top, and she nods as if she understood all along.

'Shall I continue?' She waits for me to agree, and after clearing her throat and taking a sip of coffee, she picks up the statement where she left off. *'They had caused quite a scene, and I had seen several customers leave. So when they eventually came to buy something, I didn't question it when I realised that they were buying the wrong size. I was just happy that they were leaving.'*

She rocks back in her chair, eyes me up over the page before setting it back down on the desk. 'And?' I ask. I am so used to my relationship with Elle being like this, there is nothing that seems out of the ordinary. She might as well have read, *Woman goes to shop and buys sportswear.* Although I don't remember being the one who selected the leggings or the racer bra. I guess I can't blame Elle for that poor choice.

'Doesn't sound much like you were having a nice time. Her begging you. You being . . . what did he say?' She looks back down at the statement and smiles when she finds it. 'Oh, that's it. Tired of Eleanor's begging.'

'But that's Elle. She forces stuff on people, pushes them. I didn't want to go to the gym.'

'But you told me you had a nice time there.'

'Yes. It was OK. But that doesn't mean I wanted to go. If I had wanted to go to the gym in those few days, I would have taken sportswear with me, right?'

She shuffles through the file and produces another sheet of paper without giving away any opinion. 'I'll read another statement for you. From the gym: *Everybody knows Elle. She is a happy-go-lucky type. She gets involved in lots of activities and charity events. She is a bit socially awkward, but her heart is always in the right place. I think she is lonely because she seems to want to latch on to men. I think she is looking for a boyfriend. Must be hard living with your folks. I heard she was trying for a baby at one point but her boyfriend at the time backed up. Weird, she has a lot going for her.'* Forrester sips her coffee without looking at me. I reach for mine and bring it to my lips, but it is cold so I set it back down without drinking. 'You want another one?' Forrester asks, pointing at the cup. I shake my head. 'So, does that sound like Eleanor to you?'

'Not much,' I say.

'Not to me either. But only if I believe the version of Eleanor that you have described. Here's another. Now this one is from a psychiatrist,' she says as she slides another piece of paper from the file. 'You will want to listen to this one.' I nod my head energetically, certain that she is right. If anyone can shed light on Elle it will be a psychiatrist. I edge forward in my seat. 'It says: *I have known Elle in the capacity of her doctor since last year. She first came to visit me because she was struggling with the idea that she would never have a child. She was moving from one meaningless relationship to the next, looking for somebody to love her. I concluded that her relationship with her mother was poor, but that she adored her father and was in many ways looking for a replacement. She was doing well in life, socialising at her local gym and working as a volunteer at the local cat and dog sanctuary. She was financially secure, her income coming from the family estate. She required minimal assistance and guidance with understanding that not every man was a potential candidate to be the father of her child. Her biggest issue, besides the poor relationship with her mother,*' and this is the point that Forrester looks up at me, '*was her sister.*'

I must look dumbfounded, because she gives me a moment to take that in before she continues.

'*Elle describes her sister as a loner, not keen on family bonds. She has made several attempts at forming a relationship with her, and has spent the last six years trying to reach her, to no avail. She blames her mother for this loss. She describes her sister as bitter, spiteful and crazy.*'

I can feel a bead of sweat forming on my brow, and I reach up to wipe it away. Elle has made me out to be something I'm not, and these idiots who have made statements are providing the foundations for her imaginary world. Of

249

course she would be able to fool a psychiatrist. It's so obvious, yet I never imagined it. Never saw it coming. This was her plan all along. She's fucking set me up.

'I'll have another coffee,' I say.

29

Listening to Forrester read out the statements makes me feel ill. I want to run. I want to be sick. I want to scream at her that she couldn't be any more wrong. I do none of those things. I am wrapped up in Elle's web of lies, so much so that I am starting to wonder if they are my own.

'Now that doesn't sound much like Eleanor either, does it?' She ignores my request for a coffee and pushes a photo of Elle towards me, taps out each word with her finger. 'At least not according to you.' *The tall pretty one* runs around in my head. *She describes her sister as bitter, spiteful and crazy.*

'No,' I say. 'No, it doesn't.'

'Plus there is no record of her ever having received treatment for mental health issues in the past. We have a full disclosure of her medical history and there is nothing in there except a couple of visits to her GP, and this doctor who made the statement. He saw her privately, and essentially concluded that she was fine.'

'That's impossible,' I say, remembering her telling me herself that our parents had placed her in a clinic. 'She has had treatment. Must have. I know she has.'

'How can you be so certain? You haven't seen her in

years, according to this. Even now, when she is missing, you haven't tried to call her. Have you called anybody else?'

'Yes.' I jump, pointing a finger at her, which looks a bit too accusatory. She holds her hands up in a way that suggests I back off, as if I was about to attack. I sit back down, calm myself. 'Witherrington. I know who he is. He's the lawyer dealing with my father's estate. I spoke to him.'

'We know very well who he is, Dr Harringford.' She pulls out a photocopy of what looks like my father's will, highlighted with yellow and pink lines, little sticky Post-it notes marking important and interesting segments. I spot that Article 4 has been both highlighted *and* emphasised by a Post-it note. 'The reason we know of him is because of this, a will signed by your father the day you arrived in Horton. It was found at your parents' home. Now your home, right? I presume you have seen it before.'

I consider lying, but figure there is little point. It could do me more harm than good. 'I have seen it, yes.'

'And you didn't think to tell us? It cuts Eleanor out, doesn't it? I can't imagine a better reason to be upset and feel vulnerable.' There's that word again, the word that reminds me how far they are from the truth. 'After losing both her parents, she finds out that your father has cut her off financially. And we have just heard how she was financially secure because of your family. This is like a smack in the face, isn't it, after everything that happened? Can you see this?' she asks, pointing to a section with a pink Post-it note next to it. 'Maybe you can't because this is a copy, but there are wrinkles in the page. Watermarks. We had them analysed and found that they were tears, Dr Harringford.

No doubt your sister's. On the will made by your father, whom she adored, and with whom she had a good relationship. All backed up by a statement from Eleanor's psychiatrist. Yet right after you turn up, he cuts her out. How do you explain that?'

'I can't.'

She slides the statements back into the file and sips her cold coffee. Her tired, birdlike eyes stare at me as she sits back and folds her arms like a fat Texan sheriff. 'Why did you change your flight home on the night before your father's death?'

'I didn't change it. I missed it.'

'You sure about that?' She pulls out another sheet of paper and I feel myself flush, because even though I know that what I have said is the truth, I have a horrible feeling that she is about to prove me wrong. 'We got this from the airline.' It looks like a screenshot, topped with a logo declaring: *Internal Air, a flight in the right direction!* She pushes it my way. I see the words *Manage My Booking*. I read on and see that apparently I changed my flight to the following day. Did I do this? I don't remember doing it, but there is a lot I don't remember doing that night.

'I didn't do this,' I say, not sounding certain. I bring my fingers up to my nose, sniff at the nicotine. 'Elle must have changed it.'

'You have to have the booking details in order to change the flight. Could she have had access to those?'

I think about the bag sitting in my room with everything in it. She could have dug out the flight details. But she could also have got them from the study, where I left them during my mother's wake. I got sloppy, forgot how to play the game. I look down at the page and scan the information. Time of amendment: 16.35.

'Elle did this.' I rub my fingers on the desk, scratch at my head. I'm falling apart, unravelling stitch by stitch. 'She must have gained access to my things and made the changes. Online you can be anybody, you must know that. At this time we were together at the house.'

'But you didn't remain at the house all night, right? You were at a hotel with a man named Matthew.' She slides an image taken from some grainy CCTV footage across the desk. There is no doubt it is me; my face attached to his, him holding me up as if I am about to slump to the ground. 'You were seen kissing him in the foyer, and then, a little later on, you were caught on the third-floor landing doing other things that involved your mouth. I can prove that too if you would like?' I bring my hand to my mouth, cover it as if I'm about to be sick. Perhaps trying to conceal the evidence. She holds up another photograph, turns it away from me so that I can't see the image. 'But I'd much rather you just admitted it. Save us both the embarrassment.'

Elle has planned it perfectly. By screwing Matt, all I have done is reinforce my guilt, polish her innocence. I've played straight into her hands. I have to make out that it wasn't important. 'Admit what? That I screwed another guy when I was away from home. I wouldn't be the first to do that. It doesn't mean that I had anything to do with the will or my father rewriting it. It doesn't prove that I was the one who changed my flight. I paid for another ticket the next day. Why would I have done that if I knew I had changed my flight?' I try to sound defiant, but being caught out, hand in the cookie jar, never feels good.

'No, you wouldn't be the first. And to be quite honest, I don't care who you fuck. What I do care about is this. Let's assume that what you've told me is the truth. I'll recap.' She stands up, starts circling the room. 'You have no feelings for your mother, yet you rush to fly up there when she dies. You say it was to support your sister, yet this is the same sister that you refused to have a relationship with for years before that. You spend the next few days bitching at her as she tries to spend time with you. You act like nothing important has happened, visiting the gym, going out for drinks. Then, after your father alters his will and subsequently commits suicide, you change your flight home and end up blowing a stranger in the corridor of a hotel.'

'I didn't change the flight,' I shout. I slip down in the chair, seeing how badly this whole thing is playing out before me. She doesn't pay me any attention. Instead she continues recounting the facts as she knows them.

'Your father kills himself with a Valium overdose, something he doesn't have a prescription for and for which we cannot find a box or bottle. Not even a shred of foil from a blister pack. And you know what, your sister with the psychiatrist, even she doesn't have a prescription for it. But you're a doctor. Anaesthetist, isn't it?'

I nod, and she leans in, the smell of coffee pungent on her breath. I am wondering if this was Elle's plan all along, to screw me over right from the word go. Perhaps she's been trying to wrap me up in trouble since the days with Margot

255

Wolfe and Robert Kneel. Maybe she got our father to change the will just to set me up.

'You have access to medication like that, I presume? I could look at the controlled drugs records at Queen's, if you like. That's where you work, isn't it? Queen's College Hospital?' She doesn't wait for me to answer. 'Then your sister disappears, something you seem to want to explain in terms of mental illness, yet other than seeing a shrink for a few months last year because she wasn't handling the idea that she might not become a mother, there is no history of mental illness recorded in any of her hospital documents. And oh, surprise, surprise,' she holds up her hands, 'the missing sister is the only relative who could possibly contest the will. A will that was written days before your father died, leaving you, the daughter he kicked out when you were three years old, with everything. Something doesn't add up, Dr Harringford. Explain it to me.'

'Do you think I've hurt my sister?'

'I didn't say that. This is not an interview under caution. You are here voluntarily.'

I am so frantic, I am barely listening, but I do just about hear the word *voluntarily*, which calms me a little. I could leave, in theory, and that helps. I need to change direction. 'Joyce, the housekeeper, was there when I left. She can vouch for me that Elle was still alive. And she made it pretty clear that Elle was the one with the problems. She'll be able to tell you. She knows everything that happened in that house. If you are accusing me of something, I want to know whether I need a lawyer.'

'Do *you* think you need a lawyer?' Forrester asks me, as

if such a need would prove my guilt. She is just waiting for me to make the request.

'No,' I plead, lifting myself up. Before I know it, I am on my feet, and I hear the chair crash to the floor behind me. 'But you are making out like I planned this whole thing. That I planned my parents' deaths and then did away with my sister in an effort to get my hands on their money. But my mother died before I even saw her. Plus my father killed himself, and nobody knows what has happened to Elle.'

'Somebody knows what happened to Elle. And you know how I know that? Because somebody always does.' After a pause in which she shuffles her papers back and forth, putting them into an unnecessary order, she looks up at me, motions for me to relax. 'But no, I don't think you are involved in your sister's disappearance. The team in Edinburgh have spoken to Joyce. She told them that you left straight away. Seems quite taken by you, in fact. Plus we have a definitive sighting of Eleanor after you left Horton.' When I don't sit down straight away, she motions again for me to relax. 'I personally spoke to Joseph Witherrington, and he also seems to back you up on knowing nothing about the changes to the will. But this situation doesn't make much sense to me, and I don't think you are telling me the truth. You know more than you're letting on. That makes me suspicious because that's what I am trained to be. So start being straight with me so that I can be straight with you. Why did you go there?'

I take a long breath in and reach for the chair. I pick it up and take a seat. I begin slowly, painfully, hate for this woman oozing out of me for making me admit the truth.

'Because I wanted to see my mother. Dead or alive. I couldn't remember her face and it was my last chance. Curiosity, I guess.' DC Forrester seems to relax a little. 'I wanted to know why I was given away. I have never known the truth.'

This she seems to accept, tracing a finger along the edge of the file. 'You look a lot like her, you know.'

'Yes, that's not the first time somebody has told me that.'

She is softer now, leans across the table. 'What am I missing, Dr Harringford? Tell me what is going on. Do you care about your sister?'

I think about all the times Elle has done something randomly weird to which I once aspired. Done something outright crazy when I was older that pushed me away. I think of all the times I have cut her out and then felt miserable because she wasn't around. I think of how I still have the prepaid phone, just in case she calls. I get it out and show Forrester, setting it down on the table.

'I threw this away so she couldn't contact me. I retrieved it from the bin because I changed my mind. I care about Elle, I want the best for her,' I say, repeating my father's words. 'I just don't know how to let her be my sister. These people who have been describing her, they don't know her like I do. I know her differently. She isn't normal, DC Forrester. When I went there, I wasn't myself. I did and said things that aren't like me.'

'Like the man in the hotel?'

I take a shot of air, desperately feeling like I need it. 'I guess so. Do you know that she drugged me that night? You can ask Mr Guthrie, he heard her admit to it. I struggle to have Elle in my life and I push her away. I push everybody

258

away. I guess it's what I am trained to do.' She eyes me in a way that suggests I watch my smart mouth, but she lets it go. I think in this moment that maybe she likes me a little bit more. 'I want you to find her. I do. I don't want anything from my family's estate. It's like it isn't anything to do with me. I want to know she is OK, and then go back to avoiding her. I know that makes me sound like a bitch, but it's how it has to be. I can't live with her, but I—'

'Can't live without her either?' Her tone is different. She has dropped the asshole cop routine. 'You're right, it does make you sound like a bitch. But that's not a crime, and neither is fucking a stranger behind your partner's back. Drugged or not.' There is a sharp twang to that last note, just enough so that I understand she doesn't quite trust me yet. 'Now, tell me something else, now that you are being honest. What have you really been doing since you got back?'

'Hiding out. Staying in. Watching TV.' I think about leaving it out, but I consider that adding it in makes me look more pathetic, and right now, that is a good thing because I'm still concerned that she thinks I arranged this whole thing. 'Getting drunk at home.'

'With Antonio?' she asks. I catch a sly glint in her eye and wonder how this woman ever solved a crime with such a poor poker face.

'No,' I say, because I know that somehow she already knows. 'We argued when I got back. I think it was partly the guilt that I had cheated on him, and partly the fact that I felt like I had let Elle down.' That is the truth. 'Plus, the whole deal with the will, realising I had inherited everything, upset me. I didn't want it. I wanted to move on, leave the past behind. We argued, he smashed a couple of wine glasses, left at some point during the night. Or the next morning. I don't know. I woke up and he was gone.'

'So it would be fair to say that your relationship is strained. That things aren't going well.'

'That would be fair.'

'So where'd he go?'

'Italy. He withdrew money from my account and left. Came back the night before you knocked on the door.'

'For four days?' I shrug, confirming the duration of his absence. 'And he is planning to open a restaurant soon, right? He applied for a bank loan. A pretty sizeable one at that.'

How does she know about that? 'It's a dream of his. He always wanted to open a bistro. Now he has the money I'm sure he will do it. He has some savings, I think.' Most of which I assume has been siphoned off from me.

'Hm, really,' says Forrester. She pulls out another sheet of paper, thick, like the photographs from the CCTV footage. I can't quite make out the details. She ponders it and then looks at me. 'Will it be a joint venture?'

'No. I didn't even know about the bank loan. He organised it while I was away. We'd had another fight, and I think we both thought it was over.'

'I'm sorry about that. I have to ask you, does Antonio Molinaro know your sister?'

'No. They have never met.'

She is silent for a moment, and then asks me, 'You sure about that?' She slides a grainy image across the plastic desk. I see Elle's unmistakable blonde hair tucked neatly behind her ears. Even in greyscale she is stunning. Good bone structure. She is in a bar, clutching a drink. It's the same bar where we went together in Hawick. Next to her is a man, a face I recognise. At first I think it's Greg, the mind playing tricks on me. Showing me what I expect to see. But it is Antonio's face huddled in close to her ear. 'I got this through just before you arrived.'

'When was this taken?' I ask.

'The day she went missing,' says DC Forrester. She almost looks sad for me as she goes on, 'Antonio, it seems, was the last person to see her before she disappeared.'

30

The last thing I ask before I leave the station is whether they are going to arrest Antonio. All DC Forrester says is that there'd be little point in me trying to warn him. It gives me the impression that maybe they are watching him already, or waiting for a vital piece of evidence before they strike. Maybe for me to implicate myself as an accomplice so they can finger us both. Whatever DC Forrester is planning, by the time I leave the police station, the air thick and muggy, all I can think about is how I am returning to a life that doesn't mean what I thought it did. A life that's over.

Let's start with the facts. Number one: Antonio is a liar. He hasn't been in Italy. He has been with her. In a bar. And let's not pretend that he wasn't huddled in close enough to lick the sweat from her skin. He was nestled into her neck, whispering in her ear. It could have been the briefest of moments. It's possible that DC Forrester printed off that specific snapshot to make him look bad, like a hot-off-the-press celebrity exposé. Maybe she thought it would introduce doubt, that I would feel betrayed, reveal a damning truth and solve her little mystery by confessing. After all, that's why she got me there first, right? See if I'd give him up like a woman scorned, fire-angry, willing to ruin herself if she can take her cheating man down with her. That's the problem with a photograph: it's so momentary that your mind takes the luxury of filling in the hours before and after until you have got yourself a whole story. And in my story Antonio is a liar. He has been meeting with my sister. He hasn't been to Italy. He's going to be taken in for questioning. Antonio is a fucking liar.

Another fact: my father left me the best part of the family inheritance. The money, save a small fund so that Elle doesn't starve, and the house. All my mother's jewellery, which, considering the fancy necklace I spotted on her stiff dead neck, is probably a sizeable collection. All the time I wanted something more from my family, and now I've got it. What a haul. Problem is, I don't want it any more. I wish he hadn't bothered.

Because my final fact, the cherry on top, the real kicker of the story, is that *I* look like a liar. Everything that has happened, from me going there in the first place in a reckless attempt to uncover the truth, to my decision to leave right after my father's death, makes me look like I planned this whole thing. DC Forrester has managed to interpret every action since the moment my mother died as an attempt to secure the family inheritance. Despite the fact that she told me she doesn't think me responsible, I know that all she is waiting for is the evidence. Like I'm some kind of kingpin, able to manipulate lives and deaths from a distance and really cash in. *Ker-ching!* I hit the fucking jackpot.

I sit in my car, look down at the prepaid phone, my only connection left to Elle. I pick it up, dial her number and listen as it begins ringing. DC Forrester is right about one thing. I really should have called her already. The voicemail picks it up and I start to leave a message.

'Elle, hi. It's me,' I say, voice sweet, kind, like I am trying to coax a kitten down from a tree. The victim. I can play that role if it makes her show her face. 'Everybody is really worried about you. The police are searching for you. I'm worried too. I need you to get in touch. I . . .' I pause a bit while I think of what else to say. When the words don't come, I hang up.

I throw the phone back down on to the passenger seat and grab the wheel with both hands, tighten my grip. It has started to rain, and as I pull on to Brixton Road, I can feel the car slipping, the ground slick with late-summer drizzle and dust. The wipers bat left and right, and for the briefest of moments I can barely see a metre ahead of me as the rain buckets down. I pull over into the bus lane and reach for the phone. I punch the keys until I am dialling Elle's number again, and when I hear the voicemail pick up I leave the message I really wanted to leave the first time.

'Elle, where the fucking hell are you? It looks like I set this whole thing up. Don't you dare disappear on me now.' I slam the phone down on the seat and pull back on to the road, feeling better.

I park and run through the rain to Starbucks, nestled just alongside the tube station. I order an espresso and take a seat at the bar in the overcrowded coffee shop, which smells like a combination of hot cinnamon and vanilla. From my seat at the window I watch people passing by, staring through the condensation-drenched windows. A street florist opposite hurries to rearrange pots of daffodils and tulips and sprays of gypsophila. People are rushing and dashing; everyone has somewhere they should be. Some hurry inside to escape the downpour, laden with shopping bags, bringing with them the scent of summer rain. One of them is a mother with a child in a buggy. Some people help by clearing a path, shuffling their chairs out of the way. But the kid is crying, screaming out as if it is in pain. I watch the woman as she buys a drink, a cookie for the kid, which he proceeds to smash against the table, sending crumbs high in the air like wedding confetti. She looks close to tears, beyond hassled. Yet she scoops that kid up, bounces him on her knee. Such a simple thing. A few minutes later he is asleep. She catches me watching her, smiles awkwardly in my direction. How hard can it be? I turn away, stare instead at the mottled reflection of my face in the window, not sure I even recognise who I am.

An hour passes like this before the rain eases off. The café empties gradually, the mother and child among the first to leave. I try a smile as she is on her way out, but the moment for friendship has gone and I end up turning back to my reflection, feeling awkward. I've never been very good at making friends, which is why I suppose I don't have anybody to turn to now. I guess I never did learn how to integrate, despite Aunt Jemima's best efforts.

I drive home, reminding myself on every corner of exactly where that is. *Home. Home. Turn left towards home.* I check the prepaid phone before I step from the car, but there is no reply from Elle. To fill the time, I call the number left by Miss Endicott.

'Yes, hello?' She answers in her very best telephone voice, a softening of her Scottish accent. She sounds so different that at first I'm not sure it's her.

'Hello, Miss Endicott? This is Mrs Jackson.' Confusion on the end of the line as I keep up the pretence. 'We met at the school a couple of weeks ago.' There is silence while she thinks, so I try to jog her memory. 'I was searching for a placement for my child.'

'Oh, yes,' she says slowly, as if the parts of the jigsaw are starting to move into place. 'I wasn't sure you would return my call.'

'Your message sounded important. You told me there was some information I should know.' I'm not sure why I am skirting around the subject. I would love to just blurt it out, tell her that I saw her at the funeral, that really I am related to the family from *Mam Tor*, the place that is not for sale. But I remember just how strange Elle's reaction was when she saw Miss Endicott arrive in the church, so I stick to my false identity, wear it like a bulletproof vest.

'Yes, I did, Mrs Jackson. It is regarding that house you mentioned during your visit. It has become vacant, but,' and she pauses, a last breath before she lets herself fall without a net for safety, 'I think we both know that already. I wanted to warn you in advance that pursuing that house could be very difficult.'

'Oh,' I say, feigning surprise, clinging on to my own lies even though I am sure she has all but admitted she knows who I am. 'Well, I will bear your advice in mind. Have the residents moved on?'

'The residents have indeed moved on. Before their time.

There is a daughter in the picture, but rumour has it she is not set to inherit the house.' She whispers this last part as if it is hot news, salacious gossip burning her tongue, steam coming off her sizzling words. I can hear voices and laughter in the background and I realise I have lost track of the days. I glance at the clock and see that it is Tuesday.

'I'm sorry, Miss Endicott, but are you working at the moment? Perhaps there are people there and you can't talk?'

'Yes, that's right, my dear. Now listen. The house is empty, but might not go forward for immediate sale. I believe somebody else is set to inherit it,' she continues, ignoring my question but somehow also answering it. I go along with her coded conversation.

'Who will inherit the house?'

'Mrs Jackson, I am good friends with Mr Witherrington. Just friends, mind. I don't want there to be any confusion.' There is no confusion. 'Mr Wittherington is the lawyer who has been charged with handling the estate. But you might already know that,' she murmurs. I imagine her turning away, her usual brusque, overbearing nature reduced to huddling in a corner with her hand cupped over the mouthpiece.

'Yes, I do know that.' I am losing my patience and can't keep up the pretence any longer. 'Please, Miss Endicott, you known damn well who I am,' I snap. 'That's why you called me. Get to the point.'

Silence for a minute, save the background voices still joking around. I wonder if I have blown it, whether I misread the conversation and have given myself away. But then Miss Endicott chuckles as if we have just shared a joke. I pull out a cigarette and light it quickly, cracking open the window. Breathe in. Breathe out. Water drizzles in, chilling my leg as it falls. 'Oh yes. Of course, Mrs Jackson. You gave me all the details when you came to see me at the school. I understood perfectly.'

'So,' I say, happy to be on the same page, 'if you know who I am, tell me what is going on. You must know that my sister has gone missing.' I puff hard on the cigarette, close the window a little to stop the rain from falling inside the car.

'Why yes, dear. Of course. And that is why I had no choice but to call you. Mr Witherrington is dealing with the transaction, but I must stress that I would advise you against following it up. You see, there is an issue regarding the inheritance of their firstborn daughter.'

'Miss Endicott, be straight with me. What are you trying to tell me?' I stub the remains of my cigarette out. I don't understand. In one breath she is trying to help me, but in the next she is being so cryptic. At the funeral she didn't even speak to my father, so why is she so concerned to help me now? Does she know something about Elle that I don't? About her disappearance? Why would she hide it if she did?

'I just think that you should let that property go, Mrs Jackson. It's not worth the risk. But of course, if you were to come here, I would gladly meet with you and try to help you find the missing pieces of your jigsaw, so to speak.'

'Are you suggesting I come to Horton, Miss Endicott?'

'Well, yes, of course I'd be delighted to meet you again. Any time you are able to stop by. Thank you for returning my call, my dear.'

'Wait, Miss Endicott, don't go yet.' But she has already hung up. I dial her number again, but she doesn't answer. It doesn't even go to voicemail.

31

I think about starting the engine, driving straight up there. Whatever it is she has to tell me is important enough that she has to cover it up on the phone, secrets that perhaps she doesn't want overheard. But I see Antonio waving from the window, and decide there are other things that demand my attention first.

I step from the rain and into the house, the hallway dark, humid. I can hear the tinkle of a spoon in a teacup, the shuffling of a liar's feet across the tiles of the kitchen. I think about his plans to open a restaurant and wonder if he told me he had the loan or if he had only applied for it. I wish I had read the letter from the bank when he'd given it to me. Forrester certainly didn't seem convinced that it had been approved. I try to focus on anything I know as fact as I close the door behind me. Trouble is, the only facts I know just seem to make things worse.

Antonio is a liar.

He's going to be questioned.

He hasn't been in Italy.

He was with Elle.

I walk through to the living room, stand next to the couch

where we made love, the spot where I harboured desperate hopes that life was going to get better. The same place we have snuggled, watched movies, dropped popcorn. The room still smells like our hot bodies, the smell of sex on the furniture. I hear him coming towards me, cup of tea in hand, and so I sit down, my clothes still drenched. Rainwater drips to my shoulders, runs through my hair and across my scalp, falling like tears down my cheeks. I see his raincoat, the one I paid for, draped over the back of an old leather chair. Why would he have bought that to go to Italy in the summer? There's another fact for you. I'm gullible and stupid.

I think about what I am going to say, playing out at least five different scenarios in my head. But when he arrives in front of me, all of my caution, careful questioning and plans to get him to trip himself up fall apart. I blurt everything out.

'You weren't in Italy,' I say before he has even set my cup down. He stares at it for just a little too long, looking for answers that he never expected he would need to find.

'What do you mean? I went to Italy,' he replies. But he hasn't looked at me yet. He is avoiding eye contact. Eventually he manages a quick glance. His nose twitches, mouth pulls up slightly at the side. I know immediately he is lying.

'You are lying,' I say, unblinking, unflinching. 'I know where you were.'

He smiles, laughs, as if it is a case of, *OK, caught me.* I am almost waiting for him to raise his hands, as if I am holding a tiny concealed gun like a James Bond villain. 'You don't know where I was,' he says, pantomime fashion. He picks up the raincoat and reaches into the inside pocket, bringing out a small red box.

There are not many things he could have produced to stop me in my tracks, but this is one of them. I see the familiar smirk he gets on his face when he feels pleased with himself, when he knows he has shocked me or done something to make me happy. Under normal circumstances he is satisfied by both results in equal measure. The first night we slept together he did things with his tongue that made my body shake. It's that face I see now, the same one that loomed over me after I came, wiping his mouth with the back of his hand.

'What is that?' I ask.

He doesn't say anything, but the smug grin fades to one of hope. Pitiful hope. He opens the box and drops to one knee, and inside I see a tiny diamond set on a beautiful mount. It's the kind of diamond that says, *I don't really have enough to offer you, but I am making my best effort. My best and final offer.*

'I want us to be married. Now that the thing with your family is over, we can move on. Be our own family with a big wedding in Italia.' I become even more nervous now that he has started substituting Italian for English, because he only does that when he is really excited, or really angry. He isn't angry. He actually means this.

'Just exactly how did you conclude that the *thing* with my family is over?' He is still crouching on one knee, holding the box up to my face. I can see from the way his smile has disappeared – even the pitifully hopeful one has slipped – that this is not going how he pictured it.

272

'Your parents have passed, and your sister has finally disappeared from your life. You have what you always wanted. Now you can move on.'

'My sister hasn't disappeared from my life. She has disappeared completely.' But he is undeterred and edges towards me, still down on one knee. I push the box away from my face. But I am shocked because it seems that even Antonio never realised that it was all a big game; me running, hoping secretly that they were on my tail. Doesn't he understand why I went there? In my astonishment he manages to wriggle the tiny ring on to my finger. He takes my lack of resistance as a good sign and kisses my cheek.

'It looks good,' he says, a tear forming in the corner of his eye.

'No, Antonio,' I say shaking my hand out from his. 'I didn't agree to marry you.' I try to pull the ring off, but my fingers are swollen and the ring is too small. It is stuck. 'Where did you get this idea from? That everything was over, settled? It is so far from over.' I make another attempt to pull the ring off, and when I fail, my hands drop to my sides as if I have given up. 'I know where you were, and you were not in Italy buying this tiny thing. You were in Horton, with my sister. And don't pretend that you weren't. I have seen the pictures with my own eyes. Why did you lie to me? How did you find her?'

He stands up and moves over to the other couch. He sits down and tosses the box on to the table, just forcefully enough that it rattles towards me, landing open-mouthed and empty. He runs his hands up through his hair, then pulls at his T-shirt like he wants to rip it off. Now he is angry.

'I didn't find her. She found me. You called me from her phone, and that's how she got my number. She wanted to get to know me.'

I think back to my phone when I found it on the driveway, the broken screen, the precise way in which it was smashed. As if on purpose, perhaps with a stiletto. When did she have time? I don't know when she slipped outside and did it, but I know it was Elle. Just one simple move was all it took to cut me off, then bide her time, snare his number. 'How many times did you speak to her?'

'Seven, maybe eight while you were there. She called me in the evenings, asking about you. Asking about our life together. I thought I was helping.'

'Helping?' I hang my head in my hands, thinking of all the effort I went to in order to keep them apart. 'What did you tell her?'

'Just simple things at first. Things that sisters would want to know. What kind of house you lived in. How many hours you went to work. How many on-call shifts you had to do. She wanted to learn about your life. She asked where we went on holiday, about my family, about Italia.'

So now I know how she seduced him into talking. He loves rattling on about his overextended family with eight grand-mothers and a gazillion aunts. Oh yes, nice, kind, poor misunderstood Elle and her simple interests. I can hear him now, sighing about how fucked up I must be to have cut her out.

'You said *at first*,' I say as he reaches across the table and recovers the box, perhaps embarrassed by its presence. He closes it and sets it down next to him on the cushion. 'What about after that? How did it stop being simple?'

'Her questions became more personal.' He makes an effort to close the gap, inching towards me. Something holds him back. 'But she didn't seem crazy like you said she was. She was kind, friendly, told me she was worried about you.' I avoid breaking eye contact in the hope that it is my cold, ice-hard stare that is keeping him from standing up and reaching out to touch me. 'Then she told me that you weren't coping well. That you were behaving strangely.' A tear breaks free and he brushes it away. 'I was worried about you.'

'Of course I was behaving strangely,' I shout. 'How else would I behave while I was there with *her*? Have you forgotten everything I ever told you about her?'

'But that's the problem, Rini. You never told me anything.' His head drops to the back of the couch, and I can see that this isn't the first time he has realised what a stupid idea it was to meet her. I know the look, the feeling of being weighed down by something Elle has said or done. It sticks with you like an albatross lashed to your leg. The feeling of joy she brings with her when she first makes contact is short-lived. But by then she has got you, already got her claws stuck in your flesh, dragging you down beneath the waves that she, no doubt, has created.

'I only told her a few personal things,' he says as he braves his way towards me. 'I wanted to help. Like the fact you always wanted to know who you looked like, what foods you liked as a baby, what your childhood room was like.' Maybe all the time we were together it was just one long script she was working from, filling in the gaps as Antonio presented them. Same with the butterflies on the wall, her fluttering fingers against my skin, the insects she drew on my casts. A theatrical seduction to win me over. Another mind trick that I soaked up, believed, made real.

'You're so stupid,' I say, shaking my head, wiping away my own tears. I don't feel good about crying, but there is no covering it up. Not this time. 'She only wanted to know those things so she could use them against me. Anything she knows about my life has potential to her. It is something she can manipulate to get to me. And she did. She used those things to soften me to putty. So she could mould me, lure me into her world.' How easily I fell into her plan. *Just one drink. A last goodbye.* She used that night to isolate me from the only thing left that I was connected to. Antonio. Without him she knew I was alone. Without him I would need her. Without him I would be hers and for once in our sorry lives I would start chasing her.

'No. She was trying to get close to you.'

'God, Antonio, don't you get it? Do you know what this looks like? That I organised the whole thing. That I wanted my family dead so that I could inherit the house. The money. That this is a crime for inheritance.'

'But that's ridiculous. Is that what DC Forrester said?'

'She didn't say it, but that doesn't mean she isn't thinking it. And yes, it's ridiculous, but that doesn't stop her believing it. You know what isn't so ridiculous, though? The fact that everything I have done makes me look guilty. I don't have a relationship with my family, but as soon as my mother dies I am straight there. My father changes his will and then commits suicide with Valium, which nobody but me has access to.' He has started stroking my leg, and I don't stop him. It helps. Soothes me. 'But you know what is even better?' I say, pushing his hand away as I remember the facts. 'They think you were in on it.' He stands up, straight as a lamp post. 'They have pictures of you, Antonio. You lied to me. You weren't in Italy. You were the last person to see her.'

'They think I have something to do with her disappearance?'

'Yes. That we both do, maybe. They probably think I put you up to it. Why did you go there? Why did you meet her?'

He crashes back down on the other sofa, his T-shirt parting from his trousers, exposing his olive stomach. He looks so good, and yet I can feel him slipping away from me. I know there are more lies beneath the surface. Scratch at it for a bit and they will all come bubbling out, like the tiniest prick on a septic wound, opened up and spilling pus.

'She told me that you hadn't handled your father's death very well. She suggested I go there, that we could talk about how best to help you. She told me she had seen you like this before, many times. That she always knew how to help, but that she wanted me involved. Oh, Irini. Why didn't you tell me she was sick?' He sits up, reaches forward. There is a pile of magazines on the table between us and he fiddles at the edges, straightening them up. 'I was desperate. It was that or we were finished. I didn't want to lose you.'

'They have pictures of you in a bar. Nobody has seen her since.'

He punches the couch in frustration. 'But that's impossible. I left her at the hotel and there were—' He stops mid-sentence.

'You were at a hotel together? Antonio, did you . . .' I

say, but I leave my question to fade to nothing because the answer is written all over his face. 'Oh my God,' I whimper as more tears start to flow. 'You had sex with her, didn't you?'

'It wasn't like that. No. NO! It wasn't like that.' I jump up from the couch to get away from him because I can already see what it was like: her nuzzling up to him, looking for a hero. Him stepping up. How good it must have felt for him to know what to do for once, how to make things right. He must have thought it was all so fucking easy in comparison to me. Just a brief kiss, then another, and before you know it her hand is down his trousers looking for the on/off switch to his brain. I pull desperately at the ring, his stupid, pathetic, guilt-carved ring that was supposed to help make up for what he did. I run to the kitchen, grab the soap and squirt it all over my finger, pulling and twisting. 'Rini, no,' he begs, following me. 'It's not what you think. Please,' he says as he grabs my shoulders, spins me round. Water splashes over us, mixing with my tears. 'I didn't sleep with her. I didn't.'

'But something happened, didn't it? Something happened that you don't want to tell me about. Did you kiss her? Did she kiss you?'

'I didn't want it. She tried. She wanted to have sex with me, but I stopped it. I told her no.' He is snatching at my hand, trying to stop me from pulling off the ring, as if by forcing me to wear it we can forget everything that has happened and the future will happen just as he wishes it to.

'And where were you when you told her no? You weren't at the bar, were you?' He can't look at me. He is gripping me, clinging to what he knows will be his only chance to save us. 'You were at a hotel. You were going to do it and you changed your mind. I'm right, aren't I?'

He lets go and flops down in one of the plastic kitchen chairs, green liquid all over his hands. He drops his head into his slick palms, the soapy, apple-fresh fingers sliding into his hair.

'I was at a hotel with her. She kept talking about you and telling me things, stories from the past, and I felt so close to you. She knew all these things, like what colour your baby clothes were, what milkshake you drank, the kids who bullied you because of the way you walked.' I wrap a protective hand around my hip, as if it has been offended. I hear *Bison* in my head, the voice of Robert Kneel, the grunting of his buddies, the snorting and whinnying as I get close. 'It was like all the things I ever wanted to know about you were right there on offer. I had the answers. It was like she was you, and I got confused.'

'You expect me to believe you thought it was me? That you got *confused*?' At that moment the ring slips from my finger. I slam it down on the table.

'She kissed me, and I let her. You look alike, you know. Not superficially, but you do. You have the same Cupid's bow,' he says as he raises a finger to his lips, traces the triangle beneath his nose. 'And your ear lobe. It curls at the back the same way.' When I can't bring myself to look at him, he drops his head. 'But then she told me that I was better off with her. That I should stay with her. Do all the things I wanted but that you wouldn't do. Like kids. That she would give me what you wouldn't. That she would marry me, and you never would. I figured you must have told her about not wanting kids, because I hadn't mentioned anything that personal.'

'I never told her about not wanting kids.'

'Well, she knew. She knows you better than you think.' He grabs a towel, wipes the soap from his hands. 'I got up to leave. She started shouting, screaming at me that I was just like all the rest. That she would ruin me to make me pay. That she would make you leave me. She started telling lies about how you had been fucking around. But I left. I left straight away.'

I try to stop myself crying, but I can't. I shake when I cry, so I wrap my arms around my chest and try to stem the movement. Part of it is guilt, knowing that she told him the truth and he didn't believe her. Some of it is anger. But mainly it is sadness. Something else coming to an end. 'She had a lot to say considering you left straight away,' I stutter. 'To manage to say all that as you stormed out would have been quite something.' He hangs his head in shame and I know I am on to something. 'Did you have to get dressed? Is that why she had all that time? All those threats and accusations thrown out while you had your fucking trousers around your ankles?'

He picks up the ring and fingers it for a while, knowing that hope, and that last chance, has been lost. He slips it in his pocket. He must have envisioned tonight so differently. He looks up at me, tears streaming down his soapy face, and nods his head.

Fact. Antonio is a liar.

32

'You have one hour,' I say as I walk away, straight up the stairs with big, false-confident strides. I want to get away from him, because I am sure that with the slightest effort he could break me. With only a little bit of pleading I would beg him to stay. I might have treated him badly, cut him out over the years, but when it comes to being alone, I would do anything to avoid it.

'Rini, please. I won't just go. Not before you talk to me.'

He has said this a few times. From my barricade in the bathroom I can hear him shuffling about in the hallway. When it goes quiet, I press my ear up to the door, listening out for a hint that he is still there. When I hear the floorboards creak, or hear his body move against the door, I flinch back, pleased that he hasn't gone and yet too proud to ask him to stay. If I had a girlfriend to call for help, that friend who drops everything when you need her, maybe I wouldn't feel so alone. Maybe if she were to suggest I kick him to the kerb, or *once a cheater, always a cheater*, I would nod my head with dignity and never speak to him again. But I don't have that friend. And besides, that's not who I really think Antonio is. I think the same has happened to him that happened to me. He got caught up in Elle's promises and in her world. Got lost somewhere between fantasy and reality, and is now struggling to find his way back.

'Rini, please talk to me.' He knocks lightly. I hear him slump against the door, and his body blocks the flash of light from underneath it. It is not hard to see how she lured him in with promises of getting closer to me.

I am lying on the bathmat when I hear knocking on the front door. I must have fallen asleep, cried out to the point of exhaustion. I look at my watch and realise that I have been here for nearly two hours. I hear Antonio – still there, bless him – trailing down the stairs to answer the door. When I hear that it is DC Forrester and DC McGuire, I swallow my pride, remember what she told me at the station regarding Antonio's exploits in Scotland. I take one quick look in the mirror, realise there is no amount of sprucing I can do to make me look like I haven't been crying, and head downstairs.

When I arrive in the sitting room, it appears that they are waiting for me.

'Hello again, Dr Harringford.' Forrester smiles at me, but I can't make out whether it is genuine or not. She is getting better at this. Perhaps just getting better at reading me, learning how to act.

'Hello,' I whisper from a croaky throat, scratched by all my screaming. I see them glance around at the untouched drinks on the table, the ring box still on the couch where Antonio left it, the red wine stains splashed up the wall.

'Celebration?' she asks, eyeing up the box, and then my bare ring finger. She looks up at Antonio and I follow her gaze. His face is swollen and red. There is no doubt that we have both been crying. 'Obviously not. Well, I'm sorry to interrupt. It's just there are a few things we would like to talk to you about, Mr Molinaro.'

'With me?' he asks.

'What about?' I say at the same time, as if I don't know. Neither of them looks at me.

'Perhaps you would rather do this at the station, Mr Molinaro?' DC McGuire asks.

Antonio shakes his head. 'No. Anything I have to say, I can say it here.' He glances at me in a last-ditch attempt to look honest. As if he wants me to know that he has already admitted everything.

'Very well,' says McGuire.

'Mr Molinaro,' says Forrester, motioning for us all to sit. I do as she asks. 'Can you account for your whereabouts over the last week?'

'I was here for most of it.' He snatches a glance at me, as if telling me to brace myself. 'Before that I was in Horton. With Eleanor Harringford.'

'So you admit to being with Miss Harringford?' Forrester looks to McGuire, purses her lips in a surprised fashion.

'Yes.'

'And to being at her house? *Mam Tor*, Horton,' she says as she flicks through her small pad. 'Eleanor and Irini's family home.'

'You were at the house?' I ask, breaking my silence.

'Yes,' he says to me, and then repeats, 'Yes,' for the police. 'I was there.'

DC Forrester flicks through a few pages and adjusts her position to get comfortable. Antonio's cheeks are flushed, but the rest of his face is sickly white, the shine of a fever glossing over his skin. 'In which case, you'll not be surprised to learn that somebody fitting your description was seen there on two separate occasions. Once with Eleanor, and once alone. A white Jeep was also seen. The description matches a vehicle parked outside this property. I'll assume it is yours unless you tell me otherwise.' She closes her pad and slips it into a suit pocket. DC McGuire takes over.

'The witness gave a good description of the man in question. Do you think it could have been you?'

'I don't know. It might have been,' he says as he looks at me again.

'Did you stay the night?' DC McGuire asks.

Antonio shuffles in his seat before eventually saying, 'No, no. I didn't,' but we all know he is lying.

'We have an inventory of the house from your family's lawyer, Dr Harringford,' Forrester says, looking to me. 'It would seem your father was well organised when it came to his possessions. Knew where everything was. Had a safe full of jewellery, too. You know what, Mr Molinaro? That safe is empty now. Not a dot in it. Pearls, gold, diamonds. You know anything about that?' Antonio shakes his head. 'There was a diamond ring in there. Belonged to Dr Harringford's mother,' she says, looking at the red box. 'Mind showing me what's in there?'

'There's nothing in there,' I say, chipping in. I picture the bistro he wants to own, the loan that might not yet have been approved. The diamond in his pocket.

'I have a picture of the ring. Here.' DC McGuire pulls a few photographs from his pocket, selecting the right one.

There is a stamp on it that reads *Witherrington & Co.,* but it is the image that stands out as he holds it up for us to see: the same tiny diamond that was on my finger only a couple of hours ago.

'Elle gave me the jewellery,' Antonio admits. 'It's in the car. She was angry, she said it was hers.' He points to me. 'That everything was hers, thanks to their father.'

'Only Miss Eleanor Harringford isn't around to back up that claim, is she, Mr Molinaro? What we have found are signs of a struggle in her bedroom. Broken glass on the floor, sheets crumpled from where more than one person rolled around in them.' DC McGuire pauses, before adding, 'We found traces of blood and semen.'

'It's not what you think,' says Antonio to me, not paying any attention to the police.

'You might be surprised at what I think, Antonio,' I say. I'm not sure how much I believe. Truth that comes out at moments like this is always tempered, the dangerous edges smoothed off, details forgotten on purpose. I don't doubt that a good forensics expert could trace him to that bedroom, but I do doubt that he has hurt Elle. Any struggle would have been consensual.

'Mr Molinaro, we have cross-checked the blood with Miss Harringford's health records. It was her blood on the sheets, and we believe you were the last person to see her before she disappeared.' They step towards him, DC McGuire pulling a set of cuffs from his belt. He dangles them, showing Antonio that using them is an option. 'On that basis, I am arresting you in connection with the disappearance of Miss Eleanor Harringford.'

My ears fuzz over, and I watch as they attach the cuffs. Antonio is staring at me, mouthing something. I try to fight my way back, desperate to hear the last words he will ever say to me. Because this is it. Whether he did it or not, Elle has found her latest victim. But I don't hear anything, and only a second later the police have manhandled him through the front door.

33

The night out in the club just before I went to university was the beginning of the end for me and Elle. Up until that point I'd wanted her near, craved her despite the instability she brought with her. But by the end of that night I knew that desire was drawing to a close.

What I told Antonio about that night wasn't exactly a lie. I woke up as she was being kicked out of the club. She was causing a scene, and shouting about the injustice of it all. The bit I left out was about the man who was with her.

I followed behind as they stumbled along, her boob tube askew, her hot pants riding up higher than intended. He was there at her side, edging her forward, helping her stand. It wasn't quite a cuddle, and he wasn't laughing. There was an uncomfortable level of control, like he had hold of her. She kept apologising to him, saying she was sorry if she had ruined his plans. He was smiling and friendly, but I got the impression he was the kind of charmer who had loads of friends who all believed him to be a nice guy, but who behind closed doors would regularly beat his wife.

'You're going to need to wait here, all right?' he said to

me as Elle ate a kebab and chips. I was sitting opposite her in the cheap takeaway restaurant. He was standing next to us, somehow managing to block our way out. I nodded my head to agree to his terms. I was only eighteen and low on confidence. I wouldn't have dared disagree. 'Elle has some work to do.'

She looked up at me, just an eyeball really, from where she was slumped on the table. It might have been imperceptible to him, but regardless he grabbed her arm and pulled her to her feet. She was still high, that was for sure, but not enough to deaden how she really felt. I was gripped by this overwhelming knowledge that I should be stopping her, and yet I said and did nothing. She shovelled a handful of chips into her mouth, adjusted her boob tube and very softly stroked her hand across my cheek.

'Won't be long,' she said, and for a moment I thought she was going to cry.

I watched as they left. Just before they disappeared from view, I saw him slap her across the face. I jumped up from my seat, my intention to help, but he saw me. He pointed his finger and mouthed the words *Wait there*, and I did exactly as he said.

She came back about an hour later without him. She grabbed me by the arm and marched me out like a parent retrieving a wayward child. She didn't speak for another hour, not even when I asked her if she was all right. She just kept snivelling, crying, hyperventilating. I didn't know what to do so I suggested we go home, but she refused. She looked dishevelled, her hair knotted, her mascara smudged. As another hour passed, us sitting on the edge of the kerb, watching cars go by, I realised that her eye was starting to swell. Her lip too. When she flicked her hair back from her neck there was a bruise just below her ear, something that resembled a love bite.

'Elle, please talk to me.' I edged a little closer and dared rest a hand on her arm. She flinched, but she didn't push me away. 'Are you all right?'

She wiped away a tear, took a swallow of watery Coke, spilling some of it down her front. 'No, Rini.' She turned to face me. Her pupils were black like a shark's, so large I could barely see her irises. 'I'm not all right.'

Relieved to have an answer and to know that something at least was wrong, I pushed further. 'Who was that man?' I let my arm rest across her shoulders and she surprised me by nestling her head on to mine. 'Where did he take you?'

'He's a good man,' she sniffed. 'He gives me stuff. Stuff I need.' I was naive about a lot of things, but I had seen them together in the club. I knew what kind of stuff he was giving her.

'I don't think he is,' I whispered. 'He's your dealer, isn't he? You don't need that stuff. It doesn't help.'

'I wish he *was* my dealer.' She started crying again, picked up a handful of cold kebab and threw it into the road. 'What would you know, little goody two-shoes? I don't have anything else.' I turned to her as she looked at me, her big doll-eyed pupils and pink hair, and watched a tear roll down her cheek. 'I don't even have you any more.'

'What do you mean?' I tried to joke, but we both knew. I would be gone soon, a new life at university.

'You're leaving, remember. You'll meet new people. How

will I ever discover the truth if you're not here with me?' She nuzzled in, kissed me on my neck. It was just a peck here and there, nothing too weird, yet still it was enough for me to edge back. 'You see,' she said, disappointed. 'Even that freaks you out.'

The following day I was watching children's BBC with a headache when somebody knocked on the door. I opened it to find the man from the night before standing there in a white suit, the jacket big at the waist, double pockets. His hair was a dirty blond, and it was slicked back to reveal an unfortunate male-pattern hair loss. It made him appear as if he had one giant widow's peak. My first thought was that I wished Elle was awake.

'Irini, babe. Can I come in?' He was perhaps my first brush with adulthood outside of my immediate family, and I didn't want to appear childish. So I stood back, let him pass. He waltzed up the windowless hallway as if he was in the market to buy the place, his hands tucked in his pockets, nodding as he glanced around. There wasn't much to see, just a dusty old mirror and a picture of a countryside duck pond. He turned back, smiled, and walked through to the lounge. I quietly closed the front door, praying that Elle would wake up soon.

'Can I make you a cup of tea?' I offered from my position of safety in the doorway to the living room. He was already sitting in the armchair, flicking through the channels of the television and holding a cigarette between his fingers. He eventually settled on an episode of *Sweet Valley High*, and seemed disappointed that it was finishing. The coverage of the Ashes series was about to start.

'I love that show, don't you?' he asked as he swung around to face me, pointing at the television with the remote. 'Which one do you think is prettier, Jessica or Elizabeth?'

I wasn't much of a *Sweet Valley High* fan, and wasn't even sure which twin was which. But I felt an urge to answer, as if it was necessary, though I also knew there was a distinct possibility that my answer could be wrong.

'I guess Elizabeth,' I said as I moved through the living room and into the kitchen. Halfway there, he joined me, blocking the doorway just enough so that I had to squeeze past. I caught a whiff of cigarettes on his breath. I was close enough to see the pimples on his nose. I dodged past, grabbed the kettle and filled it with water, set it on the side to boil.

'You're probably right,' he said, leaning against the wall, dragging on his cigarette. 'But that other one is a minx. I bet she'd fuck like a professional.'

I didn't know what to say. I could hear the intro music starting in the background so I suggested, 'The cricket is about to start,' hoping that he was the kind of man who watched it. Uncle Marcus was, and that was all I had to go on.

'So it is,' he said, turning around to take a look. 'But Thorpe was out before we even got started, and the Aussies have won the first three tests. What's the point?' He watched as the players came out while I rustled up two cups of tea.

'Sugar?' I asked. He was still leaning on the door frame. I had no other way out. I tried to remember that Elle had told me he was a good man. But it seemed so hard to believe.

He chuckled to himself and dropped his cigarette on the floor. I smelt a whiff of burning carpet before he ground it out with his foot. 'I don't remember saying I wanted a cup of tea.'

'Sorry, I just assumed . . .' I stirred a large spoonful of sugar into my own cup, as loudly as I could in the distant hope that Elle would wake up. But she hadn't surfaced before midday any day this week, and after last night's efforts I doubted I'd see her until the evening. As he walked towards me I kept asking myself, if he wasn't her dealer, then what was he? He looked like a dealer, at least how I imagined a dealer to be. 'I just thought when you didn't say no . . .' I said, but I let the sentence drift into nothing. He stopped just short of where I was standing. I gripped my tea as tightly as I could.

'Well, let this be a little life lesson. If somebody doesn't say they want something, it doesn't necessarily mean they don't want it. Do you get me?'

I could feel my heart racing. He was tall, and standing right next to me, he towered over me by a good foot. 'I'm not sure I do.'

'Well let me make it clear. Did I tell you that I wanted a cup of tea?' He stepped forward, one foot either side of mine. I could feel his body up against me, and my hip was throbbing. I shook my head. 'And did you tell that boy from the club you wanted him to fuck you a couple of weeks ago? No? Exactly,' he said as he picked up the second cup and sipped. 'I take one sugar.'

I struggled to turn, still confused, but managed to grab the sugar bowl and drop a spoonful into his tea. How did he know what had happened?

The talking on the television had stopped, and all I could

hear was the deep clunk as bat struck ball. He hadn't taken his eyes off me once. He put his cup back down behind me, then took mine and set it on the side next to his.

'Shall we go into the living room?' I asked. 'Watch some telly?'

'Is that what you want?' I nodded, although I wasn't sure what I wanted, other than to get away from him. But he shook his head. 'Don't you remember? People don't always say what they want.'

With that he brought one foot between my feet and kicked my legs apart. I knew what was coming, and that it wouldn't be like the first time. I didn't want my second time to be with this man. My mind raced to the knives, the forks, a frying pan. What could I hit him with to make my escape? I reached for the nearest drawer and managed to pull it open. But he struck his fist against the back of my hand, slamming the drawer closed. I yelped in pain.

'I don't want this,' I said, trying to push him away. But he was too strong. 'Elle will be awake soon.' I didn't know if bargaining with my sister was acceptable, but it was all I had.

'Maybe. Maybe not,' he said with a smile on his face. 'Maybe I'm not interested in Elle. You'd fetch a nice price yourself now that you've been broken in, you know that?' He grabbed my cheeks and forced my lips up into an abstract smile. 'See, you like it. You want it.'

He tugged at my pyjama top, something with a Forever Friends bear on it. One breast escaped, but I managed to grab the material and pull it back down. He slapped me hard across the face and I screamed.

'Who are you screaming for? There's nobody here to help you,' he spat in my ear. I could feel the wetness of his lips. He pushed himself against me and there it was, the bulge between his legs, digging against my hip.

'Elle,' I screamed, but he just laughed.

'You think she'll wake up after what she took last night?' He pushed me backwards and yanked at my shorts. But what he didn't know was that I wasn't screaming for Elle. I was screaming because she was already there.

He felt the knife as she jabbed it at his neck, and backed off. I screamed again when I saw the trickle of blood running from the tip of the blade, dripping on to the collar of his white suit.

'Now relax, Elle,' he pleaded. 'I was just fucking around.'

He held his hands up in surrender, but Elle didn't care. She reached back and grabbed the kettle, and before he could push past her, she had showered him with the contents, his skin instantly pink as the hot water washed across his face. Then she smacked him over the head with it, so hard it smashed into several pieces. He fell to his knees, crying out in pain. That was when I noticed that his belt and flies were already undone. She had saved me.

'Elle, thank you—' I began, stepping towards her. But she swung around, narrowly missing me with the knife. 'Elle, watch it. Be careful.' The blade was only inches from my face. Why would she threaten me? What had I done? I pushed myself back against the counter. Somewhere in the distance I could hear applause.

'You think you can fuck my boyfriend, huh?' She lowered the knife, pointing it right at my chest. I swallowed hard as

I tried to back away, but there was nowhere else to go.

'No, Elle. I never—' but she didn't let me finish.

'Oh no, Elle,' she mocked. 'I never wanted to do it. He was forcing himself on me.' She jabbed the knife forward but not close enough to touch me. 'You think you can leave me and take everything I have left with you?' I looked down at the man she was claiming as her boyfriend. He was rolling on the floor, whimpering rather than moaning, trying to stagger to his feet. She kicked him once in the head and I immediately thought of her dead dog. He dropped to the ground, out cold.

'He *was* forcing me,' I protested, and she jabbed at me again with the knife, this time just catching my arm, drawing a prick of blood. I snatched my arm away and saw the smile spread across her face as I winced, clutching at the wound, warm blood pooling beneath my fingers. Now I was crying. 'He was trying to—'

'Don't you say it. I'll fucking stick you with this, I promise you. Just like you did to that Margot Wolfe.' She waved the knife at my face, so close I could see my reflection in the blade. 'She deserved it too. Just like you will. I'll fucking slaughter you if you go near him again.'

He groaned once more, distracting her for a split second, and I slipped past her, grabbed my bag and ran. I had to get away. I could finally see that while she might have been the one person who always wanted me, she was also the one person who was always there when something went wrong. For every mistake, every incident, every time that I or somebody else got hurt, Elle was right there to orchestrate it. I couldn't let her keep that power over me any more. I had to take it back. The last thing I heard before I slipped out of the door was his moaning, and her promising him that she was going to do worse than kill him.

I didn't even stay long enough to change my clothes, preferring instead to run out in my Forever Friend pyjamas, smeared with blood from my cut arm. I didn't care that there were people watching from their windows. I left for university that day, believing that if I stayed, she would kill me, either now or later. I have been running ever since.

34

I watch like a nosy neighbour from the window as a team searches Antonio's car, while DC Forrester and DC McGuire escort him away. Another team comes in, searches the house. They tell me that somebody will be back the next day to take a further statement. With my permission they take files of paperwork and my computer, items of Antonio's like the new coat he purchased. I can imagine the nearby curtain-twitchers watching from the shadows, making up stories. Maybe they think he has killed me. They are probably expecting a couple of uniformed officers to turn up, tape off the entrance. They'll sit there for hours waiting for the body bag to be carried out. That's what we do, us humans. We wait for the negativity to flare up in somebody else's life and then sit back and watch the show, voyeuristic fucks that we are.

It's only now that I realise how strange it is that I never saw Elle's room in that house. But I can imagine it; in fact I haven't stopped since the police let out the snippet of information about what they found there. I picture a big double bed, everything that is usually neat and orderly pulled out of place. Sheets full of wrinkles, the way my bed always looked on the nights when I couldn't sleep for questions about my parents. Perhaps a row of teddy bears in various states of collapse, a few fallen to the floor, kicked there by stray impassioned feet. A water jug like my father's, smashed. Glass on the floor. I imagine the room dated as if it belongs to a fifty-year-old woman with saggy tits and menopausal sweats. The crumpled sheets covered in traces of blood and semen.

I attack my own bed like it is to blame, pulling the sheets from it so hard that one of them tears. I ram them into the washing machine, put them on a ninety-degree wash. I kick a standard lamp next to the couch and it falls over, the bulb smashing on the floor. The electrics fizz a bit until they eventually give up. I pick up the ring box and toss it across the room. It strikes the wall before falling, landing on the edge of the waste-paper bin before dropping to the floor.

I grab a CD, something angry by Metallica, and get wasted on a bottle of bourbon I find in the cupboard. Within a few songs my throat is burning from too many cigarettes, a stacked-up ashtray growing at my side. I fall asleep, but not for long enough for the night to creep away or the sun to rise.

When I wake, I splash my face with cold water. My mind wanders to Antonio held at the police station, and I force myself on to a different track. I need to find Elle to prove that he had nothing to do with her disappearance. I can't let him become another one of her victims. Because I know he didn't hurt her. There was only one place the blood could have come from. The only thing he is really guilty of.

I grab my keys and the copy of my father's will. I don't want to wait for a flight, so I drive, my AA road atlas circa 1997 on the passenger seat of my red Fiesta. I never bought a satellite navigation system, never having wanted to find my way anywhere badly enough. I was never heading towards anything; happy always to be moving in the direction of *away*.

I suppose this is why Antonio was sucked in by Elle. If you push somebody away for long enough, your connection to them gets frayed. Then one day it snaps like a broken thread, and somebody else takes hold of the end and draws you in. All anybody wants is to belong. I can understand that. Perhaps this is why I don't feel angry with him. But maybe it's just because of my guilt.

One of the first times I remember feeling guilty was at Aunt Jemima's house. She was dishing up dinner, all of us sitting at the table waiting. It was quiche, potatoes, peas. She segmented the quiche and began serving it on to our plates. She served Uncle Marcus, then my cousins, Jinny, Kate, Nicola, and then . . . oh! She had cut it into five. Three cousins, two parents and me, that made six. You'd think six portions would have been easier. Five required a lot more thought. I watched as she scooped up the portioned food under heavy protest, uttering some excuse about the middle not being cooked through. I knew she had forgotten about me, a fact confirmed when the quiche returned chopped up into cubes, from which we all got a helping. I felt guilty for the inconvenience, ashamed of my intrusion, the idea that I didn't belong. I was an afterthought, someone who was not supposed to be there.

After an hour on the motorway with a belly full of nausea, I pull over into the first service station, go to the toilets and throw up. It doesn't come naturally. I crouch, my hip painful because the air is damp and I have been stuck in a car, and stick my fingers to the back of my throat, bringing out whatever is in my stomach. Afterwards I sit on the edge of the seat and inspect a scrap of tissue speckled with flecks of Warholian vomit.

I pull the edge of my trousers down, look at my hip. It looks swollen, the scars buzzing, bright red like they always are when it gets painful. As if something inside is trying to burst out, break through the seal. I splash my face with cold water, and then wet a wad of tissue and press it against the scars. It cools the area down, helps. I check in my bag for Valium, but it's just habit really because I know I don't have any. My last bottle was swallowed by my father, and I haven't yet been back to work.

I head to the shop, grab the first food item I find – crackers and soft cheese – and buy it. I order a coffee and a sandwich, knowing it will be several hours before I arrive at my destination, and the ache in my stomach needs food. I munch on the crackers, flicking the radio stations as I travel through county after county with the windows down, registering the signs as I pass from Buckinghamshire to Oxfordshire, Staffordshire to Cheshire. The familiarity of the warm concrete fades, giving way to pastures of green and an imperfect landscape of hills and dales and distant mountains as daylight creeps in. As I return. The smell of wet grass ripples into the car as I pass into Scotland.

By the time I reach the exit for Horton, a carpet of crumbs covers the passenger seat and my black jumper. As I pass *Mam Tor*, the mother mountain that was my parents' house – not *my* house – I stare dead ahead, force myself not to look. An early fog lingers in the fields. The weather has changed; autumn has arrived in Horton. I wait for the interruptions to the greenery: the houses, the church, the school. All there, just as I expected, as if nothing has changed.

Exactly two weeks after I watched them bury my mother, I park the car, pull it on to the side of the road next to the church in a haphazard fashion, like I'm setting up for a 4 x 4 car show. The windy journey has done me good, cleared my head. I check my face in the mirror, certain that the hangover pallor that confronted me in the service station must have passed. Not quite, but I don't look as bad. Nothing that a good drink can't fix, so I head over to the Enchanted Swan, leaving the memories and mists of early morning behind.

It's quiet inside the pub, and I pull up a stool, which rocks on the uneven floor. I eye up Mr Riley, the landlord, and motion to the optics with a nod of the head. He checks the watch strapped to his fat wrist. His ruddy face is kind, Celtic no doubt, his hair what people call strawberry blonde, bright like gentle fire. He balances his weight on the bar, propped up by his two more-than-steady hands. Then he realises that he recognises me.

'Back again? I saw you only a couple of weeks ago.' I assume he is going to tell me that I resemble my mother, but he actually seems to remember me from my first visit. I was more than a little tipsy that night. 'Are you new here? I don't remember seeing any properties for sale.'

I consider who I could be. Mrs Jackson with the kids, maybe? A holidaymaker on an extended stay? A traveller on her way back from wherever it was she was travelling to? But what's the point? 'My name is Irini Harringford,' I say, realising that if ever I am to find the truth, or Elle, I have to start being honest with the people I meet. And with myself.

He steps back. Now he sees the resemblance. 'You look—'

'Just like my mother? Yes, I've been hearing that a lot lately.' I nod again towards the optics on the wall. 'Are you serving?'

'It's a bit early for it.' After a second longer to consider me, he grabs a tumbler, completes a fancy spin with a flick of his wrist I didn't expect. Seems out of place in this tiny village pub. He holds up the glass to the row of spirits. 'What'll it be?'

'Anything brown,' I say, and watch as he empties a double measure of Glenfiddich into the glass. He scoops up some ice, but I bat my hand to show him that I want it straight. 'How much?' I ask, keen to make the payment now so that at any point when I have had enough I can make a quick getaway.

'On the house.' He picks up a beer towel and mops the counter before me, then leans back, crosses his arms across a big, overfed gut. 'I'm sorry to hear about your father. Must be hard to lose both parents in such a short space of time.'

'Wasn't so hard,' I say as I swirl my whisky into a whirl-pool. When he looks for a further explanation, I say, 'We were estranged.'

He goes back to mopping the bar top, his gaze fixed on me. 'Yeah, I remember. Talk of the village you were at one point. Weren't nobody who didn't know about the little Harringford girl who disappeared. It was a terrible time for the family.'

'I didn't exactly disappear,' I say, taking a good glug of the fine spirit. 'I was given away.'

'I know, I know. I guess she just couldn't cope, what with

that sister of yours.' He snorts, almost a giggle, as if he has remembered something that amuses him. 'What a tearaway she was. Hair all colours, nose rings.' He quietens his voice as if there is a pub full of people to overhear. I even look around in case somebody else has slipped in. It is still empty. It's only just 11 a.m. 'Not what we're used to up here. Quite the taste for men, too.'

'Yeah, I heard that.' I take another glug and he eyes me with caution, as if he regrets offering me a double. 'It's her that seems to have disappeared now. And I really need to find her.'

An internal door bursts open and a little wisp of a woman clatters through dragging a vacuum cleaner. She smiles at us, straightens her tabard before heading into the snug. Riley thinks for a moment, perhaps assessing what harm it could do to talk to me – it happens when people know that crazy runs in your family – then props himself up on the bar with his elbows. He waits for the cleaner to turn on the vacuum cleaner and then starts talking.

'The police have been all over the village. Asking questions, snoopin' in bins. I caught one fishin' through the waste out back of the pub. Sent him away with his tail between his legs, but I told them others what they wanted to hear.' He stares off into thin air for a moment, tosses the beer towel back to the bar.

'What was it they wanted to hear?' I ask.

'If anybody had seen her. I saw her all right. Out there in the graveyard. Acting right strange she was.' I remember now that he was the one who called Joyce.

'What was she doing exactly?'

'Well, I put it down to the fact that she'd lost her mother and then her father within a few days of each other.' He picks up a big bag of nuts and fills a near-empty jar on the bar. 'That'd be enough to send anybody crackers. Still, I told Joyce about it, and she must've called the police.'

'So you think she was crackers?'

His eyebrows shoot up sky high, as if they're trying to make an escape from his face. I'm under no illusion what he thinks.

'Miss, with all due respect, everybody around here knows your sister is crackers. I heard she even spent some time as a child in Fair Fields.'

'What's Fair Fields?'

He looks around again to check nobody is there, then beckons me close. 'Old hospital. For the infirm and mentally insane,' he says, as if reading from a script. 'That place you can see in the distance from the road. Looks a bit like an old church.'

The place that Elle hates. 'Did you tell the police that?'

'Tell them what? That I heard a rumour? You can't be selling rumour off as fact when it comes to the police, lassie.' He looks at me like I am a naive little girl out on a treasure hunt, but then obviously is hit by an attack of pity. 'I'm not sure it would make any difference even if I did tell them.'

'I think it would.'

I knock back the last drops of whisky and hold up the glass. I pull a ten-pound note from my bag and slide it across the bar. Against his better judgement he fills the glass, and I take another sip. He doesn't touch the money. The smell hits me right between the eyes, the liquor burning my throat.

It feels warm in here, and I realise now as I hear crackling in the background that there is a log fire burning.

'So what was she doing in the graveyard to make you think she was acting strange? I mean, strange for a crazy person.' I flash him an asymmetrical smile that I hope he takes in good humour. He does.

'It was late, getting dark. Way past dusk. I could hear wailing. It had been a quiet night; it was raining, so not a lot of people were in. I popped my head out the door to investigate the noise, and I see Elle, your sister,' he adds for clarity, in case I wasn't sure, 'running around in circles wearing not much more than a sports bra. Bucketing down, it was.'

A couple of men, regulars by the looks of it, come into the bar. Mr Riley checks his watch then points at me, insinuating that I should wait a moment while he pulls their pints. A minute later he is back.

'So where was I?'

'Running in the rain.'

'That's right. So I step back inside, pick up a raincoat and make to head over there. But then I spot a man with her. He has a car, engine running; trying to coax her into it, he is. I figured it was just another bloke of hers, and that she was all right because she had company. Liked the fellas, that one. Last I saw he was helping guide her into the passenger seat.'

'What kind of car was it?'

'Not sure. A white one, four by four.' Jeep. Grand Cherokee. Antonio's. The one the police confiscated last night and found full of jewellery that had once belonged to my mother. 'Next thing I know, the police are up here takin' statements.'

I smile and thank him, pick up my drink and knock it back. Just as I stand up to leave he says, 'The house was crawling with police for the last few days, but they've left now. If she was going to turn up anywhere, I wouldn't be surprised if it was there.'

Outside, the air hits me, and there is still that sensation of nausea in my gut as I look across the fields to the old hospital where Elle once supposedly stayed, just visible through the low-lying mist. The whisky hasn't helped at all, not like I thought it would. But I swallow down the nausea, try to focus, and take my first steps towards the school. My priority is to see Miss Endicott, find out what it was she wanted to tell me.

'Irini Harringford to see Miss Endicott,' I say as I walk into the reception, my words out before the door is even closed. The receptionist looks at me over her glasses. She is a different woman from before, doesn't recognise me. Not at first, anyway. But then her mouth slowly curls open, her shoulders drop. 'Harringfo—' I begin to repeat, but she stops me halfway through.

'Yes, I heard you. Harringford.' The name is obviously still fresh in people's minds. 'You look just like her.'

I pull my jumper cuffs down over my hands, turn my face away.

'I came to see Miss Endicott,' I say, not altogether kindly. I take a seat on the nearest undersized chair, stare at the children's self-portraits that still adorn the walls. The receptionist stands to make her way to Miss Endicott's office, but stops halfway. The schoolmistress heard me arrive and is already on her way out.

'You'd better come through,' she says as she beckons to me.

Her office is large, oversized like her calves. She takes me by the arm to guide me into the nearest grown-up seat, avoiding the row of child-sized chairs, pastel colours lined up along the wall like a row of chewy sweets. Above them there is an ABC chart, letters made out of curly snakes, flowers and beach equipment. She leaves the door to swing closed, giving it an extra push to ensure it is shut before heading to a nearby side table with complex wooden legs. She pours me a coffee from a warmer without asking me if I would like one.

'You look like you could do with it,' she says with a smile as she sets it down on the desk. She assumes position in the chair opposite me, folds and then unfolds her arms. After a moment of discomfort she stands up, drags a spare visitor's chair next to mine and pulls a bottle of Scotch from a small cupboard under the desk. She pours a measure into her own coffee and then leans over and drops a splash into mine. She smiles, but there is no happiness on her face. 'You look like you could do with that too. Hair of the dog.' She lights a cigarette and offers me one. I take it, but then set it down on the desk. Feels wrong to smoke in here.

'Miss Endicott, let's not pretend like we did the first time I was here. You know who I am, and you told me that you had something important to tell me. What is it?'

'I seem to remember the only one doing any pretending was you, *Mrs Jackson.*' She drags on the cigarette, lets a little of the smoke go, gulps the rest down. I reach for mine and light it. 'But let's put that behind us. You look like you have been awake all night. And I can't tell you that the smell of alcohol on your breath is altogether subtle.' I pull my lips in tight, trying to stifle the smell. I realise I haven't cleaned my teeth since I was sick, and then I ate the cheesy crackers. I gulp at the coffee, hoping to disguise the reek. 'Are you sure you don't want to go home and get some rest? We can meet later.'

'I'm not sure where you think home is, Miss Endicott, but it certainly isn't nearby. I have driven for seven hours to get here. I'm looking for answers. And my sister.' I rub at my hip and she watches my every move. 'The police have arrested my boyfriend in connection with Elle's disappearance. They think she might have been harmed, but I know my boyfriend didn't hurt her. In fact, I doubt anybody did.' She drags again on the cigarette, and in spite of my breath, I move in closer. 'I need to try to understand what is going on.'

'Irini, your sister is a very troubled young lady. I have known her since she was small, and she was always the same. I'm sorry for the mysterious message, but as soon as I saw you here at the school, I knew you were the daughter they gave away.'

'And yet you didn't say anything,' I point out, looking as sad as I might have done on the very day I was handed over. 'You let me pretend to be Mrs Jackson.' In this moment I feel pretty stupid. Having pretended to be somebody else, even though I have years of practice at it, feels so degrading.

'What was the point of saying anything?' She concentrates on straightening out a pleat in her fine cotton-weave skirt.

'The fact that I knew who you were didn't change anything. You were still the Harringford child that was given away, and your mother was still dead.' Perhaps abashed at the harshness with which she stated the most painful facts of my life, she adds, 'I figured it would only make you uncomfortable.' She wasn't wrong, and I am grateful. A brief smile flashes across my face.

'Why tell me now?'

'Because now things have changed. I heard you inherited the house. Elle won't let that lie, you know that. Let her have it, and be grateful they gave you away when they did.'

Let her have it? Be grateful? Being grateful for what happened to me didn't even cross my mind until a couple of weeks ago, and only then because I saw how dysfunctional my family really was. Miss Endicott is an outsider, a bit player. Somebody who sat in the back row at my mother's funeral. But to make such a statement she must be privy to something, and I have to know what it is.

I take a sip of the coffee. 'Do you know why they gave me away?'

'Of course, my dear.' She almost chuckles at first, but when she realises that she is the only one laughing, she turns to me, her face serious and puzzled. 'Do you not?'

'No. I have been looking for answers all my life.' I guzzle down the tepid coffee. I am certain there is a definitive answer coming my way, like the last scene in *Murder, She Wrote* when the cast comes together and the solution to the crime is announced. Yet Miss Endicott's thought processes appear stymied by my ignorance, and she is stumbling for words.

'Well, it was . . .' she begins, but falls short of a full sentence. She breathes hard, tries to focus. 'It was in many ways a simple decision on their part. Your sister was a difficult child, both at home and at school. She was very troubled, spent some time in psychiatric care. Everybody knew that. Horton is a small place. But when the time came for her to return home, they realised they couldn't raise both you and your sister. They tried, but it was obvious that it wouldn't work. Elle needed a special sort of care.'

'Yes, I know about that, although the police seem to think she has no history of mental health problems. There is nothing on record.'

'Of course there isn't, dear. There was quite a stigma back then. It was a private hospital and the records remained confidential.' She looks away, bashful. 'Things were different in those days.'

'I think it was a place called Fair Fields,' I say. 'The large building you can see from almost anywhere in the village. But that still doesn't really explain why they gave me away.'

She offers me another splash of whisky, but I refuse. 'You're right, that is where Elle spent some time. As a young teacher I offered to lead a couple of classes over there. Just occasionally, mind, and it was never what one might call official.'

'You taught her?'

'Once or twice. A long time ago.' She adds a couple of measures to her own cup, but doesn't go on to top it up with coffee. 'You were a victim of circumstance, Irini. Your parents agonised while you were at home with them, waiting for your sister to return. She was institutionalised for over a year, might have been two. They knew you couldn't stay together. They had to make a decision.' She returns to her skirt, finds another offending fold out of line.

'But still, why me? If she was crazy and I was good, why not send her away?'

'Because nobody would take her. Your mother was distraught.' She drains the coffee cup. 'She loved you dearly, both of you, in whatever way it was that Elle could be loved. They were trying to protect you, hoping that they could at least give you a stable life in a stable family. They couldn't just leave Elle to fend for herself. They feared for her.'

She looks away, pours herself another shot of whisky and knocks it straight back. I wonder how she will ever manage to teach with so much liquor on board.

'I shouldn't say this, Irini, but your sister was a deeply unlovable child. She was spiteful. Vile to other children, her hatred towards them obvious. I saw it during the teaching sessions. The way she would look at them.' She closes her eyes, picturing the memory, then opens them and looks down at my hip. 'Do you know what she did to her dog? Trampled it to death. Trampled it, I tell you! You just ask Joyce. She was the one to find her with it, bloody up to the elbows and knees with a butter knife in her hand. A butter knife!' Her voice becomes a fluster and she takes a moment to calm down. She is scared of Elle too. 'Imagine a thirteen-year-old child that could do such a thing. Folk feared her. She seemed capable of things we as adults couldn't comprehend.'

I could imagine it all right. And something else I was beginning to understand was that Elle and I were not all that different. I too was a deeply unlovable child. Ask Margot

Wolfe. It's the second time I feel gratitude towards my parents for giving me away. If I'd stayed with Elle, God knows what I would have become.

'What things?' I ask. She stares at me for a while, contemplating whether or not I can stand to hear it. She needs encouraging, coaxing to spill the beans. 'Miss Endicott, with all due respect, there is no reason to hold back now. I'm well aware of what my sister is like. Last time we were together she drugged me with Ecstasy. I know what she is capable of.'

'Then there is no reason for me to embellish matters any further with opinions from the past. What you should know is that what happened broke your parents. They loved you dearly, and they tried to care for you the best they could. It was easier when Eleanor wasn't there, but even so, her shadow hung over the household.' As if on cue, a cloud casts us in shadow, and Miss Endicott shakes off a chill before swilling what is left in her cup down her throat. 'When she returned home, they had no choice. They kept her because they knew nobody would take her. They couldn't risk what might happen to you if you stayed. Keep your friends close and your enemies closer. That's how the saying goes.'

'Are you telling me they saw my sister as an enemy? That's absurd. She was a child.'

Miss Endicott rises to her feet, sighs as if she was expecting more from me. She places her hands on the desk; four whiskies in and no doubt in need of some support. 'Do you honestly think of her as just another adult? Do you not see what I see?'

I think about what it is I see when I look at Elle, remember how I was so sure that she was responsible for our mother's death. A woman who I am more convinced than ever loved me.

'I thought she killed our mother.'

'And if your dear mother hadn't been suffering with cancer, we would all have thought the same thing. Elle knew it was your father who made the decision to keep her and send you away. She never forgot that, and never forgave your mother for feeling differently.'

'But I got the impression that something happened to her. That they brought her home through guilt.'

'Nonsense. Whatever stories Elle has told you, don't believe them.'

'It was Joyce that told me.'

She shakes her head. 'A busybody, plain and simple.'

'You just told me to ask her about the dog.'

'I said that she knew about the dog. Not that she knows about everything.'

'Regardless, Elle loved me, I think. She always wanted to reach out for me.' I stand up, move in close to Miss Endicott, place my hand on her arm. The touch shocks her, and she backs away. 'That's why I have to find her now. Help her. I shouldn't have run away when my father died.'

'No,' she shouts, jumping forward. She knocks my coffee cup, the contents spilling on to a pile of papers that look like school reports. For a moment I think she is going to grab me, but at the last minute she stops herself. 'Don't look for her. Give up the house. Let them go, all of them. Leave it as it is. Don't open up the past by searching for answers. You never know what you might find.'

'Might open up old wounds?' I ask sarcastically, and she

313

looks again at my hip. She knows more about me than I do myself. But she is struck by a pallor, her face white as fresh snow, her eyes like two little piss holes.

'What about old wounds?'

'Nothing,' I say. 'Just something my father said.' I set what is left of my coffee down, brush some drips from my knee. 'But I have to find her, because the police have arrested my boyfriend. They found her blood in the house.' Miss Endicott's brow furrows, anxiety spreading as if perhaps she has underestimated the nature of Elle's disappearance. 'But Antonio is innocent. He didn't hurt Elle.'

'They found blood, though. Maybe I am wrong. Maybe she really is hurt.' She backs away, one hand coming up to her lips. 'Oh, I should never have said anything.'

'She isn't hurt, Miss Endicott. She is sick. Mentally unwell,' I say, tapping my head. 'Tell me about the old psychiatric place. Fair Fields. Maybe I can prove to the police that she has mental health issues so they understand they are reaching the wrong conclusions about my sister.'

She shakes her head. 'Fair Fields is just a shell. Nearly burnt down about fifteen years ago. A few patients died. There is nothing left inside. Not even the records.' She must catch a look on my face, something that passes before I even realise. Like when I know Antonio is lying before he knows himself. When I know there is more to a story than I am being told. 'Yes, there was talk about who was responsible. Everybody in the village was aware that Elle had a troubled history, and a few knew where she had spent time as a child. There was a lot of talk about the kind of things that went on in that place. The early eighties in psychiatric care was not a happy time, Irini. Many put Elle's promiscuous ways down to experiences she may have suffered in the hospital. Of course, I never saw any evidence of that myself.'

I think back to Elle's interest in matches, the smell of her burning fingernails. 'You think she burnt it down?'

'It doesn't matter what I think. It matters only what you do. Do you love this boyfriend of yours, the one the police have arrested?'

'What does that have to do with my sister?' I ask, finding a fold in my own clothes that suddenly requires attention.

'I mean is he important to you? Could you live without him?' When I fail to answer, she makes assumptions. 'Then forget him. He came up here, Irini. I saw them together. He got himself into this mess, and by all accounts he was none too well behaved.' She sinks into her headmistress's chair, folds her hands together, her fingers like a nest of gnarled snakes. I hear the wind picking up outside. 'Your parents tried to keep Elle away from you for a reason, and I suggest you keep as much distance as possible. Don't try to save this Antonio if to do so means having to find her.'

35

As I approach the house, creeping along the driveway in my car, I see the gates are closed, remnants of yellow police tape attached, flickering in the breeze. When they don't open automatically, I stop the car, get out. I yank on the latch and push both gates open until they sit against a backdrop of conifer trees. I wait for somebody to stop me, but nobody does.

I turn back to the car, and that's when I remember. I don't know if it's the line of oak trees swaying at my side, or the muddy track bisected up the middle by a stretch of grass. It could be the sound of the gravel as it crunches underfoot where the driveway begins, or the soft chug of the engine as it ticks over. It is likely all of these things that transport me back to that moment when my mother placed me in Aunt Jemima's car. This is where the exchange happened, right on my own doorstep. I can almost picture the car ahead. I look at the house and wonder if my mother said it had to be done here, how I would be calm close to home.

I get back in the car and drive in, park outside the garages like Elle always did. I knock on the door to the apartment above, hoping that Frank or Joyce have been taped in like objects from a crime scene. Nobody answers. I slip around the side of the house, towards the kitchen. I find the door taped but unlocked. I push it open, duck inside. I am in.

The only sound is the tick-tock of the old grandfather clock in the hallway. I listen for the sounds of my memory, my mother's words of encouragement as I pull myself along on the kitchen floor. Nothing comes to mind, as if the whole place has died, memories included. I glance towards the stairs that lead to my bedroom, but I do not take them; instead I head into the house, towards the main corridor.

I poke my head into the sitting room where the coffin once sat and see that everything appears just as it was: the settee pushed aside, the floral pillows scattered in clusters of three, freshly plumped ready for use. The pictures all remain in place, the heavy curtains half drawn, the pelmets hanging above, limp as droopy eyelids. I step backwards, head towards the study. The police have been here. Little Post-it notes adorn the telephone and bookshelves, and traces of fingerprint dust still coat the door handles. I look down, find I have a smear of it on my hand. On the far wall there is a picture frame that hangs like a door, revealing a safe behind it. Empty, the contents in Antonio's car, I realise. I brush my hand against my leg, leave the study behind.

I head up the stairs. On the banister there is a smudge of blood, a sticky yellow note positioned just to the side. I push on, arriving at my father's bedroom. I consider going in, rooting through his things. Maybe I can find something of my mother's, a dress that smells like her, a favourite piece of costume jewellery that wasn't deemed fit for the safe. Maybe I'll find a bundle of letters all for me, written over the years, that she never had the courage to send. But right now I'm not sure I'd have the courage to read them either, so I close the door behind me and continue along the corridor.

I open two more rooms, both of which look undisturbed, before I arrive at the final door. I push it open, see the bed, a double, sheets all wrinkled and pulled. I see the splatters of blood, just a few tiny drops. They are not from a struggle or a fight. These are consensual wounds, the type a woman accepts with a smile. The type that come from the pain we say we like because we think it makes us more attractive to the man we are with. There are handcuffs hanging from the frame of the bed, traces of blood on the edge from where they have cut into skin. Red smears on the pillow, too.

The room doesn't fit the house, like French lingerie on a woman too idle to pretty herself up. Above the bed there is an image of Elle, a blown-up portrait, black and white, her face cast in complimentary shadows. She is tipping her head back, her naked arms gripped seductively around her chest. Reminds me of Madonna in the eighties. The room, too, that faux-glam eighties plastic, lots of pastel peach and cushions, strip lighting around mirrors. Like a time warp. Not how I imagined it.

There is a CD player on a small cabinet just inside the door, and next to it a selection of CDs. I pick a few up and shuffle through them. Puccini's *Madam Butterfly*. My mother's favourite. I open the case but find it empty, so I turn the CD player on and press play. Soon enough, just as I expected, the room is filled with the anguished refrain of a female soprano. I listen, remembering the story: a mother who has to say goodbye to her child, a wish that he might remember her face. I think of the times my mother must have listened to this. Was she thinking of me, praying that I might remember her? What did Elle mean when she said that it was our mother's favourite even before? Before what? Before we said goodbye?

I leave the music on low, dodge the blood to sit on the edge of the bed. I lean backwards, rest my head back, my eyes to the ceiling. I smell him as if he is here. The scent of ginger mixed with cardamom, the spicy neckline that I have nuzzled into so many times. I know he was here, rubbing himself all over her and the sheets, leaving his scent. I reach up, flick on the lamp. The same black dust covers the bedside table, fingerprints picked up on the glass and the receiver of the beige plastic phone. Is this the telephone she used to speak to him, to entice him to visit? Is this where she called me from on so many occasions? There is a dish next to it overflowing with the little black twigs of fully burnt-out matches. I finger a handcuff hanging from the bed and look up at the portrait.

'Where are you?' I ask.

I pull open her bedside table, looking for anything that might help me. Inside I find a few magazines, one of which is unsurprisingly called *Elle*. Main story? *How to start over*, and then a subheading: *Everything you need to make a clean break*. There is a selection of body creams, at least five hand creams, and a bottle of eye drops. A couple of bracelets. A box of matches nestled under an upturned jewellery box. Further back, a vibrator and a tube of lube.

There are a couple of framed pictures, both of Elle. In one of them, from childhood, she is staring at the camera. No smile. I pull it out, try to prop it up, but the leg of the stand falls off. I pick up the frame and find the whole back casing is hanging loose. I pull at the edge and it comes away, revealing three more photographs inside. Polaroid pictures. It is her, naked, here in this bedroom. In one she is smiling at the camera. In another she is on all fours, a close-up taken from behind with the tip of a finger in the frame. In the third she is strapped into the handcuffs, her body writhing about while whoever is behind the lens looks on. I drop them back into the drawer, kind of sad, kind of embarrassed. She would do anything for anybody, just to be wanted. We are not so very different. But then I wonder if it was Antonio who took these pictures, and if it was, perhaps it would prove to the police that she was a willing participant. I look at the tip of the finger caught in the frame. Antonio's? Maybe. I snatch them back up and stuff them in my jeans pocket.

As I stand back up, I notice something on the floor. It is almost hidden by the bedside table, only a corner poking out. I crouch down, nibble at it with my fingertips, use my shoulder to push the bedside table back and free the card underneath. Anything hidden has the potential to be useful.

When I wriggle it out from underneath the furniture, I realise that I recognise the blue lettering and the name. 'Gregory Waterson, Investment Banker,' I say aloud, remembering that I have Matt's card. I slide it out from my jacket pocket, the edges dog-eared and dirty. I stand up and silence the music just as it is reaching its devastating climax. Without thinking, I take out my phone and dial the number.

'Hello, Matthew Guthrie.' He answers after only two rings. He sounds distracted, and noise fills the background.

'Matt, it's me, Irini.' He doesn't say anything for a moment, and I suddenly feel stupid for calling. Like maybe I missed the part where he was only being nice by giving me his card, and there was an unwritten rule that I wasn't supposed to call. 'We met a couple of weeks ago with my sister, Elle.' The background noise quietens and I hear the click of a door.

'Irini, I remember who you are. I just didn't expect you to call. But I'm glad you did.'

'Matt, there is a problem with my sister.'

'Aye, I know.' I hear the creak of a chair and the whistle of wheels as he sits down in it. 'I saw it on the local news, and the police came to my house yesterday to speak to me.'

'What did they want to know?'

'About the night we spent together. About Elle drugging you.' He lets out a heavy breath. 'I thought they were going to arrest me on suspicion of rape. I think they thought I might have been in on it.'

I fiddle the card over my fingers, tap it against the cupboard. 'Have the police spoken to Greg?'

'Aye. He's devastated. He's been trying to help, but he was away for the weekend with his fiancée. He hasn't seen Elle since the hotel. Where are you? Are you calling from London?'

'No. I'm calling from the family house. I drove up here.' I should tell him about Antonio and his arrest, but although it is right there on the tip of my lying tongue, I can't. 'I just wanted to be close in case there were any developments.'

'There are a lot of rumours going around, Irini. About your sister, about Greg. About your parents. Your father and Elle's inheritance.' I wish I could tell him everything I know, but I'm back to feeling like the liar, the one who is trying to keep two lives separate. 'That's the thing with small villages,' he continues. 'People talk.' He pauses for a second, and when I don't interrupt he says, 'I'm so sorry for what your father did, Irini. It looks like you were best off out of it all.'

'Maybe. It seems I was given away because of Elle's mental state. You were right when you said that something happened to make them do it. It was Elle that happened. She came home from a mental hospital and I was the victim. As were my parents.' I am surprised to think of them this way. Perhaps I could already accept the idea of my mother being a victim, the good wife going along with her husband's plan. But perhaps my father was also trapped by his decision. By Elle. His hand forced to do something that not even he thought was right. I try to imagine how it must have felt to be them, to have a disabled daughter they loved, and another in psychiatric care. Knowing that when one came home, the other couldn't be cared for. It was nothing to do with depression like Aunt Jemima said. I try to put myself in my mother's shoes, easier than my father's, and I can't even do that. It is too big for the scope of my emotional maturity. 'But whatever happened back then, it doesn't matter. Right now, I have to find Elle.'

'How are you planning to do that? As far as I understand it, there's no trace of her anywhere.' For the first time I wonder if I really have a plan, and I'm not sure that I do. So I focus on one thought: prove that Antonio isn't to blame.

'Didn't you grow up nearby?' I ask.

'Hm,' he says, sounding surprised. 'You remember that? Aye, I did. Why do you ask?'

'Do you know a place called Fair Fields? It was an old hospital.'

He pauses for a moment, takes his time to think. 'Everybody who grew up nearby knows it. Big old place not too far from Horton. You can see it from the village. It's not a hospital any more. Part of it burned down in the early nineties and it was later closed.'

'Only part of it?' I look at the pile of burnt matches on the bedside locker, and then up to Elle's smoky portrait. If only *part* of Fair Fields was damaged there might still be something useful to be found there. 'Do you know if they moved the old records before it closed down? You see, the police believe that Elle has no history of mental health treatment. But they can't find the records because it was all private care. If I can prove them wrong about that, then maybe they'll see that they could be wrong about other things too. They are holding a man. They think he hurt her.'

'Antonio? Your boyfriend?'

I'm speechless for a moment, and swallow hard before I can carry on. 'How do you know about him?'

'Elle told me.' I hear a knock in the background of the call, and the squeak of the chair as Matt stands. I listen as he tells whoever has arrived that he can't speak right now, that he is taking an important call with a very important client. I get lost in thoughts of how easily I paved Elle's way back into my life. If she had realised that all it took was a death, I'm sure she would have bumped our mother off years ago. 'Sorry about that,' he says, returning to the phone. 'Elle told me about him.'

I sigh. 'Yes, she spoke to him on the phone while I was here. I guess I'm not surprised she told you after what happened between us.'

'No, Irini. I mean she told me before you even came here. That her sister had a boyfriend called Antonio. That he was an Italian and that you lived together. I just assumed that you didn't want me to know about him. I took it as a good sign.'

He tries a light giggle to lighten the mood, but I cut him off. 'Before I came here? But she didn't know anything about Antonio before I came here.'

'Well, she told me about him. Weeks, maybe even a month before. She told me that you were a doctor, that he was a chef who was opening his own restaurant, that you lived in London and that soon enough you'd be visiting.'

'What? But that doesn't make any sense. You told me—' I begin, but I am distracted when I hear the latch of a door. I stand bolt upright. 'Hang on. Did you just open a door?' I whisper.

'No, I'm sitting at my desk. Why?'

I hear it again, a door hitting something, then another sound. Something smashes.

'Rini, I heard that. What was that sound?'

'Somebody's here!'

I creep down the stairs, past the faces of my ancestors, anxious to turn the dog-leg corner. My body is shaking, breaths firing in and out like a jackhammer. Matt is talking, but the phone is down at my side and his words are nothing more than a distant mumble. I feel the chill of the wind and hear the rustle of the conifer trees before I even see the open door. The grandfather clock ticks the seconds away. Then, as I approach the hallway, I see the police tape fluttering, the same way that Elle once fluttered her fingers over my leg like a butterfly flapping its wings.

One of the Chinese urns is lying in pieces, particles of dust swirling in the air above it. The door is swinging on its hinges, knocking against the obelisk. I hear my name being called from the phone. I bring it up to my ear in a daze.

'Irini, are you all right?'

'Somebody was in the house.' I run down the last steps, my hand brushing past the smudge of dried blood, sending the sticky note floating to the floor. By the time I make it to the door, there is nobody to be seen.

'Get out of there. Don't stay,' Matt says.

I reach into my pocket to pull out my keys and hobble out to the garages, my hip more painful than ever, the scars throbbing hot in my jeans. I jump inside my car, toss the phone to the passenger seat and stick the key in the ignition, then spin away, a cloud of gravel dust kicking up behind me. I swing out of the gate and take one last look in the mirror. When I see Elle standing in the dust storm, her hair slapping against her face, eyes dark and skin dirty, I slam on my brakes, skidding along the dirt track. I reach behind the passenger seat and swing myself around, looking left and right, but sure as I was that I saw her only a moment ago, now she is nowhere to be seen. I slump back into my seat, hit the central locking and floor the pedal.

With the pictures that I am certain Antonio took in my

back pocket, I drive away from the house and head for the hill that climbs out of the village. I can see the old hospital in the distance, the white boards glistening in the sunlight, mist rising from the ground like steam.

Matt is calling me, the phone buzzing desperately at my side. But I can't answer. I have to focus. I have only one aim. The truth. I must start right back at the beginning of our family's story, and for that there is only one place to go.

36

I drive through capillary country roads swamped in green, a canopy of autumn blue above. I pass intersecting streams, a couple of farms, and yellow fields full of rapeseed. With no idea of where I am going, I follow the intermittent flashes I get of the white steeple rising above the treeline. 'House of the Rising Sun' plays on the radio, followed by 'Hotel California'. Halfway through the second chorus I see the old building appearing in full view as the trees thin out and the overgrown ground flattens out. Up ahead is a broken sign, aged wood with faded letters, the words *Fair Fields Rehabilitation Hospital for the Infirm and Mentally Insane* just visible.

I shut off the engine at the end of a fractured tarmac road. The music stops, leaving nothing but the wind rustling through the grasses and the whistling of a few birds overhead to break the silence. I check my phone but find that I have no signal. Regardless, as I step from the car, I slip it in my pocket.

The perimeter of the compound has been fenced off, the metal meshwork covered with hazard signs: *Keep Out!* They flap frantically in the breeze, as if they are trapped and are trying to fly away. From where I am standing the land appears flat, without dimension, and in the distance I see the main building of the hospital nestled between other smaller buildings. The bracken snags at my feet as I navigate the perimeter until I find a gap in the fencing. I drop down and push through, snagging my jumper on a fault in the meshwork. I get to my feet, dust off my blackened knees. Now that I'm on the other side, the central building feels bigger. A threat as it rises above me.

I arrive at a small building, the blackened smudges of fire damage licking up the side of the wooden boards covering the walls. I look through a broken window and see that it is nothing but a shell, just like Miss Endicott said, the inside of a cavernous black wound. It still smells of soot and burnt wood. Was this where the fire started? The fire that Elle may or may not have been responsible for?

I continue to a clearing overlooking the main block. Close up, it has an impressive look about it: columns at the front like the Parthenon, covered by a flaky mixture of grey and green age spots. I can imagine my father here, impressed by the extravagance of the place as he was driving towards it. The imposing columns and high windows; the ornate steeple that I have followed to get here erupting proudly through the roof. I think he would have taken one look at it and been certain it was a good idea. Because even though it was him that wanted to keep Elle rather than me, I am also sure that he would have chosen here over home for her. He was a fixer, a decider, a doer. He saw a problem and found a solution he could stick to. Just like he stuck to shutting me out.

I move up the steps towards the front door, the huge arcade swallowing me up. The door is small in comparison to the rest of the building, almost doll's-house-like. There is a sign that reads *Keep Out*; I shove against it, breaking the rules. But a chain, thick and heavy, locks the door shut. I would need bolt cutters to get through it. I rattle it a bit, then let it drop. It clatters against the door, and I watch as more dry paint flakes away.

I follow the line of the building until I broach a corner. Underneath a mass of ivy I spot an old wrought-iron railing marking another entrance. A set of steps descends to a basement. A small metal sign directs me: *Visitors*. I follow the arrow, edging my way down the creeper-covered steps, clinging on to the railing, which is fortunately still solid. I arrive at the bottom step and test the door handle. Seems loose. I brace my shoulder against the door and with one strong effort break through, sending sprigs of ivy and clouds of dust into the air. I slip inside, my heart racing. I'm in.

And now, standing here alone in the dark, I remind myself why I've come to this godforsaken place. It isn't only to prove that Antonio didn't hurt Elle. I also need to prove to myself that Elle really is crazy. To hold in my hand the evidence that backs up the story of why I was given away. Because all the years of separation have left me marked, stigmatised as the one who wasn't wanted. Now, the possibility that somewhere within these walls lies the answer to everything, the single cog that drove my life forward, is exhilarating.

I pass through several dingy corridors until I come across a large bath standing in the middle of a room, flanked by thick green rubber curtains that are falling apart in places. The walls are covered in peeling paint, as if they are shedding their skin. Perhaps an old hydrotherapy room. Dust clings to every surface, and from somewhere I can hear water dripping. I look towards the next room and see rows of Victorian sinks all lined up alongside each other, still beautiful, like the kind somebody would fit into an old house to restore the period features.

I head along another corridor, up a set of stairs, where the rooms open up and the sunlight gains access. It dapples through in faint bands of light, illuminating the grey fingers of dust that snap at my feet as I tread through years of filth. It is cooler up here, and there is a breeze filtering through broken windows. The walls are painted in myriad colours, as if by children. In squiggly, childish letters somebody has painted the word *recover* in the centre of a yellow sun. It reminds me of the paintings on the wall in Miss Endicott's reception area. When I think about Miss Endicott, it reminds me that this place, unlike the first building, isn't as damaged by fire as she would have had me believe. Was that a mistake on her part? Why was she so sure there was nothing left?

'Must be the children's wing,' I say to myself as I walk through into what looks like an auditorium. There are chairs stacked along the walls, and some left higgledy-piggledy on the floor, scattered about as though a freak tornado hit the room. The windows that remain are dirty, partially covered in threadbare curtains. I fear that if I was to touch one, it would disintegrate in my hand.

The excitement I felt at my proximity to the truth when

I first arrived has long passed, sucked out of me by the claustrophobic nature of this forgotten place. It's as if it's constricting around me, the sensation of being trapped with no way out. God only knows how it must have felt as a patient. But the paintings on the walls give me hope that it was better than I imagine it to have been. Even so, the smell of damp and bodily functions is hard to ignore. I hold my hands up to my nose and try to breathe through my mouth. But the taste gets the better of me and I nearly choke on it as it hits the back of my throat. I pull my jumper up over my mouth, and then cover that with my hand for good measure.

There is graffiti, too. Somebody has painted an elaborate mural of crucifixions with words over the top that read: *You will pay for what you did to me here.* As I move through the maze of rooms, passing upturned desks and abandoned belongings, the image is repeated time and time again. The words remind me of something that Joyce once said. Something that would explain Elle's pain. *He didn't feel it right after learning what they were doing to her. They had to bring her home.* Is that what was happening? Was Elle being mistreated while she was staying here? Abused by those who were supposed to be caring for her?

I pass into a narrow corridor, dark, with only a little light streaming through a solitary window. On one side there are cells, some padded, some concrete. The isolation cells. All the doors are open; one of them is snapped in two, as if somebody broke through. Inside that cell the graffiti reads: *This is where you will be judged.* I fight back a tear, certain for the first time that Elle's life might have been harder than

331

mine. Certain that she must have felt as let down as I always have.

I climb a creaky staircase and it becomes clear that I am in an administrative section. I open flimsy doors with glass windows, uncertain what I am looking for. I am moving too slowly, but it is because I am now sure that this is the place where my family was destroyed. Something happened here that my parents discovered, and it changed everything. I don't want to miss what that was. Within these walls the seeds were planted, watered and matured until my sister was spat out, ruined, destroyed. Without this place, perhaps we would have all lived together. I let go of my jumper, breathe in the stale air.

Then as I push open the next door I am met by a wave of hope. This is without doubt the records room, a gaping cave stacked with rows of files like a library. I rush across to the first shelf, pick up a dirty beige folder with a number on the front. But then my excitement fades. There's no name on it. I pick up a second, and again I find only a number: 0021-94-59. Without names, it will be impossible to find Elle's file.

I open the first folder, the pages brown, dusty. It belonged to Charlotte Green, diagnosed with manic depression. 'They'd call that bipolar now,' I mutter. There is a grainy, faded photograph tacked to the inside, and the sense of hopelessness on little Charlotte Green's face washes over me. 'What a stupid system.' I toss the file down and open the next. This one has a picture of a young man on the inside cover. 'Green, Christopher, 26, admitted in 1959, schizophrenia.' I remember the name in the first file. I reach down, grab it just in case I have made a mistake. But I haven't. I'm right. Green, Charlotte. Green, Christopher. It's alphabetical.

I move along the rows pulling out folders, checking names. I realise that some of the files do actually have names written on their spines; it's just that most are so faded they can't be read. I must be close to Harringford, so I keep flicking through, looking for where the Gs become Hs. But then another thought comes to mind. Matt. I pull out the business card from my pocket. Matthew Guthrie. He told me that he had therapy too, didn't he? Is it possible he knew Elle all along?

Part of me doesn't want to look, as if by doing so I'm snooping in something private to which I have no right. Like his bathroom cabinet. But I can't help myself, and before I have even decided whether I should or shouldn't, I'm clutching a file that has the name Matthew Guthrie written on the spine. I open it, and there staring right back at me is his childhood face, unmistakable blond curls drooping across sad eyes.

I slide out my phone and see that I still have no signal. I move over to the window and wait for the phone to register on the network. As it does, a call comes through. It's Matt.

'Oh, thank God you picked up,' he says, breathless. 'I've been trying for the best part of half an hour. I'm on my way to Horton. Where are you? Are you with Elle?'

'No.'

His breathing relaxes. 'When you heard somebody in the house . . .' he says, sounding relieved that the things he imagined possible have not come true. 'Tell me where you are. I'll come and find you.'

'I'm at Fair Fields.'

'Oh.' He pauses. 'You went there? OK, wait outside. I'll meet you on the road just before the fence.' I hear the revving of his engine as he accelerates.

'Too late. I'm already inside.' I look down at his childhood face on the inside cover, wonder just how well he knows my sister. 'I'm in the records room.'

'In the records room? What did you find?'

When he remains silent, I take a punt on a guess. 'Why didn't you tell me that you knew Elle as a child?' For a moment I listen to his breathing, the sound of his lips as he swallows. Then the line goes dead.

37

I watch from the window as Matt crosses the grounds of Fair Fields, his steps quick, just short of running. I am sitting on the windowsill, his file placed on my knees. I haven't moved since he hung up, a little over fifteen minutes ago. He must have left Edinburgh as I was leaving *Mam Tor*. He disappears from view as he nears the building, and only a minute later he arrives in the records room. He must know the layout, remember where he is going.

'Irini,' he says as he bursts through the door. His cheeks are red, his brow shiny. I hold up his file.

'I didn't read it,' I say, feeling a little guilty. For a moment he stands there, his eyes darting about the floor.

'Let me explain.' He rushes towards me, and I don't stop him when he takes one of my hands in his, just like he did at the hotel. It feels good to have him touch me, his grip tight, his strength comforting. My lack of resistance spurs him on, and soon enough he has wrapped me in his arms, holding me to his chest. When he lets me go he says, 'Thank God you are all right. I left work as soon as you told me that you heard somebody in the house. If anything had happened to you, I would never have forgiven myself.'

He finds a couple of chairs and sets them up near the window. We sit down like we are on a confessional chat show, him wringing his hands between his knees, nervous. He is dressed in his suit, a light mac over the top. He looks different from before, sharper, without stubble, but there is worry on his face. I'd love to tell him it doesn't matter, that he doesn't have to do this. Part of me wants to make it easy on him, stop him before he starts. But the other part of me needs the truth. No turning back now.

'I should have told you before. If you are angry at me, you have every right. But I didn't want to admit to having been here. In this place,' he says as he glances at the walls surrounding us. 'I was ashamed.'

'Why? What do you think I would have done?' I try to sound soft, reassuring, but I get the feeling that everything I say now sounds like an accusation.

'Maybe you'd have felt the same way about me as you do Elle. I didn't want that.' I can't deny him that. I haven't exactly been kind about Elle. 'Plus I try not to remember the things that happened here. It wasn't a great place to be.' He shakes his arms out from his jacket, loosens his tie as if it is suffocating him. 'The time I spent here was hard.'

'I need to know what happened, Matt.'

He sits back, his hands on his knees. 'Aye, I know. I was only in here for a few weeks, after my parents' divorce. The doctors said I needed to stay in; my parents believed them. They would have done anything to assuage their guilt over the separation.' He wipes a bead of sweat from his brow. 'You see, I didn't take it very well. I idolised my father, thought that without him around everyday life would be impossible. I was playing up a lot, in school, at home. They brought me here to help me work through a few issues. But it didn't help. It made things worse.' He looks to the floor, unable to maintain eye contact. I feel the urge to say something, but I'm sure that if I do, I'll tip the balance, and suddenly he'll realise that he doesn't owe me this explanation. So I wait, and a moment later he starts speaking again. 'It was in the papers, and there was an investigation. Residents chained to beds, shock therapy, beatings, violations of girls, some of them not much older than ten. Boys, too. I got a few lashes, and they tried to break me, but my parents pulled me out before it got too bad. Others weren't so lucky.'

'You mean Elle.'

'Yes,' he says, still unable to look at me. 'She was here a long time. I knew her briefly; we became friends.' I reach out, take his hand. I'm grateful to know that in the midst of this, he was with her, no matter how temporarily. 'The kids who had been hurt left this place, grew up. But they kept the scars they took with them.' He lifts a tuft of hair and points to a small triangular scar on the top of his forehead. 'Elle has one too. Hot pokers from the fireplace. Meant we were fighters.' I remember the small scar on her face, how I always wondered if it was chickenpox, and realise how wrong I was. I think back and wonder if my life was ever as bad as I believed it to be.

'I'm so sorry,' I say. I want to hold him in my arms, cradle him as he speaks. It's like finally it's all coming out. I edge towards him, but he starts up again and I hold back, give him space.

'Scared kids grew into angry adults. They wanted justice.

Some came here, wrote things on the wall, broke the place up. You must have seen the graffiti on your way up here. Others tried to press charges, but very few cases ever made it to court. I stayed in touch with Elle because we lived close by. I guess we understood each other. That's how we ended up back here. I thought we would cause some trouble. Break a few windows or something stupid. But Elle was planning to burn the whole place down. She set fire to the linen room. They chased us away before it got out of hand, put the fire out, thank God. Afterwards, I told my mother what had happened and she moved me away. Elle and I lost touch, but to be honest, it was a relief. I realised that in my effort to thank her for being there for me, I was prepared to go along with any of her suggestions.

'Then a year or so ago I met her by chance at the gym. At first I avoided her. But then Greg got involved and we became friends. When she showed me a picture of you about a month ago, said you were coming to visit and that I should be there, help her to reconnect with you, I couldn't say no. She'd been strong as a kid, helped me. I thought I owed her, so I went along with it. I wanted so much for her to be all right, knowing what she'd been through. So I agreed to show you around a bit.'

'But you told me that Elle said her sister had died.'

'I know. I know.' He picks shamefaced at his thumb. 'But she said stuff like that for attention. She would lie and exaggerate to impress people. She was always making stuff up, looking for sympathy. I felt sorry for her, I guess. I'm sorry I got it so wrong.'

I reach out, touch his knee, stroke it with my thumb.

With my parents gone, Matt is the only person who understands Elle like I do. Despite the fact that he held back the truth about their connection, I'm so grateful that he is here. 'It doesn't matter now.'

'Maybe not. But what does matter, and what I should never have kept from you, is this. Elle came to me after you left and told me that somebody was threatening her. That they were going to reveal everything that was in her file from Fair Fields. She seemed terrified. She also told me that the person who was threatening her knew about the fire we had started all those years ago, and that I was being implicated as the ringleader. She wanted to disappear for a few days, and told me that if I covered for her, everything would blow over. I didn't want anything about the fire to come out. I've built a good life for myself, and I love my job. I didn't want to risk losing it because of a stupid childhood mistake, so I went along with it. I covered for her.'

My first thought is that she must be OK. But the first thing I ask is quite different. 'What was in her file that she was so scared might be revealed?'

'I have no idea.'

I kick away the chair and dash over to the shelves, Matt following closely behind. 'Maybe her records are still here.'

'Some of them are the wrong way round,' Matt shouts as we finger our way through. I pull out file after file until I hear him shout, 'Irini, over here. I've found a file for Harringford.' I run to meet him just as he is pulling it out. He flicks it open but then stops, looks at me, confused.

'What is it?' I ask, pawing at the folder. 'Is it Elle's file?'

'No.' He turns the folder and holds up the spine so that

I can see the faded lettering. 'It's for somebody called Casey Harringford.'

'Casey? My mother was called Cassandra.' I reach over, take the file. I flick through the first pages, look at the image staring back at me. A baby, cute; close-ups of the feet and legs. Reports about hydrotherapy. 'The name can't just be a coincidence, but I've no idea who this is. She is a Harringford, but I am so detached from my family I couldn't tell you who.'

'Cousin?'

'I don't think so. And look at the date of birth.' I hold the file up and point to the details for the little girl. 'February 1984. That's nearly two years after I was born. If she was family, I'd know about her. I wasn't given away until I was three and a half years old.'

'Maybe she was given away too and you don't remember.'

I lean against the shelf behind me, the dust lifting, settling on my shoulders like falling snow. I let the file drop to the floor, and cough to clear my throat.

'It's possible,' Matt persists.

'No. There was only one Harringford girl who was given away.'

He reaches out and touches my leg as we sit amongst the old paperwork. I feel it, that spark from before. No drugs this time, just me, him and honesty. 'Yes, but there was only one person who was written into the will, remember. You. Everything left to you.'

Another reminder of just how deep I am in this mess. The will, the thing that makes me look guilty, the payout of blood money designed as restitution for my parents' sins.

I think about it in my pocket, and how the next visit needs to be to Witherrington so that I can relinquish anything my father left me and get him to talk to the police again. But then I remember the purposefulness with which it was placed in my bag. How the envelope had *Irini Harringford* written on it, unmistakably for me. I pull it from my back pocket, unfold the crumpled paper. 'Give me that file.'

Matt hands me the file for Casey Harringford and I turn the will over to find the number written on the back. I hold them up alongside each other. The handwritten number is the same as the case file. The last six digits are Casey's date of birth.

Matt shuffles up next to me and runs his finger along the numbers. 'They're the same, Irini. What is this?'

'It's my father's will. He gave it to me, and I'm sure that he wrote this number on it.'

'Then he knew about this file.' He taps at the number with his finger, and as I look up, I see fine particles of dust settling on his eyelashes. He catches me staring at him, his eyes darting away, the slightest flush spreading into his cheeks.

'Which means that he must also have known about a little girl called Casey Harringford.' Matt begins to nod, but then looks away, somewhere lost in thought. 'What is it? Did you think of something?'

He has the look of a person about to deliver bad news, his mouth hanging open, his cheeks sunken as he slips back against the shelves. 'Now it makes sense.'

'What makes sense?'

'Why Elle told me that her sister had died.' He looks

down at the file and then back to me. 'Maybe she wasn't lying. She might not have been talking about you at all. Maybe this is who she meant.'

'Another sister? Impossible. I would have known about it.'

'Don't you have any family left that you could ask?'

'Only my aunt, but she doesn't answer when I call. And a few cousins, I guess, but I don't have their numbers.'

At that moment Matt reaches up and touches my cheek, brushes something away, and I realise that in the short time I have known him, I feel closer to him than I ever have to Antonio. He takes hold of the folder and starts flicking through the fragile pages.

'What are you looking for?'

'I don't know. Maybe there's something in here that helps. Maybe a copy of her birth certificate, or an old address.' He turns page after page until he reaches the end of the file. 'Nothing.'

'Well, we know her birthday. Could we get a copy of her birth certificate online?'

'Probably, but isn't there somewhere that holds records of these things?' I remember the countless death certificates I signed as a junior doctor, how the mortuary was always nagging me to get things done quickly so that the family could register the death and arrange the funeral. 'There should be a registrar's office somewhere where they keep them. Do you know where it would be?'

'No,' he says as he stands up, offering me a hand. I take it and with his support get to my feet. 'But we can find the address on the way.'

38

We decide to take Matt's car, and by the time we are on the road I am already on the phone to the records office. They are still open, will be for another hour. But we are over twenty miles away. That doesn't give us much time if the traffic is bad. We have travelled at least five miles before I turn to face the front, but still I'm not entirely convinced that Elle hasn't somehow acquired a car to follow us. I can't help but check over my shoulder every time we turn a corner.

I call DC McGuire and tell him about the photos I found in Elle's drawer, and everything that Matt has told me since. He asks me to scan the Polaroids and email them over, so I do so from my phone. I find it hard to believe how calm I am after discovering that my boyfriend had consensual sadistic sex with my sister, but figure that perhaps it's because he's not my boyfriend any more. Whatever we once had is over.

I open the file and look at the picture of baby Casey. Maybe this child could be my sister. She has a similar nose to me, and a high hairline just like I do that I try to hide with a fringe. I flick through the pages. The records are sparse, incomplete, but as I read, I see something that is just like me. A diagnosis. Dysplasia of the left hip.

'Matt,' I say as he negotiates the turns of Johnston Terrace, Edinburgh Castle rising high above us on our left. I reach out, grab his arm as if I am trying to warn him of danger. 'Casey Harringford has the same diagnosis that I do. Dysplasia of the left hip. According to this, that's why she was at the hospital. Hydrotherapy. It looks like she was treated there for the first six months of her life as an outpatient. Then all treatment stopped.'

'What does that mean?'

'I'm not sure,' I say, but we are interrupted when the phone rings. It is DC McGuire.

'Irini, thanks. We have the photos. But we will need the originals, and I would ask you, if at all possible, not to handle them. If we can get a good print from Elle on them, it's highly unlikely she was harmed while she was handcuffed.'

For a second I'm confused, because in my mind the whole thing is already solved. 'I told you, I just saw her at the house, and that Matt confirmed her intention was to disappear. He will make a statement today if he needs to.' Why are they still looking for evidence?

'Well, there is nobody that can prove either of those claims to be true. A fingerprint from Eleanor on those photographs would really help us with the timeline.'

I can feel the disappointment swelling as we are sucked into a melee of gothic architecture. We bobble over the cobbles and weave our way through open-topped tourist buses and congested commuter traffic. 'You're not going to let Antonio go, are you?'

Matt looks at me, pulls a face, his hands raised in the air

in disbelief. He honks his horn for people to get out of his way as we travel downhill along the Royal Mile.

'I'm afraid it's not that easy.' For a moment I am sure I am on speaker phone, as if DC McGuire is waiting for somebody to give him the nod before he continues. That's when DC Forrester speaks.

'Irini, good afternoon. First things first, I did ask you to make sure you stuck around. You had no business running off to Scotland.' She lets that hang there for a while, but I offer no reply. 'But as you already have, and now that Antonio has pretty much cleared you of any wrongdoing, let me tell you where we're at down here. Mr Molinaro has confessed that Elle first made contact with him months ago. She found him on Facebook. He has also confessed to taking the pictures you sent us, and to a consensual sexual relationship with your sister.' She pauses before she says, 'I'm sorry, Irini, but his story is that Elle paid him for information and your phone number. In return she promised to keep his name out of the mud. Seems they had a few secret liaisons in London before your mother died. Elle seems to believe that she was to inherit her mother's jewellery upon her death, and she promised it to Antonio as a further payment if his information proved useful.'

She pauses again, and I glance down at my empty ring finger, and then at Matt. Twenty-four hours, and so much has changed. Forrester picks back up.

'I guess it did prove useful. You might also like to know that his bank loan was never approved, and we have tracked three bank transfers from Elle's account into his since their first meeting. Rest assured, Irini. Everybody will get what

they deserve.' I know she includes me in that, but I also feel
that she has softened towards me. She has stopped addressing
me as Dr Harringford, for one. 'I'm going to need you to
check in at the station up there, provide a statement. Matt
too.'

'OK, we'll do that.'

'And listen, Irini. If everything that we think we know is
true, you'd be best off staying away from the house. We
have no idea what Elle is capable of.'

After we hang up, I reach for a tissue in the side of the
car door. I wrap the photos inside it and place them in the
glove box.

'So they're not letting him go yet?' Matt asks as he pulls
on to the pavement outside the Bank of Scotland on
Lawnmarket. He sounds his horn again to move the pedes-
trians out of his way; people complain and curse as he
mounts the kerb. It's a side of him I haven't seen before:
forceful, making things happen, as if nothing can get in his
way. His eyes appear heavy, perhaps as if he has been crying,
but it could just be from the dust. Yet his face is still kind,
and soft. This is what safety feels like, I realise. Having a
team member on your side. Not that suffocating feeling of
losing myself like I always had with Antonio.

'I'm not sure you're supposed to park here,' I say.

'Never mind. Tell me,' he says as he pulls on the hand-
brake and turns off the engine. 'Are they letting him go or
not?'

'Not yet.' Money. Payments. Antonio sold my trust.
Bastard. 'He sold me out to Elle in exchange for money.
And sex. Maybe it'll do him good to stew in a cell for a

while.' Right now I'm thinking he deserves whatever they can throw at him. But I try to remember that he was sucked in by Elle, which makes you do things you normally wouldn't. I only have to remember Margot Wolfe to be reminded of that.

'No doubt.' He nods to the glove box. 'And handcuffs, eh? His idea, you think?'

'It would be a first.' I can't look at him when I say it. I feel so stupid. So suckered in by the pair of them. 'But at least now that Antonio has confessed his side of the story, they can see that Elle is really the one to blame, and that she was playing him to get what she wanted.' After a brief pause I add, 'Perhaps they'll see that she was playing me too.'

'What do you think she was trying to get out of it?' he asks as he unclips his seat belt.

'She wanted to get me here, prove that my father loved her more than me. Our parents might have sent me away, but Elle never believed it was what they really wanted. She always doubted their love. It was as if she needed to prove to herself that they didn't regret keeping her. But she also wanted me to need her in just the same way as I always wanted her to need me. The easiest way of doing that was by making sure that all I had left was her.'

'You think that's why she slept with Antonio, to ruin your relationship with him?'

'No. I was never supposed to find out what she had done with Antonio. That would have made it her fault. I would have been angry with her. My relationship had to fall apart because of me.' I shake my head, brush my hands over the dusty file. 'Why do you think she drugged me? Me sleeping with you was just another part of her plan. She would have told Antonio when it suited her. Once she was ready to be my hero. But my father's will changed everything. And now this file,' I say as I hold it up for him to see, 'changes everything again.'

We exit the car into a chilly Scottish breeze and I glance up at the grand building. The brass plaque outside reads *City Chambers*. Inside it is palatial, and my boots resonate in lofty echoes on the monochromatic marble floor. We pass through to the records office, stuffy, the smell of old paperwork trapped in the dry air of central heating. There is a mood of library quiet, the studious atmosphere that reminds me of university and loneliness. I take Matt's hand, and he slips his fingers through mine. I squeeze them tight.

'Can I help you?' A frail old lady is standing at the desk. She is wearing a high-buttoned blouse with frills running down the front. A small locket, no doubt containing those she loves, sits around her neck. She is not unfriendly, but she is aware of the clock, and looks at it twice before we have even spoken. We are the visitors at the end of the day that she doesn't need.

'Yes, I hope so. Anna? We spoke on the phone.' I move towards her, holding Casey's file tight to my chest.

'Oh, you must be Dr Harringford.' She perks up and shuffles out from behind the desk. She must have been on a step, because by the time she is alongside me she seems even shorter. 'I have found the records I think you need.'

She guides us over to a large oak table, the kind that would be more at home in a servants' kitchen. The old building creaks and groans as we walk towards it, the parquet floor moving up and down, especially as Matt follows behind.

'We are looking for a birth record from the year 1984,' I say as we approach the table. 'A girl called Casey.'

'Well, based on the information you gave me over the telephone, I pulled some old records, but I also did a computer search. Most of our documents dated after 1971 have been filed electronically now,' she says with a degree of pride. 'I ran a check and found a birth registered for the year 1984. The nineteenth of February.' I look down at the file and see the number: 0020-95-03-19-02-84. I angle it towards Matt, but he is already nodding. 'Here, I pulled the original document so that you could see it for yourself.'

I look down at the old register. Casey Harringford, born 19 February 1984. Mother Cassandra Harringford, father Maurice Harringford.

'My sister.' I turn to Matt, tears in my eyes. 'I have another sister.'

Anna coughs a little and I realise that I have been premature. 'I'm afraid that is not the only record I have. When I ran the computer check, two records came back. The first, a birth,' she says, tapping the book. 'The second . . .' she pauses, her lips pursed, 'a death.'

'For the same person?' asks Matt, moving in closer to me.

'Yes.' The old lady lifts a heavy green leather book from a shelf, dust flying up in clouds like smoke. She opens it at a page marked with a sticky note. 'The same little girl, it would seem. Date of birth matches. Date of death, the fourth of June 1984. It seems that she lived little more than three months.'

'Are you sure there isn't a mistake?' Matt asks, leaning in to inspect the name, as if something might change the closer he gets.

'There is only one registration for which the details match. I'm very sorry to be the bearer of bad news,' says Anna, backing away.

We thank her and retreat to the car. Outside, the afternoon shoppers are making the most of the dry weather. We are still sitting there in silence when Anna leaves ten minutes later. She waves, gets into an old Punto parked a little distance from the building, and drives cautiously away.

'What do you think?' Matt asks. 'I mean, how do you feel?'

'Confused. I should feel sad, because I have just learnt that I had a sister, and according to those records she died. But according to this,' I say, holding up Casey's medical records , 'for the first six months of her life she was receiving outpatient treatment at Fair Fields for a dysplastic hip.' I sigh. It couldn't be called a breath, because it feels like I haven't breathed for the last ten minutes. 'What I feel like hearing is the truth.'

He starts the engine, pulls the car forward and we rumble back on to the cobblestoned road. We wind through the city, passing the Scott Monument and the Balmoral Hotel clock tower, and I can't help but think of Elle, the times we sat in the park below it, the hours we wasted together in this city. Is all that over? Has she really disappeared this time? For good? After a moment Matt turns to me.

'What do you want to do now?'

I try calling Joseph Witherrington, but he has already left his office for the evening. That will have to wait until tomorrow. I consider asking Matt to drive me to Aunt Jemima's old house. I could probably still remember where it is, and just maybe she still lives there. But I'm not sure I could face a rebuttal, so I scrap that idea before it leaves my lips. We should go to the police like DC Forrester asked, but where will that get me? The police can wait.

'Did you go to school in Horton?' I ask. 'You grew up nearby, right?'

'Nearby, but not in Horton. I was living in Selkirk until my parents' divorce. After Fair Fields I moved to Peebles with my mum. Why?'

'Well, there's this woman, a teacher from the village. She's the only person who knew my family back then that I could contact. She must have known about Casey.'

'Worth a try,' Matt suggests.

I pull out my phone and dial Miss Endicott's number. There is no reply.

'Do you know where she lives?' Matt asks. I think back to our conversations in the school, how she told me that she had lived in Horton all her life. What was it she said? The little cottage on the end of the row?

'I think so.'

'Then let's go and talk to her.'

'OK. Head to Horton.'

After a few minutes of driving, he speaks. There is no warning, nothing to pave the way. 'I'm so sorry, Irini. For everything that has happened to you.'

351

I reach over, stroke his leg like Antonio used to do to me. I realise now that to comfort somebody who has suffered is difficult. There is no easy way to soften the past, or make things right. But for the first time I know I have to put my own memories aside and try. I have to do this for Matt. Because I must also learn how to do the same for Elle.

39

By the time we arrive, the sun is hanging low in the sky and the shadows are starting to creep across the fields, cast by the distant trees and the steeple of the church. We pull up alongside the stone wall of the graveyard. There are a couple of people heading into the Enchanted Swan, and another tending the grave of a loved one. Fresh, the soil still heaped on top, waiting for the land to settle. I let my eyes scan across until they find the mound that covers my mother. It will be weeks, maybe even months, before the ground is firm enough for it to be covered with grass.

'Which one?' asks Matt as he closes his car door.

I slam my door shut and move towards the front, my fingers lingering on the hot bonnet. 'I think that one,' I say when I spot a cottage decked out with colourful primroses and beautiful topiary hedges.

We walk towards the house and find all the lights off, except for a small lamp that is glowing in the downstairs window. It's a humble home, naturally beautiful in a quaint, imperfect way. The paint on the door is peeling like the walls of Fair Fields, and the garden from up close is a smidge overgrown. The edges of a once neatly trimmed lawn ragged, the almost dead buds of a dahlia clinging on to the last days of life. We walk up the pathway, closing the gate behind us. I knock on the door and wait.

'Maybe she's still at the school,' I say when there is no reply. I knock again but get the same. Nothing.

Matt checks his watch. 'It's a bit late for school, isn't it? Nearly five o'clock.' He pulls the sleeve of his mac back down, wraps the coat around himself. He peers up the side alley, looking for an answer. Knowing that he is right, I knock again, louder this time.

'Miss Endicott, hello. Are you home?' I call through the letter box.

'Irini, what did you call her?' I turn. Matt has taken a step back, is staring at me.

'Miss Endicott. I don't know her first name. Listen,' I say, turning back to the door. 'I can hear the television.'

'Maybe we should come back another time,' Matt suggests, edging away from me, towards the gate. I ignore him, step over the flower bed, a carpet of red and purple petals. 'Irini, I really think we should leave. I'm sure she doesn't know anything.'

'How can you be so sure?' I balance on an old green bench set against a black wrought-iron frame. I cup my hands around my face and peer in through the window. I see an uncomfortable-looking settee, 1950s design, floral cushions balanced along the back in neat diamond rows. Behind, a bookshelf loaded with books, and a fireplace with a roaring fire. There is a tray on the table with a plate full of what looks like roast chicken and vegetables. And then I see it.

'Break down the door,' I shout to Matt as I leap off the bench, trampling across the flower bed. 'She's on the floor.'

Matt hesitates, but then pushes past me towards the door. He tests the handle, finds it locked from the inside. He pushes against the door with his shoulder, but it doesn't budge. He grips one fist in the palm of his other hand and jabs the point of his elbow at one of the glass panes in the door, then fiddles his hand carefully through the shattered glass and finds the latch. The door pops open.

Inside we are hit by a smell: burning, charcoal, food? I am not sure what. We dash through the dated living room, towards drifts of smoke coming from the kitchen. I am the first to see it. Only seconds pass before Matt sees it too, my tongue so tied I couldn't warn him.

Miss Endicott is lying on the floor, her skin blackened, smouldering like an ember. She is bound to a chair with garden wire, red gashes circling her from where it has cut into her flesh. There is a fireplace poker sticking out of her chest. Smoke is rising from her body like an abandoned city after a night of rioting, when whole streets are left to burn.

Matt grabs the nearest towel, soaks it in water and throws it towards the charred body as if there is something left to save. Steam rises with a sizzling sound as the wet material makes contact. He looks up to me for an explanation for the inexplicable, but his eyes are drawn away and I follow his gaze, turning to see the words painted on the wall in blood: *This is where you will be judged.*

'Like Fair Fields,' he says, backing away from the body, finally realising there is no hope. Or that perhaps Miss Endicott didn't deserve to be saved.

He rushes to the front of the house with his phone to his ear. That's when I see the file sticking out from underneath the table to the side of the body. I grab the wet towel with one hand, the other clasped firmly over my mouth, then reach forward and pull at the file. It is just like the one I have in the car for Casey Harringford. The corners are blackened, but as I open the cover, the image is clear to see. Elle as a little girl. I stand up and take the file to the window, cracking it open to clear the smell. I can hear Matt in the background requesting an ambulance and the police. I turn the pages, but as I do, I see something from the corner of my eye: movement outside near the rear gate.

I dash towards the back door, running towards danger for the first time in my life. I scramble through the garden, push open the gate, looking first right, then left along the row of houses to the rear of Miss Endicott's property. I see the flash of blonde hair slip around the corner and I know it was Elle. I close the file, slip it into the back of my jeans and pull my baggy jumper down over it. Whatever she has done, no matter why she was here, I know I need to protect her. My only wish now is that I had realised it sooner.

40

We sit on the bench at the front of the house, waiting for the emergency services. We can't find anything to say, and nobody walks past us to break the silence. I watch the mourner in the nearby graveyard, focus on the sounds of cheer coming from the Enchanted Swan. When we hear the distant wail of an ambulance siren, Matt turns to me, his face ghost-white.

'What are we going to tell them?' he asks. 'They'll want to know why we are here.'

Blue lights flicker in the distance. 'The truth, I guess.'

He licks at his dry lips, but there seems to be no moisture on his tongue. 'I don't think we should tell them that I was at Fair Fields.' He looks away, wrapping his arms around his body as if he is cold.

'I don't think we should tell them about Fair Fields at all,' I say, aware of the file digging into my back. 'And we probably shouldn't mention Elle, either. Perhaps we were just passing, on our way to the pub, and thought we could smell something?'

'Thank you,' he says, but I bring my finger to his lips, and kiss him on the cheek. We stand up together to greet the ambulance as it screeches to a halt. Matt reaches for my hand. I take it, and hold on tight.

In the police station we make our statements: who we are, where we're from, what we were doing at Miss Endicott's cottage. They interview us separately; stern faces and tired eyes look back at me over the table. One of the officers has such a strong accent I can barely make out what he is saying to me. But I do catch the gist of the story from the other. It turns out that Miss Endicott's neighbour saw us arrive, and heard me calling out for her to answer the door. Plus she had heard a scream about half an hour beforehand. Her statement pretty much rules us out of any offence, so they let us go a little before midnight.

Matt drives us through a busy Edinburgh city centre, the tyres rumbling over cobblestoned streets until we arrive at his apartment. It is a beautiful building, grey Georgian elegance. I'm glad to be back in the city, somewhere I can slip into the shelter of endless brick and a populace of more than a few hundred.

The investigation into Miss Endicott's murder happens fast. I keep Elle's records hidden along with Casey's, but it doesn't take the police very long to reach a conclusion as to what happened. There have been several unsubstantiated complaints against Miss Endicott over the years, and her time spent working as a teacher at Fair Fields before she arrived in Horton is nothing to be proud of if the rumours are to be believed.

There was a series of suicides in the 1990s, victims from all over the Scottish borders. Each had been a patient at Fair Fields, each of school age at the time of their admission.

Where some of her colleagues were charged and sentenced, it seemed nobody wanted to believe what had been suggested regarding Miss Endicott, especially those that lived in Horton. Because of that, she had been allowed to remain free, and had never paid for her crimes.

Matt doesn't say much about the events of that night. He seems to want to put them behind us, move forward together, and I think I might want that too. But at some point we will have to talk about what happened, and until then we are stuck. I need to admit that I saw Elle at Miss Endicott's house, and he needs to confess everything he knows about Elle's past. By association, that also means that he must confess to his own.

I decide to hand in my notice, tell the hospital I won't be going back. The managers wrangle over procedure, tell me I can't just make a phone call and consider it finalised. But I can. I have done it already. I don't want to return to London. I need a fresh start, and for the first time in my life I think it might be within reach. I am starting to understand that I was wanted by my family, that none of this was my fault. I have no plan, no escape route, and no commitments to hide behind. I am just Irini.

A couple of nights after Miss Endicott's murder we go to Fair Fields to pick up my car, and I return to *Mam Tor*. The mother mountain, a house that, thanks to my father, is mine. I am certain that at some point Elle will come back. She is a scared little girl, running from her past. I know how that feels. I've tried to be angry with her. She is a murderer, twice over most likely. The first time she attacked the man who wanted to rape me, and I always believed she went on to kill him. But she did it to save me, and I kept quiet. Now she has killed to save herself, so I will keep quiet again, and keep her secrets safe. Accepting that she could do such a thing isn't easy. But neither is facing up to what happened to her at Fair Fields. Facing up to the number of times I abandoned her when she needed me is harder still.

Her file has answered many questions. That's why I haven't handed it over to the police. I fear they would put two and two together and come up with four. It wouldn't take a genius to work out that Elle is responsible for Miss Endicott's death, even with all the missing pages, which perhaps were deliberately lost to the fire. Perhaps those pages might have explained the missing gaps in my own history, but I guess there are some things we can just never know.

What I do know is this: Elle was admitted to Fair Fields by my parents when she was six years old, in June 1984. They complained about her destructive nature, her difficult behaviour, her desire to harm others, especially other children. In one incident she had tied a boy at nursery to a radiator and turned up the heat. She was four years old at the time. Was she aware what she was doing? With everything I now know, I can't help but think that she was.

I read the reports from the psychiatrists, and the description of the EEG they performed, which showed an increase in the delta and theta activities in Elle's frontal lobe. They proposed a diagnosis of antisocial personality, claiming that she was basically unsocialised, as if she was some sort of farm animal. They speculated about the coexistence of childhood manic depression, and that she was a self-harmer. There were other notes, written in near-illegible handwriting, that suggested she be diagnosed with sociopathic personality disturbance, but this was contradicted as inappropriate and outdated in later entries. In fact, the notes went on and on. Height and weight charts documented the passage of time. The argument concerning how to label her was never resolved, and at no point was I ever convinced that a diagnosis was made. Elle, it seemed, remained a mystery.

Then, without explanation, her treatment stopped and she returned home. No doubt when my parents discovered what was happening to her. That was right before the day I left. If there remained any doubt about why I was handed over to Aunt Jemima, the correlation to Elle's return was all the confirmation I needed. They made a choice. They kept her, gave me away.

But reading about her history is overwhelming, so not for the first time I leave Elle's records on my bed and head outside. Walking in the autumnal wind is a relief, clears my head, gives me a chance to breathe. It's becoming a daily habit, this walk around the perimeter of the house. But the temperature has fallen overnight, and after about twenty minutes the first drops of rain begin to fall, stinging my face. I run back to the house, head towards the kitchen door. I reach for the handle with my coat pulled over my head, but as I push open the door I realise that above the sound of the rain I can hear music coming from inside. For a split second I reason that I must have left something on, but even as I'm thinking it, I know that isn't the case.

I step inside, leaving the door open. The music intensifies as I walk towards the hallway, a trail of wet footprints in my wake. I recognise the urgent, tremulous arias of the final acts of *Madam Butterfly*, and I know in that instant that Elle has come back, just as I believed she would. I take cautious steps through the kitchen, glance up the stairs to my old room, but the music isn't coming from there. I pass through into the hallway, the music louder still.

'Elle,' I whisper. I look back at the open door, the rain beating down. I could leave, I tell myself as I grip the banister. I could leave right now, call the police if I wanted. Instead, with somersaults of nausea stirring in my stomach, I begin to climb the stairs.

With every step it feels as if I am being weighed down by lead boots, and each is heavier than the last. But I reach the top of the stairs and follow the music, which is coming from Elle's bedroom. The light is on, the music so loud I can no longer hear my own breathing. But I can feel it, staccato breaths stuttering in and out as I harness my courage and push open the door.

'Elle,' I say again, my voice shaky and frail, trying not to scare her. I don't want her to run. But she isn't here. At first I think the room is as I left it, the scrunched-up sheets from the sex with Antonio, the bowl of burned-down matches on the side. But as I look up at her portrait, I see it has been defaced, a deep red stain smeared across her face. Proof that she has been here. Then I freeze as I hear the crash of a door behind me.

At first I'm sure she must be there in the room with me. I'm convinced I can feel her, her presence like a weight on my body. But then I hear footsteps on the stairs. I spin around, rush after her.

'Elle,' I call, but I get no reply. 'Elle!' I scream, louder this time so that she might hear me over the music as I reach the top of the stairs. 'Wait.' But I know I'm too late. I sit down on the top step to catch my breath. That's when I notice that just around a bend in the corridor a small table has been overturned, the contents scattered about the floor. I stand up, move towards it. I crouch down, pick up a photo frame, being careful not to cut myself on the broken glass. I shake the frame clean and hold it up.

The image is from the same sequence that I was looking at in the album in the study. In this picture, Elle is sitting on my tricycle, her legs too long, her form awkward but face determined. I am standing at the side, tears rolling, my mouth wide midway through a scream. Nobody is concerned. Nobody interrupts. Somebody was watching the whole thing through a lens, relishing the memories that they would laugh about in the future. But in this final picture my mother is also in the frame, on her way towards me, her face a mixture of sorry and amused. She is glancing over her shoulder at the camera and trying not to smile. Not in a way that makes me resent her, though, because what is happening is just normality, before we all became what we became. This picture depicts a time when everybody was wanted, when nobody feared for their place in the family, and before Elle spent time in Fair Fields.

As I look again, I realise there is something else in this picture. My mother's swollen stomach, unmistakably pregnant. The baby who went on to become Casey. My lost sister. And then my eyes are drawn back to the two children; to Elle on the tricycle, and her younger sister standing nearby on her own two perfectly formed legs. Not a sign of plaster with butterflies scribbled up the sides. By the time I was three, I couldn't even walk. Nobody in these pictures has a dysplastic hip. This little girl cannot be me.

I race down the stairs and charge towards my bedroom. I slam open the door and snatch Casey's Fair Fields record, hidden underneath scattered pages from Elle's. I rifle through it for the truth, turning pages so fast that one of them rips. All the details are there. Casey is the one who was born with hip deformities. Casey is the one who was strapped in plaster soon after birth. Casey is the one who would need surgery, surgery that would leave a long vertical scar on her left hip. Casey is the one who was registered at Fair Fields Rehabilitation Hospital for the Infirm and Mentally Insane. Is Casey the child my mother was carrying in her womb when Elle stole the tricycle in the photograph? Am I Casey?

I step from the room and stare at the photographs on the dresser. Elle and another little girl. A girl I know cannot be me. I take each photo one by one, looking for the mistake, looking for me. But I don't find it. I'm not in any of these photographs.

I allow my anger to get the better of me and snatch up the heaviest frame, launching it at the dresser. It clatters forward, smashes into the back of the cupboard. I stand there in silence, shaking. But as I look up, I notice that along with the glass of the frame, part of the dresser has shattered too. Wood splinters fly up, and a chink of light creeps through the hole. I push my fingers into it and find space on the other side. I grip the wood and pull, breaking another flimsy part away. Beyond there is no wall. Instead there is a corridor, and as I put my eye to the hole, I see the same red carpet that runs underneath my feet.

I pull the dresser away and find that the corridor continues behind it, with only a narrow outline of bricks built to mask the remaining gap around the edge. I step through the space where the dresser once stood, into a side of the house that I've never been able to access from my bedroom before. I follow the corridor as it turns to the right, and at the end I see the same upturned table that I was kneeling at only moments ago. Beyond that I hear music, and I can see the open door of Elle's bedroom just up ahead.

But I retrace my steps because there is another door that had remained hidden until today. I open it, bursting through as if I want to catch somebody in the act. Before me is a room, pink, a small bed to match my own. More sad, dated furniture, everything grey with dust, as if it is slowly fading away. A large bay window with the curtains pulled shut. On a shelf there are three albums, the same size and style as the albums in the study. I pick up the first, faded gold lettering reading *1984*. My mother isn't pregnant any more. Instead there is a baby in her arms. I turn the page. The same baby, a little bigger. Two children in the background. One of them is Elle, and she is holding a red marker in her hand. There is a butterfly on the baby's plaster cast. A cast that extends all the way up her left leg, above the hip. My hip. The other little girl has her hands on the edge of my crib. She has blonde curls. Blue eyes. She is the girl from the tricycle. The girl I thought was me, but who was not.

Because I am Casey, the youngest of three, born in February 1984 with a dysplastic hip. I am the child who is supposed to be dead. But if I am Casey, who is the other girl?

I snatch at the album marked *1985*. I flick through the pages, and there I am. Bigger. Growing. Alone. No other children. My parents are there with me, pictures of them holding me, of bath time, nappy change, days in the garden. All the pictures are from the house. As if they never took me out. My parents' features are heavy. The easiness of their youth has gone. Their faces talk of the decision to exclude one of their children, and the unexplained loss of another. 1986 is the same, me with my parents, until it stops halfway through, an album unfinished. A family disappeared.

I stare at my mother, wish I could ask her what happened, beg her to tell me the truth. But it's too late to ask for the answers, because all that remains is her grave, the secrets of the past buried with her and out of reach. I remember what Matt told me: that when our parents die, they take part of us with them, the part that belonged to them all along. I wonder if the reverse is true. Perhaps they leave part of them behind with us. The part of them that was always ours to keep. Maybe if I wish for it hard enough, part of her will live on in me.

And that's when I remember. I run from the house, grabbing my keys just before I slip out of the back door. I am panting by the time I reach the car, rain streaming down my face, my heart pounding. I drive towards the village, screeching to a halt as I pull up alongside the graveyard. I hobble forward, my hip throbbing in pain as if it knows, as if it is excited that the secret will finally be uncovered. I stagger towards the muddy mound under which my mother lies, and right next to it, just as I remember from the day of the funeral, is the other grave. The headstone with no dates, filled instead with an empty promise, no stronger than the one they offered me.

I peel back the covering of moss and brush away the remnants of mud, read the engraving.

Our dearest Casey.
You live on in her.

41

It took weeks for the exhumation licence to be approved. But it came through for early November.

Who will they dig up? My bet is that we will find a little girl who once went by the name of Irini Harringford, the second child of Cassandra and Maurice Harringford. The little girl whose place I took. I'm not sure what happened to her yet, or if Elle had anything to do with it. If she was here, maybe she could help answer the questions. But my best guess is that Elle was involved with her death and that my parents sent her to Fair Fields in a desperate bid to help her. Casey's reported death at roughly three months old ties in with Elle's admission. So they passed me off as Irini, perhaps easier to convince people of the death of a baby with health problems than it was a toddler. I became Irini, and nobody became any the wiser. I inherited her name, and she inherited my health problems. But when my parents found out what was happening to Elle, they had to bring her home, leaving them with no option but to send me away, or risk losing Irini all over again.

I suppose there will be questions afterwards. The police will open an investigation, will want to know who killed little Irini, the *actual* Irini. They'll want to know who knew the truth, and who kept it hidden. Somebody must have signed the death certificate for a baby who didn't die. Somebody in the village must have wondered why Irini was suddenly kept at home. Perhaps some of them were even at Casey's funeral.

But until I know for certain what happened to Irini, I continue to live as her. Casey doesn't quite seem to fit. Perhaps it is because I am fourteen months younger than the age I have believed I was for most of my life. Aunt Jemima must have known the truth, so it's no wonder she didn't want Elle in our lives. But she can't keep hiding, and now that the police are involved she will have to face the truth. I wonder if she will want to talk to me, apologise, atone, beg forgiveness for the lies. Perhaps that is the least I deserve, but really I just want to move forward, find a new life, one that feels true to who I am. Whoever that might turn out to be.

As part of that effort, I took a trip to London with my medical records from Fair Fields to convince DC Forrester of what I believed to be the truth. Once she could smell a loose end she was all over it like a rash, screaming bloody murder at anybody who stood in her way, bothering the Scottish police to push for exhumation. But I needn't have worried, because it turned out to be hard for anybody to argue with the fact that Fair Fields had been treating somebody who had been registered as having died.

While I was in London, I saw Antonio for the first time since the police let him go. We met at my house when he came to pick up his things. He seemed desperate to make it up to me, to undo what he'd done. He even asked me, *What am I supposed to do now?* He can't quite believe how his life has unravelled. He doesn't realise that none of it really matters any more. Not to me, anyway. I spent three years trying to make him fit, avoiding his pleas to open up. I don't have to do that any more. When I realised he hadn't anywhere to stay, I offered him the house. He was only disappointed when he realised I wouldn't be there.

I stayed in London long enough to pack up most of my things, and to sign the necessary paperwork to get out of my employment contract. Now I am on the road back to Scotland, and the journey is surreal, as if for the first time I am returning to a place where I belong. A place of history.

I arrive in Horton early, three suitcases in the car. I pass the sign for *Mam Tor* and head up the driveway, the gates already open. It feels right to stay here, for now at least. Matt is waiting for me on the doorstep with takeaway coffees, as if we are somewhere alien and without supplies. But we are not. I am no longer a stranger to this place. *Mam Tor* might never feel like home, but until Elle comes back, it has to be. I know I am going to wake up here every morning, wondering if this will be the day when she returns. Until then I live in hope that my presence will lure her to me, so that I can begin to undo my part in her crimes.

I unload my clothes from the car, deposit them in one of the other bedrooms, one of the rooms that looks unused. While I have been away, a builder has worked on fixing the corridor so that it is open again, connecting my old room to the rest of the house. I have brought linen with me, starch-crisp, straight from the pack. Matt helps, and we find a degree of comfort in the fact that it feels like we are nesting. Moving forward, starting something new. We have agreed to stay here together for now. Maybe we will leave in the future, return to his nice apartment and a new life. Maybe I will leave on my own and go somewhere else entirely. I'm not sure where I need to be long-term. But for now, being here with Matt is enough. In a few months' time this house and the whole estate will be mine, and then I suppose I'll have the freedom to do anything I choose.

The shadow of tomorrow hangs over us, the day of the exhumation, but we spend our time in relative happiness. We get into bed naked and lie there, although neither of us seems interested in making love. It's like we have covered ten years of a relationship in a few short weeks and are now just happy to be free. He has told me about some of the abuse he suffered in his short time at Fair Fields, and how it makes him want to shut out the world. These are truths I believe I am the first to hear. I get to nurture him, and that seems to undo the past for both of us, one stitch at a time. Our joint story, apportioned into what we once knew as my past and his, tells the tale of Elle, a woman we both need in some way, for she validates the narrative of our lives.

As fate would have it, it is a wet morning, still dark when we leave the house. Accordingly they erect a tent large enough to accommodate both grave and spectators, but the ground was already wet and the cold nips at our toes. A few villagers linger nearby; others hurry past with shivers running up their spines, telling themselves it's just the chill of the air. I wonder how the diggers feel. Usually they just dig a hole then move on. This time there is purpose, something to discover. A real possibility of striking the jackpot when it comes to the truth.

I wait as they dig, expecting a good few hours of toil on

their part. But after little more than an hour they have reached something solid. DC Forrester, who has come up on her day off, clears us out as they uncover what they have found, and we stand in the drizzle listening to rushed instructions and the sound of shifting soil. After another twenty minutes they bring out a small wooden box. It is nothing fancy. Nothing like my mother's. No golden handles of fancy filigree. They fill in the grave, and within another twenty minutes everybody is clearing out. Forrester assures me they will have the results available within the next few weeks.

'Just got to sit it out,' she says, before making her excuses, saying she is on the next flight home. 'I'll be in touch.'

Dawn is breaking when we arrive back at the house. My feet are numb, my toes bright pink when I pull off my socks. 'I'm going to take a shower,' I call to Matt, who doesn't suggest he join me.

The water feels good, and it doesn't make me uncomfortable to be naked in this place in the way that it did before. I let the heat soak into my body, wash my hair. After ten minutes, when the water from the old heating system is starting to cool, I reach for a towel. That's when I see the shadows under the door.

Even though I know Matt is in the house, my first thought is Elle. I open the door, look left and right now that the dresser has been removed and the corridor is open. I cross the hallway, my old bedroom door already ajar. As I push it open, I find her sitting on my childhood bed. She looks smaller than before, her face dirty. I am sure she has been sleeping rough. Perhaps in the grounds, and I find the idea surprisingly comforting. I close the door behind me and speak softly.

'Elle,' I say, my breath catching in my throat. 'Where the hell have you been?' I sit down next to her. She gets up, moves to the door. She doesn't want me near. I know she doesn't intend to stay.

'You cut my time with Miss Endicott short.' There is no smile on her face, no glimmer of delight or pride. Just the facts and an accusation.

'I'm sorry about that,' I say, without finding the apology ridiculous. 'I was only ever looking for the truth.'

'Well now you have it, Casey. You know what they are going to find when they open that box.' She opens the door a crack, perhaps ready to bolt in case I have the police hidden, waiting to pounce.

'Irini,' I say, and I sense the first flicker of a smile creeping across her face. 'You did it, didn't you? You killed her. That's why they sent you to Fair Fields, and why they sent me away when you came home. They passed me off as Irini to hide your crime, kept me hidden until I had grown big enough to convince people.' I take her silence as proof of what I believe. 'Why did you do it?'

She shrugs. 'What do you want me to tell you? The explanation and logic of a six-year-old? I thought you were smarter than that.' She shakes her head, opens the door, but then closes it again and turns back to look at me, her body still angled ready to leave. How could a six-year-old girl kill a baby? I try to imagine how it could possibly have happened. But I can't, and I have to accept I will never know. 'I guess they started calling you Irini to pretend she still existed,' she says.

'No. They did it to cover up your crime. The same reason they gave me away. To protect you.'

'They tried to keep us both, you know. We were together for a while after I came home. Even after they sent you away, they still hoped that one day they might be able to bring you back. But I couldn't help myself.' She looks down at my hip, and now I see why my parents had to let me go, and exactly why they had to keep her. When she arrived home from Fair Fields she hadn't changed at all. 'I'm sorry about adding to your list of scars. I thought it might end up like a butterfly. But you should be grateful. Unlike Irini, you at least are still alive.' She looks away sadly, as if she can't quite believe how it has all turned out.

When she slips through the door, I jump up to follow her. I catch her at the top of the stairs, just two steps down. 'Why don't you stay? I will help you,' I say. Thoughts of trapping her run through my mind. I should call the police, force her to atone for what she did. For killing my sister, ruining my life. But I can't give her up now any more than my parents could.

She smiles, and there is that face I recognise, the one I could never let in. The sly grin, the emotionless eyes. I remember now why I have spent my life running, and understand why my parents sent me away to protect me. 'Would you trust me to stay?' she says. 'Hide me? Would you trust me to sleep next to you?' I know I wouldn't. When I don't answer she says, 'No, neither would I.' Then she reaches down and lifts my towel.

Her fingertips brush against the raised lumps of tissue that never really healed. Not the long, straight line that runs as vertically as any decent spine. Instead she focuses on the ragged arcs above it. The marks she made. I remain still, goose pimples running across my skin. She traces her finger along the curve of scar. Is she sad, sorry, hurt? Could be any one or none of those things. And I realise that while I've spent all my life believing that I have lost everything, it isn't the truth; I never lost my parents' love. My father gave everything he had to save me. He told me so. And deep down Elle knows it. That's why she will never forgive me, and why I could never trust her again. I fear her now the same as I did when she held a knife to my body on the day I ran for my life. With just the touch of her fingers she elicits the same unease.

'They faded, at least,' she says as she drops the towel. 'That's what our father always hoped for.' She turns, walks down the stairs.

I chase after her and catch her just before she slips outside. As I hold her arm I whisper, 'Elle, do you think our father forgave you?' She smiles but cannot make eye contact. She doesn't answer me, at least not verbally, as she disappears from my life. I'm not sure if it is for good. Her own scars run too deep just to walk away.

But although I know she doubts it, I am sure my father did forgive her. Because she was a part of him just like she is a part of me. I can't say it doesn't hurt to know that I was sacrificed for her. For the little girl who cut my leg open and killed our sister. But perhaps our parents did what they had to to save not just me, but both of us. The two children they had left. Whatever their motives, I forgive them. I will let the past go, and Elle's crimes with it. No matter how terrible or scarring their actions really were. Because we are them, and they are us.

We are family.

Acknowledgements

Almost one year ago to the day I sent the first three chapters of this book to a London based literary agency, full of hope that somebody might like what they read. The fact that I now find myself writing an acknowledgements page prior to publication is pretty humbling, especially considering that at that time I thought I had finished. How wrong I was.

So huge thanks go to Madeleine Milburn, who read my submission while she was on holiday in Scotland. None of this would have been possible without her belief, support, and absolute faith in Irini's story. I am so very grateful to have found an agent who gives such great editorial advice, and who knows how to throw such an awesome Christmas party. Thanks also go to Thérèse Coen for all the foreign rights deals and constant Prosecco top ups (*Proost!*) and Cara Lee Simpson who dealt with my constant first-time author enquiries. I'll get better at this, I promise.

I had no idea how hard-working editors in publishing houses were until I met Emily Griffin at Headline. I thought it was all about doing lunch by the Thames – now I realise that's only part of it. I will remain forever grateful to her for teaching me what it really means to edit a book. Next time dinner is on me. Also to Sara, Kitty, Jane Selley for her copy editing, and Jo Liddiard who is doing a great job with marketing. There are many other people at Headline who have worked on this book whose names I've yet to learn. My sincere thanks go to all of you. More publishing thanks go to the team at St. Martin's Press in the US, including Jennifer Weis and Sylvan Creekmore, who worked alongside the team at Headline to create the first ARC. Anytime we need a meeting in New York, just let me know.

I'd like also to say thanks to my UK based family, who will be pleased to know they were no inspiration when it came to creating the characters in this novel. I love and miss you guys very much. To my Cypriot family, I'm blessed to have been made so welcome, and thankful that you remain amused by my inappropriate mistakes in Greek. I know I am very lucky to have found you all. There are many friends who have played a part in my journey as a writer throughout the years, and thanks go to all of you for the ways in which you have helped. Special thanks go to Michelle Abrahall for the vital role she played in helping me get to this point. You were always, and continue to be, way cooler than me. There are many friends who read early manuscripts and offered me cheer and guidance, and for that I will always owe you. I am fortunate to be able to say there are too many to mention by name.

To Theo and Themis, thank you for offering me your love when you had no reason to. I am grateful for each day that I get to share part of my life with you guys. And to you, Stasinos: none of this would have been possible if it wasn't for your love, support, salary, and willingness to overlook the multitude of things I forgot to do while I was writing this novel. You are my constant cheerleader, toughest critic, and make me so proud to be your wife. More than yesterday, less than tomorrow.

Tap tap, agapi mou x